Slip

of the

Hand

J.P. Farrell

Riverhaven Books

www.RiverhavenBooks.com

Slip of the Hand is a work of fiction. While some of the settings are actual, any similarity regarding names, characters, or incidents is entirely coincidental.

Published in the United States
by Riverhaven Books,
www.RiverhavenBooks.com

ISBN: 978-1-937588-36-6

Printed in the United States of America
by Country Press, Lakeville, Massachusetts

Edited and designed by Stephanie Lynn Blackman
Whitman, Massachusetts

Cover Picture © Maleah Torney Photography

About the Novel:

Slip of the Hand is the story of a man seeking justice in a world where he sees no choice but to take the law into his own hands, regardless of the consequences.

Jeff Keller opened his eyes after thinking back, as he had countless times before, to that night six years ago. It was the last time he saw his fiancée, Laura Weston, alive. He loved her and now he was sitting in prison, serving a life sentence, framed for her murder by government insiders.

Navy SEAL Jack Bolton has barely survived his last special operations mission in the Taliban-controlled mountain ranges of Afghanistan when he receives the devastating news that his sister, a college student, is missing. He immediately returns to Massachusetts and begins an exhaustive search to find her. When he learns that she has been murdered and that the police and FBI can't develop the case for lack of evidence, he makes a life-changing decision to deal with her killers himself. That ostensibly clear-cut decision takes him on a journey that he could never have anticipated. Along the way, he discovers a shocking government plot and eventually finds himself the object of a massive manhunt, not only for taking the law into his own hands, but for what he might know. The New York Mafia, a Mexican cartel, and powerful government officials all want him dead.

Meanwhile, Jeff Keller might just hold the key to both their futures.

Also written by J.P. Farrell

The Common Cure

Chapter 1

The evening sun was disappearing behind a row of empty warehouse buildings overlooking the waterfront. A major mixed-use urban renewal project had begun in the southwest area of Washington, D.C.

Gus Banner, a tall slender man with a hardened face and receding hairline emerged from his parked car. He walked several yards and lit a cigarette while looking out over the water, waiting patiently for his contact to arrive.

On the surface, Gus was the consummate Washington insider. After graduating from Stanford at the top of his class, he joined the armed forces and, later, the Central Intelligence Agency, where he served for many years. In subsequent years, he held high-level positions in both Republican and Democratic administrations. He moved easily through the halls of power.

Within a few minutes, a slow-moving black Cadillac pulled up and stopped. Senator Sam Atkins emerged from the back seat with a tan folder in his hand. He instructed the driver to come back in twenty minutes.

Sam came from a long line of politicians. His father, George Atkins, was a well-respected and powerful senator who had retired seven years ago at age seventy-one. Sam was forty-one years old, six feet tall with athletic good looks, and well on his way to achieving the same prominence as his father. He held aspirations of someday running for president, something his father had talked about but never pursued.

He greeted Gus with a handshake and a smile; then they walked side by side along the row of empty buildings while a cool summer breeze blew against their faces.

"How's your father?" Gus asked.

"He's fine, thanks."

"That's good," he said with a smile. "I've worked with him on occasion over the years."

"Yeah," Sam replied. "He told me that, and he said you had ways of taking care of problems."

"So what's the urgency that couldn't wait for tomorrow?" Gus asked.

"I need you to take care of something for me that is getting out of control."

"It usually involves money, political influence, or a woman. Which is it?" Gus asked calmly.

"A woman."

"So she won't go away, huh? Is she blackmailing you, threatening to go to the media? Better yet, she actually thinks she's in love with you?"

"Does it really matter?"

"No, it doesn't," Gus said with a smirk. "But, I don't get you guys. You have all the money and power, yet you let women destroy you. You think you can have it all."

"I don't need a lecture, Gus," Sam said in a quiet,

controlled tone. "I need her to go away for good. I can't afford to have any questions about my character, especially if I decide to run for president down the road."

"I'll take care of it. Don't worry. I will need a picture, name, address, and where she likes to go."

"It's all here," Sam said, handing him the folder.

Gus opened it and shook his head. "How old is she?"

"Twenty-four; she's an intern in my office."

"What's her name?" Gus said, holding out her picture.

"Laura Weston."

He stared at the folder contents. "Yeah, I would say she's a real career killer, Sam. Let me ask you a question."

"What?"

"Has anybody seen you with her, or has she told anyone?"

"No, I've been careful."

That's what they always say and then something comes out, Gus thought with a half-smile. "Anything else I should know that you haven't told me?"

Sam paused, "I'm…."

"No surprises. Is there something else, Sam?" he said, looking directly at him.

"She's pregnant."

Gus turned, momentarily looking out over the waterfront, flicked his cigarette, and then turned to face

Sam. "Does she have a boyfriend?"

"Yeah… she does, she's actually engaged."

"Perfect…just give me a couple of days, and your problem will be gone."

"Good."

"Just remember, in two years when the CIA Director retires, I'm reasonably certain that I'll be appointed to succeed him," Gus stated. "I will need you to make sure there are no problems with the confirmation."

"Don't worry about that. It won't be a problem," Sam replied with a smug look.

The two parted as the senator's Cadillac arrived.

***

A late evening dinner at the Woodstove restaurant in downtown Washington, D.C., was the usual Friday night ritual for Jeff Keller and Laura Weston. When they arrived, the hostess led them to their table. They sat down and pulled in their chairs as they had every other evening. The young couple's conversation was quieter than usual at first. Jeff, dressed in a charcoal gray suit, which complimented his jet-black hair and GQ looks, did most of the talking. Laura was dressed conservatively, her long black hair tied back in a bun.

Noticing that she seemed distant, Jeff asked, "Something wrong, Laura?"

"You're always working, you never have time for

anything else," she said in a slightly agitated tone.

"I have to make my two thousand hours and, right now, we're really busy. I'm sorry. Is that what's really bugging you?"

She looked at him with a blank stare. "I'm pregnant, and I can't marry you," she blurted out.

"What…?" Exhaling deeply, he told her "If you're pregnant, we'll work through it. I love you."

"I've been seeing someone else," she said coldly.

Jeff leaned back in his chair. He was completely caught off guard by Laura's revelation. His food became tasteless, her stinging words swirling around in his head as if he had been given a fatal diagnosis. "What… you are seeing someone else? When did all this happen? Is the baby even mine? Do you love this guy? Who the hell is he?"

"I'm sorry, Jeff," she said, shaking her head.

"Are you kidding me? Who the hell is he?" he demanded, his voice cracking.

"It doesn't matter."

"I can't believe this. I just can't frigging believe this," he muttered, burying his face in his hands. Then, looking at her, he said, "So that's it. You've been seeing someone behind my back, and you're pregnant. Who the hell is he?" he repeated with a raised voice, drawing attention from people at nearby tables.

"Don't embarrass me, Jeff…keep your voice down," Laura scolded.

"That's what you're worried about?" He instantly stood up as if he were about to deliver a speech. "Hey everyone, the woman sitting down right there," he said loudly, pointing to Laura. "She just told me that she's pregnant and she doesn't want to marry me. But that's not the best part; she's seeing somebody else."

Customers throughout the restaurant silently stared. The restaurant manager came over to the table. "I'm sorry, but if you can't keep it quiet, I'm going to have to ask you to leave."

"I'm sorry," Jeff said in a lower tone, trying to regain his composure and taking his seat. "I'm in a state of shock at the moment."

"Take me home!" Laura demanded.

They exited the restaurant, all eyes watching. As they got in the car, the angry exchange continued until Laura slapped him, scratching his face. Jeff refused to just drop her off and go home; he needed to know who she was seeing. After an hour of badgering her, he left, distraught and heartbroken, still without a name.

***

Jeff opened his eyes after thinking back, as he had countless times before, to that horrible night one year ago. It was the last time he would see Laura alive. He loved her, and now he was sitting in a courtroom, accused of her murder and waiting for the jury to return with their verdict.

He anxiously looked behind him. The courtroom was filled to capacity with standing room only. His attorney placed a hand on Jeff's shoulder, signaling him that the jurors were about to file in. Jeff took a deep breath, struggling to maintain his composure.

The bailiff asked everyone to rise as the judge entered the courtroom and took his place at the bench. The foreman of the jury handed the verdict to the bailiff, who walked over and handed it to the judge. The courtroom was quiet as the judge reviewed it and then signaled for the bailiff to return the verdict to the foreman to be read aloud.

The foreman stood up and read, "We, the jury... find the defendant... guilty..."

That was all Jeff heard. He clenched his jaw and closed his eyes in dismay. His family and friends gasped. Sentencing was scheduled for another day. The trial was officially over. His life, for all intents and purposes, was over as well. Court officers handcuffed and escorted him out of the courtroom. As he was being led out, he broke down and began ranting, "I didn't do it. I didn't kill her. I'm innocent. I was framed. I loved her."

Chapter 2

Six years later, an off-campus party raged at the Beta Ki Gamma fraternity house at Wilbur Smith College in Williamstown, Massachusetts. This quaint, pastoral community in the corner of the state bordered Vermont to the north and New York to the west.

John Atkins stood at the door, collecting the entry fees from the partygoers as they came in. The ladies smiled shyly as they passed, taking note of his good looks and tall stature.

He was a junior at this small, esteemed school of 2800 students and a proud member of Beta Ki. He was the son of Sam Atkins, a prominent Democratic Senator from Washington State. Admission to Wilbur Smith had taken just a few phone calls from his father to the right people. John - an outstanding student academically- was accepted without question. He was accustomed to taking full advantage of his father's influence whenever he deemed it necessary – or merely useful.

As fate would have it, in his freshman year, John met a kindred spirit in the person of Nick Gallo, a six-foot tall, good-looking Italian kid from the Bronx whose father was a kingpin of the New York Mafia. Nick's father had big plans for his son and wanted him to get a good college education at an elite school; it was the first step on the road to a career in politics where he could legally influence the system. Also important were the lifelong connections he would make at Wilbur Smith that would serve him well in the future.

The two boys hit it off immediately and were inseparable thereafter, even pledging the same fraternity. By the time they were juniors, with the help of Nick's Mafia connections, they had a small well-oiled, gambling operation up and running. They were the toast of the fraternity. With their connections and strong personalities, it was easy to influence the people around them.

The yellow Victorian-style house, with its wide porch, steep roof, and antique rooms, added to the dark charm that enticed many girls, freshmen and townies alike, to attend these wild Beta Ki frat parties.

The party was rocking as music blared from the surround-sound speakers. Kegs of beer flowed, loud celebrations echoed through the house at the completion of random drinking games, alcohol-laden punch disappeared, and the frat brothers raised hell, making the pledges jump at their every command. It was just another wild frat party that usually carried a heavy price the next morning.

A strikingly attractive townie girl entered the party. She had dressed to be noticed, flaunting her slim physique and wearing tight-fitting jeans with a low-cut top exposing her cleavage. As John collected her entry fee, he signaled to Nick with a quick nod of the head. Nick caught the signal and immediately zeroed in on her. She would become the next victim of their insidious games.

It was Nick's turn to lure this young, naïve girl into his bedroom on the second floor. He wasted no time introducing himself and drumming up conversation with his undeniable charm. She giddily smiled at everything he said. It wasn't long before he had her drinking out of the spiked punch bowl, which the older college girls had learned to avoid from their freshman days. It was a ploy used by the frat boys to remove any resistance to their sexual advances.

As the night moved on, Nick would occasionally grin at John from afar. They had chosen the ideal victim. It would only be a matter of time before Nick would invite her to see his bedroom.

The party crowd had gradually thinned out as the night moved into the early morning hours. The remaining guests were, for the most part, too intoxicated to find their way home.

Nick made his move. He slowly maneuvered his drunken prize up the stairs to his bedroom. In a matter of minutes he had her on his bed. It started off harmlessly. She easily accepted the kisses, but his hands began to roam freely over her body. At first, there was some hesitation, but the alcohol had dampened her inhibitions.

He began to undo her pants. She pulled back, grabbing his hands, hoping that he would stop, but that only made him more determined. He yanked her pants from her body and forcefully tore off her top, completely exposing her to his raging passion. Strained pleas, begging for him to stop, fell on deaf ears.

Finished, Nick cast a look of disgust at the crying girl curled on his bed. She was too easy. But her nightmare wasn't over. As if on cue, John quietly entered the dimly lit room. The two friends exchanged sly smiles and a high five in passing, as if it were a tag-team wrestling match. The girl cried in despair, her nude body exposed, her eyes begging for mercy. But she was just another conquest to John. He proceeded to rape her. She moaned in pain, sobbing, confused, drunk, and pleading with him to stop. He ignored her pleas. And then it was over.

She was just another score. The two boys had done this often enough. They were sure she would keep her secret to herself, too afraid and embarrassed to report the rape and fearful that nobody would believe her anyway. Like many before her, she had thought she was meeting two good-looking, high-spirited, but harmless college boys, only to realize too late that they were unconscionable predators.

Chapter 3

Jack Bolton closed his eyes as the helicopter blades began to spin – his mind going back in time.

The cold wind whipped across their bodies, the light air inflated their lungs, the distant sun gleamed from the fading blue sky. It was just another day skating on the river-playing hockey. Every winter the river would freeze, allowing the neighborhood kids from both sides of the river to play hockey against each other.

Jack, an athletic eleven-year-old, and his eight-year-old brother, Tommy, never missed a day of playing hockey on the river. His father had always warned them about the dangers of skating there. The water moved just slowly enough to freeze. The hard part was figuring out whether it was safe enough for skating. It was Jack who always tested the ice while the other kids waited on shore for the all-clear signal.

Today began like any other hockey day, the rivalry between the two teams rekindled. Spirits were high. A new layer of smooth, clear ice from rain earlier in the week awaited the eager players. The contest began as they weaved their bodies in and out between each other. They laughed and high-fived on good plays and celebrated goals as their happy voices echoed through the cold air and surrounding woods.

Jack played forward while Tommy played defense. Tommy was a natural; he consistently held his own against the older kids.

The game was winding down as the sun began its slow descent behind the trees. The next goal would win. Jack hopped on the loose puck at his end, stick-handled his way through the opposing players and, with a quick flip of his wrist, sent it flying towards the net where it bounced off the inside post of the make-shift goal and ricocheted off the main playing area. Tommy scurried to retrieve it. The puck coasted to a stop on an untested piece of ice. Just as he reached it, the ice began to crack and, within a nano-second, gave way. Jack looked on in horror as Tommy disappeared from sight.

His adrenaline kicked in. He skated with lightning speed to the ice opening and plunged into the frigid water. His eyes scanned the cold murkiness, and to his left he caught a glimpse of Tommy struggling. He fumbled around until he felt Tommy's hand and grasped it. He pulled with everything he had against the slow moving current, the frigid water, and the weight of his heavy clothes. He quickly searched for the opening and moved towards the muffled voices where light was streaming through. A hockey stick suddenly protruded down into the water; he grabbed it with one hand keeping Tommy in tow with the other, as the group of kids above pulled with all their might. He emerged from the icy water, and pulled himself up onto a sturdy piece of ice, mostly with his shoulders and one elbow. He could feel Tommy's hand beginning to slip from his grasp. He reached to grab it with his left, but it was too late: Tommy disappeared into the depths of the river's current.

Jack's eyes fluttered open, as the helicopter maneuvered through one of Afghanistan's dangerous mountain ranges. He leaned back against the helicopter's insulated metal frame, his mind racing. At age twenty-seven, he had spent the last nine years of his life in the Navy, the last seven as a SEAL. It had been his goal to fight with the best of the best. At six-foot two, athletic, smart, fearless, and possessed of a well-honed sixth sense, he finished at the top of his Navy Seal class where only a select few made the grade. After two years of intensive training, he was assigned special operation missions throughout the Middle East and Africa.

SEALs were trained in all facets of how to immobilize the enemy. Jack was no exception. He was skillful with a knife, held a black belt in karate, was thoroughly schooled in the use of explosives, was self-sufficient in the harshest elements and had become an expert long-range marksman. Ironically, growing up, he hated guns, but now the gun was a major part of his life. He had succeeded in the most dangerous assignments – the quintessential SEAL.

He had seen many soldiers break down under the stress of battle and repeated deployments. Some returned home suffering from major physical and psychological impairments for which they would face a lifetime of treatment. Others dulled their tortured memories and restless nights with painkillers and sleeping pills.

He had experienced the loss of team members working alongside him. He had seen the body of one of his closest friends shattered by a well-placed IED. One minute he was talking to him; the next minute he was gone. It could have been any one of them that day.

Now, after seven years in the Special Forces, Jack knew it was time to get out before his luck ran out. He had made his arrangements and had two weeks left before he would begin a normal life and hopefully, at some point, start a family. He had seen too many people die who were close to him.

It was probably why he was so overprotective of his twenty-one year old sister, Nicole. She was all he had left. Their parents had been killed in a horrible car accident four years ago, and she stood as his one sustaining connection with normalcy. She had been on his mind more than usual in recent weeks.

She had gone to live with their grandfather after their parents' deaths while she finished high school. It was a tough period for both siblings, but somehow they managed to get through it. She excelled in school and, to her surprise, got accepted to Harvard on a scholarship. She was going to be a doctor. In a sense, they were travelling in opposite directions. Hers was the road to preserving and saving lives; he was to become a killing machine, trained by the government. They once shared a laugh over the fact that she was part of a humanity mission to the Congo to help educate neglected children at the same time that he was on an ops mission in the next country destroying a terrorist cell. His sister was right about his overprotectiveness but, with the emotional pain he had suffered already, he was determined to protect his sister. He had scared away many boys while home on leave when she was in high school, for which he always got hell from her, but she finally settled on a guy Jack actually trusted and liked. He was sure that Ted would do a good job of watching over her while he was deployed.

Jack's thoughts came back to the task at hand as the helicopter hovered above a rocky incline on the outskirts of the Paktia Province in the eastern part of Afghanistan, close to the Pakistan border. Tonight would be his last mission as a Navy SEAL.

The group of eight special-forces soldiers went through one last check of their equipment. A minute later a signal came from the pilot that the helicopter was fifteen seconds from insertion. The men undid their safety tethers and grabbed on to the hand straps. They ejected from the copter, fast roping down fifty feet to the ground below. Once they all hit the ground successfully, Jack, as the team leader, led the way. The helicopter then ascended into the night sky. The men in green and black camouflage with green and black war paint on their faces, and their communication devices firmly in place, shuffled their backpacks and pushed down their night-vision goggles over their eyes, enabling them to see everything in infrared.

They had received intelligence and satellite imagery confirming the whereabouts of a high-ranking Al-Qaeda terrorist in the camp of a Taliban group of fighters. Their assignment was to take him out. After a six-mile hike through rough terrain, they found themselves deep in unfriendly territory along the Pakistan and Afghanistan border, where a lifeline, if needed, would be improbable.

As they got closer to their target, Jack positioned himself on a rock ledge and peered through his binoculars, capturing a band of men in a camp seventy yards to the south. He zeroed in on his target and, with a motion of his hand, the target was now in play, just as the intelligence had briefed.

Oscar, who was the team's special ops sharp shooter, maneuvered into place next to Jack for a clear shot. One clean shot and they would be on their way home. The marksman modified his scope, adjusting for wind and elevation, and precisely lined up his target with his M14 sniper rifle. From seventy yards away, with the pull of a finger, the target went down. A perfect shot under perfect conditions. Now all that was left to do was hike back to the evacuation point. But then, without warning, a barrage of bullets began raining in from all directions. There was initial confusion in the moon's shadows. They were now the hunted, scurrying for cover while firing back at an invisible enemy who had the advantage of thorough knowledge of the surrounding terrain.

Being extremely outnumbered, the team quickly analyzed their best chance of survival. The squad's strength lay in the cover of darkness and the element of surprise but, once uncovered by larger forces in enemy territory, their superior skills and equipment would be neutralized. The enemy would not end their pursuit until the SEAL team was either captured or killed. Jack had always prepared himself mentally for this scene, knowing that he would never allow himself to be captured alive again by this notoriously sadistic enemy.

They found themselves pinned down in a dark, desolate mountain range, overwhelmed by the barrage of enemy firepower coming from all directions. There would be no cavalry coming to their aid.

Jack barked out orders to save ammo and stay low. He discussed strategy behind a row of rocks with Mike Brady. They had participated together in the SEAL training programs and graded out as the top two in their class with Jack finishing on top.

The mission had gone awry, almost as if someone was expecting them. Was it possible that somebody leaked the information to the Taliban? It sure felt like a set-up but for now it was Jack's job to get his men out of there. They needed to move quickly and, just as he instructed four of his men to head to the north end of the mountain range, with the remaining four staying behind to cover with automatic fire, two RPGs slammed into their location, directly hitting two SEALS. Another RPG landed twenty yards to the right, near another of his men. Jack scurried to the locations of the explosions. The three SEALs were dead. Those remaining got up from their crouches and moved quickly, ducking, and finding cover behind the rocky ledges. They moved to the north side of the mountain range where fifteen Taliban were waiting. Suddenly the darkened night lit up like a gigantic fireworks display as the Taliban opened fire at Jack's men who responded with heavy automatic weaponry, killing ten of the Taliban instantly, but a fourth Navy SEAL was shot dead during the exchange. Jack's remaining men needed to keep going but the further north that they tried to move, the more incoming fire exploded all around them. In the confusion, the four remaining SEALs became separated.

As Jack got to a steep ravine, there were no Taliban in front of him, but the other SEALs were nowhere to be seen either. It was their motto to never leave a SEAL behind, but tonight he had no choice. He heard gunfire forty yards to the east. He rapidly ran back towards the sound and saw three Taliban coming over a rocky ledge.

He opened fire, killing all three, then awkwardly slid behind a rock embankment where he came across Mike who was wounded in the leg.

"What the hell happened here, Jack?" Mike said in a strained voice with pain radiating from his leg.

Jack had no answers. "Can you move?"

Mike nodded in reply as Jack tied a tourniquet around the wound.

"Here's my backpack; take out the explosives and place them around these rocks. We'll set it to go off when I get back." Jack added in a hurried voice, "Here's another magazine clip. I'm going to find Kurt and Oscar."

Jack ran towards the sound of gunfire, ignoring every human impulse he possessed and reacting purely on his training and instincts. He randomly fired his gun, holding off the approaching Taliban, until he caught a glimpse of one of his men badly wounded but still alive.

"Kurt, do you hear me?" Jack whispered as he hit the ground and crawled toward him.

"I think I broke my ankle and I've been hit in the shoulder, I'm bleeding," Kurt said in a crackling voice with his lungs wheezing for air.

"Look, do you know where Oscar is?"

"He was about ten to fifteen yards to the east," he replied, his voice straining to get the words out.

"I'll be right back to get you. I'm going to see if I can find Oscar." Jack scurried around in the darkness looking for Oscar. He needed to find him quickly before the Taliban overran the area. Hiding and crouching along the rocks, he saw a body. "Oscar, Oscar," Jack called softly, trying to not draw attention, but there was no reply. He unleashed a fury of bullets as he moved quickly and slid next to Oscar. He felt for a pulse, but Oscar was gone.

Jack reminisced for a few seconds about what a great guy Oscar was and how he made everyone laugh, even during the roughest times. Mad as hell, Jack stepped up from behind a rock formation and unleashed another round of bullets at the Taliban, only to instantly duck down to avoid the hail of bullets coming his way. He clipped in another magazine and flat-out ran to the west to get back to Kurt.

"Kurt, you still with me?" His adrenaline was exploding. Kurt just nodded weakly and was trying to catch his breath. In one motion, Jack bent down, swung Kurt onto his back and darted towards Mike, dodging and weaving, as bullets whizzed past him. Mike emptied a clip of bullets to fend off the enemy as Jack approached carrying Kurt.

Jack knelt down next to Mike and placed Kurt down gently. "Okay, Kurt, we're halfway there." But there was no reply, not even a shallow breath. Jack looked at Kurt and realized from the blank stare in his eyes that he was gone. He looked at Mike who could only shake his head in disbelief. They had started with eight good Navy

SEALs on a relatively straightforward mission, and were now down to two. For a few seconds it crossed Jack's mind that he might be going home in a body bag but he immediately dismissed the thought.

"Are the explosives in place?" Jack asked

"All set," Mike answered with a slight smirk. "You go. I'll just slow you down."

"I'm not leaving you here." Jack stared at him intensely. "If you don't come, I'm staying right here with you."

"Okay, okay, I guess I have no choice."

"Damn right!"

"What about Oscar?"

"Look, he's dead. I wish we could take them back with us, but it can't be done. Hell, I'm not even sure we're going to make it."

"I know. I'm going to set the timer for forty-five seconds," Mike said.

An array of firepower began to descend on them as the Taliban got closer, sensing the kill like a pack of wolves chasing their prey. Mike leaned on Jack's shoulder, and they proceeded in an uncoordinated and awkward fashion down the rocky terrain as fast as Mike's good leg would allow. The Taliban followed in hot pursuit until a large explosion coming from the explosives that Mike had set earlier shook the ground stopping them in their tracks.

Jack and Mike got knocked off their feet from the

force of the blast as well, but they bounced right back up, not wasting any time as they continued to maneuver further down the desolate landscape under a now serene, star-laden sky.

Chapter 4

Tall grass rustled in the wind. An old rusty Pontiac Grand Prix, placed on cinder blocks, sat on the front lawn. Behind it stood a deteriorating abandoned Cape-style house, with peeling paint, crooked black shutters, broken windows, and a leaky rotted roof. The house was off the beaten path and secluded from the main road. It was located close to the town line, between Williamstown and North Adams, Massachusetts, and a large pond was within walking distance of the property.

Rex Saxton sat on the front porch eating a couple of burgers with french fries, staring off into space as if in a trance. He was a man who was losing the battle with mental illness, which could be traced back to a mother who did potent drugs while she was pregnant and a drug-addicted father who had no education and whom he barely knew. Rex had been a ward of the state from early childhood, moving from one foster home to another. He was now thirty-four years of age, of median height and build with long straggly hair already receding from his forehead, teeth that needed work, and facial scars from past acne. He was a typical loner, who had no friends, even in his youth. The kids shunned him because of his strange behavior, bizarre mood swings and lack of empathy, all precursors to the mad wave of terror that he was about to unleash.

He had been honorably discharged from the army after two years because of several conflicts with fellow soldiers. As the years passed, he found himself drifting from state to state with no real place he could call home. He could never keep a job long enough to stay in one place. He was skilled as a carpenter, which came naturally to him, and was able to earn some money doing odd jobs from time to time.

As he got older, his thoughts tilted more and more to the dark side until they reached a point of no return. He woke up one morning in Kentucky and began a drive that eventually took him to North Adams, Massachusetts. He drove around the area in an old beat up Ford Mustang, formulating his deranged plan. He even got a fishing license while he was in the area.

The evening sun had slipped behind the trees as Saxton stepped off the porch where he had been sitting for hours in a deep trance. He got in his car, drove a couple of miles down the road and parked close to a secluded Colonial-style house with a two-car garage. The owners, Mary and George Becket, were thought of by friends as two fun-loving, caring, friendly people who were just beginning to enjoy the fruits of their labors. They were in their late fifties and had aged in the same way, both adding pounds as the years went by. They had built a nice retirement nest egg and looked forward to traveling the world together during the next few years.

Saxton sat on a hill above, smoking one cigarette after another, watching the Becket house, and waiting for the lights to go out. He had spent a good part of the morning scouting the area. When he came across the Becket house, which showed no signs of kids or dogs, he determined that the layout of the house was perfect for an invasion and fit precisely into his plan.

The lights had gone off about an hour earlier, but Saxton just sat there waiting for the precise time to strike. He looked at his watch and when the hour hand struck one, he put out his cigarette. He then calmly placed a headlamp around his head, slid his fingers snugly into black gloves, and began his descent down the hill, running like a man possessed. He ran until he came to the edge of the house where he took out a wire-cutting tool and cut the phone line to see if it would set off an alarm. When it didn't, he removed a fan from a window in the garage and slipped in quietly. He then smashed a window into the house, using a crowbar that was hanging on the wall. His heart was racing with adrenaline as he rushed full throttle up the stairs, his headlamp leading the way, until he came to the Beckets' bedroom. He flung the door open before they had a chance to realize a hostile intruder had invaded their home.

After quickly binding the two with zip ties, shouting

at them, waving his gun, and threatening to kill them if they tried anything stupid, he led them to his car, forcing them at gunpoint to get inside. Mary was forced to drive the car, struggling with the steering wheel for a few miles until they came to a stop at the abandoned house. Saxton pulled George out of the car, leaving Mary tied to the steering wheel. He led George to the basement of the house and secured him tightly to a chair and then went back to get his wife.

Mary had managed to slide her hands off the steering wheel, escaping from the car. With her hands bound tightly, she was sprinting for her life through the field in the black of night. She had gotten about thirty yards from the car when Saxton tackled her and dragged her back to the house, throwing her on the decaying, discolored mattress and tying her hands to the broken headboard while her screams of despair went for naught, too far away to be heard by any neighbors.

He left her alone and went to the basement where he pulled out a silencer, attached it to the muzzle, and shot George three times, causing blood to splatter on the cement floor and his head to slump to his chest. He then slowly and calmly walked back up the stairs where Mary was trying in vain to escape by pulling on her ropes with every ounce of strength. He watched, amused that she was flopping around like a fish out of water. She screamed hysterically when she saw the demented killer standing over her, leering, his shirt splattered with

George's blood. At that moment she realized her demise was imminent. He then raped and strangled her.

The next morning, with no emotion, Saxton cleaned up his handy work. He placed the bodies in garbage bags, covering them with scattered debris from the cellar floor, walked out of the abandoned house, and drove away.

Chapter 5

The foliage season was in full bloom – a perfect time for Nicole Bolton to take a weekend trip to the Berkshires to see her good friend Donna Crump at Wilbur Smith College. They had graduated from high school together and hadn't seen each other in quite a while. Her boyfriend, Ted Brown, who she sometimes called "my big teddy," was only too happy to accompany her.

Ted picked her up in his late-model Ford Taurus early one Friday morning for the three-hour trip from Cambridge to Williamstown.

During the quiet moments of their trip, along the scenic parts of the winding roadway, Nicole's mind wandered to her overprotective brother Jack. Always lurking in the back of her mind was the fear that one day someone from the armed forces would knock on her door to inform her that her brother had been killed while participating in a covert operation. She and Jack would Skype at times to catch up with each other's life, and then there were his surprise visits, which always ended up with him scaring the boys away. The high school boys were surely intimidated by his Navy SEAL status. But when she introduced Ted to Jack, surprisingly Jack didn't say much, which meant he silently gave his approval.

She had never seen her brother cry until one day when she walked into his room unannounced and found him sobbing. He had received the Purple Heart for saving seven soldiers in Afghanistan. And here was this toughest of tough Navy SEALs, with tears rolling down his cheeks. He blurted out, "I failed Tommy...just a slip of the hand and he slid away from me." He also blamed himself for the rocky relationship his parents had after Tommy's death. Their mother never could get past it. She took anxiety and sleeping pills, and she would have these crying spells that came out of nowhere. Eventually their father grew tired of it, began to drink more and ultimately got involved with another woman.

Jack told his sister for the first time that day that he joined the Navy because of his failure to save Tommy and the guilt he felt from not heeding his Dad's warnings on the hazards of the frozen river.

It was after their parents' deaths that they grew closer and came to realize how much they meant to each other.

"One hour to go, Nicole," Ted said, as he rubbed his tired eyes.

Her mind had drifted... "What? Oh, okay. And don't you close your eyes," she ordered, taking over as navigator.

"I'm wide awake."

He opened the window, squirming around in the

driver's seat to keep from closing his eyes. But as the long drive continued, they began to slowly close; several times he was jolted as he felt the car swerve slightly, only to catch himself before he went off the road with Nicole reprimanding him and insisting that she should drive.

They were almost there. Nicole knew him all too well; a long drive always tuckered him out. Maybe it was the motion of the car or he didn't get enough sleep the night before, but once they got there he would perk right up. She always cautioned him, knowing this would happen. But it was minor flaw in Nicole's eyes. Other than being a little goofy at times. He had a big-heart, a nice smile, a six-foot-four frame, and, of course, he liked it when she called him "big teddy."

Meanwhile, Ted was looking forward to the weekend. His thoughts drifted. He had known that Nicole was the one from the first day that they met. It wasn't easy getting the first date, but he was relentless and eventually she gave in. She used to joke that if she said "yes" to a date that would be the end of his interest, but three years later they were closer than ever.

He almost bombed on that first date. He remembered how clumsy and nervous he had been. He burnt his tongue on the pizza, which made him talk funny. Then, he accidently spilled his drink on Nicole, but she didn't get upset. And that wasn't the worst of it. When they came out of the restaurant, he discovered that he had a flat tire. And as luck would have it, he had no spare. She just shook her head. He had to call his father to pick them up, and a good night kiss sure wasn't in the cards, just a goodbye and a "don't bother to ask me out on a date again look" as she got out of the car. He remembered how he tossed and turned and didn't sleep that night. All he could think of was how he blew it with the prettiest girl he had ever dated and how she probably thought "what a loser." But, to his surprise, she called the next day and said that she had a great time other than the flat tire. That was Nicole, she saw the best in people. A first date that would have been a disaster in most girls' eyes had been pretty amusing to her.

The car finally came to a stop outside of Donna's townhouse on the Wilbur Smith campus.

***

Cedar Tavern, located over the New York border, was a popular place where locals and college kids congregated. The tavern inside consisted of a dining area and a separate large pub which filled to capacity on most Friday nights. Cedar wood throughout the tavern gave it a quaint look. A small dance floor and several pool tables complemented the pub with adjacent tables surrounding the circular bar, which was set in the center of the room. Large flat-screen TVs were strategically placed around the bar for optimum viewing.

Nicole and Ted sat at a table with Donna and four of her roommates. They drank, laughed, and told stories, oblivious to the people around them. Off to the far right, a few of the Beta frat boys were already revved up for a big night, drinking round after round of tequila shots and twelve-ounce beers. They checked out every girl who went by, and as the night progressed, they became more obnoxious, especially with every short skirt that walked by.

Tom Mello shot a few rounds of pool at the back end of the tavern, drank a few beers, and people-watched in between turns. He noticed Nick and John and a few of their frat brother minions at the far corner of the tavern, towards the left of the ladies' room, drinking one shot after another. The more they drank, the crazier they got.

Tom, a Beta frat member, was a sophomore at the college. He was an average looking kid with a down-to-earth personality who had a lot of friends around campus. He generally accepted people at face value, never saying a bad word about anyone, but he knew all too well how Nick and John operated. While most people viewed them as well-bred college boys occasionally indulging in more-or-less harmless excursions to the wild side, Tom knew their dark side. He had seen it firsthand when he witnessed what could only be called a rape, committed by the two partners in crime. He wanted to report it to the school but the girl never pressed charges and he figured that, in the end, his life would be made miserable without anything happening to his two well-connected frat brothers. So, after a lot of soul searching, he did nothing, a decision that continued to prey on his mind.

Tom reflected on how the frat was a divided brotherhood, almost like evil versus good. You had John and Nick's group with their unethical and unsavory character, considered the bad boys of the fraternity. Most came from well-to-do families and felt entitled to do anything they wanted. Some of them smoked pot on cue, every morning at ten and every afternoon at four. They made the pledges do the most embarrassing things and sometimes it bordered on dangerous. Alcohol poisoning came to mind. If a student was pledging the frat it was a good idea to avoid this group as much as possible, especially if they had been drinking. Of course, there was also a core group of good guys, but there always seemed to be a battle for the hearts and minds of the new pledges and the middle-of-the-road frat brothers.

Tom couldn't forget an incident that happened back in his pledging days. John and Nick ordered him to take advantage of a girl who was extremely intoxicated or high on some drug by trying to have sex with her, but he refused to do it. That infuriated them because no one ever stood up to them.

So, at the next frat meeting, they tried to make him pay for his insubordination by having him blackballed out of the frat. Despite their influence, they failed to get the necessary seventy-five percent of the vote; he was too well liked by most of the other frat brothers. From that day forward, there were very few words spoken between them. Tom kept an eye on them, however, knowing that they were two very bad apples whose presence anywhere could spell trouble.

Tonight looked like it might be one of those times. Nick's group was getting louder and drunker as the night wore on. Tom took a walk over to the men's room at the same time that Nicole Bolton was making her way to the ladies room. She got stuck in the long line of waiting girls and had to endure a few whistles and shouts from Nick's group. She certainly was the type of girl a guy didn't forget. She had to be the best looking girl in the place that night. She easily turned heads with her natural long blonde hair and lean supermodel body, enticingly package in tight-fitting casual jeans and a simple white blouse, none of which went unnoticed by Nick and John's group. Combine alcohol and a head-turning girl to the mix and Tom knew for sure there was an accident waiting to happen. If history was any harbinger, Nick's and John's minds were working overtime trying to figure out how they would force their will on this stunning bombshell.

As he made his way back from the men's room, no words were spoken between him and Nick's group when he passed them. They were too busy studying the hot girl who was still waiting in the ladies' room line. The childish whistles, and, "where have you been all my life?" banter filled the air. Nicole just ignored them.

Tom continued to watch from a distance. Nicole came out of the ladies' room and made her way to the bar. Tom had a bad feeling about what might be going on in Nick's mind.

Nicole ordered a Coors Light while Nick nonchalantly planted himself next to her at the bar. In the background, the frat boys were in hysterics watching Nick maneuver with his usual self-assurance.

"What's your name?" Nick asked. "I'm Nick," he said, extending his hand.

"I'm here with my boyfriend," she replied instantly, keeping her hands to her side and hoping this guy would just go away, thinking that the beer she ordered couldn't come fast enough.

"So I see you are up here visiting some friends at Wilbur Smith?"

"Yeah," she replied, not looking at him.

"Well, we're having an after-hours frat party later on. Why don't you come over? Bring your boyfriend as well," he said confidently with his elbow on the bar and facing her. "You know you have beautiful eyes."

Nicole found herself extremely uncomfortable and, with a quick turn towards him, she caught a glimpse of Nick's eyes and remembered something that her brother always said: "Look at their eyes and you can see their soul." What she saw was someone she didn't want to be around. The bottle of beer was placed on the bar counter. She handed a ten-dollar bill to the bartender and walked away quickly, not waiting for the change. This incensed Nick as his frat brothers were laughing in the background, knowing he had gotten shot down.

"Get me four tequila shots," he ordered. Then he turned, with his back leaning up against the bar, glowering at the table where Nicole sat, as he began to plot his next move. The shots came and he delivered them to his group, but Nick silently seethed, never taking his eyes off Nicole's table for the rest of the night.

Tom sat back at the far end of the pub, working off his fifth beer. He was done playing pool and nonchalantly watched Nick from afar, nodding every now and then at the conversation around him. He looked down at his smart phone – signaling it was on low battery - as it approached 12:45 p.m. He chuckled at a joke that someone told, then noticed the hot girl and her friends getting up from their table to leave. He quickly turned his head and eyed Nick's group. He could see Nick talking to John and pointing over in the direction of the hot girl. Whatever Nick was up to, Tom knew it couldn't be good. As the girl left with her friends, coincidently, Nick and his crew put down their drinks to leave as well.

Tom wasn't too far behind as he exited the tavern.

He looked around and saw the girl of interest standing outside, talking to one of her girlfriends who was sitting in the passenger seat of someone's car. Once the conversation ended, the car pulled out, leaving Nicole to walk back to the passenger seat of her boyfriend's car. It appeared that Nicole and her friends had driven in two separate cars. Tom's eyes wandered around the parking lot until he came upon Nick, sitting in the driver's seat of his BMW Five Series, about ten parking spaces from the hot girl and her boyfriend. Tom got in his Honda CRV and just sat there observing the situation.

Nick waited patiently in his car, while the frat brothers in the back seat were becoming restless.

"Let's go," Chris Spenser said. "What are we waiting for?"

Nick looked at John in the passenger seat; both had sly smiles.

"We are going to have some fun," Nick said with a big drunken grin on his face and a crazed look in his eyes. He then pulled a 380-caliber pistol from under the seat, brandishing it around the car like a trophy.

"What the hell are you going to do with that?" Chris asked.

"Well, remember that girl over there," Nick said as he pointed over at the late model Taurus where Nicole and her boyfriend were sitting.

"Oh, yeah," Ike Smith added. "The hottie that shot you down."

"Shut the hell up!" Nick shouted angrily. "Time for a little payback, and, we are going to scare the hell out of them."

"What are you going to do?" Chris asked.

"Sit back and you'll see," Nick snapped, confident in his evil plan that John, his partner in crime, already knew.

Ted started up his car and headed out of the tavern parking lot. The alcohol had surely put them both in good spirits. They bantered back and forth. Nicole thought how good it felt spending time together with Ted in this idyllic setting away from the daily routine.

The tavern was a straight eight miles east on Route 2 back to the college. The moon was full, giving off natural light that brightened the surrounding landscape. The roads were empty at this late hour. Four miles into the drive, Ted's car slowly came to a stop at a stop sign and, without warning, a big jolt came from the back of his car.

"What the hell?" Ted muttered as his head bounced off the head rest. "You okay, Nicole?"

"I'm okay."

Ted got out of his car to see the damage. Nicole stayed in the car while looking back through the rearview window.

"I'm sorry," Nick said, standing there shaking his head at the minor damage and then turning his head and slyly smiling at John who had moved into the driver's seat of the BMW.

"There doesn't seem to be any real damage," Ted said. "Why don't we just forget about it?"

"That's a great idea," Nick said. "I'm really sorry."

"Forget about it," Ted said, as he started to walk away.

"I have to give you something. It's all my fault," Nick confessed as he pulled out his 380-caliber handgun and pointed it at Ted's head. "Now, let's go for a ride," Nick ordered, and he got into the back seat of Ted's car.

Tom slowly drove around the two cars, hoping not to be recognized, and with a quick peek he noticed Nick in the backseat of the couple's car. He drove the car around the corner and pulled off to the side of the road and turned his headlights off. About twenty seconds later both cars went past him. He started his car with the headlights off and followed, not too far behind. The cars veered off to the right of a split in the road. After six miles on the back roads of Williamstown, the two cars began to slow down and took the next right onto a dirt road. Tom pulled his car off to the side of the road where it couldn't be seen. He got out of the car and immediately began jogging down the dirt road. The full moon gave off plenty of light for him to see where he was going without losing a step.

Chapter 6

The frigid Afghanistan air had settled into their bones after two nights in the mountains. The sunrise was just breaking through the eastern sky. Jack and Mike had eluded Taliban, Al-Qaeda, tribes, villagers, and any other human being in those mountains by moving at night and hiding in rock crevices by day. Water, food, and ammo were getting low and the time had come to find the good guys.

They had finally made it out of the mountain range and into a lower elevation where fields of opium could be seen for miles. These were big operations run by drug-lords, criminal gangs, and Taliban, a dangerous place for any outsider wandering into the area. But the GPS had driven them north towards friendly forces which meant their only road to safety was through these fields.

The two SEALs crouched down and moved forward between the rows of poppy plants, their progress slowed by Mike's leg wound. It had stopped bleeding after the firefight, but the pain was radiating throughout his body and he needed medical attention soon. Ammo was short and they were sitting ducks in the open field. If they were going to get home, they needed to move quickly.

"Mike, wait here," Jack said in a calm voice. "I'm going to scout ahead."

Mike nodded in agreement as Jack, still crouched down, scurried alongside the waist-high poppy plants which camouflaged his movements. Periodically, he cautiously peered over the plants to survey the area. Eventually he came to a dirt road where three Taliban, engrossed in their task, were carefully placing an IED for the next unsuspecting American soldiers. Jack took out his fully loaded small caliber 9mm handgun. He quickly thought about his situation, especially with Mike sixty yards back in the opium field. His action would draw attention to both of them, but it had to be done. He bolted out of his crouching position and began firing at the three Taliban, causing the IED to explode and knocking him back into the poppy field. He was momentarily disoriented from the blast and the sound of small caliber gunfire could be heard in the background. His senses slowly returned. His first thought was Mike and he immediately scrambled back towards him.

The explosion had gotten the attention of every Taliban in the area. They came over the hill, guns blazing in all directions, bullets whizzing past very close to Mike's position. He rose and returned fire to keep them at bay as Jack kept low and slithered on the ground for the last fifteen yards until he reconnected with Mike. They stayed low on their bellies, both thinking of their next move. Once the ammo ran out there would be no escape.

"What do you think?" Mike asked.

"We could run for it and take our chances or stay here until our ammo runs out. Either way we are pretty screwed," Jack reasoned.

"Look, I can't move that well," Mike spit out in an uncomfortable position. "I'm not going to get very far. Let me cover you and at least you'll have a chance to get away, Jack."

"I'm not leaving you," Jack replied sharply, locking his last magazine clip into place. "If this is it, then we'll go down together."

Mike smiled. "Okay, your call."

As the Taliban closed in, the two exhausted SEALs unloaded the last of their ammo, trying to slow their advance.

Then, out of nowhere, an Army Ranger patrol that was in the area rushed to the sound of the explosion, firing their M4s at the approaching Taliban, unaware of Mike and Jack in the poppy field. The two SEALs remained close to the ground, invisible to the approaching Rangers. They were caught between the crossfire of the two groups. The Rangers' firepower drove the Taliban back into the hills. When the gunfire ceased and an eerie quietness settled in, Jack yelled out, getting the attention of the Rangers who rushed to their position.

The first Ranger on the scene yelled out, "We need a

medic." Within a short time after the area was secured, a helicopter landed and whisked Jack and Mike back to the main base.

***

The helicopter hovered above the Bagram Military Airbase in Bagram, Afghanistan. It slowly descended onto the designated area as a group of medical personnel and military brass waited, shielding their faces from the loose dust being blown around as the chopper blades continued to spin. The medical team immediately rushed to the helicopter door and whisked Mike away to surgery while a two-man team of military officers accompanied Jack to the Commander's office.

Commander Gary Armstrong, a Special Operations senior commander, greeted Jack as he entered the room. The two lower ranking officers stood behind Jack. He took a brief look around the room and caught a glimpse of the framed pictures of scenes from World War II.

"Sit down. Jack," Commander Armstrong ordered in a kindly tone. "How are you doing?"

"I'm fine, sir," he replied, as he seated himself.

The two lower ranking officers settled into chairs behind Jack.

"So what the hell happened out there?" Commander Armstrong asked. "We've been looking for you guys for two days now."

"We took out the target as planned and then all hell broke loose from every direction, sir. The Taliban hit us with rocket launchers, small arms fire, and rapid fire weapons."

"Once you didn't show up at the extraction point, and we hadn't received any communications, we knew we had a problem." Armstrong said. "I'm glad you're alive. What happened to the other members of the team?"

"Except for Mike Brady, who is being worked on by the medics, all the other members of the team are dead, sir," Jack stated, bowing his head.

"Are you sure everybody else out there was killed?"

"Yes, sir."

"You know this for sure?"

"I checked on all of them myself, sir; a few of the men's bodies were beyond recognition, " he responded in a solemn tone.

"I'll need a full report of what happened out there on my desk as soon as possible, Jack." Armstrong said, his voice a shade higher. He shook his head at the outcome.

"Yes, sir."

"Everybody out of my office except Jack," Armstrong ordered. The door shut as the last officer left. "Now, Jack, I know your time with us will be up next week; I want you to know that I consider you to be one of the finest Navy SEALs I've ever had under my command," he stated.

"Thank you, sir."

At that point, Armstrong rose from his chair and walked over to the window where he stood, looking out, as he continued to talk.

"You know this is one screwed up war and, between you and me, I have no idea what we are doing here. Nobody knows what the mission is and I just lost six very good Navy SEALs, men with families killed on an ops mission to take out a specific insurgent target, knowing all too well that he will be replaced by another. So I ask, what the hell is it all about? We have soldiers walking to nowhere along dirt roads only to die from booby-trapped implosive devices. And, I ask myself what are they dying for? Terrorism! We can't engage until the enemy fires on us first. How ridiculous is that? We're fighting what may be five thousand real Taliban we can't even see. This war should have lasted no more than two years, yet here we are twelve years later with no end in sight. Two wars, three trillion dollars of wasted taxpayer money, a lifetime of disabilities for some of these brave men, and what do we have to show for it? Absolutely nothing. And what do you think is going to happen here when we eventually pull out?" he ranted. "Look at Iraq, what the hell did we accomplish there? The place has turned into a civil war. Then ask me what happened to all the money that was supposed to rebuild that country. It just disappeared into thin air. And how does Washington expect us to win the hearts and minds of the people if they view us as conquerors or occupiers?"

"I don't know, sir."

"Well, it will all go to hell when we leave; it will be like we were never here. How damn sad!" he concluded in a tone of despair. Then, returning to his chair, he said, with his hands folded together on his desk, "Anyway, I originally wanted to talk to you about a CIA opportunity that's come across my desk or talk you into staying on with the Navy SEALs. A person with your skill set is very much in demand but, when you were missing in action, I took a closer look at your profile and realized you've had quite a few tragedies in your life. I saw that you have one remaining sister in your family and thought how devastating it would be for her to be told that you died or went missing in action. But there's something else we need to talk about."

"I don't understand, sir." Jack looked at him, thinking that he was still quite an imposing figure in his middle age, which included a well-built six-foot four frame and a shiny bald head. He had seen it all and had the reputation of a tough guy who took no nonsense. He was one of the toughest Navy SEALs in his day and here he was ranting about this pathetic war and how, in his mind, this was all a waste of time and a sad waste of life.

"Well, Jack, as you have already learned only too well, life has a way of throwing curve balls. You've been dealt some raw deals in the past which you have found a way to overcome. It says a lot about your character, Jack."

"Sir, if you don't mind my asking, where are you going with all this?"

"I'm sorry to have to tell you, Jack, that life has thrown you another curve ball."

His mind immediately raced in panic. "Has something happened to my sister?" He shuddered waiting for the commander's answer.

Commander Armstrong took a deep breath. "Jack, I got a call from a Special Agent Ryland out of the Boston FBI Office yesterday."

"What are you trying to tell me? That my sister is dead?" Jack asked, his face ashen.

"No. I mean… I don't really know. He just said that your sister is missing along with her boyfriend."

Jack shook his head and put his hands to his face. A feeling of numbness engulfed his body from head to toe. "What do you mean she's missing, sir, and from where?" he asked. "She's all I have left."

"From what the agent explained to me, the last place that they were seen together was at a tavern on the New York border near Williamstown, Massachusetts. Here's the agent's number," Commander Armstrong said as he handed it to Jack. "I can only imagine how you're feeling, Jack. I have a daughter who's in college as well and I'm always worried about her."

Jack sat staring at Commander Armstrong. All he could think of was what he had been through and survived in the mountains of Afghanistan. Now his sister was probably dead in some car wreck in the serene Berkshires.

"Jack, there's a medical plane leaving for Germany in three hours. And I've arranged a flight out of Germany to the States for you. Get something to eat, take a shower, and get that report to me before you leave."

"Yes, sir," Jack said. "How long has she been missing?"

"Three or four days."

Jack sat there, trying to hold back his emotions as best he could, but his eyes were starting to fill. He took a deep breath and exhaled as he got up from his seat, shook the commander's hand and headed to the door.

"Jack, I've put through the papers for an early release from the SEALs."

Jack turned toward his CO as he opened the door. "Thank you, sir."

"Good luck, Jack. I'm so sorry," Commander Armstrong said in a soft tone. "And, Jack, I want you to give me a call anytime if I can help you, even if it's just to talk. Also, remember there's a position with the CIA that is open for you. Think about that."

Jack nodded in agreement and headed into the darkness of the corridor.

Chapter 7

Jack got off the elevator that had taken him up to the offices of the F.B.I. in Boston where he was met by security. After the requisite screening, he was escorted to the office of Special Agent Ryland who was expecting him.

"Come on in," Ryland said quietly, the phone to his ear, as he motioned with his finger for Jack to take a seat. "I'll be with you in a minute," he whispered.

Jack sat down and looked around the office while waiting for Agent Ryland to get off the phone. The office was comfortably furnished with traditional mahogany and leather upholstery. It included a small conference area and afforded a pleasant view of the city below. A group of family pictures were displayed on a window cabinet behind his desk, a proud family man for sure.

Agent Ryland hung up the phone. "I'm sorry," he said, as he got up and extended his hand to Jack. "I'm Special Agent Ryland."

"I'm Jack Bolton, Nicole's brother."

"This must be hard on you. I'm not sure what you've been told," Agent Ryland said. "Right now, all we have is a missing person report on your sister and her boyfriend, Ted Brown."

"What's the latest?" Jack asked.

"Let me give you an overview of what I know," Ryland said, settling his sturdy frame against a bookcase while rubbing his chin. "We were called in by the Williamstown Police after they talked to Donna Crump, the friend of your sister, who reported them missing. In the absence of any other information, the consensus for the moment is that they may have decided to drive back to Boston and went off the road. Route 2 can be a very tricky and dangerous road at night, especially if they were driving after having had a few drinks. So that's where we're concentrating our resources in searching for them right now."

"Where were they last seen?" Jack asked.

"Well, from what Donna Crump told us, they were at a pub called the Cedar Tavern just over the New York border about eight miles from Wilbur Smith College, and it's basically a straight drive from the college. So it's pretty hard to get lost."

"So, I'm confused. Where were they last seen?" Jack asked with a frown on his face.

"I'm sorry… Donna told us she last saw them in the parking lot when she left with her friends."

"Is it possible something happened in the parking lot?"

"We checked with the employees on duty that night and there was nothing of significance that any of them could recall."

"So you pretty much have no idea what happened to them?"

"I wish I had something more I could tell you," Agent Ryland said sadly. "At least there's always the possibility that they're safe somewhere."

Jack leaned back in his chair and gathered his thoughts. "Your conclusion then is that there's no evidence of foul play and they probably went off the road."

"Yeah. But there is one other thing that we're looking at."

"What is that?"

"Well, we have been investigating the disappearance of a couple from their home a couple of weeks ago on the Williamstown-North Adams town line."

"You might have a killer on the loose?" Jack asked, folding his arms.

"It's possible; we haven't ruled anything out."

"Maybe they stopped to help someone out that night on the side of the road."

"Yeah, that too, is a possibility."

"So you have two couples who have disappeared from the same general area within weeks of each other. Don't you find that kind of strange?" Jack asked.

"It surely is a concern and there's always a possibility there might be some connection," Agent Ryland stated.

Jack got up from his chair, took a second look at the framed pictures behind the agent's desk, and wryly commented, "Good looking family you have there, Special Agent Ryland."

"Thanks."

"I think you should be focusing your attention on this as a crime instead of some standard missing person report. I know my sister and something has happened to her," Jack said with a tone of exasperation.

"Jack, there's no evidence of a crime yet and we are doing the best we can under the circumstances."

"What's the address of the missing couple?"

"I shouldn't be doing this, but what harm can it do?" he said, looking through a file. "Let's see, 8 Old Farm Road in North Adams."

"Thanks. Well, since it looks like there's nothing more you can tell me, I'll be hitting the road," Jack said with a disappointed look. He shook Agent Ryland's hand and turned towards the door.

Chapter 8

Jack drove the rented Chevy Impala west along the scenic, sunlit Route 2 highway. The steep hills and winding roads caused him, at times, to think back to Afghanistan. During most of the trip, he focused on looking along the route for anything out of place. He stopped a few times whenever he saw a banged up guardrail, and examined the surrounding area, but to no avail. As much as he wanted to believe that Nicole and Ted might have eloped without telling anyone, he knew deep down that they were gone.

After three hours of driving, the road changed from curving and hilly to flat and straight as he drove through the town of Williamstown, which was hidden in the valley between the mountains. The breathtaking scenery at this time of year made one think that it was impossible for anything sinister to happen in such a place.

Jack turned the car into the parking lot of a cheap roadside motel called Clarks, with painted red shutters, white brick stucco, and a large motel sign blinking Vacancy. It had been a fixture of the local landscape for over sixty years. He got out of the car and walked into the motel's front office, came out with a key, and went over to room ten. He had reserved the room for two weeks. He knew he wasn't leaving until he learned exactly what had happened to his sister. The motel consisted of twenty-four rooms, all facing the main road, the type of place where nobody was interested in exchanging pleasantries with their neighbors. Jack unloaded his suitcase and a duffle bag from the trunk and carried both items into the room, which wasn't much to write home about. It had the standard saggy mattress, worn dull blankets, cracking white paint on the walls, a basic TV, and a bathroom that had seen better days. He opened the duffle bag, examining a combination of small caliber handguns. Jack had prepared for a war as only a Navy SEAL would before a mission.

***

The morning light cut through the curtain slit, waking Jack before the alarm went off. He turned and looked at the clock; it was time to get up anyway. He showered, dressed quickly and opened the door to the refreshing morning air. He got into his car, found a fast food restaurant, and used the drive-thru to grab a coffee and a Danish. He then continued to the address that Agent Ryland had given him.

He took a turn off the main road and drove a couple of miles until he came to the *Old Farm Road* street sign where he turned left onto the hilly road, coming to a stop in front of the missing couple's home. He emerged from the car, and stood for a moment in front of the colonial-style house with a two-car garage surrounded by yellow tape. He walked around, not sure what he was looking for. He noticed a cut wire and an open window in the garage. He looked at the hill above and walked up to the top, hoping to find something. He figured that if someone were watching the house, they surely would have taken the high ground to observe. In the armed forces, soldiers never set camp in low-lying land; they always wanted to take the high ground so the enemy wouldn't have an advantage. When he reached the top of the hill, he walked around looking for any sign that someone had been there. Within a few minutes, he discovered a section of trampled down grass with cigarette butts scattered about. Just as he thought: - someone had been stalking the Beckets.

As he stood looking down on the house, he could hear dogs barking. Two black labs came running up to him and quickly realized that he wasn't a threat; their tales began to wag as he patted them. An old man in good shape caught up to the dogs. As they scurried around at the top of the hill, the man introduced himself. "Hi, I'm Mike Oar; I don't live too far from here," the old man added, somewhat out of breath.

"I'm Jack Bolton. Nice to meet you," he said, shaking the man's hand.

"You a friend or relative of the family?" the old man asked.

"Neither. I don't really know why I'm here. I'm hoping to find some clues."

"The police have been here for two weeks but I don't think they have a clue as to what happened here."

"Well, I already know that someone was stalking them."

"How do you know that?'

"Look over there in the grass; you can see that someone was sitting there for some time and there are cigarette butts lying on the ground."

"You're pretty observant; were you in the army or something?"

"Yeah. I'm a former SEAL."

"Well, a Navy SEAL man, huh? I was in the army in the fifties. I fought in the Korean war."

"That war was pretty tough."

"Sure was. I'll tell you this: if some guy broke into my house, one of us wouldn't be coming out alive," the old man said with a stern look.

Jack looked over the area while taking the final sip from his coffee cup. "Mr. Oar, it was nice meeting you." He shook the man's hand. "I've got to be going. I'm not going to find anything here."

"What are you looking for?"

"My sister came up to Wilbur Smith College with her boyfriend over a week ago and they're both missing."

"I'm sorry. I heard something about that on the news."

"Yeah, it really sucks."

"So do you think there might be some connection between the two disappearances?"

"I don't know," Jack said while looking at his cell phone. He started down the hill slowly. "It was nice meeting you."

Jack headed back towards Williamstown to see Donna Crump and made a pit stop along the way to get another coffee. He walked in and was greeted by a couple of polite young girls from behind the counter. He ordered a medium coffee and found a table where he sat comfortably enjoying it while thinking about his sister's disappearance and looking at everyone who went by as a suspect. Then he saw an expressionless character walk in and order a coffee.

The man received his order and sat at a table facing the counter girls. He sat a few tables away from Jack, but Rex Saxton just focused on the girls, with an obsessive stare, the type of stare that was far from normal. Jack's sixth sense picked up an evilness that most people would overlook until it was too late. There was something very scary and odd about this guy. It was that blank stare, the soulless eyes, and the facial expressions that made him to be something more than a patron, as if he was stalking his prey. The man was oblivious to everything around him, in a trance-like state. The man got up from the table and walked out the door. Jack's eyes followed him until the man got into his green car. Maybe, Jack thought, he was just overreacting, looking at everyone who walked by with a crooked smile as a suspect.

Jack got back into his car and headed to Wilbur Smith College. When he came to the campus, he parked his car in front of a row of townhouses. He slowly got out of the car, glanced at the time on his cell phone, walked over to Donna Crump's unit and knocked on the door. A pleasant girl with a warm smile opened it, still chattering away with her girlfriends in the background. "May I help you?" she said, her smile fading.

"I'm looking for Donna Crump. I'm Nicole Bolton's brother, Jack."

"Oh, um...Come on in. I'll get her."

Jack looked around at the spacious but messy kitchen, as he grabbed a stool and sat down at the counter.

Donna walked into the kitchen wearing jeans and a white T-shirt which fit her small frame well. Her hair was still wet and frizzed up from the shower. She was busy rubbing it dry with a towel as she greeted Jack. "Hi Jack, I'm so sorry about Nicole. Have you heard anything?"

"Donna, now I remember you. I think you and Nicole were at the house having pictures taken with your prom dates," Jack said awkwardly.

"That's right," she said. "Have you heard anything?"

"As to what I know about Nicole and Ted, the answer is very little. Right now police are just treating it as a missing person case."

"So they haven't found anything?"

"No. It's as though they just disappeared off the planet," Jack said, trying to get comfortable talking to Donna. "The reason I'm here is, hopefully, to learn if you saw or heard something that night which might have been overlooked."

"I told the police everything. We had a fun night at the pub and we left them at the parking lot; they were supposed to come straight back to my townhouse, but they never showed."

Jack rubbed his face while looking straight at Donna. "Think back to that night, Donna. Was there anything that Nicole might have said, some creep that might have given her a hard time? I'm looking for anything. I don't care how stupid or minuscule you might think it is."

Donna looked up and then paused as her eyes focused back on Jack. "Well, there was one little incident, but I don't think it was anything. It had to do with some Beta frat guy, but those guys are always hitting on girls."

"What happened?"

"Nicole just said that when she was at the bar, some guy from the Beta frat had invited her back to an after-hours party."

"Do you know who he was?"

"No, but she said he was kind of creepy."

"That's it."

"Yeah."

"Okay, where's this Beta frat?"

"Um, it's down the road here," she said, pointing to the left. "It has a sign on the house that says Beta Ki Gamma."

"Well, thanks, Donna, for all your help. I think I'll pay a visit to the frat and see if they saw anything that night."

"Good luck, Jack. I hope Nicole is okay somewhere."

"Yeah, I hope so too," he said shaking his head, knowing in his heart that his sister wasn't coming home.

Jack headed out of the townhouse and walked towards the Beta frat. It was located on a street lined with thick oak trees.

As Jack stood in front of the large yellow Victorian, with the mountains in the background, he thought that it looked like one of those houses out of a horror movie. He walked up to the porch, knocked on the front door, waited and then knocked again. Still no answer. He turned the knob, found it was unlocked, and entered. He heard laughter from the back room. He walked slowly into the foyer and then through a hallway until he came to the kitchen. He silently stood at the outer limits of the kitchen where he saw a group of frat guys sitting at a table, smoking pot and laughing hysterically. "So this is what they call a college education?" he blurted out loudly, smirking.

"Who the hell are you?" Nick said in a raised voice as he stood up from the table while the other frat brothers followed.

"Calm down," Jack said, while raising his hand in a negotiating manner. "I'm here about my sister, Nicole Bolton. That's all. My name is Jack Bolton."

Nick, John, Chris, Ike, and another frat brother strutted over and confronted Jack. "Next time, knock," John snapped.

"I did knock, but you guys were too busy studying," he said with a slight grin.

"What can we do for you?" Nick said in a more civil tone.

Jack reached in his pocket and took out a picture of his sister and handed it to Nick. "Were any of you at Cedar Tavern two Fridays ago? That was the last place anyone saw her."

Nick showed the picture to the other frat brothers. They all shrugged their shoulders with blank looks on their faces. "A few of us were actually at Cedar Tavern that night, but it looks like none of us noticed her," Nick said.

"So you're telling me that none of you saw this girl at Cedar Tavern?" Jack asked.

"I guess not," Nick said.

"Since when do college guys not notice a pretty girl?"

Tom entered the kitchen to see what all the commotion was about and grabbed the picture from one of the guys. "I saw her," he said loudly.

"You saw her," Jack exclaimed.

"Yeah. She was very attractive."

"Did you see anything else?"

"No, I just remember seeing her that night," Tom said while nervously handing the picture back to Jack.

Jack handed the picture back to Nick. "What's your name?" Jack asked.

"Nick Gallo."

"Nick, maybe you can show it around to the other guys in the frat and see if anybody saw anything."

"Sure, no problem."

"That's a nasty bruise you have on the side of your face, Nick," Jack said, standing in front of him.

"I walked into a tree branch," Nick replied.

"Well, if anyone saw anything, my number is on the back of the picture and my name again is Jack Bolton."

"Okay, I'll show it around," Nick said, focusing on the photo because he couldn't look Jack in the eye.

Jack felt something wasn't right. He sensed they were hiding something.

"That's a beauty of a shiner you got there," Jack said pointing at John.

"You should see the other guy," John joked, as the frat boys laughed half-heartedly.

"Well, thanks for your time." Jack turned and headed out the door, paused on the porch, took a deep breath and exhaled. The skills that he had developed over the years of interrogating Taliban prisoners had given him a keen sense of body language and the frat boys showed an uneasiness that was more apparent from their actions than anything they said.

As Jack got to the end of the brick walk-way, Tom came running out as if he was running a race. "Jack," he said, stopping briefly. "Can you meet me later today at Cedar Tavern around four o'clock? I have something that you might want to hear."

"What do you have?'

"My name is Tom Mello; I have to go to class. Just meet me at Cedar Tavern at four o'clock," he said. Then he jogged off

"Wait," Jack hollered, but Tom was off to his class.

Chapter 9

Jack sat at the Cedar Tavern bar, drinking a beer while waiting for Tom to arrive. He had a little discussion with the bartender and showed him Nicole's picture, but the bartender told him that he wasn't on that night.

The tavern was almost empty except for the few townies sitting around the bar. He glanced at his cell phone and it was 4:10 p.m. and no sign of Tom. He wondered why this kid wanted to meet him at the bar. He motioned to the bartender that he needed another bottle of beer just as Tom walked in. "I'm sorry I'm late," Tom said, as he took off his jacket and placed it behind the barstool.

"I didn't think you were going to show up," Jack said. "What do you want to drink?

"I'll take a Bud."

Jack motioned to the bartender again that he needed another bottle of Bud. "So what's with all the secrecy?"

Tom sat looking straight ahead. He slowly lifted the bottle of beer to his lips and took a long swig.

"Do you always drink half your beer in one swallow?" Jack asked.

"No, not usually," Tom replied and proceeded to take a second swig, finishing the bottle. He then motioned to the bartender for another.

"At this rate, I'll go broke paying the tab."

"Jack, I'm really sorry. I've been holding this in. I haven't slept for over a week. I've been drinking a lot. I'm a wreck. I can't study or think clearly. It's eating away at me and I don't know what to do. I saw what happened to your sister," he confessed, looking directly into Jack's eyes.

"What do you mean you're sorry?"

Shaking his head and not taking his eyes away from Jack's, he said. "I don't really know how to tell you this. I saw everything. I'm so sorry, but your sister and her boyfriend are dead."

The words hit Jack like a ton of bricks; he had strongly suspected that something bad had happened to them, but there was always that small glimmer of hope – until now. He looked forward, struggling to hold his emotions in check. Then, he calmly turned to Tom and, in a tone of suppressed rage, said. "I want to know every detail."

"I was here that night playing pool, minding my own business, when I saw Nick Gallo, the guy you gave the picture to, John Atkins, the guy with the shiner, and two other frat guys, Ike Smith and Chris Spencer. All four of them were hanging out near the ladies' room that night," he explained, pointing to the table where the boys had sat. "They were drinking shots and getting pretty wasted and rowdy as the night progressed. Nick Gallo and his partner in crime, John Atkins, are both psychopaths. Nick is the guy who comes up with the ideas and John is a pretty sick accomplice. Well, anyway, Nick noticed your sister that night and tried to talk to her at the bar, but she shot him down pretty quickly from the looks of it."

"So he's the guy who talked to my sister that night."

"How did you know about that?"

"It doesn't matter. Keep going with the details."

"Okay, where was I? Oh...um, your sister and her girlfriends along with her boyfriend all got up to leave and I saw Nick talking to John and pointing over to your sister. Now, when your sister and her boyfriend drove off, the four frat guys I mentioned followed in another car. I followed them. I knew they were up to no good. As I approached a stop sign, I saw both of their cars pulled over and, when I passed them, I saw Nick in the back of your sister's boyfriend's car. I pulled off the road further ahead, shut my lights off and waited for them to pass. I then followed them to a dirt road about eight miles from here. I parked my car off to the side of the main road and ran down this dirt road for about a half-mile until I came to this abandoned barn. I climbed up to the top window of the barn to see what was going on. Do you really want to hear the rest?" Tom asked, finishing off his second beer.

"You know, Tom, you have no idea who I am. I've seen and been through a lot in my life. I saw my brother die right in front of me when I was eleven. So damn it…keep the hell going."

Tom received his third beer from the bartender and took a big swig, then a deep breath. He could hear Jack's heart, or so he thought at first, until he realized it was his own. This was hard for any human being to explain, especially to someone whose sister had been at the mercy of these monsters. "I can't do it. I'm sorry, Jack," he said as he got up from the barstool.

"Sit the hell back down," Jack snapped, his eyes blazing.

"Okay, you don't need to get angry."

"Just tell me everything, alright. I want the whole story."

"Okay. So, I'm peering through these windows at the top of the barn, looking down. I see that Nick is clowning around with a gun, harassing your sister, and then, he puts it down and begins fooling around with her and she is pushing him away. Suddenly he gets crazy and rips off her shirt. She starts screaming. Then John comes over and throws her down. He's laughing like it's some type of big joke and he holds her down while chanting 'go, Nick, go' over and over again. Nick gets real crazy and rips off the rest of her clothes and you know…" he finishes in a low voice

"No, I don't know," Jack snapped.

"Um… Nick raped her pretty violently. They smacked her around a bit more for her to stop screaming and then John really roughed her up and forcefully took his turn." Tom paused, looking at Jack, hoping he had heard enough.

"Keep the hell going."

Tom sighed and continued. "When John finishes, he demands that the other two guys take a turn; they hesitate at first, but Nick and John basically strong-arm them into taking part and they very reluctantly rape her as well," Tom said. He paused and looked at Jack, who appeared to be looking right through him.

"Those bastards gang-raped her," Jack said, seething inside. He had seen this in third world countries, but his own sister here in America. Here he was, a Navy SEAL, protecting this country from the evil that percolates in other countries and his own sister was viciously raped and murdered in this quaint, serene part of the world, where no one would ever think there were monsters. It was inconceivable!

"Yeah," Tom said sadly, as he took another swig of beer.

"Then what?"

"I looked around wondering what had happened to her boyfriend. I thought about looking for him when I heard a noise from one of the cars outside. I think they must have tied him up and somehow he broke free because he ran into the barn like a wild man. First, he threw a mean punch at Atkins, knocking him to the ground. Then he tackled one of the other guys, driving him into an old rusty carriage. He then turned and grabbed the guy that was on top of your sister and threw him into one of the old horse stalls. Finally, he turned towards Gallo and charged him like a raging bull. Gallo just stood there and, to my horror, he pulled out his gun and shot him twice, stopping him in his tracks. Your sister started screaming uncontrollably, bloodcurdling screams like nothing I ever heard before. Gallo kept yelling at her to shut up, and she just kept screaming. Then, he shot her in the head. After that, there was this eerie silence."

Jack, grim-faced, demanded "What happened after that?"

"John Atkins – pretty boy - got up off the ground, his eye swollen and bloody; he grabbed the gun from Gallo and started shooting their lifeless bodies until the gun just clicked. He then started kicking your sister's boyfriend over and over again. He didn't stop until one of the other guys finally pulled him away. Unbelievably, Gallo and Atkins just started laughing like it was some sort of big joke. At that point I just wanted to get the hell out of there. So I jumped off the top of the barn and ran as fast as I could to my car. I'm sorry, Jack. I should have done something to help, but I was confused and scared."

Jack just stared ahead, took some money out of his pocket, and signaled to the bartender to come over with the tab. "And I was thinking this whole time that some serial killer was at work here and now I find out it was a bunch of college kids. What the hell is the world coming to?" he said out loud.

"I'm really sorry."

"Forget about it. You couldn't have done anything at that point, anyway," Jack said calmly. "But I need you to get a lawyer, tell him what you told me and have him report it to Special Agent Ryland in the Boston office of the FBI."

"Jack, I don't think you're aware that Nick Gallo's father is Frank Gallo, head of the New York Mafia crime family and John Atkins's father is some powerful senator," Tom expressed nervously.

Jack stared ahead and gathered his thoughts. "I know you want all of this to just go away, but unfortunately you're neck deep in it," he said. Then, in an agitated voice, "I don't give a damn who their fathers are! I just want justice. Now, you are going to take me to where this all happened."

"Now?"

"Yeah."

They both got up from their barstools, headed out the door, and drove in Jack's car to the crime scene. The car bumped along the gravel and dirt road until it came to the old red barn, which was surrounded by a field of low-cut grass. The windows were cracked; some panes were missing. The faded red paint had given way in places to worn and splintered wood. It was a relic of a simpler time – hard to envision as the scene of a vicious crime. Jack stopped the car and got out. Tom followed. The sun was fading fast behind the rolling hills. Jack opened one of the crooked barn doors, stepped inside and glanced around.

"Where did the rape take place?" Jack asked.

Tom pointed to the area near the horse stalls.

Jack slowly walked over there. "About here?" he asked.

"Yeah," Tom answered sadly.

Jack squatted down as if he was a catcher for a baseball team, studying the dirt while sifting it through his fingers.

"What are you doing?" Tom asked.

"There's nothing here. It's all been cleaned, and not by a bunch of drunken college kids."

"How do you know that?"

"I just do," Jack said as he got up and wandered around the barn looking for the smallest clue that a crime had taken place there. "Let's go. There's nothing more I need to see here."

***

Two days later, a lawyer by the name of Max Lufkin, a burly, short man with a white receding hairline, walked into Special Agent Ryland's Boston office.

"What is so important that you needed to see me on such short notice?" Agent Ryland asked.

"I represent a client who saw a horrific crime in Williamstown."

Agent Ryland perked up. He thought *this might be the big break he was hoping for*. "So what did your client see?" he asked.

"It has to do with the young couple who are missing out there," Max replied.

"Why don't you sit down while I get a tape recorder and start recording all this? Do you want a cup of coffee or water?"

"I'm all set."

Agent Ryland, after a sixty-minute closed-door meeting with Max Lufkin, emerged from the room. He never got used to senseless murders, especially when it had to do with young people. Now he had the knowledge of what actually happened to the two promising young adults murdered in a ghastly crime, but there was no case until evidence was compiled to back up the lawyer's statements. Otherwise the case might never get to trial.

The investigation began immediately based on the information that Agent Ryland had just received. It didn't take long before the old barn was filled with a forensic team going over every square inch of the barn. Pictures were snapped, soil samples were taken, and tire tracks were studied. FBI agents wearing dark blue jackets with big FBI letters on the back could be seen coming and going throughout the day. The place was like a scene from a movie except there were no media camera crews, which Agent Ryland made sure of since he didn't want the media getting involved quite yet. This case had the markings of media frenzy, especially if they got a whiff of the people behind the deaths of the missing couple.

Chapter 10

Special Agent Ryland had received the reports from the forensic team, and he wasn't surprised by the results, which showed no evidence of a crime. The FBI had obtained a warrant to search the cell phone records of the four college students allegedly involved in the crime. That information revealed the location of two calls of interest on Nick Gallo's cell phone. Those two calls were recorded in the general vicinity of the old barn on the night in question. One took place around 2:00 AM when Nick Gallo made a call to his father. The other was an incoming call around 4:00 A.M from Marty Leppo, a notorious Mafia henchman known as "The Cleaner." He would get called in after a hit and make all of the evidence neatly disappear.

After reviewing the cell phone records and based on Tom Mello's allegations, Agent Ryland made arrangements to interview the four alleged conspirators in an informal way at the fraternity house. Ostensibly, he was merely seeking information. His hope was that one or more of them might slip up and contradict another's story. Or actually crack, if he thought the FBI was closing in.

Ryland arrived on schedule and interviewed each of

them separately in a small study room. He started with John, followed by Chris, and then Ike. They each gave the same answers to his questions as if their story had been rehearsed over and over again. They said they were at the Cedar Tavern that night and came back to the frat around two o'clock. Ryland quickly dismissed any notion that he might get a break here. These boys had too much to lose to ever admit to a crime, even if it meant no jail time. The family reputation was at stake; then there were the high expectations placed on them. And, above all, the fear of the Gallo crime family. They would take the secret of that night to their graves.

Nick, the last to be interviewed, entered the study with an air of cockiness. "So, Special Agent Ryland, how are you?" he asked with a smirk, knowing full well that Agent Ryland had no case.

Ryland proceeded, well aware that he wouldn't be able to shake the ringleader. "So, Nick, I'm here just to ask you a few questions."

"Go ahead."

Ryland thought about how his interrogation of the suspects was going nowhere especially with Nick's conspirators sticking to the story. "I have your cell phone records, Nick. There were two calls in the area of an old barn about ten miles from here in the early morning hours following the night in question. That, coincidently, is the same night that two people disappeared after leaving the Cedar Tavern."

"I have no idea what you're talking about. What would I be doing out at an old barn in the wee hours of the morning? Going for a jog?" he said, with a smirk. Nick sat back in the chair wondering how Agent Ryland knew about the barn. He knew about everything, except he had no evidence, which meant he had no case. He was winging it on circumstantial evidence. But the deeper question was how did he know. Somebody else must have watched the whole thing go down. And then it hit him: he had briefly noticed Mello drive by that night; maybe he somehow followed them to the barn and saw what happened.

"I don't know, you tell me." Ryland calmly retorted.

"What…?" Nick said, as he brought his thoughts back to the question. "Maybe you can tell me what happened at this old barn that you seem so concerned about, Agent Ryland?"

Ryland paused; without physical evidence, it was going to be nearly impossible to prove a crime happened at the old barn. Nick knew this. Nick knew the ropes just from being around his Mafia kingpin father and seeing him escape prosecution one time after another over the years.

"Look, unless you are going to charge me with something, I have a class to attend and, if you want to talk to me again, contact my lawyer, Agent Ryland," Nick said defiantly.

Ryland sat there as Nick got up. "Well, Nick, I

expect that we'll meet again."

As Nick started walking away, he turned and said. "I read somewhere that a couple from North Adams is missing; maybe you should be looking into that angle instead of bothering us with some crazy theory of yours."

"Thanks for the advice, Nick. But I'm sure we'll be seeing each other again."

"I don't think so, Agent Ryland. I know, and you know, that you're just on some wild goose chase here," Nick said, glaring back at Ryland as he turned and left the room.

***

A few days after Agent Ryland had interviewed the four suspects, Tom Mello was walking briskly on the brick pavers to his first class of the day. It was just another typical day, as he made his way through the campus with its beautiful manicured green grass and brilliant colored flowers. A middle-aged, stocky, medium height guy with dark black hair walked along with him step for step.

"Do I know you?" the stranger asked.

"No, I don't think so," Tom said, moving hurriedly along the brick walkway.

"Well, I'm your guardian angel."

Tom had an immediate bad feeling about this guy. "I

don't know you," he said, trying to distance himself from the stranger.

"You know me, Tom. I'm either a friend you'll never see again or I will be your worst nightmare."

"What do you want?"

"You know what I want, Mr. Mello. I know everything about you. Where you grew up, your nice family, even that beautiful black lab you have back home. What's the dog's name?" He paused…looking in the air. "Duke, right?"

They both stopped. Tom felt his body shaking, his mouth dry, and words were hard to say. "Um…Um…"

"It's alright. Tom," he said, slicking his hair back with a comb and then jabbing his comb into Tom's shoulder. "Just think if this was a knife. Since you are going to play stupid with me, I'll make it easy for you. Just keep your mouth shut and you'll graduate. That's easy. Right, Tom?"

Tom stood there, his face ashen, his pulse racing and his heart beating loudly. His mind returned to that terrible night and he realized that somehow they knew. How they knew he had no idea, but the Gallo crime family would kill him without hesitation if Nick got indicted. This was their final warning, and if he chose to ignore it, they would take him for a long ride one day and he would never be seen again.

"Right, Tom?" the strange man demanded in an agitated loud voice.

"Yes, I understand," Tom said quickly, nodding his head, his eye twitching.

"Good, then we are on the same page," the stranger said, patting Tom on the shoulder and then disappearing into the crowd of college students walking to class.

***

After a few days of deliberations between the state prosecutor, police, and the FBI, they decided not to move the case in front of a grand jury, and to drop any further contemplated proceedings against the four Wilbur Smith College students. There wasn't any physical evidence to tie any of them to the missing couple, even with an apparent eye-witness who now had recanted his story. The prosecutor thought about serving Tom Mello with a subpoena to testify in front of a grand jury, but the defense would have ripped holes in his story. Why did he take so long to come forwarded? How much did he drink that night? The prosecutor feared he would have just stuck to his new story, even under oath and the threat of perjury, too scared of the Gallo crime family to come forward with the truth. Without the bodies, some DNA sample tying the couple to the suspects, or some compelling circumstantial evidence, there was no case.

Agent Ryland leaned forward in his chair and called Max Lufkin to tell him that even if his client hadn't recanted his story they didn't have enough evidence to move the case forward; no charges would be filed against the four college students. After the five-minute call, Ryland sat back in his chair, staring out at the city below. He realized that Jack Bolton and Ted Brown's family would never get justice, the bodies would never be found and the case would just go into the dead end file. Yet, he knew who did it, and how it was done. And he surmised that the Gallo family had gotten to the witness somehow. He then moved his chair forward, opened his file-drawer and pulled out the Becket missing person case.

***

Tom Mello breathed a sigh of relief when his lawyer called to tell him that the FBI wouldn't be bringing any charges against the four frat boys in the Bolton case. He had barely slept since the whole ordeal began. He had been conflicted from the beginning about reporting what he had seen that terrible night. He wanted to help Jack Bolton but after receiving the threat to his family as well as himself from the Gallo hit man, he advised his lawyer that he no longer recalled the events of that night. Nevertheless, it troubled him deeply. The news from his lawyer made it a non-issue now.

Chapter 11

As his cell phone buzzed, Jack picked it up and placed it to his ear. He just listened as Agent Ryland told him the bad news. There would be no charges filed against the four college students. Jack had already figured this would be the probable outcome and had planned accordingly.

He put the phone down and pulled a Glock-17, nine-millimeter gun out of his duffle bag. He twisted it in different directions while studying it like a Rubik's Cube. He felt deceived by the American court system. There would be no justice. He could feel the rage bursting within him.

He got up, leaving the gun on the bed, and moved to the bathroom where he splashed water on his face. He looked at the time just as he heard a knock on the door. "Who is it?" Jack hollered.

"Charlie Costa."

"He ran over to the door, and greeted Charlie with a big hug. "Hey, Big Charlie. It's great to see you. Come on in. How've you been?"

"I'm doing well," Charlie said, settling his large frame into a chair. I've got a job as a mechanic at a Honda dealership."

"That's great. Thanks for coming up on short notice. How's Patty doing?"

"She's doing great now that I'm out of the SEALs. And she's pregnant," Charlie said with a smile and a chuckle.

"That's great. Hey, have you heard from Brian Butler?"

"Yeah. He's almost healed from his injuries, but he's still bitter about what happened out there in the Helmand Province when we got no back-up."

"He's one guy you want next to you in a firefight."

"Yeah. He spends a lot of time in Mexico nowadays. He asked me how you were doing. He also mentioned that he owes you, and if you need anything let him know."

"He's a real good guy. Not one to go by the playbook and you've got to earn his trust."

"That's for sure," Charlie said, not sure how to approach the topic of Jack's sister. "I'm sorry about your sister. Any idea what happened to her?"

"Yeah, part of the reason why I wanted to see you."

"You know what happened?"

"Unofficial: she was murdered. Official: she's a missing person."

"Wow. That's crazy, Jack. Do you know who did it?"

"Yeah, and the FBI does too, but they aren't going to do a damn thing because they don't have any physical evidence."

"How do you know all this?" Charlie asked.

"I know someone who witnessed the whole thing," he said

"Who did it?"

"The people who killed my sister are a couple of entitled college students."

"What do you mean?"

"One kid's father is the kingpin of a New York Mafia crime family; the other kid's father is Senator Sam Atkins."

"No shit," Charlie sputtered. "Are you talking about the Gallo crime family?"

"I guess."

"You're planning something, Jack."

"I just need you to drive the car around while I teach them something about justice."

"I can't say no to you, Jack. I owe you big time but just don't do anything too crazy here," Charlie said in a sympathetic tone. He owed Jack for saving his life not once but twice during the special ops days in Afghanistan. Jack received the Purple Heart for one of those lifesaving missions. He couldn't refuse Jack, but he was nervous about what he was planning to do. Just by the look in Jack's eyes, Charlie felt the intensity of the situation.

"Don't worry, Charlie. It's just like a mission – we're out looking to get the bad guys."

Jack Bolton's campaign for justice began with Charlie driving the rental car around campus. They eventually parked fifty yards away from the Beta Ki Fraternity, right in the direct path of students going back and forth to class. Jack spotted two of the conspirators who were part of that night's crime.

He got out of the car quickly and forced Chris Spencer and Ike Smith into the back seat of the parked car as Charlie started the car. They drove to the scene of the crime. The two boys were very scared and pleaded with Jack, saying that they didn't kill his sister – stating in unison that it was Nick Gallo and John Atkins. Jack just focused on the task at hand, his face like granite. They tied both of them up to an old rusty wagon inside the barn and headed out again to look for the two ringleaders.

"Jack, this is crazy," Charlie said, as they again waited in the car fifty yards from the frat house.

"You're right. Did I forget to tell you that they gang raped my sister as well?" Jack said, as he got out of the car and started walking.

"Where are you going?" Charlie hollered with his head out the window.

"I'm going in to get them," Jack snapped, as he quickly forged ahead and marched up the porch while passing members of the frat. He walked briskly through the open door and searched around the lower floor with no luck. He took the stairs to the second floor and checked out each bedroom until he came to the last one on the right where he heard laughter and the odor of pot filled the air. The door was open a crack; Jack pushed it wide open and stood in the doorway. Nick, sitting down in a chair with his back facing Jack, couldn't stop laughing as a joint was being passed between him and two other frat brothers. The laughter stopped when the other two frat brothers noticed Jack standing in the doorway. Nick turned towards the door with a joint in his mouth and an attitude that came with being the son of a Mafia kingpin. "What do you want?" Nick asked in a casual manner while turning towards his friends displaying a cocky attitude and a wide grin.

He could barely control his mounting rage as he stood there watching Nick Gallo living life, knowing that his beloved sister who had so much to offer the world was dead, viciously attacked and murdered by this monster. "Let's go for a little walk, Nick."

Nick, sitting there, still looking at his friends, said, "I told you everything and, as you can see, I'm busy." His friends snickered in the background.

'Where's your buddy, John Atkins?"

"He went home this weekend. I really feel bad about your sister, but I told you I don't know anything and nobody else around here does either."

"Oh, you don't feel bad about my sister," Jack said in a controlled voice as he pulled a gun from his jacket pocket and pointed it at Nick. "Let's go for that little walk."

"Alright, Jack Bolton – that is your name," Nick said sarcastically, getting up from his chair. Jack waved the gun in his direction. The two other frat guys just sat there stunned.

Jack led Nick out of the frat house without incident and hand signaled Charlie to drive the car to them. A call from inside the frat house had been made to the police.

As the car stopped in front of them, Jack forced Nick into the backseat with him.

"Do you know who I am, Jack?" he asked, still maintaining his self-assurance.

Jack said nothing as Charlie drove to the old barn location.

"You don't know who I am, do you?"

"You're a murderer and a rapist and a waste of life," Jack snapped, staring back at him.

"I'm the son of Frank Gallo, maybe you've heard of him. The Gallo crime family of New York," he boasted.

Jack said nothing, looking straight ahead, his mind racing as if he was on a special ops mission.

Nick played along, confident that whatever Jack was up to it would be pretty lame and he would tell his father about this guy and he would end up like his sister. "If I were you, Jack, I would turn around and drop me off back at the frat house, and, if you're lucky, I won't mention this to my father."

The car turned down the dirt road and stopped in front of the old barn. The rain had become steady. Jack pulled Nick out of the car and led him into the barn as Charlie followed. "Does this place look familiar, Nick?" Jack asked.

Nick entered the barn and saw Ike and Chris tied up off to the side. "Hey guys," he said with a wide grin, not taking any of this too seriously, but his fellow frat guys were too scared to smile. "What are you going to do with us, Jack? Try to make us confess. Is that what you want, Jack? Will that make you feel better?" Nick's arrogance continued. "Come on, Jack, what are you going to do with us, huh?"

Jack looked around the barn and then back at Nick who was ten feet away. "Why did you rape and kill my sister?"

"You want me to answer that."

"Your life depends on it."

Nick just smirked and chuckled at Jack's request. He looked down at his two frat brothers, both tied to the old rusty wagon with a look of extreme fright on their faces.

"You got something to say," Jack asked, staring intently at Nick.

Nick stood there with his mind working overtime. He figured. What did it matter? Jack was a dead man. He wasn't going to shoot the son of Frank Gallo. "What do you want to hear, huh? That I raped your sister and shot her boyfriend and then her? Is that what you want to hear, Jack?" he asked smugly.

Jack paused then walked around the barn looking back at Nick. The rain was now dripping down through the decayed roof rafters, bouncing off his head and face. He recalled a saying from his Bible class – "an eye for an eye." There was no remorse in Nick's eyes. He was still treating the whole thing like a big joke. He was going to walk away from all of this, a brutal gang rape, and murder of two people in cold blood. That thought was killing Jack inside. At that moment, he considered the unthinkable.

"Jack, he's not worth it," Charlie pleaded loudly. "You don't want to ruin your life over this guy."

"Call your father," Jack snapped.

"You want me to call my father?" Nick said with a surprised look.

"Yeah."

"Your life, Jack," he muttered, still not understanding the gravity of his situation. He pushed a few buttons on his smart phone and put it to his ear. "Hi, Dad. I got a little problem. There's a man here by the name of Jack Bolton who has a gun pointed at me," he said, pulling the phone from his ear. "He wants to talk to you."

Jack grabbed the phone from Nick, put it to his ear and said. "Hello."

"If anything happens to my son, I will kill you personally," Frank uttered "There won't be a place in the world where you will be safe."

Jack waited for Frank Gallo to finish his rant. He knew that he would be a dead man regardless of what he did to Nick Gallo. He calmly spoke into the phone. "So, Frank, what would you do to someone who raped and killed your sister?"

There was a pause on the other end of the phone. Frank knew the answer, but this was his son; it was different. "Look, I don't know who the hell you are, but I will find you and kill you if you do anything to my son," he raged on the other end.

Nick just stood there smirking as he looked at his buddies sitting on the ground. He had seen men pee their pants when Frank Gallo walked into a room. *Jack would fall in line like all the others,* he thought.

Jack, with a crazed look now, shouted into the phone. "Frank, give me a damn answer. What would you do?" Jack thought of his sister and the killer before him. There would never be justice for Nick Gallo; he would go on abusing power and wreaking havoc in people's lives, just like his father. Charlie was pleading with him that it wasn't worth it, and Nick was smiling with a look of invincibility when Jack pulled the trigger. The sound of the gun echoed off the wooden barn walls as the bullet struck him in the head. He dropped to the ground in the same spot as Jack's sister. It was like any mission. The bad guy had been taken out. It had to be done.

A sudden quietness descended on the scene. Only the crows drying off from the rain could be heard above. Charlie shook his head in dismay. "Jack, why? You're better than this."

"This isn't any different than the bad guys we kill on missions. Is it, Charlie?"

Charlie didn't answer the question. "How about letting these two other guys go?" Charlie pleaded.

Jack turned and looked down at the two college students who were now white as ghosts. Both were terrified and afraid to look up. "We'll leave them here and we'll call someone tomorrow to pick them up." Jack's eyes said it all. He was in battle mode; there was nothing anybody could say to him now.

"What about the body, Jack?" Charlie asked

Jack said nothing as he left the barn. Charlie followed; Jack took the driver's seat. Charlie got into the passenger's seat and they drove back to the main road.

"Why did you do it, Jack?" Charlie asked.

"I got rid of a bad guy. The world's now a better place. It's no different than any ops mission when the government tells us who the bad guys are. Are the people we get rid of really the bad guys? You ever think of that, Charlie."

"That was different, Jack."

"No difference, Charlie. Just because we took orders didn't mean it was right."

"Alright, I get it. Where are we going now?"

"There's one more guy I have to get. After that I don't know what I'm going to do."

"You know the Gallo crime family will never rest until you're dead," Charlie warned.

"I know exactly what I did, Charlie. And I know that I'll be looking over my shoulder for the rest of my life now."

"He wasn't worth it, Jack."

"Charlie, I don't expect you to understand, but I have no family now; my sister was the best thing in my life. And now she's gone.

Charlie didn't answer and just looked out the window at the dreary day, knowing that he didn't want to be part of Jack's world. He had a new job and a baby on the way. He needed to cut ties with Jack as soon as possible.

"You know, Charlie, everybody always thought I was this indestructible force that could never fail. The reality was that I had already failed. I failed my little brother when he was eight years old and I lost him, something I can never forget. I vowed then that I would never fail again." He breathed deeply, sighing, while pausing before wiping tears from his eyes. My little sister was all the family I had left. She meant everything to me and that bastard back there took her away from me. She was going to be a great doctor someday, and now…" He shook his head.

"It's okay, Jack."

"You're looking at me like I'm a monster."

"No."

"I'm going to tell you something that I haven't told anyone else, Charlie."

"Jack, it's really okay."

"You remember that night a couple of years ago, the mission where I went back in to make sure everyone was out."

"Yeah."

"Ask yourself. Why did the helicopter leave me there?" I came running out just as the helicopter was leaving. Jack looked straight at Charlie. "You were there."

"We yelled at the helicopter pilot to turn around, but there was just too much incoming firepower to make a landing and we had orders to leave."

"You know what I think. I think somebody high up wanted me to be captured by Al-Qaeda."

"What? That's absolutely crazy, Jack."

"When they captured me, they spent a week going through this practice of beheading me – video and all. Then one night they took me into this room and beat me senseless, and I thought this is it, but they stopped when Omar Iman walked in."

"Omar Iman, he was at the top of the CIA's terrorist most wanted list. You sure it was him?"

"Oh, it was him all right. I remember him clearly from the briefings."

Charlie looked confused and puzzled. "What are you getting at?"

"He took me to this separate room and said in broken English he was going to let me go. I couldn't believe what I was hearing. I asked him why. Blood was oozing from my forehead, my nose was broken, my ribs were broken, and my kidneys were bruised. You know what he said to me?"

"What?"

"He said, 'Sometime it is better to show kindness. I've done some bad things that I'm not proud of, but I'm not the monster that your government wants you to believe. Your government is on my land. I had nothing to do with 9/11.'"

"So he let you go because of that."

"I'm not quite sure of his reasoning, but he went on to say that he wanted to be a college professor, but it was my government that created him. Then, he went on to explain that a drone killed his brother and sister nine years ago and, after that, his hatred for America drove him to where he is today. Now I know what he felt when he lost his brother and sister: the hatred that runs through your body for the people responsible."

"He was just playing with your mind, Jack."

"I don't think so, Charlie."

"So you really believe he was just being a nice guy?"

"The guy let me go. He went on to say that we were

94

both pawns being used by America's corrupt politicians and a World Order. He had fears for his own family and said that I should go back to my family before it was too late."

"So the most wanted terrorist wanted out."

"I don't think so."

"Why you telling me all this now, Jack?"

"Well, I told intelligence that I escaped which I did not. But, most importantly, sometimes you do things you are not proud of and are driven to do."

"Jack, I'm not judging you," Charlie said in an apologetic tone. "But we aren't in Afghanistan anymore."

Jack turned into the motel parking lot and eased the car into a parking space at the left of his room.

"Jack, I'm going to get something to eat," Charlie said. "You want me to bring you back something."

"I'm not that hungry; thanks anyway."

Charlie drove off in his pick-up truck, parked at a fast food restaurant across the street from the motel and looked at his phone. He hesitated at first, and finally pressed the 911 keys; the call went to the Williamstown police station. "I'd like to report a murder," he said, as he spoke nervously into the phone. He told them what had just happened and where they could find the shooter and the body of Nick Gallo. Charlie sat back in his truck; he hated what he had just done, but Jack was on a tear and he wouldn't stop until he had taken care of John

Atkins as well. It was wrong what Jack was doing; at least that's what Charlie said to himself, trying to justify his decision.

Fifteen minutes later, from across the way, Charlie could see the Williamstown and State Police streaming into the motel parking lot, followed by a swat team vehicle a short time later. He hated watching what was happening. He loved Jack like a brother, but it wasn't right in his eyes to be taking the law into one's own hands.

A call came in to Special Agent Ryland about the murder of Nick Gallo. He happened to be in the area working on the Becket case and immediately drove over to the Clarks motel to join the assembly of town and state police; a crew of swat team members was strategically placed to apprehend Jack Bolton.

Special Agent Ryland took over and hoped he could persuade Jack to come out of the motel room peaceably; he knew how dangerous a former Navy SEAL could be, especially if he had "gone bad." He called the motel room. After a few rings Jack picked up. "Jack, this is Special Agent Ryland. How about making this easy and just come out with your hands up? I understand how you feel."

"Agent Ryland, you have no idea how I feel!" Jack said with authority. "You have a family to go home to. I have nothing. You know what happened to my sister and you know that none of those guys will ever serve a day of prison time."

"Jack, you can't make your own laws. Jack, you still there?" Agent Ryland asked as the swat team got into position. Charlie just watched from across the street and began doubting his decision.

With a sense of urgency, Ryland called the room again, but there was no answer. Ryland received an incoming call. The rain bounced off his windbreaker and there was silence in the air as he put the cell phone to his ear. Nick Gallo's dead body was confirmed at the abandoned barn and the shooter was confirmed as Jack Bolton. Ryland just leaned on his car; at some point something had to give, but he wanted to give Jack time to think.

Thirty minutes passed and everyone could feel the tension in the air. Ryland called the room again while the officers appeared to be getting restless. There was no answer. Ryland didn't want to use force, but the next move was to force him out with tear gas. As the swat team began to prepare the gas canisters, a loud bang broke the silence and a flash of light lit up Jack's motel room. The officers all ducked down from the apparent gunshot, then looked up cautiously from their crouched positions. Did Jack Bolton just commit suicide? Ryland shook his head. He had the utmost respect for Jack, a man who had risked his life for his country many times and who had received a purple heart for his bravery. Was it all to end in a motel in Williamstown? And for what purpose? Jack's sister would never get the justice that she deserved.

As the swat team got into place to storm the motel room, Jack opened the door and stepped into the doorway holding his hands up. Agent Ryland, in a stern voice, immediately ordered him to get on the ground and lay face down. He was surrounded by a group of police officers, as one officer handcuffed him, and another read him his rights.

Charlie watched from the restaurant parking lot with sadness in his heart as FBI agents quickly escorted Jack into a waiting car and whisked him off to an unknown destination.

Chapter 12

As the cold day turned to night, Rex Saxton drove along the roads of upstate New York. He had stayed low for the past few months and felt invincible because the authorities didn't have a clue as to what happened to the Beckets. He had searched the Internet looking for any clues that the FBI might be any closer to finding the missing bodies. Every story ended the same way. There were none.

In fact, he had read with great interest the story about Jack Bolton killing a Mafia kingpin's son, believing that he had something to do with the disappearance of his missing sister and her boyfriend, which happened around the time Rex was in the area. He was a little envious that Bolton was getting all the media attention. In his deranged mind, the Beckets' demise was a much bigger story. He would show them all that he was the star, not Jack Bolton.

Driving along the quiet roads, his confidence was sky high and he began to formulate his next diabolical plan. It was just a matter of time before he would come across the perfect victim.

He entered the small town of Saranac Lake with a population of just over five thousand people around eight in the evening. He maneuvered his beat up dark green Ford Mustang into the parking lot of Joe's Tavern. It was a place where the locals hung out, far removed from the bars that the tourists would patronize. As he parked his car, he was highly confident that his plan would go off without a hitch in any one of these rural towns where their small police forces were no match for his perceived intelligence.

Saxton entered the bar, his eyes intensely combing the interior of the room like a cat searching for a mouse in the field. There, in the corner of the bar, was a middle aged woman by the name of Mary Thomas, whose age had gotten the best of her. Her face reflected a hard life. She was fairly plump, about five-foot two with long brown hair.

Saxton found a seat next to Mary and ordered a beer. It didn't take long before the lonely woman began to drum up a conversation with him. She carried the conversation, too eager to detail her hard life and her miserable relationships between shots of whiskey. She rambled on about her two broken marriages and her unemployment status. Saxton, a socially inept introvert, would throw a few words out every now and then, to show that he was interested. He nursed his four beers during the hours of conversation with breaks in between when she would go to the ladies room and then follow it up with a cigarette outside the bar. Saxton just bided his time and, as the clock got closer to 1:00 a.m. she asked in a rambling drunken tone, "Do you want to go back to my place?"

Saxton, with an expressionless face, just nodded as a sinister smile appeared, his devilish protruding eyes gleaming in the dull light, but Mary Thomas was too drunk to notice the warning signs. Of course, she lacked any shred of common sense when it came to bringing men back to her place, drunk or not. Her whole life had been a crapshoot, never worrying about tomorrow. Saxton had found himself the perfect victim.

He walked out into the cold night air, Mary following closely behind. They exchanged a few words in the parking lot. A minute later, Mary's car pulled out onto the deserted road into the dark night with Saxton's car following closely behind.

Chapter 13

Brian Butler, a former Navy SEAL, sat on a folding chair on a small third-floor balcony of an apartment building situated in a slum-ridden section of Ixtapaluca, a small city of roughly 400,000 located in the eastern part of Mexico, a short drive from Mexico City. While drinking a bottle of beer, beads of sweat formed on his forehead; the light breeze, the shade from the roof above, and the cold beer provided little relief from the oppressive heat. He had spent the last six weeks in this run-down part of the world. It was an area that he knew well from his family visits when he was a kid. His mother was of Mexican descent and still had family in the area.

Brian was a natural born-charmer with an easy going personality. Some people were intimidated at first by his six-foot plus, muscular frame, shoulder length hair and the tattoo on his arm of a large, angry seal with teeth. But not for long. He made friends easily - and kept them. He had shown his mettle many times during his years as a SEAL.

He had separated from the SEALs after his last tour of duty when he realized he could no longer accept authority with which he did not agree. There had been an incident when his team was ordered to stand down as they witnessed, from a nearby ridge, the brutal killing of a group of villagers by the Taliban because they were reading science books given to them by American soldiers. That scene continued to haunt him.

Brian felt right at home in this seedy part of the world – a stopping off place while he contemplated his future. This section of Ixtapaluca was a hotbed of organized criminal activity that included extortion, automobile thefts, illicit drug dealing, kidnapping, prostitution, and the sale of counterfeit products. But he was attracted by its harsh realities. And had no concerns that he couldn't handle whatever came along.

As he watched from his balcony, six men were delivering duffle bags into the bank across the street. This was the third week in a row, at the same time, twelve o'clock, that the same men delivered these duffle bags. He knew it was drug money, earmarked for laundering into the sophisticated, worldwide system that the cartels had devised for themselves. The bank across the street was just one little cog in the wheel.

A plan was beginning to germinate in his mind. *A few SEALs with guns could pull this off easily. The cartel would have no idea who stole their money. They could be in and out quickly and live happily ever after. He could do what he always wanted to do, a boat business on one of the islands in the Caribbean, taking tourists out on scenic rides and scuba trips. He would never have to worry about money again, just if the sun was coming out and how many tourists were looking for a good time on a boat.*

As the evening sun faded behind the mountains, Brian took a walk to a local bar. Along the way, he passed rows of housing and old automobiles, and meandered through narrow streets until he came to an entertainment strip lined with bars and call girls. He entered one of the bars, found a seat and ordered a shot of tequila. He followed it up with a Corona beer and settled in at the bar for the night. His Mexican descent enabled him to fit in, and he knew enough Spanish to carry on a conversation with the locals.

He looked forward and enjoyed the cockroaches putting on a show behind the counter. He continued drinking his Coronas while casually surveying the scene around him when he observed something he couldn't ignore. Three men rushed into the establishment with an obviously distraught, young woman, who seemed to be looking about frantically but not wanting to make a scene. Her eyes met Brian's, as she was ushered upstairs to the second floor. Brian turned towards the bartender and ordered another tequila shot. The bar was crowded with locals; nobody paid attention to the young woman. People here didn't want to know other people's business, but Brian couldn't let it go; he knew something was not right.

He pushed back the bar stool and made his way

upstairs. As he turned the corner at the head of the stairs, he was abruptly greeted by one of the men.

Brian put up his hands and in Spanish asked, "¿Donde esta el bano?"

The man pointed downstairs, in no mood for small talk, and pushed Brian forward as he turned away. Brian then turned with quick fury and head-butted the man, who instantly fell to the floor. He continued walking until he got to the end of the hallway and heard the young woman pleading with the two men to leave her alone. Brian heaved his body into the flimsy door and landed on his feet, all in one motion, surprising the two men inside. The first man jumped from his sitting position and went at Brian with a knife. Brian reacted with a quick move, spinning 360 degrees into the air, as if he were a Kung Fu expert, hitting the man squarely in the chest with both feet, and driving him through the thin wall into the adjacent room. The second man, who was at first on top of the girl, had spun off the bed half-dressed and reached for his gun on the table, but Brian tackled him before he could get it, propelling them both through the window. Brian was able to grab what was left of the window frame, while the other man plunged to the ground. Brian hauled himself back over the windowsill. The man he had slammed into the next room had regained his footing and snatched the screaming girl. Brian grabbed him from behind and threw him head first into the wall. Two more men now appeared at the door as Brian took the girl's hand and swiftly led her out the shattered open window as the two men closed in behind. They slid down the roof, both hitting the ground hard. A small crowd had gathered around the fallen man below. Brian and the girl began running hand–in-hand along the street, dodging and pushing people as they went. Two pops were heard in the background. After about fifty yards, they were able to flag down a cab. The young woman slid into the back seat first and Brian followed.

"Where to?" the cab driver asked in Spanish

"Just drive, now," Brian said in Spanish while handing the man a fifty-dollar bill through the open glass partition.

The girl sat quietly on the other side of the car, barely clothed.

"Where do you live?" Brian asked in Spanish.

She replied, quietly, "Huixquilucan."

Brian tapped on the glass and handed the cab driver another fifty-dollar bill "Huixquilucan," he said.

"Huixquilucan," the cab driver repeated, smiling at the request.

"You okay?" Brian asked the shaken girl.

She just nodded

Brian didn't say much as the cab driver drove west along Route 15, while this mysterious girl just sat quietly on the other side of the back seat. This had to be a kidnapping for ransom money or, possibly, human trafficking. Huixquilucan was a wealthy suburb, which probably meant that the girl's parents had money or were important government officials.

The young woman got more comfortable as they got closer to Huixquilucan, and she began to direct the cab driver to the location of her home. She looked over at Brian and asked in English, "What's your name?"

"Brian," he replied, surprised at her accent-free English. "Now, what's your name?"

"Maria."

"Pretty name," he said.

"Why did you help me?"

Brian paused for a second... she knew little about him. "I saw your eyes. I knew you were in trouble and your life was in danger. I couldn't walk away."

A single tear rolled down her cheek as the cab rolled to a stop in front of a gated community. She reached over and hugged him and said, "Thank you for saving my life. You were my guardian angel tonight. I'll pray for you."

He just looked at her, trying to find some words to say as she pulled away and opened the car door. She turned and, with a beautiful smile, waved as she reached the security gate, Brian impetuously jumped out of the cab for one last goodbye, but she ran off as the gate closed. He felt some sort of connection as crazy as that seemed, and he watched her disappear into the night. He then spoke in Spanish, directing the cab driver back to

Ixtapaluca.

On the return trip, he couldn't stop thinking about her beautiful eyes and lovely smile. He felt a connection to her, as if he knew her from some past life.

The taxi dropped him off a half mile from his apartment. Brian ran to the apartment at a fast pace and reached it as the clock struck midnight. The excitement of the night had passed, but he knew that there would be retribution for his actions. These people, possible cartel members, would be looking for him and there was always the possibility someone had a photo of him.

He entered his apartment and packed what little clothes he had in a backpack. He then left the apartment and ran about another mile to a relative's house where his motorcycle had been stored in a safe place. Brian thanked his relatives, unlocked his bike and drove off, heading back to the United States.

Chapter 14

Inside the dimly lit pub called "The Place" on the outskirts of the city of Cleveland, where pictures of gangsters and athletes lined the walls, Brian Butler sat at the bar nursing a beer, as he waited for his friend and former Navy SEAL, Joe Cap, to arrive. He took a shot of tequila and then chased down the aftertaste with a swig of beer, while thinking about his golden plan.

It had been five months since he had returned from Mexico. He had spent the last few months travelling around the country on his big Harley, and looking up old military buddies. He talked about his plan to the few whom he thought would want to join him in carrying it out. He had laid the groundwork with an executive at a large agricultural bank in Indiana who had a talent for laundering money and he had opened a Cayman Islands account. All that remained was for him to assemble his chosen group of six former SEALs. He was half-way there.

The news from Boston about Jack Bolton being charged with murder was a shocker. Jack wouldn't do something like that unless he had good reason and, from what Charlie had told him, there was reason enough. If that was the case, in Brian's eyes, what Jack did made total sense.

He started thinking again about how lucky he was to still be alive. He owed his life to Jack. With no regard for his own safety, Jack had risked his life to save Brian and six other SEALs from certain death. Brian wanted with every fiber of his being to repay that debt.

Momentarily, his thoughts wandered back to Ixtapaluca and Maria, the young woman he had rescued there. He thought about her from time to time. *Did she think about him? Did those people go back after her again? Was she okay?*

Joe Cap entered the bar, smiling widely at Brian who stood up immediately to give Joe a big hug. Both exchanged pats on the back, smiles, and handshakes as they settled down onto their bar stools.

"Hey, I'm really sorry about your brother," Brian said.

"His life was too damn short, Brian. George was only thirty-three when he died. Can you believe it? Just thirty-three!"

Brian nodded sympathetically.

"He served in Afghanistan and Iraq and never got touched by a bullet. He came back home and got engaged to a beautiful girl. He had a good job with the CIA. His life was really good. I'd never seen him so happy. Then he's coming home late from his girlfriend's place one night and he gets run off the road and hits a tree."

"That really sucks," Brian said.

"I got to see him right before he passed and it was really sad. There weren't enough tissues in the room to hold back everyone's tears. Just seeing him drugged up on morphine was hard."

"Did they find the other driver?"

"Of course not. Do you think the cops care? Nobody cared, just another statistic. And my mother, who was battling cancer, couldn't handle it. She passed away six weeks later."

"I'm really sorry, Joe."

"It's okay. It's life."

"How's everything else going?" Brian asked.

"I've been staying with my dad, you know. Helping him around. Just keeping a low profile. And I've been helping out in my cousin's landscaping business every now and then to make a few bucks. Obviously, it's not much.

"Well, there's not much work for someone with our skill set unless you want to live overseas," Brian said.

"Yeah." Joe nodded.

After listening to Joe, Brian figured this was as good a time as any to find out if he was interested in making the score of his life. "Joe, the drinks are all on me tonight."

"No, I'll chip in," Joe said. "Hey, did you hear about Jack Bolton?"

"Yeah, I talk to Charlie Costa every now and then

and he told me that the guy Jack killed had it coming. He raped and killed Jack's sister."

"Shit. If someone did that to my sister, I'd have killed the guy too," Joe exclaimed, shaking his head.

"Yeah, he doesn't deserve to go to prison. That's for sure. We owe him."

"We sure do. We wouldn't be here if it wasn't for him."

Brian decided this was the time to disclose the plan. "There's a particular reason why I wanted to meet you tonight, Joe. I have something that you might be interested in doing with me. But keep this to yourself, okay?"

"You know me. I won't say a word to anyone. What is it?"

"I need someone with SEAL experience, not that we would even need to use it, but just in case. I was down in Mexico for a few months and I accidentally came across these guys bringing full duffle bags into this small local bank. They did it every Tuesday, right at twelve o'clock. It's usually about eight to twelve duffle bags full of money."

"Drug money, huh?"

"It sure is, and it looks like they use this little bank to launder some of it. Also, from what I saw, they're pretty nonchalant about security. They must think nobody is going to hit the cartel."

"So we go in, grab the duffle bags, and we're gone?"

"Yeah. The way I look at it, Joe, I need six guys. I have three guys who are in; you would be the fourth."

"Who's in?"

"Dan Milton, Bob Rodriguez, and myself."

"I know both of them… they're good guys."

"The advantage we have here is that we are trained to go in fast and get out fast."

"How much money are we talking about?"

"I'm figuring fifteen million, maybe more. So we are talking almost three million apiece."

"Wow. Where's the catch? "

"No catch. We just need enough fire power in case something goes wrong. This is basically our back-up plan. Otherwise, we're in and out. I've found a pilot who owns a small aircraft to take us over the border and back. Then, when the job is finished, we all go our separate ways and that's it. Nobody will be the wiser, except you just need to keep a low profile with the money."

"Sounds simple."

"It is. I'll put all the details together and you just need to show up when we're ready to go."

"Well, I'm definitely in.

"Good. Welcome aboard."

***

Ned Johnson sat at the bar across from Brian and

Joe, observing them with curiosity. His smartphone vibrated as he got the bartender's attention for another beer. He got up from the barstool to take the call. "Tony, did you get the pictures okay?"

"Yeah. The man's name is Brian Butler, a former Navy SEAL. They were in the same SEAL unit."

"Well, it sure looks like they're just reminiscing about old times. So what do you want me to do?"

"Just continue to watch Cap."

"He still hasn't done anything unusual."

"It's not your job to think – just keep watching him for anything out of the ordinary."

"Okay, okay. I get it. How much longer do you think I need to observe this guy? I've been watching him for seven weeks now. I've gone to two funerals; I've watched him work on more yards than I can count. We've bugged the house and nothing but boring conversation. Whatever you guys are looking for, he sure doesn't seem to know a thing?"

"Just keep watching him until we tell you otherwise."

"Alright, alright, I'll keep in touch."

Chapter 15

The media was all over the sensational trial of Jack Bolton; it was nine months to the day since the murder. It had all the intrigue of any of the big name trials that had found their way onto Court TV. "A former Navy SEAL who was the recipient of the Purple Heart for bravery, was now standing trial in the State of Massachusetts for the murder of a notorious Mafia kingpin's son." The real question was not Jack Bolton's guilt, but how long he would survive in prison with Frank Gallo and his Mafia lieutenants hell-bent on killing him.

Charlie Costa was the last prosecution witness to be called.

The prosecutor began his questioning. "Mr. Costa, you were there on the day Jack Bolton shot Nick Gallo. Is that correct?"

"Yes."

"Why don't you tell the court what happened that day?"

"Okay," he exhaled and began his testimony. "Jack called me to meet him at the Clarks motel in Williamstown."

"Did he tell you why?" the prosecutor asked.

"No, sir. But when a guy who saved your life calls you for a favor, you want to help him out," he stated to the court.

"Okay, please continue," the prosecutor ordered.

"So he told me that he needed me to just drive around. He said he had to teach a couple of guys a lesson. I didn't think much about it. I thought he was just going to scare these guys. He grabbed two of them at the college and we tied them up at the barn."

"Did you find that strange? To tie up these two guys at this barn?" the prosecutor asked with a frown.

"No. I thought if he wanted to scare them, this was probably a good way to do it," Charlie said.

"Fair enough. Now please continue with what happened next."

Charlie took a sip of water; he could feel the perspiration from his armpits dripping down his sides. "We went back to the campus where Jack found Nick Gallo at the frat house and forced him into the car at gun point. Then, we drove back to the barn."

The courtroom was extremely quiet. The jury didn't take their eyes off Charlie, as he continued his testimony.

"Now, Mr. Costa," the prosecutor continued," were there any signs at this point that Jack was going to shoot Nick Gallo?"

"No, none at all. I still thought that Jack was just going to scare them."

"What happened next?" the prosecutor asked.

"We were in the barn and Jack started to get agitated with Nick Gallo's attitude. The guy acted untouchable, bragging about who he was, who his dad was. Jack told him to call his father."

"Let me get this straight; he asked Nick to call his father? The notorious Frank Gallo?" the prosecutor asked with a puzzled look.

"Yes."

"Did you find that odd?"

"I don't know what I thought at that moment."

"Did his father answer?"

"Yes."

"What happened next?" the prosecutor asked

The courtroom was remarkably still. "Jack asked Frank Gallo what would he do if someone raped and killed his sister?"

"Did he get an answer?"

"I think they were both yelling at each other on the phone. Jack just kept yelling over and over again, 'What would you do if someone killed your sister?"

The prosecutor walked around, stopping in front of Charlie. "Were you concerned at that point that maybe this situation was escalating?"

"Yes, I was concerned...I said to Jack, don't do anything stupid; it's not worth it. And then a few seconds after that, he pulled the trigger."

The prosecution rested after Charlie Costa finished

his testimony, sealing Jack Bolton's fate.

***

The next day a circus atmosphere engulfed the Suffolk County Superior Court in downtown Boston. Hordes of reporters converged on the courthouse. The jury had notified the court, after an hour of deliberation, that it had reached a verdict. The prosecution had rested its case after three days of overwhelming evidence pointing to the defendant, Jack Bolton, as the triggerman. Once the prosecution had called the three main witnesses, Charlie Costa, Ike Smith, and Chris Spencer, it was pretty much a slam-dunk case, reinforced by Jack's own self-incriminating testimony.

The prosecution had wondered why Jack Bolton didn't take the plea deal of twenty-five years. But as the trial proceeded, it became clear. Most defendants, on the advice of their defense teams, elect for the defendant to waive their right to testify, but Jack insisted on taking the stand, and then his reason for doing so became quite clear.

While on the stand he related in graphic detail why he shot Nick Gallo. His testimony was riveting and, no doubt, elicited sympathy from some jurors. The jury and the general public now knew the entire horrifying story. But the prosecution reacted quickly and objected to the motive as fictional. It was all a figment of Jack Bolton's imagination, as far as they were concerned. The judge immediately ordered that Jack's testimony about the motive for the killing be stricken from the records.

"It was hearsay," the judge stated. He went on the offensive and ordered the jury to disregard it.

But the damage was done to Nick Gallo's reputation, even though it had no bearing on the case.

As he left the stand, Jack deliberately smiled at Frank Gallo who stared back at him, silently seething. A sharp reporter caught the exchange and used it as a lead headline in the Boston Ledger the next day with a full-blown picture of the two caught in an intense eye lock. It read, "If Looks Could Kill."

The overflowing courtroom was packed with both local and national media types, as well as Nick Gallo's extended family, which took up most of the remaining seats. Jack's 80-year-old grandfather was the only remaining member of his family there to support him.

The jury, after an hour of deliberation, had notified the judge that it was ready to announce its verdict. After five days of opening statements, presentation of evidence, examination of witnesses, lawyer conferences with the judge, delays during the trial, closing arguments, and the judge's final instructions to the jury, it was all now coming to an end.

He sat quietly next to his lawyer as they waited for the jury to file in. As he looked around the room, his eyes once again met those of Frank Gallo, glaring fiercely at him.

Frank mouthed the words, "You're a dead man."

Jack ignored him and turned his attention to the jurors who were filing in.

The twelve jurors filed into the jury box, studiously avoiding eye contact as they took their seats.

Jack looked away from the jurors and noticed his old pal, Brian Butler, seated in the far corner of the courtroom. He smiled warmly at him. He was one of those guys that you thought might get kicked out of the SEALs because of his head-strong personality, but somehow he managed to barely escape that distinction. Of all the Navy SEALs he had spent time with, Brian Butler was the roughest around the edges. He was always second-guessing authority, only because he thought he had a better way, but then he would reluctantly follow orders to the letter, except for one time that almost cost him his life and barely avoided a court martial. Brian had served four tours of duty in Afghanistan, twice suffering gunshot wounds, and then he was asked to leave quietly. He might have been a rebel, but he was the one guy you wanted next to you when the going got tough.

Once the twelve jurors had settled into the jury box Judge McClain, who presided over the case, took his place at the bench. The courtroom became silent. Judge McClain then asked the jury if they had come to a verdict, and the foreman responded with a "yes." The bailiff received the verdict from the foreman and handed it to Judge McClain who reviewed the document for a few short minutes and then signaled to the bailiff to return it to the foreman to be read aloud. Judge McClain then stated, "I will note for the record that all are present."

The foreman stood up as the courtroom media, family, friends, and general public quietly waited. A larger than usual platoon of court guards and state police were posted at the back and sides of the courtroom. Jack just stared straight ahead, already expecting the guilty verdict.

The foreman then proceeded to clear his throat and announced the following; "We the jury... find the defendant... guilty of murder in the first degree."

The reporters immediately fed the guilty verdict to their newsrooms. A large roar erupted throughout the courtroom as Gallo's family and relatives reacted. The Gallo family was all too familiar with the court system. They were usually on the other side of the law, but today the opposite was true, and the verdict, in their view, was a victory.

Frank, however, was raging inside; it was his own flesh and blood and no verdict could bring his son back. His face reflected the hatred he had for Jack Bolton. And he vowed to himself that he would get revenge in his own way.

Jack just looked at the jury as the verdict was read.

He couldn't help but think how the system had it all wrong and no one cared about his sister or her boyfriend. They were the innocent victims whose lives were cut short. The court had it all backwards. He was the good guy, not the other way around.

Jack stood tall in his navy blue suit as Judge McClain began to announce his sentencing. "In Massachusetts, Mr. Bolton, anyone convicted of first degree murder is automatically sentenced to life in prison without parole."

Jack didn't hear another word. He would rot in prison for the rest of his life.

As Frank Gallo emerged from the courthouse into the fresh air, the reporters immediately surrounded him with cameras flashing. The imposing Mafia kingpin was in no mood to talk to them. Then he heard one of them call out "Frank, do you think Jack Bolton's sentence was fair?" As his lieutenants pushed them aside, he stopped in the middle of the swarm of reporters and turned back towards the direction of the voice. "Do I think the sentence was fair? Hell no," he blurted out. "My son was just an innocent victim of that crazy Navy SEAL who probably thought he was still on a special ops mission. He took out the frustration of his missing sister on my son, maybe because he somehow thought it was okay to kill Frank Gallo's son. Well, the only thing that would be fair here is if the man was put to death – just like he executed my son in cold blood."

Frank descended down the stairs with the media following closely behind, trying to get more vintage comments from the "Don" as some would call him. Frank for the first time in his life had gotten a dose of his own medicine and he didn't like it, especially when it came to his own flesh and blood. It burned him inside thinking of what Jack Bolton had done. He had big plans for his son and now it was all gone. Frank had taken the lives of so many men, some who were trying to seize power, others for betraying him and some who were just in the way. Of one thing he was certain, Jack Bolton was going to pay for what he did. It didn't matter if Bolton was in prison; he would find a way to get it done. Ideally he wanted to do it himself but, unfortunately, it would have to be done quietly and efficiently in some obscure place in prison.

***

Special Agent Ryland sat in his office watching on Court T.V., as the guilty verdict was handed down to Jack Bolton. Then, it was over and he was led away to begin his life sentence. Ryland couldn't help but shake his head at the final outcome of this heinous crime which took the lives of two outstanding young people. Three of the four perpetrators were walking free and a national hero, who had exacted retribution from the fourth, had just been sentenced to spend the rest of his life in prison.

Ryland understood what drove men like Jack Bolton to do what he did. The system failed him. The only recourse, in his mind, was taking the law into his own hands. And he was trained to kill.

He sighed and turned his attention to the large map of the United States hanging on the wall. It was studded with markers in certain locations that represented unresolved disappearances which appeared to share certain similarities. Four of these cases were of particular interest to him. The first one began ten months ago when the Beckets, a retired couple, disappeared from their home in North Adams, Massachusetts. Following that, Mary Thomas, a middle-aged single woman, disappeared from her home in Lake Saranac, New York. She was last seen drinking with a man who, according to the bartender, was in his middle thirties, of average build and height, with a receding hairline and black stringy hair – and a stranger to the area. The next report of similar interest to Agent Ryland was that covering a woman missing from Arnold, Pennsylvania; and following that, the most recent incident which took place in Austin, Indiana, where an elderly couple mysteriously disappeared.

Agent Ryland was drawn to the fact that all of these disappearances were reported from small, rural towns and involved single women or senior citizen couples. His gut was telling him he had a serial killer on his hands. Although early, he sensed that a sinister pattern might be emerging. At least that was his initial analysis, but there were no bodies, no evidence, just a description from a bartender of a potential suspect. That was all they had at this point.

Chapter 16

Jack had begun the adjustment to his new life in maximum-security at MCI-Cedar Junction in Walpole, Massachusetts. The amenities in his cell consisted of a desk, toilet, sink, and a hard bed. At night, he would lie there thinking about how his life was no longer his. The decorated Navy SEAL was a thing of the past. He would never see his sister's smile again. He was alone; he would have no family visits. What he did for the country no longer mattered. He was just a number, another convict with a sad story to tell and no one to listen.

He had been placed in a single seven-by-ten foot cell, and was rarely seen by other inmates, probably for his own protection. The authorities were surely aware that Frank Gallo wanted him dead. There wasn't any real free time. He was under lockdown most of the day, but he was allowed a daily shower and an hour in the "yard" a few times a week, always accompanied by a correctional officer. The *yard* was nothing more than an outside cage where he could walk around. His meals were brought to his cell.

Two weeks after he entered MCI, he was notified that his eighty-year old grandfather had passed away from a gun-shot wound, received when he surprised someone breaking into his home. That was the official story. But Jack was almost certain that Frank Gallo had something to do with it. He had tried to get protection for his grandfather but the authorities denied it. They didn't care. He tried to persuade his grandfather to move but he said he had lived in the house all his life and wasn't leaving for anybody. Now he was dead and Jack's last blood relative was gone.

It wasn't until he received a letter a few weeks later with no return address that his suspicions about the housebreak were confirmed. He put down the book he had been reading and opened the letter. It contained a handwritten note that said "Sorry to hear about your grandfather. My deep regrets. If you think I've forgotten you, you're sadly mistaken. I hope to send you another message very soon. I will, however, understand if you can't read it." Jack just stared at the signature. "Hope to see you soon, Frank."

After ten weeks at MCI, a notification letter was handed to him by one of the correctional officers. It advised him that he would be transferred in two weeks to Shirley Super Max prison in Shirley, Massachusetts. It mattered little to him. The humdrum daily routine wouldn't change. The cells would all look the same. The food would still taste bland .The fences and barbed wire would enclose the facility in the same way, and the correctional officers, as well as the prisoners, would be indistinguishable from one institution to the other. Just a formality, where he still would have no control and they would watch his every move.

***

One of the guards came over to Jack's jail cell around 10:00 o'clock one morning and announced. "Jack, you have a visitor."

"A visitor…huh. Now, who would be visiting me?" he said out loud.

The guard accompanied him to the non-contact inmate's visitor's room where a glass separated the visitor from the inmate and a phone was used for communication.

Jack sat in a small cubicle, waiting with great curiosity for the mystery visitor to appear. Only the glass separated him from the free world. Jack's eyes opened wide when Brian entered the room. Jack grabbed the phone with a big smile, "Brian!"

Brian picked up the receiver. "Hey, Jack," he said shaking his head. "You doing okay?"

"I'm doing okay. Every day is the same, of course. And they watch everything you do."

"That really sucks. Hey, I've been talking to some of the guys."

"What guys?"

"Well, Joe Cap, Dan Milton, and Bob Rodriguez. They all wanted me to tell you to hang in there."

"Yeah. Well, you tell them I miss my SEAL days with them."

"Hey, don't get sad on me, Jack. Look, if it's worth anything to you, I would have done the same thing."

"I don't regret what I did, Brian," he said, looking through the glass. "It's my sister who got the short end of all this. She was a beautiful person who I'm never going to see again."

Brian took a deep breath…"I know. I'm not going to forget about you in here," Brian said. "You're like a brother to me. I'll visit whenever I can."

"It's okay. We've all got our lives to live. Anyway, they're moving me to MCI Shirley in two weeks."

"How are they moving you?" Brian asked.

"How do I know?"

"I was just curious how they move inmates?'

"I see that mind of yours working. What are you going to do? Break me out, Brian?" he said laughing, which caused Brian to start laughing out loud

"Yeah! A bunch of former Navy SEALs are going to fast-rope down from a Black Hawk helicopter and break you out, just like the old days."

Jack couldn't help but laugh and Brian chuckled along with him.

***

A few days later Brian was driving his motorcycle

through the back roads of Maine until he came to the town of Brunswick and found the Oakwood Grille. Mike Stanley was already sitting at the bar waiting for him.

"Hey, buddy!" Brian said, tapping him on the shoulder.

Mike turned around and gave him a big hug. "It's good to see you."

"You look good. How's the leg?"

"My leg is pretty good now," Mike said. "But just not quite up to SEAL standards."

"You know, Mike, I was in the Navy for fifteen years. I got injured on a mission, which I had bad feelings about. Of course, I didn't recover fully and what did they do? They rejected my disability claim. Can you believe that? Five more years and I would have had a full pension."

"I don't get it," Mike said. "Why the hell are they so tight with the money when we risk our lives so many times?"

"Because they don't give a damn," Brian said. "Once you are used up, they just move on to the next guy."

"So have you seen any of the other guys?" Mike asked.

"Yeah, I keep in touch with a lot of the guys. I just visited Jack Bolton in prison."

"How's he doing? I can't believe what happened to him."

"Yeah. But if someone raped and killed my sister, I would have done the exact same thing as Jack."

"Is that what happened?'

"Yeah."

"I see your point."

"Anyway, I wanted to throw something out there for you to think about."

"What?"

"I was down in Mexico a while back and saw a way to make a lot of money."

"Let's hear it." Mike said.

"I'll be upfront with you. I need six guys. I have four, but I could use you. There's a Mexican cartel that's laundering money at a small bank outside Mexico City. We just go in, hold them up, and take the duffle bags of money. In and out, no big deal."

"I don't know, Brian. I mean, it sounds crazy."

"Well, if fifteen million dollars is crazy, I guess it is crazy," he said with a laugh.

Mike laughed along with him. "I can't do that. I just can't do it. I mean, what if something goes wrong or these guys come looking for the money. I'm sorry; it's nuts."

"I'm telling yah, you won't have to worry about money ever again."

"I can't do it, Brian. I just can't."

"Okay, I respect your decision. I don't want you doing something you don't want to do."

"I'm sorry. I wish I could."

"There's one other thing. I haven't told anyone else yet."

"What's that?"

"In ten days, they're transferring Jack Bolton to a prison in Shirley, Mass. I want to intercept the transfer."

"What? You want to break him out of prison!" Mike said in disbelief.

"Yeah."

"That's crazier than your first idea."

"Let me put it this way: We wouldn't be talking here today, if Jack didn't save our lives. He doesn't deserve to be there."

"I know. He saved my life twice."

"Look, the guy he killed was the son of Frank Gallo, a Mafia kingpin. How long do you think Jack is going to last in prison? Eventually they're going to kill him."

"You're right. The Mafia will never let go until they get him," Mike said.

"I got ten days to put it all together, but we can break him out, hit the cartel money, and be back in the states before anyone knows what happened. Nobody will know who broke Jack out or who hit the cartel. I think we owe it to him."

"Damn, Brian," Mike said, taking a swig of beer. "You sure this can all work? You make it sound so easy."

"I can't guarantee anything, but I can't let Jack

spend the rest of his life in prison. I just can't. I owe him big time."

"Who are the other guys who are in?" Mike asked.

"Cap, Milton, Rodriquez, myself, Bolton - though he just doesn't know it yet - and you would be the sixth guy."

"You got a good crew."

"I'll take care of all the operational stuff. You just have to show up," Brian said as he flagged the bartender for a couple more beers.

"Okay, okay, I'm in. Hell, I can't let Jack just rot in prison," Mike said shaking his head. "You are one crazy bastard, Brian."

Brian grinned. "Excellent. To our success," Brian said, as they clanked their beers together, patted each other on the shoulder, and followed up with a long swig.

Chapter 17

They flew in from different parts of the country, except for Mike who took a bus and was picked up by Brian at the Boston Greyhound station. The five members of the group, Joe, Mike, Dan, Bob, and Brian, registered at the Hilton hotel in Dedham, Massachusetts. Brian had set up the hotel reservations, arranged the air flights, and organized a plan to break Jack Bolton from prison. They had two days before Jack was to be transferred from MCI Cedar Junction to MCI -Shirley.

They ate at the restaurant inside the hotel. They found a secluded corner where their conversation could flow easily without being disturbed or overheard by customers. The night was just beginning, and drinks and appetizers were being consumed with great enjoyment in short order. The customary reminiscing of special ops missions, the sad story of Jack Bolton in prison, and the camaraderie from their days in the SEALs kept the conversation flowing, along with the many laughs.

Brian had held off telling everyone except Mike about his plan to break Jack out of prison. They had asked him earlier in the day why he wanted all of them to come to Massachusetts. He just told them he would tell them tonight. And he was now waiting for the right moment.

As the meal came to an end and the last few drinks were being consumed, Brian got the attention of the group. "Well, you're probably all wondering why we aren't on our way to Mexico quite yet," he said in a low voice, as blank stares looked back at him. "I've put a lot of thought into this and it's the right thing to do regardless of the consequences, at least for me. You all know that Jack Bolton saved the life of everyone that's here tonight. Now, unfortunately, he is sitting in prison for something that any of us might have done."

"Where are you going with this, Brian?" Bob asked

Brian paused, took a quick swig of beer and then said quietly, as the guys at the table leaned in, "Okay, in two days, Jack is going to be transferred from MCI Cedar Junction in Walpole to MCI-Shirley. I have a plan to break him out during the transfer. He's our sixth guy and, if everything goes according to plan, nobody will know that we broke him out. We'll then head to Mexico, hit the cartel, and be back in the states in no time, living happily ever after with a lot of money."

"Wow!" Dan said. "Sounds like you got this all figured out, Brian. But it's one thing to hit a cartel, but to break Jack out of prison, I mean this is a little crazy, don't you think?"

"Look, I understand, if some of you decide not to do it, or have serious doubts about doing it, but this will be the only opportunity we have of getting Jack out of prison before the Mafia finds a way to take him out - or he rots in prison."

"I'm in," Joe Cap said firmly. "I wouldn't be here today if it wasn't for Jack. So yeah, I'm in all the way."

"I'm in as well," Mike said.

Bob looked straight at Brian. "This definitely confirms you are crazy, but I wouldn't miss this for the world. I'm totally in. I love the action."

Brian looked at Dan. "Well, Dan, you're the last man standing."

Dan looked at the group with a straight face. "Of course, I'm in," he said with a wide smile. "Do you think I'd let you guys go without me? Who the hell is going to keep you all out of trouble?"

The group erupted with laughter. "Just like old times," Brian said, high-fiving Dan. Then added, "Time for a small toast, to Jack." They hit their glasses together and finished their drinks.

***

The smartphone vibrated while Ned Johnson sat at the bar in the Hilton Hotel. He got up and walked to a quiet area outside the bar to hear the conversation. He had been watching Joe Cap for ten weeks now and was waiting to finish his assignment. He had no substantial information of any kind to forward to his superiors. "Did you get the pictures, okay?" Ned asked.

"Yeah."

"Looks like a reunion."

"Nice pictures. We've identified everyone. They were all in the same SEAL unit."

"Well, you want me to continue to follow Cap? He's done nothing out of the ordinary."

"Yeah, we'll let you know when the assignment is over."

Ned went back to the bar and observed the group while nursing his beer. They all looked like they were having such a good time, but he had to watch from a distance, wishing he could join in. He actually joked to himself that maybe he should send a round of drinks over and they would respond by inviting him over. Needless to say his superiors would not approve of such a tactic.

Chapter 18

At 9:20 a.m. two correctional officers escorted Jack from his cell, down a long corridor, through a series of metal gates, and then to a waiting armored car. He was led into the back of the vehicle where he was securely ankle-chained to a metal bench and handcuffed, as he sat down. A correctional officer sat at the opposite end of the bench. Jack listened to the rain beating down on the roof and watched as they escorted another inmate, Igor Barinov – a bald, muscle-bound guy with a tattoo on his neck, who looked like a Russian weight lifter - into the vehicle and seated him opposite Jack.

Dean Ray, a first-year correctional officer, then knelt down and chained Igor's ankles and handcuffed him in the same manner as Jack. While doing so, he furtively slipped a shiv inside the man's sleeve. Then, he stood up and went over to Jack to make sure that he was securely fastened to the metal bench. "Both inmates are secure," he called out through the small partition to the two guards in the front seats. Finally he sat down alongside the other correctional officer. A few minutes later, the armored car left the prison yard escorted by a state police cruiser which led the way.

Joe Cap sat in his car, drinking a cup of coffee while

waiting on the side of the road on Route 1A for Jack's transportation vehicle to drive by. He checked his watch. It was 9:35 a.m. They had spent the previous day going over the plan. Brian covered the route that the prison vehicles would take and how they would intercept and extricate Jack from the armored car. Brian supplied the automatic weapons, the plastic explosives, the two cars with GPS, the cell phones, and the jumpsuits with masks. It was exactly like a SEAL mission, except now they were going against the system. Every detail was discussed, memorized, and questioned. They couldn't fail. There would be no second chance. Joe sat watching cars pass and wondered if this could all go off as planned. What if something went wrong? What if they had the wrong day? What if the security detail went a different route? What if Jack wasn't in the vehicle? What if...Then, just as Brian had described, a state police car, followed by an armored car, pulled out onto Route 1A. Joe immediately called Brian. "They've just pulled out onto Route 1A."

"Okay," Brian replied.

"It's a go, guys," Brian said, back in Shirley, as the adrenalin began to kick in. He opened the trunk and passed out semi-automatic weapons, jump suits, and masks.

"This is really happening," Mike said.

"It's going to be fine. Trust me." Brian said. "It's like any mission. We're pros at this."

An hour and ten minutes had gone by when the cell phone buzzed. Joe said, "Brian, they're about one minute away. I'm behind the armored car and we will be turning onto South Street any second."

They got into position. Brian drove one of the cars onto the middle of South Street and parked on an angle between the two lanes of traffic at the same time that the state police and the armored car entered South Street. When he saw the approaching state police car in the distance, he laid flat on his belly against the pavement in front of the driver's side of the car with the door wide open. The rest of the team hid on the side of the road. Both vehicles came to a stop fifteen feet in front of Brian.

Meanwhile, inside the armored car, Igor suddenly bent over, moaning and complaining of stomach cramps. Dean went over, pretending to attend to him, and surreptitiously unfastened his ankle chains and handcuffs.

"I'm okay," Igor grunted. With a nod, Dean went back to his seat.

***

The state police officer on the passenger side of the cruiser jumped out and walked briskly to where Brian lay in the middle of the road. Bending over him, he asked, "You okay, sir?" He lifted Brian's wrist, feeling for a pulse.

At that moment, Brian flipped over onto his back and pointed a gun at the officer. "Take your gun out of your holster and put it down slowly. Now," he commanded, while rising to his feet. The rest of the team moved in swiftly, semi-automatic handguns drawn, and disarmed the other officers.

The men inside the armored car were oblivious to the drama unfolding outside. Igor suddenly lunged at Jack like a cobra striking its prey. Before the correctional officers could react, Jack's quick reflexes deflected the shiv, but Igor was able to wrap his fingers around Jack's neck, choking him. At that moment, an explosion rocked the armored car. The back doors flew open, throwing Igor and the correctional officers to the floor. Igor paused for a couple of seconds, shook his head like a snorting bull, and snatched the blade from the floor. He lunged at Jack again. Two gunshots rang out. Igor slumped to the floor, the blade dropping from his hand onto Jack's chest.

Brian raced to the back of the armored car, unsure what had just happened. Joe disarmed the two correctional officers who were sitting up, still in a fog, their ears ringing and faces covered with soot from the blast. He signaled them with his hands to lie down.

"What the hell just happened, Joe?" Brian asked, peering into the vehicle, gazing at the prisoner dead on the metal floor.

Jack's restraints were unlocked and he was escorted out of the back of the vehicle and into the backseat of one of the getaway cars. He was still dazed, trying to grasp what had happened. "What the hell?" he muttered, repeatedly, clapping his hands to his ears as though to clear it.

The police and correctional officers had been disarmed and tied securely to trees on the side of the road. Jack had been rescued, and now the cars were driving off, all within a minute and a half of the initial contact.

The two cars drove west. Jack was seated in the back seat still wearing his orange jump suit and shaking his head and rubbing his ears. Finally, Joe and Brian flipped off their masks. "Hey, buddy, surprise," Brian said to Jack, laughing.

"You weren't kidding about breaking me out," Jack said, breaking into a smile.

"You should know by now I never kid." Brian smiled wider

The two cars proceeded west.

"Thanks for breaking me out, but none of you should have done this for me," Jack continued, shaking his head.

"We didn't do it just for you, Jack. We need you for another little caper in Mexico." Brian replied, keeping his eye on the road.

"What caper?" Jack asked, his head getting clearer.

"I'll explain once we get out of here," Brian said,

142

looking out for police. "So what the hell happened back there, Joe?"

"I don't know, but it looked like the other guy was trying to kill Jack." Joe explained, still holding his gun. "So I had no choice but to shoot him."

"Jack, it looks like Gallo had his own plan for you today," Brian said, taking a quick look at Jack

"Yeah, I think so," Jack replied. "One of the correctional officers went over to the other inmate who was complaining about being sick. It looks like he unlocked his handcuffs and ankle chain while giving him a blade to use on me."

"Maybe it was a good thing we came along when we did," Brian declared, turning to Joe, who nodded.

"Yeah, thanks, Joe. You probably saved my life today." Jack said.

"I owed you big time, Jack," Joe said, turning his head. "I was just doing my job."

Jack smiled, thinking sometimes it's hard to take the SEAL out when you come back to civilian life.

After driving for seven miles, the two cars turned onto a dirt road, drove a half- mile into the woods, and pulled into a small clearing overlooking a pond. They got out of the cars and congratulated each other, just as they had done after a successful mission back in the old SEAL days. They all hugged Jack as if he were a lost soldier. After high-fives all around, they took off their black jump suits and changed quickly into street clothes.

143

Dan approached Brian, smiling "I really didn't think we could pull it off, but we were damn good."

"Other than knocking off a Mafia hit man, the execution was flawless," Brian said, containing his emotion.

The jumpsuits and the masks were thrown into the cars. The crew began pulling and lifting off the fake white plastic paint that had been applied to both cars. The original black color now shone brightly on both vehicles; the fake license plates were replaced with the originals.

"Where we going, Brian?" Jack asked.

"I'll let you in on everything while we're driving," Brian said, his voice brusque. "We don't have time to be shooting the breeze. Every state police officer and FBI agent is going to be looking for us."

"I have some unfinished business to attend to," Jack said, looking like a man who had only one thing on his mind.

"Jack, this ain't the time for revenge or whatever you're thinking," Brian said.

"I told you, I have unfinished business." Jack said.

"Whatever you need to do, can't it wait?" Brian said, looking out at the pond.

"Brian, you'll never understand until you lose someone very close to you." Jack said, standing next to Brian.

"We don't have time to debate it." The one thing

144

Brian hated was a change in plan because it increased the odds of failure. But he couldn't abandon Jack, either.

"Then don't. I don't need your help, Brian."

"Dan, Joe, Bob, and Mike, you take the Ford," Brian barked. "Jack and I will take the Chevy. We have unfinished business to attend to. We'll meet you guys in Laredo at the designated location. Just put the location in the GPS. Do not use your own cell phones; use the ones I gave you to contact me."

Jack climbed into the passenger seat of the Chevy. "Go west."

Brian drove the Chevy Impala west on Route 2. "Where we going, Jack?"

"Wilbur Smith College. I told you. I have unfinished business."

"I know all about what happened up there. I talked to Charlie."

"Then you know why I have to go back," Jack said without hesitation.

"Just forget about this Atkins guy, Jack."

"I can't. Every time I think of my sister, I picture what these guys did to her. I can't let it go, Brian."

"You do what you have to do. But it won't make you feel any better. Most missions we went on, we did what we had to do. How did you feel afterwards?"

"This is personal, Brian. I've had plenty of time to read about political corruption and the Atkins political history while in prison. This kid is going to be just as ruthless and corrupt as his senator father someday, maybe worse. You should read about Senator Sam Atkins. There was a rumor out there years ago he had an affair with a young intern."

"Big deal. All these politicians have mistresses on the side."

"It's more than that."

"What do you mean?"

"This intern just disappeared."

"So you think Atkins killed her?"

"I don't know, but she was pregnant according to her boyfriend, Jeff Keller, who was convicted of killing her."

"And let's just say the senator did it. Atkins is still a senator and you are not going to change that."

Jack turned his gaze to Brian. "The boyfriend is in prison and, according to this book I read, he swore that he loved her and that he was innocent. The author of the book had him take a lie detector test and he passed."

"Wow! That would suck if he was framed, huh? Then again, maybe he fooled the lie detector test." Brian said, keeping his eyes on the road. "So, is the boyfriend still in prison?"

"Yeah. He got a life sentence."

Brian shot a glance at Jack. "Well, I still think we have our own problems here to worry about first. Right now, you are going to be on every police and FBI agent's radar, not to mention the Mafia. "

"Frank Gallo killed my grandfather." Jack blurted, thinking how it was all his fault.

"How do you know that?" Brian asked, his eyebrows arching.

"He sent me a condolence letter."

"Sorry to hear that. This guy is never going to stop until you're dead."

"So, you were telling me about some caper in Mexico."

"This is the plan." Brian said, using one hand to steer and gesturing with the other. "I've been down in Mexico from time to time and, the last time I was there, I came across a cartel money-laundering operation that takes place at a small bank every week at the same time. So I put this plan together to break you out of prison, hit the cartel for the drug money, and then live off the money for the rest of our lives."

"You always make everything sound so easy," Jack said, rolling his eyes.

"Hey, I put a lot of planning into this. We got you out, didn't we?"

Jack nodded with a grin on his face. "You always had a better plan."

"I did."

"I know. So now I'm going to add a cartel to my list of people wanting me dead," Jack said, chuckling. "And I was worried about the Mafia."

Brian smiled as they continued on Route 2 to Wilbur

Smith College. "It could be anywhere from fifteen to eighteen million to split six ways."

"That's a lot of money, Brian." Jack ran his hand over his head. This cartel isn't going to miss it?"

"They are never going to know who stole it."

"I hope you're right," Jack said.

"I also got a guy to create new identities for us."

"What are you planning on doing if we actually get out of Mexico alive?"

"I'm going to live on one of the islands and start a tourist boat ride business and forget about the world," Brian chuckled. They continued driving through the Berkshire Mountains. Although the rain had stopped, the dreary day overshadowed the beauty of the scenic hills.

"It sounds good," Jack said. "But I don't think it's going to work out like that for guys like us."

"It is for me, Jack. And when this heist is all over, you should just find a quiet place somewhere, like Canada maybe, and settle down. You'll have plenty of money and all that hatred that's now running through your veins will subside."

Jack peered out the window, looking at the scenery without really seeing it. He realized that Brian had hit on something. He rubbed a finger over one eyebrow. He could finish this last payback before the one big hit in Mexico and then disappear for good. It just sounded too easy and nothing in his life had ever been easy.

As they got closer to Williamstown, Jack sat quietly,

thinking about Nicole, and contemplating his next move. He looked over at Brian and couldn't help but shake his head. If there was one person who could have pulled off breaking him out of prison, it was Brian. Then the idea of hitting a Mexican cartel could only have come from Brian. His imagination had no limits. *If you could think it – it was possible*, he would say.

After a couple of hours of driving, they had reached Wilbur Smith College. Jack's demeanor changed as he focused on retribution for his sister. He loaded the semi-automatic handgun and cocked the hammer. The car stopped a hundred yards away from the frat house.

Brian glanced at Jack. "You sure you really want to do this?"

Jack opened the car door and turned to look back at Brian. "I don't have a choice."

"Well, make it quick. If he's not there, you have to leave. It's only a matter of time before this place will be crawling with troopers. Jack, I mean it. We can't be here long."

Jack closed the car door and walked with fire in his eyes toward the frat house. His mind filled with thoughts of his sister and what she might have been thinking those last few minutes of her life. Did she wish her brother were there to protect her? The closer he got to the fraternity, the more he thought of her and his eyes filled. The rain started up again mixing with his tears.

He entered the fraternity and walked around at a

quick pace, drawing glances from fraternity members. As he climbed the stairs, he came upon Tom Mello, who was on his way down.

"Jack! What are you doing here?" Tom asked warily. "Aren't you supposed to be in prison?"

"I'm here for Atkins," he mumbled in a trance-like state. He moved past Tom, who stood in the stairwell, following his progress. Jack searched the upstairs until he came to a closed door where laughter could be heard. He pushed open the door and stood in the doorway, his gun pointed at the two individuals lying on a bed.

"What the hell?' John muttered. His girlfriend rolled off the bed, clutching the sheet to her chest. She scrambled to the closet.

"You must be surprised to see me, John," Jack said, his finger on the trigger.

"I had nothing to do with your sister's death," he blurted.

Jack pulled the trigger twice. The two pops echoed through the house. The half-naked girl started screaming hysterically as Jack left the room. He strode past Tom, still standing on the stairs. Frat members scurried from his path like mice at the sight of light. He exited the house, marching faster until he was sprinting to Brian's car as the rain came down harder. He opened the car door and plopped down in dripping wet clothes, staring straight ahead. The car pulled out and sped off.

Brian turned towards Jack. "You okay?"

"I did what I had to do." Jack replied, grim-faced. "I don't want to talk about it."

"Okay." Brian pulled onto the highway, heading southwest to Texas.

Chapter 19

Special Agent Ryland was getting ready to board a plane in Boston to go to Indiana to investigate the unresolved disappearance of a couple that appeared to have similarities to the Becket case in North Adams. Ryland's smartphone started vibrating and he stepped aside, placing it to his ear, just as he was about to enter the plane.

"Hey, Alex," Ryland called to Agent Hawkins who was about to board the plane. "You are going to have to go to Indiana without me."

"What's going on?"

"Jack Bolton just broke out of prison."

"What? I can't believe that," Agent Hawkins replied.

"When you get to Indiana, just keep me in the loop if you come across anything," Ryland ordered.

***

Agent Ryland arrived an hour later at the crime scene in Shirley. The news media had already arrived. The media had not forgotten Jack Bolton's sensational trial a couple of months back. Reporters swarmed around Agent Ryland as he got out of his car.

"Is it true that Jack Bolton was killed?" a female reporter called out.

Agent Ryland ignored the question and walked briskly through the crowd. He looked over the crime scene from a distance. The area had been cordoned off with yellow tape.

"Special Agent Ryland," Sergeant Mark Sullivan of the Mass State police yelled with a wave. "Over here." He shook Agent Ryland's hand as he entered the crime scene area.

"It's been a long time, Mark. How have you been?" Ryland asked.

"Can't complain, Paul" Sullivan said.

"What do we have here?" Ryland asked.

"We've been interviewing the officers who were transferring Jack Bolton and we have a dead inmate in the armored car."

"It's not Bolton?" Ryland queried, as they walked to the back of the vehicle.

"No," Sullivan replied instantly.

Agent Ryland stood at the rear of the vehicle, peering in. "Was he killed intentionally from what you could tell?"

"It looks like he was shot from close range," Sullivan replied. "Two bullets in the back."

"In the back, huh?" Agent Ryland said. He stood next to the Sergeant, viewing the position of the dead inmate's body and observing the damage to the back doors of the armored vehicle. "Looks like plastic explosives."

"Yeah, this was a professional job, no question about that," Sullivan stated, standing next to Ryland. "We interviewed the police and correctional officers. They said five guys held them up with automatic weapons and broke out Bolton in about a minute and a half. It happened so fast, they couldn't even respond."

"Did anybody see their faces?" Agent Ryland asked

"No, they wore masks and were in some sort of black jump suits," Sullivan replied. "They also zip-tied the officers' hands, tied them to a tree, and took off in two cars."

"Did we get a description of the two cars?"

"Well, we have a description, two white cars. But how many white cars are there out on the road?"

"So they could be anywhere at this moment?" Ryland said. "Has anybody notified officials at the US and Canadian borders. They have a three-hour head start, which would get them to the Canadian border right about now if they go through Derby Line, Vermont."

Agent Ryland stepped up into the armored car while Sergeant Sullivan barked out orders to a few officers to issue descriptions of Jack Bolton and a gang of five men to border authorities. Ryland studied the dead body in the back of the armored vehicle from different angles while the forensic team snapped pictures, analyzed the surroundings, and took prints. He wondered why the inmate was in such an awkward position, his back turned to the back doors, when he was shot in the back. Then it dawned on him. He wasn't handcuffed. And why weren't his ankles shackled to the metal bench? "Hey, Sergeant Sullivan," he hollered.

"Right here," he answered, suddenly appearing outside the armored car. "What is it?"

"Did anyone touch the crime scene?"

"No, this is the way we found it." Sergeant Sullivan replied. "Why you asking?"

"Well, why is the inmate not handcuffed and shackled to the bench?"

"That's a good question."

Ryland rubbed his chin, perplexed by what he saw. Something wasn't right. A crazy thought came to mind. Was it possible that Frank Gallo had sent people to break out Jack Bolton just so he could kill him with his own hands? Why would he have killed the inmate, unless there was more to all this?

"Oh, the forensic team found a homemade blade on the floor in the armored car," the Sergeant said.

"That just adds to the mystery," Ryland said. "I'm starting to think that this guy was trying to kill Bolton."

"Do we have anything on this dead inmate?" Ryland questioned.

"The guy was serving a life sentence for murder," Sergeant Sullivan responded. "His name is Igor Barinov."

"Any ties to Frank Gallo?" Ryland asked, moving out of the way of the forensic team and stepping down and out of the vehicle to converse with Sergeant Sullivan.

"Well, he does have connections to organized crime," Sergeant Sullivan said. "That's all we know at this time."

"Let me ask you a question, Mark."

"Sure."

"Shouldn't this guy have been handcuffed and secured to the metal bench?" Ryland asked

"Yeah, I would think so."

"Where are the correctional officers who were in the back of the armored vehicle?" Ryland asked.

"Over there by the police cruiser," Sergeant Sullivan said, pointing to the two correctional officers, who were leaning against one of the police cruisers on the side of the road.

"I would like to talk to them." They walked together to the two men, who straightened when they saw Ryland approaching.

"I'm Special Agent Ryland. How you guys doing? Tough day."

"Yeah," they both said, nodding their heads.

"Look, I'm not going to take up much more of your time. I just have a few questions and then you're both free to go."

The two correctional officers shrugged.

"Maybe you can clear something up for me," Agent Ryland said. "The inmate, Igor Barinov, wasn't handcuffed or shackled. Can somebody tell me why?"

There was a pause as they both looked at each other.

"Well, shouldn't he have been handcuffed and shackled or am I missing something here?" Ryland asked looking directly at Dean and then the other correctional officer.

"Yes, sir," Dean answered.

"Okay. So, why was the inmate not handcuffed or shackled?"

"He somehow broke free," Dean replied.

"He somehow broke free," Agent Ryland repeated, looking confused. "Okay, so who secured him?"

There was silence.

"Well?"

"I did, sir." Dean said. "I guess I did a lousy job,"

"We found a blade in the vehicle. Do either of you know how it got there?"

Once again, there was silence.

Ryland's voice had taken on a hard edge. He repeated. "Any idea how that blade just happened to get in the vehicle?"

"No, sir," they replied together.

"All right. I'm done with questions for now, so you're free to go, but we'll be in touch," Ryland said curtly. "Don't leave town."

As Sullivan and Ryland walked side-by-side,

looking over the crime scene, Ryland said, "I need you to do background checks on both of those men. "They know more than they're saying."

"Do you really think they're hiding something?"

"Well, was it a mistake or did one of them purposely unlock the handcuffs and ankle chains? And how is there a homemade knife in the vehicle?"

"We'll get that information to you as soon as possible," Sullivan said.

"Thanks," Ryland said as his smart phone vibrated. "I've got to take this. I'll be right with you, Mark." He listened, not believing what he was hearing. He clicked off the phone and looked out at the media trucks dotting the landscape. A frenzy would ensue, once they heard this news.

The call was from the FBI director, ordering him to go to Williamstown immediately. Jack Bolton had done the unthinkable. He had killed John Atkins. Now, Ryland had to call the boy's father, Senator Sam Atkins. Normally, this kind of news would be delivered in person but it had to be done quickly before the media pushed it through the airwaves. His day had gone from bad to worse.

The theory that Frank Gallo might have been behind the breakout of Jack Bolton so that he could kill him himself was put to rest. Five trained heavily-armed men broke Jack Bolton out in quick time without breaking a sweat. Surely, there was a connection between the men and Bolton. The pressure to find him would intensify with the death of John Atkins. The powerful senator would exert unrelenting pressure on the agency to track down his son's killer and bring him to justice as quickly as possible.

Sullivan, standing off to the side of his police car as Ryland walked over, asked, "Everything okay?"

"Well, I have to go to Wilbur Smith College immediately."

"What's going on?"

"It looks like Jack Bolton has shot and killed John Atkins."

"Wow, that's the Senator's son, right?"

"Yes, and I have to call the Senator to give him the bad news."

"Do you think Bolton is still heading to Canada?" Sullivan asked.

"Yes. Let's focus our resources on the border for now," he said. "So I'll be in touch. At some point, we'll need to hold a press conference."

"Just let me know when and where you want to do it," Sullivan said. "Good luck."

"Thanks, I'll keep in touch." Ryland jogged to his car, dreading the phone call he was about to make.

Chapter 20

Senator Sam Atkins was sitting in a scheduled meeting of the Senate Finance Committee, of which he was chairman, when his phone buzzed. His secretary told him that he had an urgent call.

"I can't take it right now," he said emphatically. "Tell them I will call them back after the meeting."

"He said it's urgent," she repeated.

Sam excused himself and walked through the door. "Do you know who it is?" he asked the secretary.

"He said his name was Special Agent Ryland from the FBI," she explained, handing him the phone.

"Hello," Sam said.

"Hello, Senator Atkins. I'm Special Agent Ryland of the Boston FBI office. I'm afraid I have some terrible news for you. Your son, John, was shot this morning at Wilbur Smith College."

"What?" he said, his body numb, his mind frozen, words suddenly hard to find. "What the hell are you trying to tell me?" he demanded, raising his voice to another level.

Ryland's mouth went dry. He struggled to find the proper words, but there are no words to soften this kind of a blow. "It appears from eye witness reports that your son was shot by Jack Bolton," he said. "I'm sorry to have to tell you this, but John died as a result of his wounds."

There was silence on the other end of the phone.

"Senator Atkins?" Ryland asked softly.

Atkins sat down, stunned. He tried to gather his thoughts. "Are you telling me that Jack Bolton murdered my son?" he said, with authority returning to his voice.

"It would appear so, Senator."

"How the hell did he escape without anybody notifying the college or myself, especially after what he did to Nick Gallo?" he asked, his voice rising.

"It was a mistake, Senator."

"A mistake," he said angrily. "A mistake is a damned understatement." He slammed down the phone.

"Hello…hello, Senator Atkins," Ryland exhaled. He knew there would be extreme pressure to bring Jack Bolton to justice swiftly. But now there were other accomplices to identify. Who were the people behind Bolton's breakout? That was the question that needed to be answered.

With only the steady swish of the wiper blades to distract him, Ryland was in deep reflection as he drove west along Route 2, his thoughts racing back in time, back to the day twelve years ago when he was a twenty-seven-year old patrol officer in Hudson, Massachusetts. It was a day he would never forget.

A frantic alert came over the scanner that the then

young Patrol Officer Ryland responded to immediately since he was in the general vicinity of the emergency call. A passerby had stopped to help a hysterical ten-year old girl on Douglas Road at 8:30 at night. She said that a guy had kidnapped her and her mother at knifepoint from the mall and forced them to drive their car until they came to a secluded area just down the road from where the passerby was calling.

Patrolman Ryland's cruiser reached the abandoned SUV on the side of the road within a minute of the call and he was the first officer at the scene. He rushed out of his patrol car with his gun drawn, his heart racing and adrenaline pumping. He was unprepared for what he saw, especially in this small town where petty theft was pretty much the extent of crime.

As he secured the area, looking for any trace of the abductor, he looked in the side window of the car. He saw the young mother slumped down with her hands tied and blood covering the seat. She had been stabbed multiple times. He opened the back door of the SUV and placed his hand on her neck to feel for her pulse. She was dead. His emotions, in those few seconds, got the best of him. He pulled away from the vehicle, bent over, and threw up Luke's Café meatloaf dinner.

It was Ryland's first experience with death, never mind murder. Things like this didn't happen in the small town of Hudson. - a young mother murdered by an evil psychopath in front of her young daughter, who struggled with the attacker and managed to escape.

Ryland had regained his composure. He grabbed a flashlight from the cruiser and continued to survey the area with the help of a full moon. A light snow was falling. Footprints could be seen leading into the woods. He radioed in that he was in hot pursuit of the suspect. He followed the footprints at a fast trot. Rage flowed through him. He was determined to find this monster before he could do any more harm. He became angrier as he ran. He was running on total adrenaline and, there in the shadows of the moon, the despicable creature emerged from the tree line into a field.

The killer was running, holding his side, about twenty-five yards in front of Ryland who yelled, "Stop, police, put up your hands where I can see them." The man could not run any further; he was gasping for air. Ryland had gotten his man. The suspect turned to face him and put up his hands, dropping the knife in the field

The man, in his late twenties and of medium build, was trying to catch his breath while holding up his hands, as he slowly walked towards Ryland. "You got me," he said loudly, flashing a wide smile, captured in the moonlight. Ryland paused, then fired two shots, hitting the suspect in the chest. He staggered for a few seconds and fell to the ground

Officer Ryland was suspended with pay for two weeks while an internal investigation of his actions was conducted. The investigators went through the motions, *but he was eventually cleared of any wrongdoing and looked on as a hero forevermore by the town folks. Nobody was going to question his motives that night. Those heroics, ironically, helped him in his FBI career advancement.*

He thought about his situation twelve years earlier and compared it to Jack Bolton's situation now. Here was a guy whose sister had been raped and murdered by people who were so well connected politically and criminally that they never had to worry about the consequences of their actions. Jack even tried to go through the court system and, when that failed, he decided that he had to take the law into his own hands, knowing that his sister's murderers would never be brought to justice any other way.

Like Bolton, Ryland took the law into his own hands that dreadful night, and he never questioned his decision to kill the deranged suspect. Although he could sympathize with Jack Bolton and his actions, it was his job to bring in this decorated former Navy SEAL. In Ryland's eyes, the only crime Jack Bolton committed was to bring to justice two sinister college students who did the unthinkable and got away with it.

Chapter 21

The next morning at 10 o'clock sharp, Special Agent Ryland and Sergeant Sullivan held a press conference in Boston. They stood behind the podium and were flanked by members of the state police and agents of the FBI. A swarm of reporters were in attendance with microphones poised and cameras focused, eager for more information on the story that had hit the national newscasts the day before.

"I'm Special Agent Ryland, the lead agent on the case, and next to me is Sergeant Sullivan of the Massachusetts State Police." Ryland gestured toward Sullivan. "I'm going to start by giving everyone a timeline of the events that took place yesterday. Afterwards, Sergeant Sullivan and I will answer questions.

"At approximately 9:30 yesterday morning, a state police cruiser accompanied an armored prison vehicle that was transferring inmates Jack Bolton and Igor Barinov from MCI Junction in Walpole to Shirley MCI in Shirley, Massachusetts. At approximately 10:45, the vehicles turned onto South Street in Shirley, Mass. Within a half mile on that road, a car was stalled in the middle of the road and a man was lying face down on the street. The lead vehicle stopped, and the officer in the passenger seat of the cruiser got out of the car to check on the individual who was lying in the street.

"As the officer bent down to see if the individual was okay, the man on the ground turned over and pointed a gun at the officer. Simultaneously, four other individuals came out of hiding from the woods bordering the road with automatic weapons drawn. They disabled the other officer in the state police cruiser and the two security officers in the front seat of the armored car. Plastic explosives were placed on the back doors of the armored car, blowing the doors apart. The two security officers inside, who were temporarily disabled from the blast, were disarmed and, at that point, the suspects grabbed Jack Bolton and drove off in two large, four-door white cars. The other inmate, Igor Barinov, was shot and killed inside the armored vehicle by the people who broke Jack Bolton out."

Ryland paused for a moment, looked out at the assembled reporters and continued. "Thereafter, at approximately one o'clock in the afternoon, John Atkins, a college student at Wilbur Smith College, was shot and killed in his room in the Beta Ki Fraternity. The shooter was identified by eyewitnesses as Jack Bolton."

He paused again. "This is a general overview of what took place yesterday and I would like to say one other thing. There is a two hundred thousand dollar reward for information leading to the capture of Jack

Bolton. Now, I'm ready for questions."

He was immediately bombarded with questions from all directions, and all at once. "I can only take one question at a time," he shouted. "Yes, you with the blue blazer."

"Can you confirm for us that John Atkins is the son of Senator Sam Atkins?" the first reporter asked.

Ryland looked forward, his hands holding the podium…"Yes, that's all I'm going to say about that," Ryland said. "Next question."

"Special Agent Ryland, how many men helped Jack Bolton escape?"

"And were they wearing anything to hide their faces?" another reporter shouted.

"There were five men with semi-automatic weapons and they wore masks to cover their faces," Ryland replied.

"What type of semi-automatic weapons did they use?" a female reporter asked.

Sergeant Sullivan stepped in. "We can't answer that question at this time. I'm sorry."

Agent Ryland pointed to another reporter, who held his hand in the air.

"Any idea who the men were who helped Jack Bolton escape?"

"We are actively looking into all possible leads and it is too early in the investigation to even try to give you an answer on this. Next question," he said, pointing to a reporter wearing a red baseball cap.

"Do you know why Igor Barinov was shot and killed? And is organized crime involved?"

There was a pause. Ryland didn't want to go into too much detail at this point in the investigation. "Igor Barinov was shot twice by a semi-automatic gun. At this time, we are not sure why he was shot. As far as any organized crime involvement, we are actively looking into that. Our main concern right now is getting Jack Bolton back behind bars and prosecuting the people who were responsible for helping him escape."

The reporters kept yelling questions that Ryland tried to sort out. "Look, we can only answer one more question and then we have to end the press conference." he said. "You, in the red jacket."

A female reporter in a red jacket had waited patiently. Her question seemed designed to stir up the drama. "What was Jack Bolton's motive for killing John Atkins?'

Ryland brushed his hair back. "As for the motive," his mind raced trying to find the right words.

The crowd of reporters grew silent, expectant. Ryland envisioned Senator Sam Atkins staring at the TV, waiting for a reply. But before he could answer, Sullivan stepped toward the podium, as if he were a political handler. "We are still trying to determine the motive behind the shooting," he said.

Ryland knew exactly why Jack Bolton shot John

Atkins, but he wasn't ready to share that information with the media. Sullivan's response was perfect. "So, as Sergeant Sullivan stated, we are still working on the motive," Ryland added.

When the topic turned to the Senator's son, the shouted questions intensified. "Did the Senator's son have something to do with Bolton's missing sister?" "Did you talk to the Senator personally?" "Did the Senator's son have a Secret Service detail?" "Was John Atkins notified that Jack Bolton had escaped?"

Ryland ignored those questions. It was time to end the press conference. They were heading into a sensitive area, and the last thing he wanted to do was upset the Senator.

"I would like to thank you all today. As we get more information, we'll share it with you," Ryland said, looking over the media. "As for any information that the public might have on the whereabouts of Jack Bolton, please call the state police hotline or contact the FBI-web-tips online site and follow the prompts."

Chapter 22

Brian and Jack rolled into the parking lot of the Days Inn hotel in Laredo, Texas, at 10:00 p.m. the next night, two hours after the rest of the crew arrived. In a day and a half of non-stop driving, each taking turns at the wheel, they drove over two thousand miles. After a quick meeting with the crew, they retired to their room.

They got up early the next day and checked out of the hotel at 6:00 a.m. There would be no time for taking in the sights. It was all business. They drove east on Route 83, turned onto Route 20, and drove north five more miles until they came to a gas station and a small breakfast café. They parked their cars and walked into the restaurant where Brian greeted a lean man in his mid-sixties with long gray hair and a gray beard, his arms covered with tattoos

"Brian, I didn't know if you were going to make it," he said, pulling away from a bear hug.

"Long trip, but we are here," Brian replied. "Everyone, this is Buck Sanders who's in the transportation business."

He smiled at them, a front tooth missing, and pushed his long gray hair out of his eyes.

"This is Bob, Mike, Dan, Joe, and Jack," Brian said,

introducing each to Buck.

"Former Navy SEALs. So this is Jack Bolton, the most wanted guy in America," Buck stated with a grin.

Jack glared at Brian.

"Buck here is a former Air Force pilot. He flew hundreds of missions in Vietnam. And he knows this area like the back of his hand," Brian said.

"I tell you; out here, it's the Wild West," Buck said, amusement in his voice. "You have drug cartels, human traffickers, small-time drug smugglers, and two-bit criminals all trying to make a buck. It's pretty wild, but it looks like you guys will fit right in."

They all listened to the pep talk from the guy who looked more like a crazy grandfather than an ace pilot who made his living off the crime-infested Mexican border.

"Brian, just follow my pick-up truck and we'll be on our way," Buck directed, as they left the small café and got into their cars while following Buck out onto the main road.

Two miles down the road, a Cessna 208 Caravan sat on the makeshift runway ready to roll. They got out of their cars and started loading the plane with automatic weapons, bullet-proof vests, explosives, GPS equipment, communication headgear, water, and food. Brian left nothing out. He was prepared for a war, just in case something went wrong. Once the cars were emptied, two associates of Buck drove them away. It was a first-rate operation, nothing left to chance.

Buck fired up the engine of the Cessna as the crew boarded the plane. Jack sat in the front passenger seat next to old Buck.

Buck prepared the plane for takeoff, as the engines roared. The plane slowly rolled and then picked up speed. Within seconds, they were airborne, flying at a low altitude to keep from being detected by radar.

"This is your captain speaking," Buck joked. "The weather is dry and sunny with a slight breeze. We should be arriving at our destination in about two hours."

"I love doing that," he said, turning toward Jack.

Flying at 200 miles an hour was just another routine trip for Buck. "Hey Jack, Brian told me all about your situation. I would have done the same thing."

Jack just nodded.

The mood was quiet on the plane except for old Buck. He rambled on for the next hour talking to Jack about his exploits in Vietnam, which he compared to Afghanistan and Iraq. He railed about how the Internet was destroying humanity, and how the kids of today would become acclimated to the will of the government at an early age by the constant brainwashing of the media,

Jack listened quietly to Buck's jabbering, trying to keep his eyes open, as the plane approached its destination.

"Between smuggling illegal aliens and bales of pot, I do pretty well. But I won't smuggle heroin or cocaine."

"Well, at least you have some principles, Buck," Jack said with a hint of amused sarcasm in his voice.

"I don't need that stuff on my conscience. And what does a little pot hurt? It's basically legal in the States now."

"If you can't stop it, you might as well tax it," Jack snickered.

"It's only a matter of time before the government will have drones flying around here. I'm hoping to be out of the business before that happens. It's coming, though. Some day you'll see a drone accidently take down a commercial airliner. Mark my words."

"Drones," Jack mused. "Who would have ever thought that the government would have drones flying in the skies over America."

"I'll tell you something, Jack. The government wants to control your mind and soul. They are going to watch everything you do through drones. Add in the fact that they already have control of the Internet. They don't even have to read you your rights anymore. I'm telling you, it's going to be a very different world in the future."

"You sound like Brian."

They both laughed, "Nobody can sound like Brian," Buck answered.

"That's true."

"Look, these guys in Washington sold out the country a long time ago. They play both sides of the game. They're aiming for some kind of new world order where a few power brokers will control everything and America will be like any other country," Buck ranted.

"You believe that crap about some new world order?" Jack asked.

"Damn right, I do. Why do you think they want to ban guns in America, watch everything you do on the Internet, and not even need a warrant to arrest you?"

Jack didn't say anything, but it was entertaining listening to the old man's rants on the world. His own experience with the Navy SEALs, and his interaction with that Al-Qaeda terrorist, lent credence to what Buck was spewing.

"Hey Jack, you think I'm some crazy old man, right?"

"No… you make a lot of sense."

"Yeah, right. You'll see. Apple pie, the American flag, and baseball are all going the way of the Edsel."

The plane soared to its destination. "Please buckle up as we prepare to land. Thank you for flying Buck Airlines," he said with a sly smirk.

The plane touched down on a deserted road fifteen miles outside of San Luis Potosi, Mexico. They were two hundred miles from their destination of Ixtapaluca.

A Chevy Suburban was waiting just as Brian had instructed. The six men unloaded the gear from the airplane into the Suburban.

"Now remember, I'll be here from four to six tomorrow. If you don't show up, I'm gone," Buck said. "I'll just figure something went wrong. You'll need to call me to rearrange a new pick-up. So good luck guys," he said, shaking hands with each man.

"Hey, Buck, thanks for the view of the world," Jack called as Buck headed to the plane.

Brian took the wheel of the GMC Suburban and drove south, while the rumble of the Cessna heading north could be heard overhead.

***

They arrived in Ixtapaluca in three hours and unloaded the Suburban. Brian had kept the same run-down apartment that he had used to observe the bank a few months earlier. It was cramped, hot, and stuffy, but it would have to do for the one night. They stayed in and kept a low profile.

Brian pointed to the bank below and carefully reviewed each detail of the plan, including their approach, their positioning, the cartel members' proximity and the ideal moment to subdue them. He left nothing to chance. After a long day of flying, driving, and planning, the crew turned in.

***

The next morning, they woke as the sun poked through the clouds. The first part of Brian's plan had worked pretty close to script, except for the unexpected shooting of a Mafia henchman and the side trip to satisfy Jack's need for revenge. It was always the unexpected event that could throw a monkey wrench into a plan. He could only hope that the cartel hadn't changed their routine or added more men than he anticipated.

The six friends ate, cleaned their guns, and chatted away. As it got closer to show time, they prepared as they would for any special ops mission. Brian was certain he wasn't the only one with butterflies in his stomach.

Brian sat quietly on the balcony overlooking the bank. They were one big score away from the good life. He looked at his watch. It was 11:50 a.m. In ten minutes, two white SUVs would pull up to the bank, unload their bundles of cash and leave.

"Okay, this is it," Brian hollered. "Mike, you'll take the balcony up here, the rest of us will take our positions below."

Each man was dressed in street clothes with bulletproof vests under their loose fitting sweatshirts, wore Ray-Ban shades, and carried semi-automatic 9mm handguns. They took the stairs and made their way to street level.

The weather was cool, without a cloud in the sky

now. The street was eerily deserted, lined with beat-up cars. Even the locals knew it was wiser to be off the streets when the Moreno cartel made their weekly drop-off. Brian couldn't help but think the scene was something out of an old Western film.

Their getaway car, a large, deliberately beat-up Chevy Suburban, fit in nicely with the other cars in the area. It was strategically placed near the bank entrance for a quick escape. Brian headed into the bank while Jack took a seat on a bench thirty yards to the left of the building. Joe, Bob, and Dan crouched down in the Suburban, ready to spring out once the cartel arrived. Mike watched from the balcony with an M4 automatic assault weapon by his side.

Once inside the bank, Brian made small talk in Spanish with a customer. He glanced at his watch. It was two minutes past noon. Mike waved, holding up two fingers as a signal to Jack, who was positioned across the street. Two white SUVs approached from the north. The two vehicles stopped in front of the bank. A man exited the front passenger side of the car and walked into the bank. Five other men disembarked from the vehicles and immediately began to unload duffle bags from the back of the first vehicle. As the first three men entered the bank with the initial load, the two other men began to pull duffle bags from the back of the second vehicle.

Dan, Bob, and Joe jumped from the Suburban, guns

raised, cutting off the two men before they could enter the bank. They ordered them to lie down and to drop the duffle bags on the ground. Dan quickly zip-tied the two men. Jack walked past the men on the ground and went into the bank as Joe followed.

Brian moved quickly into position and pointed his semi-automatic handgun at the three men just ten feet from the bank's entrance. He ushered them to the side of the bank, barely out of sight of the people behind the teller windows. He ordered them to drop the duffle bags and to lie spread-eagled on the floor.

Jack and Joe pointed their automatic weapons at the three men lying down on the bank floor and surveyed the interior of the bank. Jack began to zip-tie the men. Brian immediately moved closer to the teller windows and pointed his gun at the two men behind the counter.

"Raise your hands where I can see them," he shouted in Spanish.

Mike, looking from the balcony, saw several cars moving at a high rate of speed, one from the south and two from the north. He signaled to Bob and Dan below with three fingers that hostiles were coming from each direction. Dan yelled to Brian and Jack inside the bank that they might have company. Two of the cars stopped approximately forty yards away in each direction while one of the two cars from the north kept on going until it stopped in front of the bank. Traffic became impassable.

Two men got out of the car, smiling and holding out

their hands in greeting to Bob and Dan. Mike had his finger on the trigger when a third guy with an assault rifle crept out of the back seat of the car, crouching down so as not to be seen as he maneuvered into a position to take out Bob and Dan. At this point, Mike realized he had no choice but to take out the three men.

Mike unloaded his M4 on the guy who was behind the car and then took out the other two guys before they could even respond.

"Let's get the bags into the car," Brian yelled.

Joe tried to keep his assault rifle focused on the guys on the floor and on the two men behind the teller window, while gunfire erupted outside. The men from the cars that had stopped further away were now firing at Mike, Dan, and Bob.

Bob put down his gun to assist Brian in moving the remaining duffle bags from inside the bank to the Suburban under incoming fire. Jack took Bob's assault rifle and began exchanging fire with the men on the street outside. Bullets flew from both directions as Mike from the top balcony kept the newly-arrived cartel men from advancing.

As Brian picked up the last duffle bag inside the bank, a man charged in from the stairwell firing his gun. Joe unloaded his clip, killing him instantly. As soon as he looked away from the two men behind the teller window, both men whipped out handguns and started firing.

Jack reentered the bank with guns blazing, killing the two men behind the glass. During the exchange of gunfire, Joe fell to the ground, bleeding profusely from the groin. From the amount of blood loss, it appeared that his femoral artery had been ripped open by one of the bullets. Jack took off his sweatshirt and wrapped it tightly above the wound as a tourniquet.

Mike continued shooting from the apartment above, covering Brian and Jack as they carried Joe to the Suburban, which had been loaded with ten duffle bags of drug money. Mike jumped off the balcony, landing in garbage bags below. He scrambled out and ran crouched over and limping toward the Suburban. He leapt into the back of the vehicle as it pulled away.

Brian drove, ramming the vehicle through the cartel blockade. Bullets careened off the car. He maneuvered through the street as if he were driving in the Indy 500. Once he got out onto the open road, the cartel was no longer in his rearview mirror.

The sunlight streaming in through the sunroof showed Joe Cap's dire condition. Jack's sweatshirt was soaked with blood. "We have to get Joe to a hospital right away or he isn't going to make it," Jack hollered to Brian.

"Jack, I'm not going to make it," Joe murmured with great effort.

"Hang in there," Jack pleaded. "We are going to get you to a hospital."

"No, Jack, but it's okay," Joe whispered. "Look, I want you to look into my wallet. There's something my brother gave me before he died."

Jack reached into Joe's back pocket and took out his wallet.

"There's a business card with a safe deposit box number on it, along with a key," Joe said in a low, raspy, barely audible voice.

"Where's the bank?"

"Multibank of Washington in downtown Seattle," Joe muttered.

"What is this?" Jack asked

He struggled to say the words "It… has…something to do…with the…"

"Something to do with what?"

"CIA," Brian said, his breathing growing shallow.

"Hang in there, Joe," Jack said.

Joe's eyes fixed in an unseeing stare and his face turned ashen.

"Joe…Joe," Jack said, his eyes filling up. He pounded on Joe's chest, then pulled the tourniquet tighter. But it was futile. Joe was dead.

Jack stared out the window with a heavy heart as the Suburban headed north. He wondered what life was all about. He was tired of death following him. He just wanted to go somewhere and live a normal life and forget about his past, but those thoughts seemed more like a dream.

***

Jose Moreno was the head of the Moreno cartel. It was the most savage and powerful cartel in Mexico. He leaned back in a comfortable chair on the terrace with a drink in his hand, enjoying the warmth of the sun and the view of his Olympic-sized pool on the western coast of Mexico. Armed associates stood sentry around the secluded hideaway. One of his lieutenants walked briskly through the maze of bodyguards until he was standing in front of Moreno.

Moreno enjoyed seeing the anxiety in a man's gaze. He was proud of his reputation as an articulate and ruthless leader. "What is it?" Moreno asked.

"Mr. Moreno, somebody hit our money laundering operation in Ixtapaluca," the lieutenant cautiously informed him.

"What?" he said in a loud demanding voice.

"They stole about eighteen million dollars and killed eight of our men."

There was a pause as Jose Moreno pondered the situation. "I want to know who did this," he demanded, his voice booming out into the courtyard. "What cartel …Mendez? Vega? Ortega?"

Another man, wearing a white suit, walked out onto the patio and sat down next to Moreno.

"I don't think it was any of them," the lieutenant

said. "They appeared to be Americans."

Moreno paused and turned to the well-dressed man who sat next to him. "Can you believe this shit?" he said. "Americans…"

"There's more," the lieutenant continued.

"What do you mean more?" Moreno snapped back.

"Your brother, Pedro, was killed."

Moreno slammed his fist on the table, stood, and walked over to the rock wall surrounding the terrace. He looked out at the ocean as he put the glass to his lips and downed the whisky all in one gulp. He turned back to the well-dressed man at the table. "I want to know the people responsible for this," he growled. "I want every one of them dead."

"It will take some time," the well-dressed man calmly replied.

"Just find them and then kill them. If they're Americans, talk to your government friends in America," he commanded. "Nobody gets away with this. I'm Jose Moreno. These people just made a very big mistake."

"Okay, I'll take care of it."

Chapter 23

Frank Gallo, drinking a beer and surrounded by his lieutenants, sat at a corner table at a local club watching a few of his Mafia boys drinking heavily and yakking it up as they played pool. He was still reeling from the botched attempt to take care of Jack Bolton three days earlier. He couldn't get his son's killer out of his mind. The more he thought about what Bolton did to his son, the angrier he grew. Especially given the way he did it - calling him on the phone and then shooting his son in cold blood. Every favor at his disposal would be used to track him down now that Bolton was out. It would be only a matter of time before he found him.

The cellphone buzzed. Frank answered it as he usually did. "Frank." He paused and listened, then put the phone down and turned to his first lieutenant "Ray's been taken care of." The lieutenant nodded, smiling.

A man walked into the bar. He was unsmiling and his eyes showed no expression. He wore a blue blazer with high-top sneakers - a strange-looking character, indeed. If it weren't for his apparent lack of emotion, he could have passed for a harmless nerd on a computer project. But there was something eerily different about him.

184

Frank waved him over to the table. "Gino, why don't we go in the backroom and discuss our business," he said.

Gino and two of Frank's lieutenants followed him into the backroom.

Frank leaned back in his chair as Gino took a seat in front of him; the other two soldiers shut the door and leaned against the wall.

"How was Sicily?" Frank asked.

"I don't think you have me here to talk about Sicily," Gino said stoically.

"Okay, let's get down to business," Frank snapped. "Rocco tells me you're good and can be trusted. So, I need this Jack Bolton guy taken out. Preferably, I would like you to bring him back to me alive and I'll kill him with my own bare hands."

Gino shook his head. "Well, it's so much cleaner to just take him out, but if you want him alive, the price is double - $300,000. Just to kill him, it's $150,000, plus expenses."

Frank looked at his guys with a smirk and then a sly grin. "I don't care about the money. I just want him here so I can hear him beg for his life before I kill him."

"Well, bringing him back to you, I might need more resources. But I will say this: if it becomes too difficult to bring him back, I'll kill him myself."

"That's fine. Whatever you need," Frank said. "A dead Bolton is what we all want at the end of the day."

"I take my money up front," Gino said, pulling out a card and handing it to Frank.

"What this?

"The card has the instructions on how to send the money to my Swiss account. Once the money hits the account, I'll start my work. If I take him back, I'll need final payment before I hand him over to you."

"What happens if someone gets to him first, hypothetically?" Frank asked.

"I'll send you back half your money. I don't work for free."

"Fair enough. What's the time frame?"

"I can't give you one. Sometimes people just disappear. I'll be in touch once the money hits my account."

"Why don't you stay for a drink?"

"I don't mix business with pleasure. I'm sure you can understand that," he said, standing up from his chair.

Gino walked out the door. Frank watched him leave and then turned to his lieutenants, "Not much of a personality, huh?"

"He's quite the oddball," one of his lieutenants muttered.

"Don't let his looks deceive you though," Frank said. "From what they tell me, he's a real psychopath but very good at what he does."

Chapter 24

A large map with locations circled hung on the wall behind Special Agent Ryland. He stood, sipping his coffee as he looked out his office window, watching the morning sunrise. He had been working sixteen-hour days since Jack Bolton had broken out of prison. He was under intense pressure from his superiors to find Bolton and the people responsible for his escape. The death of the Senator's son just added to the dynamics of the case. Not to mention the national media that was all over it, adding to the sensational story with constant inquiries.

If that wasn't enough on his plate, he still had responsibility for tracking down the Beckets' killer which, in the absence of any worthwhile leads, was temporarily assigned to Agent Hawkins.

Ryland mused about where Bolton might be. *He was probably long gone and, with a different identity, enjoying himself on some beautiful island, drinking umbrella drinks, never to be heard from again.* He had talked to Charlie Costa, the former Navy SEAL who had been Bolton's friend and who had been present at the killing of Nick Gallo. But nothing came from it. Charlie said he knew nothing and, if Ryland wanted to talk to him again, to contact his lawyer.

There was as much pressure to find the people who broke him out as there was to find Jack Bolton himself. Ryland had tossed around the idea that the people who aided him in his escape had to be people he knew. The finely executed plan had military experience written all over it. His mind kept coming back to the conclusion that it had to be former Navy SEALs. The more he delved into it, the more he focused on Jack's heroic rescue of seven SEALs in Afghanistan, for which he had received a purple heart.

Ryland's phone buzzed; he answered it. He listened intently as Sergeant Sullivan filled him in on the latest developments. One of the correctional officers, Dean Ray, had been reported missing, which meant either he had skipped town or he was lying at the bottom of the ocean.

Ryland pressed off the phone and then called one of the agents to start looking at every former Navy SEAL that Jack Bolton might have been associated with at one time or another, beginning with the seven men he had saved in Afghanistan.

Ryland walked over to the map on the wall, looking at the locations of missing people that he suspected might be connected. He was no closer to a resolution of the Becket case than he had been nine months ago. His phone buzzed again. He didn't recognize the number. He pressed the button and put the phone to his ear. "Special Agent Ryland."

"Special Agent Ryland, this is CIA Director Gus Banner."

"What can I do for you?' Ryland asked, surprised by the call.

"Well, it's what I can do for you," he replied. "I have some very good information you might find helpful in the apprehension of Jack Bolton and his cohorts."

Ryland paused, and then asked, "What sort of information?"

"I'd rather talk to you in person. How about we meet at my office in Langley tomorrow morning around 11:30?"

"Okay. What about travel arrangements?"

"I'll have my secretary arrange your flight and send the information to you later today."

"Great, I'll see you tomorrow then." Ryland ended the call. He could only wonder what the CIA director could have that was so important. Sam Atkins was a powerful senator and was probably calling in his favors to get Bolton back in prison as quickly as possible.

***

Gus Banner swung on his trench coat and headed out the door. A small black limo picked him up in front of the Central Intelligence Agency and drove him twelve miles to a cemetery outside of Washington D.C. where the funeral of John Atkins was being held. He got out of the vehicle and made his way towards a large crowd of people under an oversized black tent. It was a somber scene. Drizzling rain added to the gloomy day.

A congregation of dignitaries, friends and family attended the funeral. Sam read a final eulogy at the foot of the casket where an abundance of flowers had been placed. Tears rolled down the cheeks of John's mother, sisters, and relatives. Gus watched the proceedings from the outskirts of the tent.

When the funeral ended, Gus made his way toward Sam to offer his condolences. Sam, who usually looked younger than his age, looked old, his eyes glassy and lines running deeper in his face.

They shook hands and hugged. The mourners, holding their umbrellas, slowly dispersed. Gus's old friend, the senior George Atkins, came over and clutched his hand.

He pulled Gus close and said in a raspy whisper, "Jack Bolton needs to pay for this."

The rest of the Atkins clan left while Sam stayed back, staring at the casket. After the crowd of people paying their respects had left, the men from the cemetery began to prepare the gravesite for the placement of the casket into a six-by-four-foot grave. Sam struggled to hold back tears.

"Let's go for a walk," Gus said softly.

They walked side-by-side, trailed by two Secret Service agents. "You know he was going to follow in my footsteps, just as I followed my dad," Sam said, his voice cracking with emotion.

They stopped at the top of a hill, looking out at a sea of gravestones.

"John would have continued the family tradition and done whatever was necessary to keep the country strong." Sam explained. "He would be working with the same people we trust, who share our beliefs. But I lost that continuity because of Jack Bolton."

Gus lit a cigarette. "Yeah, it's pretty tough losing a son."

"That Bolton guy, he's a real piece of work. He thinks he can take the law into his own hands. He's a danger to what this country stands for."

"He sure is," Gus said, exhaling a puff of smoke.

"He must think we'll never find him. He's in for a rude awakening."

"I have some good news about him and his band of merry men."

"What do you mean?" Sam asked.

"Well, we're all too familiar with the 'Phoenix Project.' We've talked about it many times."

"That was in the best interest of the country," Sam stated.

"Of course. We both know it was the right thing to do, but some people don't share those beliefs."

"What are you saying?"

"We learned that a few of our guys who were

involved in the project wanted to go to the media about it."

"Why didn't you tell me this, Gus? We don't need anything coming out, especially now. We have some important people who have put their money behind me and I'm very close to announcing my presidential bid. "

"Don't worry, I have everything under control. Why bother you with something that I have under control?

"Do you know the ramifications of something like this getting out?" he said, his voice rising.

"There's nothing that can implicate you, so stop worrying."

"You don't think so, huh?" Sam said, shaking his head. "It wouldn't take them long to figure out the connection. Even a perceived relationship would be devastating. I can't have anything screwing up my presidential bid."

"I've got it all under control," Gus fired back. "Look, if the people who were part of this just happened to have accidental deaths… problem solved. Now, one of these guys had a brother, and we wanted to make sure he didn't know anything. During surveillance on him, we stumbled upon this group of former Navy SEALs."

"What are you getting at?"

"This group of SEALs just happen to be the guys who broke Jack Bolton out of prison."

Sam turned towards Gus. "So you know where he is?"

"Yeah, one of my guys put tracking devices on the cars used in Jack Bolton's escape.

"Explain that to me," Sam demanded with intense eyes.

"Look, Sam, I know what you're thinking, but my guy didn't know what they were exactly up to."

Sam shook his head. "Come on, Gus," he snapped. "This guy of yours couldn't figure out what was going on?"

"Hindsight is twenty-twenty, Sam. To be fair, when was the last time a bunch of former Navy SEALs broke someone out of prison in America?"

"Well, when was the last time there was a decorated Navy SEAL in prison?" Sam snapped. "It is what it is. I just want Bolton. Now tell me where he is?"

"My guy tracked them to Laredo, Texas, where he lost them."

"What do you mean your guy lost them?"

"The cars were there, but they were not."

"So where did they go?"

"They went somewhere in Mexico, but a day or two later they came back. So my guy is tracking them, as we speak."

"What the hell did they do in Mexico? And why did they come back?"

"We ask ourselves the same questions, and you are going to find this amusing." Gus said with a smirk. "One of our intelligence guys is hearing that the Moreno cartel had around eighteen million dollars in drug money stolen from them by some Americans."

"I can't believe this. We can't have former Navy SEALs running amuck?"

"Of course, we can't. I've set up a meeting tomorrow with the lead FBI agent on the case. I'm going to make it easy for him."

"I just want Bolton."

"We'll get Bolton."

"No, I want him dead," he said, staring straight at Gus.

"Sam, just let the FBI take care of it and, if they don't get him, there's plenty of other people who will."

Sam looked back at his son's grave as the cemetery workers piled dirt onto the casket. "I want your men to take care of it, and I want to be there."

Gus looked puzzled. "You don't need that aggravation, Sam. Forget about him."

"Forget about him!" he repeated. "Look down there," he shouted, pointing to his son's gravesite. "What do you see?"

Gus knew at that point what had to be done. "Okay, give me a few days and I'll let you know when we have him."

"Good. I'll be looking forward to your phone call, Gus."

Chapter 25

The sun had set. Jack and Brian drove north on I-71 to Ohio. They had been taking turns driving for almost twenty-four hours straight. Just a day earlier, the plane had landed in Texas. After hugs and words of consolation about the passing of Joe Cap, the men departed in two separate cars. Mike, Dan, and Bob left in one car, while Brian and Jack accompanied Joe Cap's body in the other car.

They were now millionaires, and had the freedom to do whatever they wanted. No more worries about bills or waiting for the next paycheck. But it all came at a cost. Joe Cap was dead and he wouldn't be part of the dream. There was also the fear that the FBI would piece together who broke Jack out. And, of course, the Mexican cartel might someday knock on the door. Life is full of calculated risks and Brian's plan had almost worked to perfection…except for Joe Cap's lifeless body lying in the trunk.

Brian continued to drive, finally passing a sign that showed 20 miles to Brooklyn, Joe Cap's hometown.

The conversation between Jack and Brian had been non-existent for most of the drive. It gave Jack time to think about his life, which was filled with death and sadness. He wished it were different, that it had all been a bad dream. He would wake up and find his family sitting around the table. His brother would be talking about how many goals he'd scored in his high school hockey game. His sister would be bragging about how high her grades were and how he could never keep up with her. His parents would be smiling at each other, gushing about how lucky they were to raise great kids. But the future was sealed the day of his brother's death.

The reality of being a fugitive was starting to sink in. He was a killer in some people's eyes. His mind started racing. He didn't want this life. Maybe he could turn this all around for something good. But, first, he had to find out what was in George Cap's safe deposit box. And, there was also his thought of setting someone else's life back on track, namely, Jeff Keller who was sitting in prison for a murder that he surely didn't commit. All for the benefit of Sam Atkins. An idea had occurred to Jack that might allow Keller to get a reprieve from prison, even if it meant giving up his own life.

Brian saw the sign that indicated Brooklyn was the next exit. "This really sucks, Jack."

"I know. How are we going to do this?'

"I'll take care of it. I'm responsible for this," Brian said

"We'll both do it," Jack replied.

"I mean, how do you do something like this, Jack? I have no idea how Joe's father is going to take it."

"Well, I wish we didn't have to do it, too."

"Yeah, I wish Joe was cracking jokes in the

backseat."

The car eased to a stop in the driveway of Joe's home. The porch light was on.

They looked at each other and exhaled at the same time. Then they pushed the car doors open. Brian stood for a second and stretched his legs before walking slowly up the front steps. He paused before knocking, as Jack opened the trunk.

Carl Cap walked out from the kitchen to the screen porch and opened the door. "Can I help you?" he asked.

"I'm Brian Butler. I was in the same SEAL unit as Joe."

"There's something wrong, isn't there?"

"Um…" Brian paused, trying to find the right words.

"Joe's dead, isn't he?"

"Um… Um… I am so sorry, Mr. Cap," he said, his voice cracking.

Carl shook his head. "He always told me everything, not like his older brother who held things in. He told me he was going to Mexico with you and some other former Navy SEALs to hit a cartel. I tried to talk him out of it."

"I feel responsible. I'm so sorry." Brian breathed deeply and struggled to control his emotions. "We brought Joe's body back."

"I was so afraid this would happen," Carl muttered. "Joe never gave me an ounce of trouble growing up and he told me everything and he was just a great, great son." Mr. Cap rubbed his reddened eyes while looking over at the car.

He followed Brian down the porch steps to the open trunk. Jack stood tall as Mr. Cap approached the car. He shook Mr. Cap's hand. "I'm so sorry, Mr. Cap," he said, feeling uneasy.

Mr. Cap stared down at his son's body for a minute. He rubbed his face and released a long, heavy sigh. "He was a crazy, fun-loving kid with a good heart," he said, shaking his head. He then bent down and kissed Joe's forehead. "I don't blame anyone for this. He was a big boy. I always thought I was going to get a knock on the door from the Navy when he was serving with the SEALs."

Brian went around to the side and opened the car door. He pulled out a duffle bag and held it out to Joe's father. "Mr. Cap, this is Joe's share of the money. He'd want you to have it."

Carl held up his hands, palms forward. "Whoa, I don't want any drug money," he said emphatically, walking away from the car.

Jack and Brian looked at each other, not sure what to do next. They started toward the porch.

Mr. Cap stopped and turned to face them. "Bring my son into his bedroom," he ordered.

The trunk was lined with a body bag filled with ice to slow down decomposition. They zipped the body bag back up and each took an end, carrying him up the porch stairs, through the front door and past the kitchen. They turned right into a hallway that brought them to Joe's room, where they placed him gently on the bed.

Mr. Cap then instructed, "Remove the body bag."

They took the body out of the bag and placed Joe as best they could on the bed. They glanced at each other, their eyes filled with sadness. Mr. Cap motioned for them to leave the room and go back to the screened porch to wait for him.

Jack thought about how crazy this all was. He had been expecting a different reaction from Mr. Cap, but he seemed to have taken the news rather well. He wasn't sure how they were going to handle Joe's body. It would only be a short time before it would break down. It couldn't be left there long. He would need a proper burial with friends and family being notified. There would be questions and investigations, if the authorities got involved. A death certificate would need to be issued by a medical examiner.

Jack whispered to Brian, "How are we going to handle Joe's body? We can't just leave it in the bedroom."

Brian shrugged. "I don't have a clue," he whispered.

Mr. Cap walked back out to the porch. He sat down across from Jack and Brian with his arms folded. "So, Jack, how was prison?" Mr. Cap asked.

This caught Jack by surprise. "I don't know what to say."

"What? You didn't think I knew, huh?" Mr. Cap

said looking at each of them in turn. "I knew Joe was involved when I saw it on the news. Don't get me wrong. I'm glad they broke you out, Jack. You didn't deserve to be in there. I'm sure a man like you had good reason for what you did. But it's not for me to judge."

Jack sat stone-faced. Mr. Cap was blunt. The guy was no- nonsense. Even with hearing aids in both ears, a small wiry frame, and a slight limp, he still looked pretty tough. He was a former Marine who had fought in the Korean War. He had lost his wife to cancer a couple of months ago and both of his sons had died in violent ways. Yet, he had a strong character. Like Jack, he was suffering inside, trying his best not to show it.

"Don't get too comfortable, either of you. This isn't the way it should have ended for Joe. He didn't deserve that."

They both nodded, frowns on their faces.

"Now, I'm not going to let you guys off easy. I have a dead son in the bedroom," Mr. Cap continued, getting up and closing the front door while they sat.

Jack and Brian both looked at each other. Grief, uncertainty, and guilt shadowed their expressions.

Mr. Cap pulled a small device from his pocket that had wires sticking out. He set it on the small coffee table between them. "Do either of you know what this is?" he asked.

"It looks like some kind of listening device," Jack replied.

Mr. Cap smirked. "Why would a listening device be in my house?" he asked. "I found it by accident a few weeks ago. The light went out in the kitchen. So I stood up on a chair to change the light bulb and, for some reason, it was tough to turn. My hand slipped and hit the ceiling panel and this gadget fell to the floor. I picked it up and inspected it. Then it all made perfect sense."

"What do you mean?" Brian asked

"You know, Joe's brother George worked for the CIA and he died in a car accident. They never found who ran him off the road, of course. But when he was home, he told me he was part of some business that troubled him and it went way up the ladder. He told me that three of the guys he had worked with on a project had died. But he never told me what he was involved in, other than mentioning the three colleagues. I was stupid. I didn't realize he was scared, and he wanted to tell me. But I never pushed it, and he never told me."

"So you think these people wanted to know if you knew something, Mr. Cap?" Brian asked.

"Yeah, but he told me nothing. That was George. He always kept things to himself, not like Joe who told me everything."

Jack sat back. He realized now that the key Joe gave him held a very big mystery. In fact, whatever Joe's brother knew had people worried enough to put a listening device in his father's house. Whatever was in that safe deposit box had somebody worried. Yet, here he was… a fugitive. He needed to get to Seattle to find out what these people were trying to protect. His bucket list was growing. He was going to make things right until either Atkins henchmen or the FBI stopped him. That would be his mission. Jeff Keller deserved his life back. George's family deserved the truth.

"Are there any more of these devices in the house?" Jack asked

"I don't think so," Mr. Cap replied. "I went through the house and didn't find anything. But, just as a precaution, I'd rather talk out here."

While Mr. Cap reminisced about Joe's life, his eyes welling with tears, a black hearse drove up to the house. Jack and Brian exchanged surprised glances. A man emerged from the front seat and walked up to the porch. Mr. Cap greeted him with a hug, a small discussion ensued that brought tears to both men's eyes. After a few minutes more of hushed discussion, George introduced the man. "Jack and Brian, this is Joe's uncle, Troy."

They nodded solemnly and shook his hand.

"You guys look surprised," Mr. Cap said. "My brother here is in the funeral business. So we'll be able to give Joe a proper wake and funeral and, hopefully, get the legalities worked out."

The men helped move Joe's body into the hearse. After Mr. Cap and his brother hugged and shook hands, Troy got into the hearse and drove away. Jack and Brian shook hands with Mr. Cap, apologizing repeatedly for Joe's death.

***

After leaving the Cap residence, Brian plugged an address into the GPS.

"Okay, where we going, Brian?" Jack asked. "Can you pull over to the side of the road? We need to talk."

The car pulled off into a strip mall. "You need a new identity, Jack. I know an old friend in Washington, D.C., who we can trust. He's going to help us out."

"That works, but I have my own agenda here."

"That's fine, Jack. You want to go to Canada or wherever, that's great. You need a new identity or you aren't going to last too long out here. Also, you can't be lugging around millions of dollars in drug money. I have someone who can launder the money for twenty-five percent on the dollar. Jack, I did a lot of planning before breaking you out. You are just going to have to trust me on this."

"Brian, I'm sure you covered all the angles but I don't know. I'm tired of all this shit. I want to do a couple of good things here and you don't have to be part of it. They're just looking for me, not you."

"What are you talking about?" Brian asked in a frustrated voice. "We are in this together. I think you really need a few beers and a hot woman."

"Remember when I told you about Jeff Keller?"

"The guy in prison?"

"Yeah."

"Okay, what are you going to do? Break him out of a maximum prison? Come on, Jack. Come to your damn senses. You can't make the world right. Go to Canada or an island and forget your past, meet a nice girl, start a family, live happily ever after."

"Sounds great, but I just don't see it," he said in a soft voice. "I've done some bad things."

"What? Killing those two despicable college kids? Stop feeling guilty about what you did. They had it coming. Forget about them. Live your life. You're an awesome guy, and you deserve a good life."

"Well, maybe so, but I'm helping this guy get out of prison for something I believe he didn't do."

"Fine!" Brian snapped. "I would love to hear the plan to break him out."

"You really want to hear it?"

"Yeah, I do."

"I'm going to do this diplomatically."

"What the hell does that mean?"

"I'm going to see his lawyer and present a plan for him to give information to the feds on my whereabouts."

"And the feds are just going to let him walk?"

"There's something called Rule 35 that I read about somewhere. It allows inmates to reduce their sentences or even get out if they have information on people like me."

"There's a rule for everything, huh?" Brian said, frowning. "But, you're not really giving yourself up."

"I might have to."

"That's crazy…No, that's absolutely stupid."

"There's something else."

"There's more?"

"Before he died, Joe Cap gave me his brother's safe deposit box key for a bank in Seattle, Washington.

"So now you want to go to Seattle, right?" Brian asked incredulously.

"Like I said, I don't need you to get involved. I have an idea how I'm going to do all this."

"This is great. I have James Bond here who is going to save the world, or maybe I should be calling you Houdini because you are going to need a lot of tricks to pull this all off."

"That's what I'm going to do, Brian."

"I thought I was the guy with all the crazy ideas, but I'm staying with you until we crash or burn," he said with a large grin. "Hell, the boat business can wait, and now I'm curious what's in the safe deposit box. So let's get you a new identity and find Keller's attorney."

They drove for a few more hours until calling it a night in a town a few miles from the West Virginia border.

Chapter 26

At ten o'clock the next morning, at CIA headquarters in Langley Virginia, Special Agent Ryland waited outside the office of the director, Gus Banner. Ryland had never met him but had been told that he was a quick-tempered, hard-nosed guy, who had been known to throw people out of his office on occasion.

The secretary picked up the phone and motioned Agent Ryland that it was okay to walk in. He entered Banner's office where he was greeted with a smile and a quick handshake.

"Special Agent Ryland, I'm so glad you could make it on such short notice. I know how busy you guys must be up there in Boston trying to find Bolton," he said. "Why don't we sit down at my desk so we can go over a few things."

"Nice office you have here."

"Yeah, I've got a good decorator, my wife," he said. "Sorry, I have nothing to offer you."

"That's okay. I'm more than a little curious as to why you requested I come down here."

'Well, this Jack Bolton case you're working on is the type of case that makes or breaks careers, if you know what I mean."

"Not sure I do, sir," Ryland replied, thinking to himself, *Every case is important.* But the special attention being given to this one, a crime against the perpetrator of another more egregious crime, was hard to digest.

"Okay, let's just cut the bullshit," Gus snapped. "Let me get to the point."

"That's why I'm here, Mr. Banner," Ryland said, trying to get comfortable where few could.

"When you have a senator's son killed by a rogue former Navy SEAL who broke out of prison with the help of a crazy group of former Navy SEALs, it's not good for the country. Can't have that crap happening. So the sooner you wrap this up, the better for everyone."

"So, are you telling me that you have information that a group of former Navy SEALs broke Jack Bolton out of prison?"

Gus smirked. "I sure am, Agent Ryland. That's why you're here." Banner tossed a folder across his desk and leaned back in his chair.

"What's this?"

"Open it."

Ryland leaned over and opened the folder. He studied the five pictures with keen interest. "These are former Navy SEALs, right?" he asked, as he flipped through the pictures.

"You catch on quick, Agent Ryland," Gus replied with a half-smile. "These are the guys who broke out

Jack Bolton. There's also a bio attached to each one of them"

"How do you know that these are the guys?"

"Well, I'm not at liberty to say, since it's an ongoing investigation. Let's just say that these guys happened to fall into our laps accidently. What I can tell you is that these are the same guys he saved in Afghanistan, for which he was honored with the Purple Heart."

"Do you know where they are now?" Ryland asked.

"You'll have to figure that one out for yourself," he replied, sitting up straighter in his chair. "That's all I've got. I'm short on time, Agent Ryland. So unless you have something else, I think we're done."

Ryland was taken aback by the abruptness; Gus could have over-nighted the pictures instead of wasting his time to come down here. There surely had to be a reason. Then, his eyes caught a glimpse of a picture off to the right behind Banner, which was hard to ignore. It now made sense why he was called in. The photo showed a picture of Gus Banner, Sam Atkins, and the FBI Director, Shone Williams, all centered around a large swordfish.

"Well, if you've got nothing else, then, I'll be on my way. " Agent Ryland stood up and leaned over, shaking Gus's hand. Then he turned and headed for the door.

"Agent Ryland, there is one last thing," Gus said. "We're hearing that a group of Americans hit a Mexican cartel for millions of dollars shortly after the breakout."

Agent Ryland stopped and turned around "Are you saying that this group of former SEALs did that as well?"

"You're a smart guy. If it was them, they'll have the means to disappear. If I hear anything new, I'll let you know."

"Thanks for the info."

"Remember, there are a lot of very important people watching how you handle this case."

"You don't have to remind me, Mr. Banner, I know how to do my job," he replied, thinking to himself how much he hated this guy and his condescending manner.

Chapter 27

Early the next morning, after crashing at a low budget motel for the night, Brian and Jack were back on the road. Brian drove with Jack as his wingman. Everything was paid for with cash; they drove within the speed limit so as not to attract attention. They knew Jack was on every state and local police radar. One slip-up and the game would be over; the contents of the safe deposit box in the bank in Seattle would remain undiscovered and any chance for freedom that Jeff Keller might have had would be lost.

After a few hours of driving, the GPS had directed them to the town of Arlington, Virginia, the home of Aaron Greenberg's law practice. He had represented Jeff Keller in the original trial and during the appeals process. In the absence of any error or any new evidence to refute the overwhelming circumstantial evidence presented at the trial, the appeals were denied.

Jack had read the book *I'm Innocent,* which told the stories of innocent people serving time in prison. One of those stories was that of Jeff Keller. Now, Jack was about to present an idea to Jeff's attorney that would later be viewed as brilliant, if it worked, and as insanity, if it didn't.

Brian waited in the car as Jack walked across the parking lot and into the law office of Aaron Greenberg. A friendly female receptionist greeted him "Can I help you?"

"Yeah, I'm looking for Aaron Greenberg."

"Do you have an appointment?" she asked with a smile.

"I don't. Please just tell him it has to do with Jeff Keller."

Aaron Greenburg was reviewing a case as he typed on the keyboard when his secretary walked in. "I have a man out in the waiting room who would like to talk to you about Jeff Keller."

Aaron put down his glasses and leaned back in his chair. "Did he say what it was about?"

"No."

"Just give me a few minutes and I'll come out."

"Okay."

Aaron's mind raced. It had been a while since he had talked to Jeff. He remembered vividly every detail of that trial which took place six years ago. It was the only trial he had ever lost. The system had put away an innocent man for life.

He had gone through the drill a few times over the years when a reporter or a young lawyer would come into his office asking questions about the case. A trial law class from a local law school used it as a case study during one semester. But it had all quieted down in the last few years since the court denied the last appeal.

Greenberg walked out of his office to see who was interested in talking about Jeff Keller.

Jack got up as Aaron Greenberg entered the room. "Hello, Mr. Greenburg."

Aaron stood in the doorway as Jack walked toward him. "You a reporter? Help me out; you look familiar."

"I'm Jack," he said shaking his hand. "I'd like to talk to you in private about Jeff Keller."

Aaron led the way as Jack followed him into his office. Aaron closed the door and swung around to his desk. "Take a seat, Jack. You want anything?"

"No, thanks. I'm a little pressed for time."

"Do you have some sort of identification? I'd like to know who I'm talking to." Aaron said, leaning back in his chair, waiting for an answer. "Do I know you? You look familiar."

"I'm here for a reason. But let me just get this out in the open. I'm Jack Bolton. I'm sorry but you are going to have to take my word for it. I didn't have a chance to pick up my license when I escaped from prison."

"I guess I'll have to take your word for it. Jack Bolton, of all people," he said, thinking there was a massive manhunt going on for this guy and here he was sitting in his office. "Wow! Are you turning yourself in? You want me to represent you? What brings you here?"

"I'm not turning myself in at the moment. And I don't need you to represent me quite yet."

"So what brings you here when the world is looking for you?" Aaron cautiously asked.

"I'm here because of Jeff Keller."

"Well, I don't see how Jeff Keller is going to help you," he said, leaning back in his chair with a slight smile. He's serving a life sentence."

"I'm here to help Jeff Keller get out of prison."

It took a few seconds for the words to sink in, but Aaron couldn't help but chuckle at Jack's statement. He sat up. "I'm sorry, but I'm not sure what you are getting at."

"You familiar with Rule 35?"

Aaron's smile disappeared, as he looked straight at Jack and leaned in, "*Rule 35?*"

"Yeah, *Rule 35.*"

"You know something about *Rule 35?*" he questioned. "I'm listening,"

"Jeff Keller is going to rat me out." He pulled an envelope from his side pocket and placed it on the desk. "In this envelope is all the information that the FBI is going to need to take the deal. You, in return, are going to notify Special Agent Ryland in the Boston office that your client knows where I am."

Aaron was trying to recall the *Rule 35* motion; after all these years a fugitive walks into his office and presents a plan that is a longshot at best. "This is very interesting. I don't know. It could work, I guess. Let me understand this: in this envelope is the place where the feds will be able to pick you up and you're okay with this?"

"Yeah, though I'd like to ask you a question."

"Go ahead."

"Is Jeff Keller innocent?"

Aaron leaned back in his chair, nodded his head, and then spoke softly. "Keller was framed by powerful people. He's not a killer."

"How do you know that for sure?" Jack replied.

"Mr. Bolton."

"Call me Jack."

"Okay, Jack. I don't take a case unless I feel the person is innocent. I knew the case would be tough to win based on the overwhelming circumstantial evidence, but I had him take a lie detector test and he passed with flying colors. I was determined to beat the charges. It was all too neat and clean."

"So then how did they convict him?" Jack asked.

"The night of her disappearance, it just so happened that Jeff and Laura were seen together at a downtown restaurant in Washington D.C. They had a big public argument that started at the restaurant. In fact, she told him at the restaurant that she couldn't marry him, she was pregnant, and she was seeing someone else. He didn't take it so well. He made a scene in the restaurant, which was understandable under the circumstances."

"What type of scene?"

"The type of scene that people don't forget. Let's

just leave it at that."

Jack just nodded as he listened to Aaron recall the case.

"They continued to argue as he drove her home. She slapped him in the face, accidentally scratching him. The scene at the restaurant and the scratch on his face were just the warm-up material used by the prosecution. Laura's body was never found, but the prosecution had enough circumstantial evidence to convict him."

"What circumstantial evidence could they possibly have had?" Jack asked with a confused look.

"Amazingly, the prosecution produced a murder weapon with his DNA and fingerprints and her blood on it. It was a perfect set-up. Irrefutable. The jury deliberated for a day and found him guilty. He was sentenced to life in prison. We exhausted all avenues of appeal. They went nowhere. But now here you are offering a 'Hail Mary' pass."

"That's me," Jack said with an amused look in his eyes.

"Do you really think they'll go for this deal?"

"I'm betting on it."

"You have greater faith than I do," Aaron said, smiling slightly. "Now tell me why you're doing this? What's in it for you?"

Jack half-chuckled. "Nothing. Let me set the record straight. I killed those two college kids because they raped and murdered my sister. "

"The media hasn't reported much about that."

"I know, I appear to be a monster in some people's eyes," he said, his voice a shade weaker. "But back to your question. I'm doing this because I don't like what I've done. I can hear my sister telling me, 'It's okay, Jack.' So I'm hoping that out of all this violence, something good can come of it, by giving an innocent guy a chance to get his life back."

"That's it?"

"Yeah."

"There's something else," Aaron said, as he got up from his chair and walked over to a file cabinet. He flipped through a few files and then pulled out two pictures and handed them to Jack.

"What's this?"

"You tell me."

Jack studied both pictures closely. "Where did you get these pictures?"

"Funny you asked," he smirked. "They came in the mail a year after the trial with no return address."

"Are these pictures of Jeff's girlfriend with the Senator? Do you think her death has something to do with him?"

"He was framed, like I said, by powerful people. And I'm sure that's one of the reasons you're here," Greenberg said with a slight grin.

Jack handed the pictures back to Aaron and stood up. "I've got to get going, but all the information is in

216

the letter."

"Thanks, Jack. I'll start the ball rolling. I hope it works out for all of us."

"Yeah, me too."

***

Later that afternoon, Brian left Jack back at a run-down motel off the beaten path in Arlington, Virginia, while he drove into downtown Washington, D.C. looking for an old friend, Carlos. Carlos was someone he had met back in the days when he visited Mexico with his mother. Years later, Carlos made his way to America and, with Brian's family's help, he settled into his new life.

One of the money-making skill sets that Carlos brought with him from Mexico was the ability to produce complete new identities, which turned out to be a lucrative trade with an endless clientele, mostly made up of illegals and people on the run.

Brian needed two new identities: one for himself and one for Jack. After a couple of hours, Brian had what he needed – a new passport with a handsome snapshot and a new license for each of them.

On his return from Washington, Brian's car rolled to a stop in the motel parking lot. He was getting closer to his dream life. He just needed to launder the cartel money at an Indiana bank and accompany Jack to

Seattle to examine the contents of Cap's safe deposit box. Then he could start his dream life in the Caribbean. But, he had a bad feeling about this trip. There were just too many people who wanted Jack dead and the authorities were looking under every rock to find him as well.

Brian emerged from the car, took a brief look around, and headed for the motel room. He knocked on the door, but there was no answer. "Hey, Jack, it's Brian; let me in," he hollered. He waited a few seconds then slid the key card into the slot, pushing in the door while brandishing a handgun. He pointed it all around the room, his heart thumping loudly. He went through the whole room, his worst fears put to rest. He quickly checked the air vent where the duffle bags were stored. They were still intact with the money. The question was: where did Jack go? *He couldn't have gone far unless the unthinkable happened.*

Brian took a jog over to the main office where a musty odor filtered through the air. A plain looking young kid with straggly long hair sat at the information desk. He was playing a video game on his smartphone with his ear buds in place.

"Hey, kid, have you seen or heard anything strange today?" Brian asked.

"What?" the desk clerk asked, pulling out his ear buds.

"I said did you see or hear anything strange?"

"Nope," he said disinterestedly.

Brian pulled out a picture of his friend. "Did you see this guy around at all today?"

"Nope."

The kid was useless, he thought, standing there for a second, thinking about what to do next, when the desk clerk's phone rang.

The desk clerk picked it up. "Sir, is your name Brian Butler?"

"Yeah."

"It's for you,"

Brian looked surprised and reached over and took the phone, expecting Jack to be on the other end. "Jack," he uttered.

A strange deep voice replied, "You have about forty minutes before your friend is dead."

"Who's this," Brian snapped.

"Listen, your buddy is about eight miles from the motel, on Industrial Road, in or behind one of the abandoned buildings. And, you have a GPS tracking device attached to your car."

"Who the hell is this?" he shouted into the phone. The voice was gone. Brian handed the phone back to the desk clerk. "Do you know where Industrial Road is?"

"I live a few miles from there," the desk clerk replied, seeming to be a little more helpful. "It's eight miles down the road; take a left once you get out of the parking lot onto Arlington Boulevard. Then, there's a sign that says Industrial Road on the left, and it's about two miles from there. If you go over the Potomac River, you've gone too far."

"Thanks," Brian said, quickly paying the clerk for the room. "We won't be staying." He hurriedly raced to his motel room. He grabbed their belongings threw everything into the back of the trunk and hopped into the car. And then quickly got out, remembering what the man had said. He looked under the carriage of the car until he got to the back bumper and felt underneath, and there, just as the man had said on the phone, was a little GPS tracking device. He stuffed it into a flowerpot and got back into the car, racing out of the parking lot.

***

Jack's opened his eyes, his senses groggy, and his head hurting. He looked up at the high rusty metal ceiling, trying to get his bearings, not sure what had happened to him. One minute he was walking to get a bucket of ice at the motel and, the next thing he knew, he was coming to with his hands tied to some contraption and his ankles tightly bound as well. The harder he pulled to get free, the tighter his bonds cut into his limbs.

"He's coming to," a voice whispered.

A couple of well-dressed men walked over. "Jack Bolton," a voice rang out in the decrepit metal warehouse. Tall, thick metal supports extended to the ceiling, evenly spaced throughout and anchored into the cement by rusty bolts. The walls were lined with a configuration of old cast iron pipes, no longer protected by asbestos coverings. The dim light was slowly fading as the last of the sun's rays penetrated through the small broken windows above. Three men leaned over him, as if they were surgeons getting ready to do a major procedure. "I got some good news and some bad news, Jack," one of the men stated matter-of-factly.

Jack's senses slowly returned, his first thought was that somehow the Mafia had found him and Frank Gallo was about to make an appearance.

When he was finally able to refocus, he asked, "You're Mafia, right?" He felt pain radiating from his face and the aftereffects of some type of knockout chemical.

Laughter erupted from the three men. "We're not Mafia, Jack," one of them said. "Let me tell you the good news first. The nylon rope digging into your arms and ankles, that will subside and the grogginess you're feeling is temporary; but the bad news is you're going to be dead shortly. Sorry Jack."

As the men walked away, Jack tried to assess his situation. Was there a way out? He still had too much left to do. His thoughts were abruptly interrupted as two of the men came back and flipped the board he was laying on upright. He was still slightly disoriented. It was as though he had been hit over the head with a hammer.

The thought of escaping faded from his mind. *Who were these people,* he wondered. If they weren't Mafia, they certainly weren't FBI, and they definitely weren't a Mexican cartel.

At that moment, a man wearing a custom-made suit pulled away from another well-dressed man in the background. He started to walk towards Jack. As he got closer, he looked familiar and Jack remembered the pictures. It was the senator, Sam Atkins.

"Do you know who I am?" the senator asked.

"Yeah, I do."

"Good, then there's no need for introductions."

With that, he struck a hard blow with his clenched fist to Jack's face. "That's for my son, you bastard. Who the hell gave you the right to kill my son?" the senator snapped angrily, shaking his hand from the punch. Then, turning to the three men who were standing there, he ordered, "Kill this piece of crap," before walking away.

Jack spit out blood, as the men looked on. "Hey Senator," Jack hollered, "is this what you guys did to Laura Weston?"

The senator hesitated for a second but then kept walking.

"Your son raped and murdered my sister," Jack bellowed.

But the senator kept walking, and did not look back.

One of the men made a gesture to Banner who had accompanied the senator, indicating that they were waiting for their next order. Banner, in turn, signaled fifteen minutes with his fingers, as he accompanied the senator out of the building. The two men entered a Cadillac, sitting idle with its engine running. After a few moments, they drove off.

"Well, Jack, it looks like you pissed off the wrong people," the head guy said.

"How do you guys sleep at night?"

"We just take orders, Jack."

Jack, still groggy, and with blood rolling down his cheek, recapped his close calls as a Navy SEAL. Now death was staring him in the face once again. It didn't matter that he was a former decorated Navy SEAL; he might as well have been a terrorist.

From ten feet away the head guy facing Jack pulled out a silver handgun and cocked it, pointing it at Jack's head. The other two stood, one on either side of him, waiting to remove his body once the fatal shot had been fired.

"Anything you want to say before I pull the trigger?" the man with the gun asked, pointing it at Jack's head.

"What does it matter?" Jack mumbled. "Just do it!" he snapped.

"Have a good ride, Jack."

Jack closed his eyes as the noise from the gun echoed off the hollow metal structure; two more pops went off like firecrackers. Jack opened his swollen eyes in bewilderment. All three men were now lying motionless on the ground. Three unerring shots had been fired from one of the open windows above.

A few seconds later, Brian entered through the side door of the warehouse. "Jack, you okay? I almost didn't find this place in time."

"Untie me." Jack snapped.

"That's all you've got to say after I saved your life again?" Brian laughed.

"We're even. How the hell did you find me?"

"I got a strange phone call telling me where you were and that you would be dead in forty minutes. I cut it a little close, but all that matters is I got here in time."

Jack rubbed his wrists as Brian untied him. His head was hurting. His face looked as if he had just lost a twelve-round boxing match. Jack bent down, checking on the three men. "Brian, one is still alive!"

"Let's find out who they are," Brian replied.

Jack knelt down close to the man, who was barely holding on. His breathing was getting uneven and shallow. "Who do you work for? Who do you work for?" he repeated, shaking him in the process.

The man, with his last gasp of air, mumbled "CIA." Then his face slowly turned a pale gray as his eyes froze in place.

"CIA. What the hell?" Brian said. "I was thinking I saved you from the Mafia."

"Well, you missed who was here just before you arrived."

"Hey, you're lucky I found the place."

"Senator Atkins oversaw these guys."

"I can't believe he would condone this."

"I can't believe the CIA would actually do this for him."

"The senator was actually here! Unbelievable," Brian exclaimed.

"It's all crazy to me. You don't know who the good guys are anymore."

"We're the good guys, Jack," Brian said with a chuckle. "By the way, I got you a new license and a shiny passport," he said, pulling out the IDs from his pocket and flipping it to him.

He took a quick peek. "My name is "Jack Riley?"

"Yeah, no exchanges."

"What's yours?"

"Brian Shore. Now, let's get the hell out of here."

Chapter 28

Agent Ryland sat at his desk in the Boston office, preparing to leave for Brooklyn, Ohio in a few hours. He had formed a unit of FBI specialists to track down every lead that came across their desks regarding the apprehension of Jack Bolton and those who were involved in his escape. He had the list of former Navy SEALs that, according to the CIA Director, were very much involved in this nationwide story. This key information would be a good start. There was always a weak link. He just needed to weed out the one who would break. Once he did that, the group would fall like dominos. His first stop on the list was Joe Cap.

As he continued his preparation, a strange call came in, forwarded by one of the specialists. "This is Special Agent Ryland."

"My name is Aaron Greenberg. I'm the attorney for Jeff Keller. I would like to talk to you about a deal for my client who has information on the whereabouts of Jack Bolton."

"Who do you represent again? Maybe you've got the wrong department," he said, making a contorted face at the specialist standing up at the front of his desk.

"You're the agent in charge of apprehending Jack

Bolton, correct?"

"Yes, tell me again who you represent?

"Jeff Keller. He has crucial information on the whereabouts of Jack Bolton"

Ryland wrote down the name. "Is that spelled K-E-L-L-E-R?"

"Yes."

"I just need an address and age."

"Fine. He's thirty-two years old; his address is the Haynesville Correctional Center, Virginia."

Ryland paused, then wrote the rest of the information down on a piece of paper and said, "Can I put you on hold for a second?"

"Sure."

Ryland looked at the specialist in front of him. "Find out everything you can about this guy, Keller," he ordered, handing him the piece of paper. "I'm not sure how he can help us with Jack Bolton." The specialist nodded and quickly left the room with his instructions.

He put the phone back to his ear. "I'm sorry, Mr. Greenberg, but you said his address is listed as a prison. I'm confused."

"Well, my client is presently serving a life sentence for murder and would like to make a deal with you in exchange for giving up the location of Jack Bolton."

"How would your client know where Jack Bolton is hiding out, especially when your client is serving a life sentence in prison?"

"I can only tell you that we have reliable information on the whereabouts of Jack Bolton and until you're willing to make a deal with my client and get the prosecutor to file a *Rule 35* motion, there's nothing more I can say here."

"So, based on your client's information, you want me to talk to the Commonwealth Attorney of Virginia and see if we can make a deal for a reduced sentence for your client? Is that what you're seeking?"

"Yes. We can negotiate a reduced sentence when the time comes, if you agree to a deal with my client," Aaron said. "Here's my direct cell number."

"I'll get back to you." Agent Ryland replied, taking Aaron's number down.

As Ryland was getting ready to leave for Brooklyn, Ohio, the specialist walked in. "You'll want to hear this," he said.

"What did you find out?"

"Jeff Keller was a lawyer for a prestigious law firm in Washington, D.C. He finished at the top of his class at Georgetown Law School."

"He sounds like a pretty smart guy," Ryland quipped. "So what the hell is he doing in prison?"

"He was found guilty of murdering his fiancé six years ago."

"So he has a mean streak. Where's the punch line?" Ryland asked with curiosity.

"Well, here it is. Keller's fiancé was an intern for

Senator Sam Atkins."

"That is interesting," Ryland said, sitting back in his chair, trying to grasp what all this meant.

"It sure is. This guy Keller always swore he was innocent and that he was framed. His criminal record is spotless from what I can tell. And the girl's body was never found."

"Did you find anything where Keller and Bolton might have crossed paths?"

"I didn't find anything," the specialist said. "But I'm still looking."

"I've got to go. Keep me up to date," Ryland said, heading out the door. While being transported to the airport, sitting in the backseat, he pondered over this new information, trying to get a handle on what Jack Bolton was trying to do. *What if this Jeff Keller was really innocent? Then who killed his fiancé? Was their some connection to Senator Atkins?* And then the unthinkable struck like a thunderbolt: *What if the senator had something to do with the girl's death?*

Chapter 29

Jeff Keller, at the age of thirty-two, serving a life sentence in the Haynesville Correctional Center, could only reminisce now about the good times he once enjoyed with his friends and family. His once fit body and summer tan had given way to flabby abs and a pallid complexion. He had traded in his finely tailored business suits for a bright orange jumpsuit. His view from prison consisted of barbed-wire fencing and guard towers manned by men with rifles, quite a difference from his days at the law firm where a view of the White House could be seen in the distance.

He sometime fantasized about escaping, an exercise in futility, to be sure. Coming from a privileged upbringing, he was surely out of his comfort zone. He had no choice but to learn to adapt to the harsh reality that he faced every day.

A population of over eleven hundred inmates called the place home. It was a place you never got used to - the daily routine of living within cement walls and bars with no natural light, the sound of electronic gates opening and closing, the sight of inmate's ghastly tattoos, the cramped cells, the pitter-patter of mice that scurried along the cement floors at night, the lack of privacy, the bi-polar mood swings of inmates, the bland food, the vulgar language, the constant stress of watching one's back, and the reality that your life was now owned by the state of Virginia. This had been his world for the past six years.

His appeals went nowhere; the circumstantial evidence was too strong and no serious errors of law were found. It had been a slam-dunk case for the prosecution.

Jeff grew up in the prestigious suburb of Great Falls, Virginia, a bedroom community of fifteen thousand people with a median income of over one hundred-fifty thousand, and just eighteen miles from Washington, D.C. His father was a successful lawyer, his mother a former nurse, and his three older sisters were now married with young children.

Straight A's were the norm in Jeff's academic life. He was a star baseball player from the time he was a young kid, one of those kids that people saw running around the neighborhood with a bat and glove in hand at all times. He was the class president at Langley High School and had been voted "Most Likely to Succeed" by his classmates.

He was the all-American boy envied by his peers. He had it all: the loving family, the good looks, the beautiful girlfriend, and a promising career that he had just begun. And then came that terrible night. The night he would never forget. The night that Laura blind-sided him with the worst news of his life; he could still feel the sting of her words, "I can't marry you; I'm seeing someone else." Those words had never left him.

They had met as freshmen at Georgetown University. Both were Political Science majors, and it wasn't long before they started dating. One could say it was "love at first sight." They never had a bad date. They truly enjoyed each other's company. They would walk the beaches hand-in-hand in the summer months, while watching the sunsets. They would ski during winter breaks and cozy up to the fireplace with a glass of wine. They laughed at each other's humor. They were never at a loss for words. They would even go to the college library together, making faces from afar in between long study periods. Then, there were all the crazy parties, and the college sporting events that they attended without ever a fight, an argument or even a brief jealous outburst from either of them accusing the other of flirting. Marriage would surely be in their future and living happily ever after. At least, that was the way Jeff saw it and Laura never disappointed in the way she acted around him.

Jeff was a star pitcher for the Georgetown baseball team and he had dreams of one day playing professionally. But that all came crashing down in his senior year in the game that he would never forget. He had pitched brilliantly for six innings against the top-rated college team in the country. He had mowed down one batter after another, which had the big-league scouts up on their feet. But as fate would have it, the pitcher on the other team was almost as good.

As Georgetown went into the last inning leading 1-0, the unthinkable happened; Jeff heard something pop in his arm after throwing a ninety-four-mile an hour fastball. With a perfect game at stake against the premier team in college baseball and a one run lead and two outs left, he was determined to finish the game. He walked the next batter with pain radiating down his arm. But, with one swing of the bat, the next batter knocked the ball downtown and handed Jeff's team a loss. Losing the game paled into insignificance when, a few days later, he was diagnosed with a blown rotator cuff, an injury from which he never fully recovered, and which ended his dream of playing professional baseball.

After college, Jeff went on to law school while Laura tried different jobs, looking for the perfect one. Finally, a likely prospect presented itself. He remembered it well; she was so excited - an opportunity to be an intern for Senator Sam Atkins. She told Jeff she never expected that Senator Atkins would drop in during the interview. She couldn't believe he shook her hand and asked her a few general questions; she didn't even remember what they were. Shortly after that she got the call from the senator's office that she had the job. She was beaming.

The timing of Laura's internship fit perfectly with

Jeff's new job as a junior associate at Bain, Strong, and Crosby, the top law firm in Washington, D.C.

For a young couple, both now working in the top political city in the world, times couldn't have been better. One evening they decided to go out to dinner at one of the more expensive restaurants along the Potomac River, not too far from downtown Washington. Jeff had a surprise for her. He had secretly put together a ten-day trip to Italy.

Laura loved Italy. It was her favorite place in Europe. After dinner they went to the piano bar for after-dinner drinks. The room was surrounded by a wall of glass, which gave the patrons a beautiful view of the Potomac. The subtle lighting and the mellow sounds of the piano enhanced the mood of the evening. After a couple of drinks, the time was right to present the Italy trip to Laura. Her beautiful smile had lit up the room all evening.

He presented the envelope with the next drink.

"What's this?" she asked, smiling.

"Open it," he said with a straight face.

She opened it and exploded with excitement. She hugged and kissed him as if he was the only man on earth. Jeff just soaked up the moment. She even told the other patrons around them, who were only too pleased to be part of this happy moment. There was absolutely nothing that could top this evening - except maybe a ring.

He had picked up the ring that day and originally thought he would propose to her in Italy but, now, caught up in the mood of the moment, he knew this was the perfect time. He loved her, she was the one, and there would never be anybody else. Why wait?

He pulled out the shiny white box and put it down in front of her. She was so busy trying to absorb the trip that she didn't notice it until she reached for her drink. "Jeff, what…"

He sat watching her react. She was momentarily speechless and then she opened the box. He knelt down to the left side of her bar stool while a crowd of patrons encircled them.

"Will you marry me?" he asked, in his best stentorian voice, just as the music tapered off to a lull.

He waited for her response and then her voice crackled with a resounding, "Yes, of course I'll marry you, Jeff," she said without hesitation, hugging and kissing him all over again. The crowd of patrons who witnessed these events gave them a standing ovation. It was a night that Jeff would never forget – easily the best night of his life.

Jeff had replayed the memory of that night many times over the last six years, as well as the memory of the worst night of his life, which took place only eleven months later in the Woodstove Restaurant where he made a terrible scene in front of another group of patrons. There was no standing ovation that night - just a broken heart, shattered dreams, and the last time he would see Laura alive.

That memory was inevitably followed by reflections on the trial and how the prosecution focused on him as the only suspect, ignoring his claims regarding the mystery man that Laura was seeing.

After Laura's disappearance, the police found no evidence of another man in her life. The cellphone records were clean, the computer had no record of any new relationship. A thorough search of her apartment gave no answers. There was not a text, an email, or a picture. Absolutely nothing. So the police focused on him as the jealous boyfriend who lost it and killed his girlfriend in a fit of rage at the thought of losing her. It didn't help that the night she disappeared was the same night he made the big scene in the restaurant, which the prosecution used to great advantage. They called witness after witness, all of whom said essentially the same thing - that he was a distraught, angry man who had lashed out at his girlfriend. He had cringed as each witness repeated the same embarrassing scene.

That testimony gave the prosecution motive but was not its primary strength. Although Laura's body was never found, the circumstantial evidence, usually much harder to prove, was overwhelming. Her blood was found in his car. He had no idea where it came from. The murder weapon, a hatchet, was located underneath his car frame with his DNA and fingerprints all over the handle and Laura's blood on the blade head. He was at her condominium the night she went missing. He had no alibi. Add in the scratch mark on his face that was clearly visible in his arrest photo, which was shown over and over again to the jury, and the prosecution's case was made.

He had taken the stand with the hope that he could present a different picture of himself than the one painted by the prosecution. They grilled him about that evening. He denied, denied, denied. He never saw the murder weapon. He had no idea how Laura's blood got in his car. The scratch mark on his face was easily explained; his DNA, fingerprints - all some sort of set-up created by someone else. That was what his defense team tried to prove. He presented to the jury that she had told him she was seeing someone else and that she was pregnant; this is what led to the fight in the restaurant. But, at the end of the day, the prosecution just threw water on the "other guy theory" because there wasn't one shred of evidence supporting it. The defense team tried for a dismissal based on a lack of direct evidence and the possibility that a third party was involved, but their case was too weak while the prosecution's case was ironclad.

Chapter 30

The years had dragged along. Jeff thought about the timing. Right about now, he would have been coming up for partner. Sitting in his jail cell, his mind often wandered to what life might have been. He imagined coming home to Laura, maybe with a little boy waiting for his dad, even a German shepherd waiting enthusiastically at the door. But that life was just a dream.

Except for his family, very few people visited him now. Most of his friends had moved on with their lives. Some even thought he might have done it. Laura's family believed he was a despicable human being who had murdered their beautiful daughter in cold blood; during the trial, he had felt their rage every time they walked into the courtroom.

Today his lawyer was coming by to see him; he usually dropped in every six months or so, just to see how he was doing. Jeff knew Aaron felt badly that he had lost the case, but the deck was stacked against them from the start.

As he was being escorted through the maze of electronic gates and signoffs on his way to meet his lawyer, the image of the person Laura had been seeing, unbeknownst to him, reappeared in his mind. It all started to make sense when Aaron showed him the pictures he had received in the mail with no return address about a year after the trial. They showed Laura with Senator Sam Atkins, both smiling like lovers. It was heart-wrenching to see the smile that Laura once reserved for him, now directed towards someone else. Those pictures told the story. It all made sense. Powerful people framed him for the murder of Laura Weston. He was the perfect victim - engaged to be married to the woman he loved, unaware that she was being seduced by the Washington limelight and a powerful senator. Her pregnancy, and whatever she was feeling for Atkins, couldn't go on. At some point, Atkins made the decision that his future aspirations and image were more important than Laura's life.

He couldn't stop thinking about Laura today. Her bubbly personality had begun to change a few months after she started working for the senator as an intern; Jeff thought it was just the stress of a new job, but it was so far from the truth. She was never home, always saying she had some important project to complete and the heavy demands of his own job kept him from focusing on their relationship. Her initial excitement in planning for the wedding had faded as the months went by. She was just going through the motions. Her sisters appeared to be more excited about the wedding than she was. He wished he reacted to what his gut was telling him, but he thought somehow it would all fall into place because they loved each other. Looking back, he should have said something, but he never did.

The electronic gate opened and there, waiting for him in the visitor's room, was his lawyer, Aaron Greenberg, seated in the far corner. With his wide glasses and receding hairline, he looked more like a bookkeeper than a lawyer who had lost only one case in his entire career. Unfortunately, that one lost case just happened to be Jeff Keller's. Aaron got up and they both shook hands as the security guards looked on.

"It's good to see you, Aaron. At least, you still come by."

"Jeff, I know we've had a lot of disappointments along the way."

"Well, that's pretty much an understatement, but, after all the setbacks, I've accepted it."

"I'm here on business today."

"What? Another attempt at an appeal or did they find Laura alive?" Jeff said sarcastically. "I'm sorry, Aaron; it's this place. I'm glad you came. It's always good to talk to you."

"I understand completely how you feel, but I have something that might cheer you up."

"What?"

"I don't want to get your hopes up too much, but I have something." He reached into his briefcase, pulled out a white envelope, and slid it across the table in front of Jeff.

"What's this?" Jeff asked with curiosity.

"Read the letter inside," he said with a smug look.

Mr. Greenberg took a look around the visitor's room knowing that his client didn't belong here. It burned him up to see him in jail. Jeff would need a miracle to get him out.

Jeff put down the letter. "Is this some kind of joke?" he asked with a blank look.

"No. What does it say?"

"You didn't read this?"

"No. The letter was addressed to you."

"Well, to sum it up, this guy Jack Bolton is going to turn himself in based on me telling the FBI where he's going to be in approximately ten days."

"Well, the good news is this, I got a phone call from the Commonwealth's Attorney before I got here, and he's willing to file a motion for a reduced sentence based on the apprehension of Jack Bolton; anything short of that and there's no deal."

"So telling the feds where Jack Bolton is going to be in ten days, based on this letter, and they'll reduce my sentence?"

"Sounds too easy, huh? That was my thought as well."

"What are the chances this guy is going to carry through with this? And why? I don't even know him."

"I'll give you a little background on him. First, Jack

241

he was in my office the other day."

"He visited you?" Jeff asked with a surprised look.

"Yeah, he sure did. I've never had a fugitive in my office before. We had a nice chat," Aaron said. "He was pretty straightforward and presented this idea of giving himself up for your freedom based on your innocence."

"What did you tell him?"

"I told him you were framed and showed him the pictures of the senator and Laura together; then I explained how we got the pictures with no return address."

"I can't believe this," Jeff said, leaning back in his chair and folding his hands behind his head. "I'm confused, and I have a couple of questions."

"Ask me anything,"

Jeff leaned in close to Aaron. "First, who is this guy? Second, why does he want to help me? And third, this envelope gives a location of where he's going to be in ten days, and the feds are just going to pick him up and they are going to just let me go. I'm missing something here; where's the catch? There has to be a catch," Jeff said rubbing his forehead, not sure what to think.

"Your first question: Jack Bolton was a decorated Navy SEAL who broke out of prison and is on the run. The feds want him badly, but the Mafia wants him dead as well."

"What do you mean?" Jeff asked, leaning in to hear the rest of the details with utmost interest.

"He was serving a life sentence for killing the son of a Mafia kingpin," Aaron stated clearly. "He broke out of prison and then killed John Atkins."

"Is that the senator's son?" he asked with a surprised look on his face.

"Yes. He killed both of them because he believed they raped and murdered his sister."

"Wow!" Jeff uttered, shaking his head. "But what does this have to do with me?"

"The senator's son, I guess. I showed him the picture of Senator Atkins and Laura together and explained to him that we had no idea who sent it."

"It looks like the apple didn't fall far from the tree, huh?"

"It sure looks that way."

"I still don't get it, though. Why is he giving himself up, just so he can go back to prison?" Jeff questioned. "It doesn't make any sense."

"As I said, he killed those two guys because they raped and murdered his sister; that's what he believes anyway. He also said that his sister would want him to turn himself in for your release. And he didn't feel good about what he had done and he had read something about your case while he was in prison. But that being said, I'm not sure what he's really up to. We can only hope he holds up his end of the bargain. He seems like a sincere guy who doesn't go back on his word."

"I'm not going to get my hopes up, Aaron," Jeff said

quietly, staring around at the place he called home. "It sounds, from what you're telling me, like this guy might not even make it to Seattle before the feds pick him up."

"Well, he's the only game in town. The good news is the feds want to make a deal. There's a lot of pressure on them, I'm sure from Senator Atkins, to get Bolton back in prison."

Chapter 31

The evening sun was slowly fading as Agent Ryland and Agent Hawkins's dark sedan pulled up to the Cap residence. They exited the car, walked up the stairs, and knocked on the porch screen door. The light came on as Carl Cap entered the porch and peeked through the screen door. "Can I help you?"

The two FBI agents, standing at the top of the stairs, pulled out their badges. "I'm Special Agent Ryland, and this is my partner Agent Hawkins; we're looking for Joe Cap," Agent Ryland replied.

"You are going to have to speak up," he said, pointing to his ears, both of which held hearing aids.

"I'm sorry; we are looking for Joe Cap," he said loudly.

"I can hear you; you don't need to yell," Mr. Cap replied. "Well, he's not going to be able to help you."

"We just need to ask him a few questions," Hawkins said in a louder than normal voice.

"My son passed away a few days ago; he was buried earlier today."

"I'm so sorry," Ryland expressed, with a surprised look. "What happened?"

"His time was up," Carl answered.

"May we come in and ask you a few questions, Mr. Cap?" Ryland asked softly.

"Come on in; we'll just sit out here on the porch, if you don't mind."

"That's fine," Hawkins replied. "Mr. Cap, how did your son die?

"He died in his sleep."

"He seems a little young to die in his sleep, especially being a former fit Navy SEAL."

"What are you getting at, Agent?" Carl Cap snapped as he rose from his chair. "I'll be right back."

Hawkins sprang to his feet, always on guard for the unexpected, while Ryland sat in a defensive position. Carl came back a minute later with a section of the newspaper. "Here's his obituary," he explained, handing the paper to Hawkins. "What did you guys think, I was coming out with a gun or something?" he joked.

"Just standard protocol, Mr. Cap, you just never know," Ryland said.

"Hey, I understand."

Hawkins handed the paper to Ryland who reviewed it quickly. "Mr. Cap…" Ryland said in a loud firm voice. "The reason we're here, Mr. Cap, is we believe that your son was involved in helping Jack Bolton escape from prison in Massachusetts."

"He's a big boy; what he does, or did, was his business. I can't help you with that."

"Mr. Cap, you understand, we can get a search

warrant to exhume your son's body," Hawkins snapped.

"I guess you have the right to do anything you want, but let me tell you my son was a good kid and wouldn't have done anything he didn't think was right, and I'm insulted that you would even suggest that you would actually exhume his body; he fought for this country."

"Mr. Cap, we're just trying to find Jack Bolton and the people responsible for his escape," Ryland said, apologetically.

"I know you have a job to do; I know that."

"Look, Mr. Cap, we are very sorry about your son, but we need to find Jack Bolton," Ryland stated. "He's a fugitive who murdered two young people. He needs to be put back behind bars, and if you know anything about this, we would like to hear it."

"As I said before, I can't help you."

"Let me show you something, Mr. Cap." Hawkins pulled a manila folder from a briefcase and plopped it on the coffee table."

"What's this?" Mr. Cap asked.

"These are the guys we believe were involved in helping Jack Bolton escape."

Carl looked over the photos in the folder; he knew two of them. But he wasn't going to mention it to the agents. He didn't trust the government. He could only speculate that every one of these guys was part of this, but he had a deeper thought: how did they know? "I'm sorry, but these photos don't mean anything to me."

"Mr. Cap, there's something else you should know, just in case your memory isn't very good," Hawkins said.

"And what's that, Agent Hawkins?" Mr. Cap shrugged.

"Well, we have information from reliable sources that these guys also hit a cartel in Mexico. I know it all seems crazy - a bunch of former Navy SEALs breaking out another SEAL from prison, then hitting a cartel for millions and apparently riding off into the sunset. Sounds like a movie, huh?"

"I've lost my wife and both of my sons all within the last few months," Carl said, not blinking, and handing back the folder. "I'm just a little too tired for any more drama in my life at the moment, which I think you can both understand. But I do have something for you, Agent Ryland," Carl reached in his pocket and tossed a miniature black device with wires protruding from it onto the coffee table.

The agents stared at the device. They both looked puzzled, not sure what to say. They knew exactly what it was.

"I found it in the ceiling a couple of months ago; I think it was connected to the phone line. But I ask myself why would I have a device like this in my house? I have nothing to hide. Now, I had a son who worked for the CIA and who is now dead. And, coincidently, three other people that he worked with on one of his assignments suffered fatal accidents as well.

"I don't know what to say, Mr. Cap," Ryland said softly.

"I'll give you my opinion. Whoever is feeding you information, Agent Ryland, is afraid of something," Mr. Cap said with a smirk. "Maybe you're going after the wrong people."

"I think we're done here, Mr. Cap," Ryland said. "Thanks for your time, and I'm sorry for your losses."

Both agents stood up, and shook Carl's hand and headed out the door.

The agents entered their car and drove off.

"What do you think?" Hawkins said.

Ryland, sitting in the passenger seat, responded, "I think he knows more than he told us. I'm sure his son is dead, but I think he was killed in Mexico and Bolton and his buddies took him back to his father and, somehow, they were able to arrange a funeral."

"That must have been quite the conversation."

"I'm sure it was."

"We can get a court order and have the body exhumed by tomorrow morning," Hawkins suggested.

"He was a Navy SEAL and fought for this country. This just opens another can of worms," Ryland said with a serious face. "He deserves better than that, and what do we get out of it? He can't tell us anything and it would just be wasting our time."

"Yeah, you're probably right."

"These guys who helped Bolton - it's going to be pretty hard to prove they conspired to break him out, unless we can get one of them to turn on the others. I doubt that's going to happen, but you never know."

At that moment, Ryland's phone buzzed; the Commonwealth's Attorney from Virginia was on the other end telling him that the Rule 35 motion relating to the case had been filed.

"Who was that?"

"The Virginia attorney. He filed a motion to make a deal with Keller. He and Keller's attorney are coming up to meet with me tomorrow morning."

"Well, that's good."

"Maybe. I'm just not sure what Bolton is up to."

"Why Keller?"

"That is hard to figure, even if Keller is innocent. His girlfriend's body was never found. She worked for Senator Atkins. Bolton killed Atkins's son because he participated in the rape and murder of Bolton's sister. What the connection is between the two cases is still a mystery." Ryland's phone buzzed again. This time it was the FBI office in Indiana. A nineteen–year old female college student was reported missing from Notre Dame University yesterday. The call ended. "Looks like you're going to Indiana."

"We have something?"

"Yeah, we have another missing person, but this time we might have some footage of the abductor.

They're going to send the video file; at least we can use that to see if there are any connections to the missing people in the other locations."

"That's going to be a lot of work."

"Yeah," Ryland nodded. "I hope we find that one needle in the haystack."

Chapter 32

Early the next morning, on short notice, Aaron Greenberg and Cliff Rider, the attorney representing the Commonwealth of Virginia, arrived at Agent Ryland's Boston office. The three men settled into their seats at a round table, prepared to hammer out an agreement. A federal judge was on standby to facilitate the agreement, once reached. They sat across from each other, their expressions as watchful as players in a world-class poker game. The drama had begun. Aaron knew the political pressure they were under and he felt he had the upper hand. What did they care about Jeff Keller? It was all about capturing Jack Bolton. Aaron's objective was to secure a deal for Jeff Keller that would insure his immediate release upon the capture of Jack Bolton. There would be nothing to negotiate beyond that point. And he was well aware that even if he was successful in the agreement he sought today there were many reasons to be concerned that Bolton would be killed, wouldn't show up, or that something that he couldn't even imagine would happen.

After formal introductions and some small talk, they got down to business. "So, Mr. Greenberg, what do you have for us?" Cliff asked.

"I'm going to cut to the chase," Aaron replied. "The letter I'm holding explains where Jack Bolton is going to be on October 8th. So time is getting short."

"Let's take a look at it," Cliff said with a grin.

Aaron smiled at that suggestion. "Let's work out the deal first, and then I'll be more than happy to give you the information on his whereabouts."

"It's just a matter of time before we get Jack Bolton, with or without your help, Mr. Greenberg," Ryland interposed.

"Then, maybe you should take that path," Aaron countered.

"Your client, Jeff Keller, has only served six years, hardly enough time for the murder of his fiancée," Cliff replied.

"That's six years too many. My client is innocent; he was convicted on circumstantial evidence and was framed for the murder," Aaron stated matter-of-factly.

"Unfortunately for Mr. Keller, the jury didn't see it that way," Cliff fired back.

"Regardless of what the jury saw in the case," Aaron replied, "he's innocent. Now, what I'm looking for is this. Once you have Jack Bolton in custody, that is when you have handcuffs on him, you immediately send me and the warden of the facility where he is being held, a signed fax or email authorizing the immediate release of Jeff Keller from prison."

"I don't know if we can do that," Cliff said with a

smug look. "Your client was found guilty of murder and sentenced to life in prison; we came here prepared to reduce his sentence to fifteen years. That's just nine more years, which I think is fair."

"Not even close," Aaron said, steadfastly.

"Well, I don't think Laura Weston's family is going to be too happy if we just let Keller walk," Cliff stated.

"Let me ask - how did your client obtain this information," Ryland interjected. "Do they know each other?" he added.

"Does it really matter, as long as you get Jack Bolton back in custody? Or, should I add, if he is accidently killed at the location we give you?" Aaron replied in a slightly annoyed tone. He had no intention of telling them Bolton had paid a visit to his office or whether they knew each other; it was irrelevant to the negotiations and the less they knew, the more they would be willing to accede to his demands.

"Let me ask you another way," Agent Ryland continued, not giving up on the question. "If your client doesn't know him, why would Jack Bolton give himself up for him?"

Aaron took a sip of his coffee; he wished he knew the answer to that question. "I don't know the answer to that," he replied honestly.

Agent Ryland's cell phone buzzed; he picked it up and excused himself from the room. It was the FBI Director. He asked how the negotiations were going and

Ryland said they were working out the terms of the deal. Ryland just listened as the FBI Director gave him orders to take whatever Keller's lawyer was offering. If Bolton showed up, that would be the end of it; if he didn't, Keller would still be behind bars. He also wanted a detailed report of everything that took place at the meeting. Ryland could only think that there must have been pressure from Senator Atkins to wrap this up as quickly as possible. He walked back into the room. "So where are we?" he asked.

"We are hung up on a fifteen-year sentence," Cliff said.

Ryland looked at him. "Can I talk to you outside for a moment?" As Cliff got up, Ryland turned to Aaron. "We'll be right back; sit tight."

After a couple of minutes, they returned to the negotiating table. "What's it going to be?" Aaron asked.

"Well, we've decided that we are going to agree to your terms, Mr. Greenberg," Cliff said softly.

Aaron wasn't about to ask any questions; he couldn't believe the change of heart. It was almost too easy. "Okay, we've got ourselves a deal," he said. "One more thing."

"And what would that be?"

"The moment Jack Bolton is handcuffed, or if he is killed, I want the call to be made to release Keller, not one second later," Aaron replied, knowing anything could go wrong in the transporting of Bolton.

"Okay. We have ourselves a deal," Ryland said.

"Let's put the agreement together right now on the laptop and I'll print it," Cliff said. "Mr. Greenberg, you can review it and bring it back to your client to sign off."

"I have Power of Attorney to sign for Mr. Keller," Aaron replied.

"Good, then we can finalize this pretty quickly," Cliff added. "In fact, we can go over to the federal building, where a federal judge is available to review it this morning."

"That's quick," Greenberg said with a puzzled look.

Cliff just smiled. "Oh, yes, this is a very high profile case and the only reason why the terms of the agreement are what they are. Also, we were fortunate enough to get a judge on short notice who was willing to make time to approve the deal. So this is pretty much Mr. Keller's lucky day, all things considered," he said. "Now, I don't have to remind you that if Jack Bolton is captured or killed prior to the designated time or doesn't show up as stipulated in the agreement, there is no deal for your client."

Aaron looked him straight in the eye and said, "Just print off the agreement so we can finalize it."

After outlining and discussing the exact wording that should be on the agreement, the deal was almost complete. But even the feeling of winning the negotiations didn't give Aaron a feeling that it was time to celebrate; it was all such a long shot. He didn't want to get Jeff's hopes up, but at least the first part of this bizarre deal was almost complete; just the signing of the agreement and the judge's approval remained. The final part, the actual execution of the plan, was the real cliffhanger.

As Cliff and Ryland got up from the table and shook hands, Aaron got up from his chair and asked, "Can I talk to you privately, Agent Ryland?"

"Sure, what is it?" he said. Cliff walked into an adjacent room to print off the agreement.

"I want to show you something; please, take a seat."

As they sat down, Aaron pulled two pictures from a folder in his briefcase, the same ones that he had shown to Jack Bolton. He pushed them over to Ryland who scrutinized them carefully. *An attractive woman*, he thought to himself. He was already grappling with the question of why Jack Bolton was doing this. And now, these pictures lent more credibility to the possibility that Senator Atkins was somehow connected to the death of Laura Weston. Ryland asked, "Where did you get the pictures, Mr. Greenberg?"

They were sent to me a year after the trial by some unknown person, no return address. Two pictures by themselves don't mean much in a court of law, but I think they speak for themselves."

"So why are you showing them to me?"

"Why? Because I want you to believe that my client is innocent. Keller took a lie detector test and passed. I

257

believe he was framed; he's an innocent man serving time for something he didn't do. I want you to understand how important this is to Jeff Keller. It's his last chance for freedom. I also want you to make the phone call to free him as soon as Bolton is handcuffed and taken into custody."

"What are you worried about?"

"I'm worried about a lot of things."

"Well, we'll know how it all plays out on October 8th," Ryland said. They both then stood up from the table and, after another handshake, Ryland left the room, and Cliff walked back in with the final agreement.

***

Ryland headed back to his office and, within an hour, he received an email from Cliff Ryder stating that the agreement had been approved in principle by a federal judge. Ryland had never seen such a fast turnaround. Of course, he figured that, in a high profile case with Senator Atkins throwing his weight around, federal judges became available on short notice.

The exact location of where Jack Bolton would be in seven days was revealed. On October 8th, at 10:00 a.m., Jack Bolton would be at "The Cup of Joe" coffee shop located in downtown Seattle on University Street. Ryland pushed his chair forward, closer to the computer, and fired off an email to the FBI director. It included the details of the meeting and the exact location where Jack Bolton would be taken into custody.

A few minutes later, an encrypted email with an attached video of a possible suspect in the disappearance of an Indiana college student arrived in Ryland's email box. This might be the first real break in the series of disappearances he had been following since the Becket case opened up in North Adams. Mass. He opened the attachment and looked at the suspect on the screen, zooming in and out, and then he forwarded the video file off to his task force team in Quantico for further analysis.

As he stared at the computer, he noticed a headline running across the screen: "Senator Sam Atkins has announced his candidacy for president and should be considered a front-runner to win the Democratic Party nomination."

He leaned back in his chair and thought about the photos he had just seen of the senator with the young woman. *Were they just harmless pictures or evidence of an affair that needed to be kept quiet at all costs? Was Jeff Keller really a killer or just a guy who had been framed to protect the presidential ambitions of a ruthless politician?*

He had a late night flight booked for Seattle and wondered if there was any significance to the location. He circled "Peace Arch Crossing" on the border of Canada and Washington State, just two hours from

Seattle. He suspected that, inside Bolton's plan to get Jeff Keller out of prison, there was a scheme to escape to Canada and disappear. The question of how he was going to pull all this off tugged at Ryland's mind.

The entire day had been busy from the start. Ryland arrived at Logan Airport and proceeded to board an eleven thirty a.m. shuttle flight to LaGuardia Airport in New York. Sergeant Sullivan and a detective lieutenant of the Massachusetts State Police accompanied him. A meeting had been arranged for 2:00 that afternoon in the heart of Manhattan at a restaurant owned by Frank Gallo.

They arrived right on schedule at the cozy little Italian restaurant called Gallo's. The staff, dressed in white attire, was busy, serving the late lunch crowd. A well-dressed man led them to a backroom where Frank Gallo and his attorney sat at a table. After introductions, they got down to business.

"I thought you guys would never show. I would offer you something to eat, but I don't like you," Frank said with a chuckle. If he was concerned at the sight of the authorities, he sure didn't show it. He turned on the charismatic smile and seemed to be enjoying the attention. Behind the smile was a bona fide killer who had climbed through the Mafia underworld, crushing his adversaries. The government had failed in its quest to put him behind bars and, after each failure, his power grew. He had eluded conviction based on witnesses either recanting their testimony or disappearing altogether.

"That's okay, Mr. Gallo," Ryland said. "You have plenty of company."

Frank sat straight up. *They had nothing on him, a bunch of useless questions would be asked, and then they would give the standard line: don't go too far. The same old questions, just another wasted visit by the feds*, he thought. "So what brings you here from Boston to my lovely restaurant?"

Ryland leaned back in his chair with his arms folded, as the State Police detective took the lead. "Well, Mr. Gallo, I have just a few questions."

"What are you waiting for? I don't have all day; I've got a restaurant to run," he replied, trying to intimidate his questioner. He grinned smugly at his lawyer.

"The day of Jack Bolton's escape, we found a homemade blade in the transfer vehicle," the detective said.

Frank interrupted him immediately. "So what? You came all the way from Boston to tell me that?" he snickered.

"Igor Barinov, the man who was killed that day, was a known associate of yours."

"Big deal," Frank said.

"We had to dig a little bit but, Dean Ray, one of the correctional officers who was in the vehicle transporting Jack Bolton, mysteriously disappeared two days after the event; and it just so happens that he has a cousin in organized crime," the detective stated, then added under his breath, "What a coincidence."

"Again, what does that have to do with me? Am I supposed to care?"

"Maybe you should care," Ryland interjected.

"I don't care," Frank said, keeping his composure. "I hope you didn't come all the way over here just to tell me this." Frank said, a look of arrogance on his face. He was in complete control, or so he thought.

"Mr. Gallo, I'm guessing you have no idea what happened to Rick Bolton, Jack Bolton's grandfather," Ryland stated.

"I read that someone broke into his house and killed the guy. Couldn't happen to a nicer family."

"It happened in a pretty quiet town; the first murder in that town in twenty-five years," the detective said.

"What's your point?"

"The *point*," Ryland said, "is that we have someone of interest in custody whom you know. Does the name Joe Russo ring any bells?" The smug look on Frank Gallo's face disappeared. "I know him. So what?"

"You look a little surprised that Russo is in custody," Ryland said.

Gallo's lawyer interjected. "Look, unless you guys have something of relevance to discuss, my client is done talking."

"Just a few more questions and we'll be done here,"

Ryland appealed.

"I got nothing to hide; you guys have been trying for years to get something on me." Gallo said. "I make an honest living."

"I'm sure you do, Mr. Gallo," the detective snapped with a smirk.

Gallo shook his head. "You guys really think you're so smart."

The meeting tilted towards hostile as Gallo's thoughts turned to the ramifications of Joe Russo turning to the feds for his protection at the expense of his Mafia friends.

"We are just doing our job, Mr. Gallo," Ryland said. "As for Mr. Russo, he made the unfortunate mistake of selling cocaine to an undercover cop. Then he compounded his misfortune by having twenty grams of cocaine on him. So now he's looking at a ten-to-twenty-year sentence if convicted.

"So what do you want from me, Agent Ryland?" Gallo snapped.

"Well, I'm just giving you an opportunity to come clean. Tell us anything you know about Joe Russo and what he was doing in Massachusetts. And what happened to Dean Ray or Rick Bolton?"

"You can go to hell," Gallo, no longer smiling, fired back, glaring at Ryland.

"Alright, Mr. Gallo. That's fine with us," Ryland said. "But you may be interested to know that Russo has been asking about the witness protection program lately. My feeling is that he doesn't want to die in prison, and we both know he's a heart attack waiting to happen."

"I'm done," Gallo fumed. His mind focused on Russo. The Mafia code of silence was big; anybody who broke that rule was a rat. Violation of that code meant that you would be found floating in the ocean or buried in some dark hole. Russo over the years had killed a few men just for that reason. But Russo told Gallo years ago he wasn't going back to prison, so now he was going to sing like a canary. The guy had killed maybe twenty-five people. He knew too much about the organization. Gallo didn't want to believe Russo would turn on his friends; he was a loyal and trusted soldier, a person he could confide in.

Maybe the feds were making it all up. Russo took care of the dirty side of the business; there were numerous hits, bodies buried in places that only Russo would know. He knew the fine details of how Bolton's sister and her boyfriend were disposed of and his first-hand knowledge of Dean Ray's disappearance and Rick Bolton's death would be a prosecutor's dream. His testimony would crush the organization for years to come, and they would all be put away by the time he was done. Ironically, Russo had a hit list greater than the "Rolling Stones" and he had the potential to leave it all behind and just walk away into the sunset.

Agent Ryland got up from the table with the two

officers following; there were no handshakes or goodbyes, just stares that said it all. They had set the wheels in motion; Gallo was on notice that he was about to be brought down from his high horse by an insider. Russo was the Fed's ace in the hole; his testimony would end Gallo's reign and he knew it. They had rattled the unflappable Frank Gallo.

Gallo turned to his lawyer after the authorities had disappeared. "We're screwed if Russo turns against us. He knows everything," he said, wincing at the thought.

"They're probably bluffing," his lawyer replied.

"I haven't heard from Russo in a couple of days. And if he is in custody, why hasn't he called me."

"That's a good question."

"So, he's going to take us all down and disappear into a witness protection program." Gallo got up and paced around the room, as two of his lieutenants entered. He pointed to the lawyer. "I need you to go to Boston and find out what's going on."

"He might not want to talk to me."

"Well, if he doesn't want to talk to you, then we'll know."

"Then what?" the lawyer asked.

"We all know what needs to be done to a rat to shut him up, but we'll never get close enough," he said angrily in a raised voice, his rage building. He suddenly pounded his fists on the table and swept a pile of folders off the table and stormed out of the room.

Chapter 33

Agent Paul Ryland had returned from New York in the early evening and was racing home to see his family. He had a scheduled flight to Seattle leaving at 11:00 p.m. from Boston. He hadn't seen much of them in the last few weeks, having spent endless investigation time on the effort to locate Jack Bolton and his cohorts as well as a possible serial killer roaming the countryside. And now, by a stroke of sheer luck, the chance of a lifetime had dropped into his lap. Joe Russo, Mafia big-fish and close associate of Frank Gallo, was sitting behind bars with a virtually ironclad case against him and getting ready to talk. The witness protection program was looking like his salvation. Agent Ryland was on the verge of bringing down Frank Gallo where many had failed. He was very close to linking Gallo to the murders of Jack Bolton's grandfather and the missing correctional officer.

But all of this was taking its toll on Paul's family life, especially his marriage. As he drove home from the office, he was exhausted from the morning conference with Keller's attorney, his one-hour flight to New York, the tug-of-war with Frank Gallo, and, finally, his quick flight back to Boston. His tie hung low. He looked more like a man coming off a drunken binge rather than a guy running an FBI operation. He was trying to think of the best way to tell Donna, his wife, that he was taking a late night flight to Seattle and would be gone for a week or so. He would fall back on his usual reasoning and say to her: *What do you want me to do - quit? Leave at five and let the bad guys get away? Things don't pay for themselves you know.* The list of excuses would be endless, but he feared her reaction would make for a very uncomfortable evening. Of course, having three young boys who needed a lot of attention didn't help the situation since Donna wasn't getting any downtime with him working long days and weekends.

He eased the car into the driveway and parked. He lived in a suburban neighborhood of beautiful homes and manicured lawns on the outskirts of Boston. On the surface, it appeared he had it all: three young sons, a beautiful wife who was his college sweetheart, an exciting job. He often boasted about not having one of those boring desk jobs, but sometimes when he went off to work on a Saturday morning, he would see some of the neighbors playing with their kids and the guilt would begin to eat away. The idea that a person could have it all didn't exist as far as he was concerned; there were sacrifices one had to make in life to get the desired results.

He was working so that his family could have a good middle-class life. He came from a family where his dad was never around when he was a kid. They never did without; his father was a cop, worked a lot of overtime and was able to save up enough money for their college tuitions. His father retired with a good pension while his mother was the rock who kept everything together when he was growing up.

As he rounded the mailbox, he grabbed the contents and headed for the front door. His thoughts turned back to how he should tell Donna about the Seattle trip, but as he walked in the door, he forgot all about it. His two little guys were waiting for him and immediately greeted him with hugs. He threw out a couple of high fives to his four-year old son who was followed by his two-and-a-half year old brother. The four-year-old had his baseball glove attached to his hand. The third little guy was fast asleep in his playpen

"Dad, can we play catch?" the four-year-old said.

A quick glance at the clock, and Paul said, "You bet, buddy." A smile formed on his son's face. "I just need to eat and talk to your mom for a few minutes, okay?"

There was some left over pasta. He grabbed it and plopped it on a plate as his wife entered the kitchen. Paul couldn't help but notice how good she looked in a pair of jeans with a long red shirt and her frosty blond hair pulled back in a ponytail. You wouldn't know she had popped out three kids. But there was no big greeting, no welcoming kiss like the days when they were first married. Reality had set in: being married for eight years; his job taking a lot of his time; her holding the house together and managing the kids. The smiles seemed harder to come by, both falling into the same rut with date-night always getting canceled for one reason or another.

"Tough day, honey?" Paul asked.

"What do you think?" Donna replied.

"I was just asking. You don't have to be sarcastic."

"Well, you should try staying home for a day and see what it's like."

"I know. I know. It isn't easy," he said, nodding his head.

Then a slight smile emerged on her face. "I'm sorry honey. There were some funny moments too. Jake decided to smear poop all over his face. Although it wasn't funny at the time," she said, shaking her head while now chuckling at the memory.

"You see what I missed?" he said with a sly smile.

"Yeah, right."

"You're right, I'd rather chase the most dangerous bad guys than clean up poop."

"Well, Matt is hauling around a pretty good one right now that you can change."

"Great," he said good-naturedly, rolling his eyes. It was enough to ease the tension a bit.

"So, I was talking to my mom today and she can come over this weekend and watch the kids, which means we can get out and have some fun. And God

269

knows we need it."

The moment of truth had just landed, loud and clear. A nervous twitch from nowhere pulsated on Paul's eyelid. Donna went in to check the boys while Jake was still snoozing; she walked back into the kitchen as Paul had just emptied his plate into the sink.

"So what do you think, honey. Good idea, right?" Donna asked, looking for confirmation.

"Yeah, it's a real great idea," Paul said in a less than enthusiastic voice.

"Okay, you are not working again this weekend, are you?" She asked, glaring at him. "Wait a minute, I don't care if you work late Friday night, even Saturday during the day, but we are going out Saturday night. I don't care. If you want this marriage to work, you have got to put some effort in, Paul. I don't care that your job is so important. I'm sick and tired of being here all by myself. I need to get out once in a while without the kids."

Paul was now beaten before he even started to explain. He should have told her sooner about the trip to Seattle, but here he was once again in retreat mode.

"I can't this weekend, honey."

She was ready to pounce "I knew it. You always put your job ahead of the kids and me. You know what; forget about it." She said in a raised voice, then, folding her arms.

"You think this is easy for me, Donna."

"It's damn easy for you, Paul. Your job comes first.

Why don't you just say so?"

"Look, I should have told you sooner, but I didn't know. I know how much you want me to work some nine-to-five job and be like the neighbors, but it's not that easy. Don't you think I miss you and the kids? I'm just doing my job to the best of my abilities. And it pays the bills, doesn't it?"

"Told me what, Paul?" she said, looking at him intently.

"I have to fly off to Seattle tonight," Paul said, his voice a shade lower. He was thinking that he might be able to catch criminals, but he was no match for his wife.

She stood looking at him, shaking her head.

Paul thought for a moment that he could see actual steam coming from her head, but, of course, it was from the kitchen teakettle in back of her.

"I know this is a big case and you need to go to Seattle to save the country," she said sarcastically.

Paul walked over to the teakettle and took it off the stove. He hated this part of the job, always defending it. "I'm going to make this all up to you. Maybe we both need to take a trip together, just you and me. Then we'll take the kids somewhere too. I'm sorry but this is what I do; I don't have a choice. If I can't do it, they'll get someone else who can."

A sense of calm came upon her; she had accepted the inevitable and knew there was no point in arguing about the weekend

"That's not the point, Paul. It's not just about this weekend. Your phone is buzzing all the time - whether we're out somewhere or not - all hours of the night, even during the birth of our kids. It never stops. I'm tired of it. Your mind isn't even here half the time, Paul. Your boys are growing up without you. You know, Todd will sit on the front steps with his glove and ball in his hands waiting for you to come home at night."

"I'm sorry," he said. "You're right. I know."

"Do you really want to work so much that you'll never be close to your boys? Do you even care about me? Who will care if you ever get shot, Paul? It sure isn't going to be the agency. Then you'll really understand that family is all you have. But hey, we all make choices in life."

He didn't know what to say as she went into the den to check on the kids. He heard little Jake stirring. She had basically read him the riot act in such a way that he couldn't argue back. She was right and he knew it. His father was never around when he was a kid, but that was just the way it was back then. This wasn't what he wanted for his family.

She returned with Jake in her arms. The little guy had a big smile when he saw his dad. "Why don't you feed him while I clean up a little bit around here? And take care of Matt's diaper, and don't forget about Todd: he's aching to play catch with you."

"Yeah, I know," Paul replied, taking the little guy to the changing table and buckling him into the high chair.

"How long are you going to be in Seattle?" she asked.

His eyes squinted, trying to find the right words. "A week," he stated meekly. "The case is all coming together; once it's over I'll be able to take some time off and we can get away. I promise you."

"A week, huh? Whatever," she said calmly.

Paul fed the little guy and then went out and played catch with Todd as they enjoyed the remainder of a beautiful fall evening. He closed out the night by making up with Donna, reading the boys a bedtime story, and then making his flight to Seattle.

Chapter 34

Jack sat in a corner chair with his head down, engrossed in a local newspaper. His face and eyes were still swollen from that near death experience at the hands of Senator Atkins's henchmen two days earlier. He kept his head down to prevent the cameras from getting a clear shot of him while he waited for Brian in a sunlit mezzanine on an early September morning at University Farm Bank outside of Granger, Indiana. The town had a population of thirty thousand people and was located fourteen miles from South Bend, Indiana, the home of Notre Dame University. The bank was an agricultural powerhouse; millions of dollars of farm money flowed through it daily. Another six or seven million would not attract attention.

Brian carried the two duffle bags of greenbacks while he accompanied Larry Crosby to his office. Brian took a seat, and dropped the duffle bags next to him, as Crosby began hitting keystrokes on the computer at his desk. Within a few minutes an account was created in the name of Grainger Agricultural, a fictitious entity with two fictitious names listed as owners of the company. The two duffle bags that Brian delivered were now taken to a vault where the contents thereof, U.S.

dollar bills in varying amounts, were processed through counting machines. Computer entries were made and a passbook reflecting a balance of $3,375,000.00 net of Crosby's 25% cut, was issued to each "co-owner." Crosby, a high level executive, handled the transaction as if it was regular bank business. He had no interest in the source of funds and assured Brian that there was no chance of it being discovered.

Grainger Agricultural was now open for business. Brian wondered how many of these fictitious accounts existed. Crosby had his system down to a science, a slick operation to be sure; but Brian was aware that the most carefully designed systems could be blown out of the water by some unexpected event. The first chance he got he would transfer the money to his Cayman Island account and advise Jack to move his money as well.

When Brian finally saw the amounts in the passbooks, he almost couldn't believe it. He was getting close to his dream of living on some exotic island, but he still had to deal with whatever was in that safe deposit box and Jack's plan to turn himself in.

While Jack waited for Brian, he came across something in the newspaper that mesmerized him. He stared at a photo on the front page and followed the story to the next page where more pictures were posted. A Notre Dame girl was missing. Authorities believed that the photos were those of a possible suspect. Jack studied each and every photo. It was a face that he had seen somewhere before, and then it struck him, like a bolt of lightning; Williamstown, Massachusetts, the coffee shop, the blank stare, the soulless eyes. The man had the look of a stalker. The pictures didn't lie; he was their man. Jack took a closer look at one of the pictures and there, in the background, was the green car.

Brian walked into the lobby and tapped on Jack's shoes. "We're all set, buddy."

"What the hell? You startled the crap out of me."

"Yeah, well, take a look at this, Mr. Jack Riley." Brian was as proud as he might have been if he were the owner of a company and they had just made a big sale. He tossed the passbook in Jack's lap.

"What's this?"

"Open it."

Jack took a quick look; he had never seen so many numbers. "Wow!"

"That's all you've got to say is wow?"

"No, this is great, Brian."

"You're damn right it's great. We are millionaires, man."

Jack put his excitement on hold for a moment. "Brian, you see the picture of this guy," he said, pointing to the newspaper. "I saw this guy in Williamstown. Now, I think he's the one who killed that old couple up there."

"I don't think we have time to go looking for him, Jack," he said sarcastically. "Let's get out of here before someone figures out who the hell we are."

The car rolled onto I-90 West, a two-day journey to Seattle for the two millionaires. After a quick conversation with Aaron Greenberg, Jack got off his prepaid cell phone.

"So what's going on?" Brian asked

Jack, in deep thought, responded, "What?"

"Is it all set?"

"Yeah."

"The feds are actually going to make a deal?"

"Yeah."

Brian rolled his eyes. "I can't believe they actually agreed to it."

Jack gazed out the window, looking at the scenery, not saying much.

"What the hell is bothering you?" Brian asked. "We're millionaires. Forget about Keller, head to Canada and start a new life. For God's sake, you have plenty of money now."

"What the hell are we doing, Brian?" Jack asked, turning his head towards Brian.

"What do you mean what the hell are we doing? Snap out of it. We are so close, I can taste it."

"I have a bad feeling about Seattle."

"Well, you should. Turning yourself in is crazy. If you don't think someone might just put a bullet in your head in Seattle, you're obviously not thinking clearly.

"I know."

"Look, if you want to find out what's in the safe deposit box, fine. I'll even drive you to Canada and then you can just disappear, but I can't be part of you turning yourself in."

"It's not that easy."

"It's real easy. I told you. Forget about Keller. You owe him nothing. You don't even know the damn guy. I tell you, it's suicide to turn yourself in."

"Atkins is running for president and has a good chance of winning."

"So what? Forget about Atkins and Keller, forget about all of them," Brian insisted. "Just go to Canada."

"I can't, I just can't, Brian." Jack said, shaking his head.

"Look, it's your life. I just don't want to see you on the street in a pool of blood."

"You know, when I was a kid, my parents took me to Florida to visit my aunt. My brother and I would go outside looking for things to do. I think I was probably ten years old and I could catch anything; frogs, fish, snakes, turtles, and even birds. But when I was in Florida there were these little black lizards and they were so fast and quick, no matter how hard I tried, I couldn't catch the little things. It was so frustrating, but I was determined to catch them. But everything has a weakness and, sure enough, I noticed one day, when it rained those little lizards dug into the bark of palm trees, an easy target for someone like me. Those little lizards, without knowing it, had trapped themselves with no way out; their quickness was neutralized and I must have caught twenty of them that day. Of course, I dropped them in my aunt's garage and she was really upset."

"So what's your point?"

"There might be a way to get Keller out and for me to get away."

Brian started laughing

"What's so funny?" Jack asked.

"Here's my take. Sometimes you need to know when to fold, take your winnings and leave the table. That's the difference between good gamblers and bad gamblers. Or, in your case, the difference between being dead or alive."

The day turned to night as they drove along I-94 west to Seattle. The conversation had died out hours ago. They were travelers on a journey, both thinking about what the future would bring. Brian was thinking about some fabulous island, while Jack was trying to figure out whether he was running out of luck or if he could make it all work out. He even considered whether it would be better to just turn himself in and end the chase.

They were somewhere on the outskirts of Bismarck, North Dakota as the hour was getting close to 10 PM; twelve hours of driving and it was time to call it a day. The gas tank was close to empty and they got off at the next exit.

After a couple of miles, they pulled into a well-lit, but deserted gas station that was getting ready to close. Brian went into the convenience store to pay while Jack grabbed the pump and began filling the tank. The moon was full and the sky was filled with stars, just like in Afghanistan on his last mission. Jack stared at the sky, thinking that at least he was far from the chaos of the battlefield.

While filling the tank, he turned his head towards a strange looking man sitting on a bench in front of the convenience store. He observed the man as he stamped out a cigarette and lit up another one. He couldn't help but recall the cigarette butts that he had found at the top of the hill overlooking the home of the missing couple in Massachusetts. He finished filling the tank and returned the gas handle to the pump as Brian came out of the store with his hands full of junk food.

They pulled out of the gas station. There were no other cars in sight. "I think we should drive another hour and call it a night," Brian said, rubbing his eyes.

"You okay driving another hour?"

"Yeah, look at all this junk food. I've got plenty of energy now."

"Where the hell are we now, Brian?"

"We are somewhere in North Dakota. Hey, you should have seen the girl behind the counter at the gas station. I was trying to signal you, but you were off in space."

"Was she the only one in there?"

"I don't know. I didn't see anyone else."

"Turn the car around."

"What?"

"Just turn the car around."

"Why?"

"My sixth sense is kicking in. The guy at the bench just didn't look right."

"You want me to go back because you saw a creep out front. It's probably her boyfriend." Brian slowed the car down and suddenly did a U-turn as the wheels bounced around the shoulder of the road. He drove two miles back the other way until they returned to a now closed gas station.

"Jack, you're killing me, you know that? Okay, the gas station is now closed. Nobody is here. Can we get back on the highway… now? I'm exhausted."

"Just catch up to the car that went by us the other way a few moments ago."

"So what do you want to do? Pull them over, draw our guns, and give them heart attacks or cause them to go off the road because you're looking for some deranged killer?"

"Just drive, Brian," Jack snapped.

Brian pushed the pedal to the metal; the car picked up speed until they were within a few car lengths of the other vehicle. "Okay Jack, what do you want to do now?"

"Can you tell the color of the car?"

"I could get closer, but it looks like a Ford Mustang, if that's any help."

"Just stay back, let me think. I don't want to overreact."

"You think. I don't feel like joy riding in North Dakota," Brian said, thinking how foolish this whole exercise was.

The car ahead slowed down and then turned left onto a dirt road. "What's the plan, Jack?"

"Just keep driving." After a few moments Jack ordered, "Stop." The road was deserted; the orange moon was displaying an unusual brightness. It was larger than normal and appeared as if it were almost touching the treetops. "Let's turn around and go down the dirt road where the car turned."

"You sure you want to do this?"

"I'm sure. Let's go, come on." Jack said. "Keep the headlights off."

The car slowly rolled along the bumpy dirt road for about a mile. The full moon gave them all the light needed to see where they were going. They had passed one house but kept going, looking for the Ford Mustang. As they approached a Cape-style house with the car lights off, Brian stopped the car. "This is crazy, Jack. Let's just go."

"No, we came this far. Just be quiet."

They got out of the car. Both Jack and Brian packed

MK25 9MM pistols. "Do you really think we need guns here?" Brian asked.

Jack said nothing as they approached the house; the lights were out, and a green Ford Mustang sat in the driveway. Jack went around back, while Brian stayed in front. *The guy just came home, why are the lights all out?* Jack thought. A small light glowed in the cellar; Jack pressed his face against the screen, trying to get a good look at what was in the cellar. He heard a door open at the top of the stairwell; and a dark figure walked slowly down the stairs and into the dim light. He walked to the far end of the cellar, Jack's eyes following him. Jack squinted, trying to catch what the man was doing and, there in the dim light a woman emerged, her left arm chained to a pole. The man stood over her and said a few words, which Jack couldn't hear, and then turned and went back upstairs. Jack's instincts had been right on the money. This guy was some sort of freak show.

Jack ran around to the front to find Brian. "Jack, what the hell are we doing here?" Brian sputtered.

"Brian, the guy is a psycho – he's holding a woman downstairs chained to a pole," Jack whispered.

"Are you kidding me?"

"Look, I'll go in through the cellar window and then go up the stairs from there."

Brian took out his 9mm handgun from his side holster and inserted a magazine. "Okay, I'm locked and loaded. I'll go through the front door. Now, I think we should take this guy alive; I'd hate for you to be wrong in your assessment."

"That's fine: remember I'm coming up the stairs, so don't confuse me with this freak."

"How long have I been doing this, Jack?"

"Okay, okay."

Jack ran around back and cut the screen of the cellar window and slid the glass pane to the side; it was just wide enough for him to slip through. His heart was racing, eyes intense, adrenaline pumping. It was just like a mission, except there was no Intel, no plan, and no layout schematics of the house. No idea what they were walking into.

He wedged his body through the window and fell awkwardly six feet down onto a pile of bags, which broke his fall. In the back of his mind he wondered what if this was all some crazy mistake, but that thought quickly passed when his hand pressed against one of the bags. It felt like a watermelon, he ripped it open and was shocked to see the bloody face of an elderly man. Then he ripped open a second bag and the head of an elderly woman rolled out. His insides almost came up on him; he gagged at the sight while his throat burned from stomach acid and his heart raced. Even after all he had seen in battle, he wasn't expecting anything like this. He was in some sort of house of horrors, run by some sicko who needed to be removed from the world.

He walked towards the light, his gun drawn. In the

shadows, he could see the young woman, chained, drugged, and in a trance-like state, too messed up to know what was happening.

He quickly turned towards the stairs and quietly started up. He wondered where Brian was in all this. *Did he realize what they were dealing with?* As he placed his foot on the second tread, two shots rang out on the floor above. The quietness of the night was broken. Jack immediately raced up the stairs and opened the stairwell door to the living room with his gun drawn. He scanned the area quickly, noticing another young woman bound and gagged on a sofa.

Then Brian's voice shattered the air: "He just went out the kitchen door."

Jack raced to the kitchen and yelled over his shoulder as he went out the door. "Stay here, Brian, I'll track him down."

Jack jumped over the back steps, landing on his feet all in one motion. He caught sight of the man just as he was entering the woods. The full moon radiated a spectrum of light through the trees, giving him a view of what was ahead. Jack raced into the woods, keeping himself low to the ground with two hands on his gun. He scurried in a southerly direction, stopping at ten-second intervals, his eyes peering in all directions, his ears tuned to the slightest sound. He stood in a crouched position and, within seconds of hearing branches break, the man from the house lunged at him with a large gleaming knife.

Jack, with a quick reflex, turned and upended his advance, flipping him to the ground. The man was stunned, lying in a pool of leaves and dead branches, trying desperately to find his knife. Jack stepped on his arm and crouched down, pointing his gun to the man's head.

"Let's go," Jack said angrily, pulling the man up by the collar and pushing him forward in front of him. They emerged from the woods and walked back towards the house; Brian waited by the kitchen door and greeted Jack with a wide grin.

"What are we going to do with this sick freak?" Brian asked, grabbing the guy by the throat and then pushing him forward through the kitchen door and throwing him face first onto the kitchen floor.

"I'm not sure yet. It would sure be easy to put a bullet in him and save everybody the aggravation of this scum ever walking the earth again," Jack said, as he entered the kitchen, waving his gun at the man on the floor. In the light, it became unmistakably clear who this man was. *This is impossible*, Jack thought. But it wasn't, this was the same man he had seen in the coffee shop in Williamstown. He was also the same man whose pictures were in the Indiana newspaper. These two women were knocking on death's door and they were rescued by a force greater than could ever be understood or explained.

Brian stepped into the living room and untied the young woman on the sofa and removed the gag out of her mouth. She was disoriented and appeared to be in a drug-induced stupor. She was the girl from behind the counter at the gas station. He recalled her warm smile and friendly demeanor at the counter, probably too naïve to know when to turn it off. And choosing to work at a secluded gas station at night wasn't a great idea either.

While the young woman tried to gather her senses, sitting upright, still in a groggy state, Brian went and got her a glass of water. He then did a quick search around the house and found a bag full of zip ties, along with a collection of pills - most likely used to knock out his victims. He also found masking tape, knives, a Colt 45 handgun, handcuffs, and other deadly utensils and chemicals that only a psycho would have in his possession. Brian grabbed the handcuffs and walked into the kitchen where Jack had his eye on the monster lying on the floor.

Brian knelt down and handcuffed him. "What do you want to do with this piece of crap," he asked.

"First, you need to go downstairs to the cellar, unchain the girl down there and bring her up here," Jack advised.

"I'm confused; you're telling me there's another girl downstairs."

"Yeah, I guess you weren't listening. There are also at least two dead bodies in the far end of the cellar."

"What? Who are they?"

"I'm guessing that they're the owners of the house."

"Is that so, asshole?" Brian asked, looking at the man on the floor, who smirked but said nothing while staring at the two imposing figures above him.

"Where's the key to the lock on the chain?" Jack snarled at the killer.

He just pointed to the counter. Jack looked over and grabbed the key lying on the back of the stove and handed it to Brian.

Brian headed towards the cellar door while Jack leaned his back against the counter, keeping his eyes on the killer, and pointing the gun at him. "You killed the couple in Massachusetts, didn't you?"

There was no reply, just a sneering grin.

After a few minutes, Brian emerged from the cellar, helping the other young woman maintain her footing. She was in the same drug-induced stupor as the girl in the living room. Brian led her to the couch and seated her next to the other girl.

"Jack, what the hell do you want to do with this guy?" he hollered from the living room as he walked into the kitchen. "He's a real sicko, Jack." Brian stared at their prisoner intensely. "Let's just put a bullet in his head and get these girls to the authorities."

Jack paced the kitchen, trying to figure out what to do with the deranged killer. "Um… Brian, take the girls back to the gas station and call the police," he directed.

"What about you?"

"You just call the police as you leave the gas station and come back and pick me up."

"What about him?"

"I haven't decided what I'm going to do with him yet," Jack admitted, pondering his next move. "Let's bring him to the cellar and chain him up."

"Alright. Get up," Brian snapped, jerking the man up from his sitting position, his hands tightly secured by handcuffs.

Brian pushed him towards the cellar door, his gun drawn, keeping him in front and not taking his eyes off of him. They entered the stairwell, and marched down the stairs. When they reached the bottom, Brian pushed the man onto the bed, grabbed the chain and clamped the metal ring around his leg. "So now what?" Brian asked.

"Take the girls back to the gas station and then come back and pick me up before the police get here."

"Okay, I'll see you in a bit." Brian headed upstairs and, within a few minutes, he was gone.

Jack sat there in a run-down chair opposite the killer. The man had said nothing, continuing to display the blank stare and the sneering grin.

Then, in the quietness, the killer broke his silence. "I know who you are," he said, sitting up against the backboard of the bed with his legs crossed and his handcuffed hands in his lap staring back at Jack.

Jack said nothing; he had no intention of getting into

289

a conversation with this psycho.

"You killed those two college guys because they killed your sister, right? I read all about it," the killer laughed sickly. "You took the headlines away from me."

Jack tried to hold back from saying anything, but he couldn't. "What's so funny?"

"We are both alike, you know?"

Jack smirked disgustedly and shook his head. "We are nothing alike; that's for sure."

"We really are, Jack. I'll bet you've killed more people than I ever have."

Jack found himself getting sucked into a conversation with this monster and curiosity began to get the best of him. *What made this guy tick? Why did he do these horrible things?* he asked himself.

"Everybody I've killed had it coming. You, on the other hand, killed innocent people for fun or whatever your sick mind drew up – there's a huge difference – you really need psychological help."

"Okay, you think what you want. You know, I was in the army for a little while and got discharged."

"Good for you. I can see why you got discharged."

"Yeah, I've never fit in anywhere my whole life. I don't belong here. I was always considered a weirdo, a loner, you know. And, as I got older, I just got these urges, and with it came power. It's funny how people treat you when you have the power. All these people I killed wanted to be my friend, pleaded for their lives, would do anything for me. Funny how that works."

"I don't want to hear how your sick mind works," Jack cracked.

"I want to make a deal with you."

"What type of deal?"

"I want you to shoot me, end my life. In return, I'll give you the list of places where you can find all my victims. "

Jack got up from the chair, looked around, and noticed a pen and piece of paper on an old coffee table. "Start writing," he ordered.

"Can you take off the handcuffs?"

"No, do the best you can."

"You know, you probably don't think I believe in God, but I do now. I never did until I grabbed the girl from Indiana. Her damn faith; I was going to kill her, but I never could at least not until I proved my point."

"What do you mean by that? Hey, don't stop writing."

"I was going to kill her like all the others, but she prayed and prayed. So I told her, 'Hey, honey, no one is coming for you; there is no God.' That's what I told her. So I said I'd give her four days, just to prove my point. And look who shows up here – you, of all people. The chances of us crossing paths were almost impossible. You were sent by God to save her. There is no other explanation. Now, I want to be forgiven for all my sins. You see, if I didn't go out tonight, we wouldn't have crossed paths. But I'm curious, how did you know?"

"Keep writing." Jack got up and paced the floor, he was anxious to be far away from this scene. "How did I know? Well, you're a chain smoker, right?"

"How do you know that?"

"You were on top of the hill, chain smoking away the night you killed that couple in Massachusetts. And you were doing the same at the gas station."

"Wow, you're good, Jack; you really are good. God sent you; that's the only reason you're here. Think about it, if your sister never got killed, we never would have crossed paths."

"How's the list coming? I don't have much time and neither do you."

"I hope that means you're going to carry out our agreement."

"That's the chance you'll have to take."

"Let me tell you something, Jack. This is how it's going to work in the court system. I'm going to plead insanity and, with my history, they are going to commit me to some psych ward. They'll have me working with some state psychiatrists who think they can rehabilitate me and, after ten years, somebody is going to feel confident that I can go back into society as long as I take my meds and it will start all over again. And, if you're still around, you'll be wishing you ended it right here."

Jack plopped down on the worn-out chair, thoughts racing. *This guy should never go back into society. I can't dismiss the thought that he is right. He is smart enough to manipulate the shrinks; he would be on his best behavior; he would learn to smile at the right time, be polite, never show a fit of anger, play his cards close to the vest and someone would buy it and it would start all over again.* Jack saw the black hole in the man's soul. And, he thought, these two girls that this guy didn't get around to were his sister's age.

Jack's phone buzzed, and he answered it. "I'll be there in two minutes," Brian said.

Jack hung up. "You almost done," he asked as the man kept writing.

"Just about," he replied.

A minute later he handed the piece of paper to Jack. He looked down at the list of fifteen people, killed in twelve different states. He paused, digesting what he had received, thinking how the FBI hadn't even gotten close to this guy. Some of the people might never have been missed, while family members of the others would spend their lives wondering and grieving. "Did you put all of them on the list?" Jack asked.

"Sometimes I get confused, but I think I got it all," he boasted. "Now, remember our deal."

Brian drove up to the house and was about to get out of the car and finish the job himself when he heard a pop and saw a flash from the basement. A few seconds later, Jack emerged from the house and quickly opened the passenger-side door and jumped in.

Brian accelerated and drove at a high rate of speed onto the main road. It wasn't long after that, the quiet, little dirt road was lit up like a Christmas tree and a small army of criminal investigators were combing every inch of the Cape-style house.

Chapter 35

Driving along I-90 west the next day, somewhere in Washington State, three hundred miles east of Seattle, the conversation had gone stale. The sun was setting behind the treetops. Brian, still behind the wheel, was exhausted.

Jack's gaze followed the spectacular orange-colored remnants of the setting sun while he thought about his agreement with Aaron Greenberg. In six days, he would be put back behind bars for the rest of his life. He had called Aaron Greenberg a day ago on his prepaid cell phone to confirm the deal. Greenberg informed him that they had agreed to Keller's release based on Jack's capture or in the event of his death at the scene. He explained that it was a pretty easy negotiation.

Nobody gives in on anything unless there's a bigger benefit to him or her, Jack mused. Yeah, there was pressure to bring him in, but maybe there was more. They didn't care about Keller. They wanted Jack Bolton, preferably dead. Agent Ryland probably had the pressure of the world on him, but he was just a pawn being used by the people in charge. Actually, he was just as expendable as any soldier who served in the armed forces.

Jack had been to a few ceremonies for fallen soldiers. The politicians' speeches were always the same, in one way or another. They talked about the courage and heroism of the fallen soldier. But how many times were the missions just a political maneuver, and the soldiers just pawns? Not to mention the idea of fighting a war where they couldn't engage the enemy unless they were shot at first, which was ridiculous in itself. How many times were they told to stand down? Who were the winners in all this? It surely wasn't the soldiers. Nothing had been learned from Vietnam, and how could a war continue if there was no real objective. And surely Iraq and Afghanistan fit into that category, which Commander Armstrong reiterated in a rant on that dark day in Afghanistan.

Brian rubbed his eyes. The miles of driving were adding up.

"You getting tired, Brian?" Jack asked. "You want me to take over?"

"I'm fine. I think another thirty minutes or so and we'll call it quits."

"Sounds good to me."

"I need a drink. I've never done so much driving," Brian said with a chuckle.

"I was thinking about some of the soldiers who fought in World War II or the Korean War."

"What about them?" Brian asked, keeping his eyes on the road.

Jack just played out his thoughts. "You know, some of these guys survived situations under the most hostile conditions. They saw their buddies die right in front of them. In some cases, after a moment of casual conversation, each of them telling the other about their future dreams, maybe they talked about their girlfriends, their family, and their life aspirations."

"And what's your point?" Brian said, sensing that Jack was feeling the pressure.

"Well, think about all the horrible memories, and in some cases under impossible odds, and they survived. Can you imagine what it must have been like to storm Normandy Beach in World War II with all that lead coming at you and then to survive in one piece?" Jack said without expecting an answer.

"That had to be hell."

"These Army vets survived all this madness. Then you read about one of them getting hit by a car or getting killed in some other mundane way," Jack said. "Don't you find that strange?"

"I've never thought of it that way," Brian said, staring at the road ahead. "Where do you come up with this stuff?"

"I don't know," he said, glancing out the window. "I was just thinking about my brother, my sister, my parents, Joe, Oscar, and the day Rob got blown up by an IED right in front of me. It should have been me, but Rob, for whatever reason, jumped ahead of me and

297

stepped on that IED and took the fatal blast. Or the time I got captured by Al-Qaeda and they beat me senseless for a week and then just decided to let me go."

"Well, if you die by getting hit by a car in your old age, then I guess you can consider your life a success."

"I guess that would depend on what demons you're carrying."

"Yeah, but you need to focus on the task at hand and start thinking about yourself or you are never going to have to worry about getting hit by a car in your old age," Brian reasoned.

"So I'm thinking you're adamantly against me turning myself in."

"You know where I stand on that," Brian said, rolling his eyes.

"So what do you think is in that safe deposit box?" Jack asked.

"I haven't given it too much thought. I really don't want to think about it. I just want to go to an island and forget about this world."

The car headlights illuminated the deserted road in front of them as Brian drove.

"Another twenty minutes of driving, you think?" Jack suggested.

"Yeah."

As the conversation between the two of them dried up, flashing blue lights lit up the rear of the car. Brian glanced in the rearview mirror, "Oh, shit."

Jack turned his head, "We have a state cop behind us."

"No kidding; I'll handle this," Brian said decisively.

Brian slowly pulled the car into the breakdown lane and rolled to a stop. The cruiser stopped behind them. The trooper emerged from the patrol car. He appeared larger than life in his standard French blue uniform and royal blue campaign hat as he approached the car. His shadow was immense from the glaring headlights of the patrol car. He walked slowly and cautiously to the rear of the car, stopping at the side to peer into the rear window.

"License and registration," the trooper said in a deep voice as he stood alongside the driver's window

Brian fumbled in his wallet, looking for his license. Jack pillaged the glove box for the registration.

"Officer, any reason why you're pulling us over?" Brian asked. "I was going the speed limit."

"Your back taillight is out," the officer replied. "Now, where are you boys heading so far from Massachusetts?"

"My aunt's home outside of Seattle. She's dying of cancer." Brian tossed the fib off the top of his head while handing over his license.

The officer glanced at the license. "So Brian Butler, where's the registration?"

"It's coming. We're still looking for it, officer," Brian said.

Jack was scrambling through the logjam of paper "I don't see it, Brian."

"I don't have all day," the officer said testily.

"I'll be right with you, officer." Brian grabbed the stack of documents from Jack. "It has to be here," he muttered.

"I'll be right back," the officer said and walked briskly to his patrol car. He paused abruptly as a 10-24 echoed off his shoulder mike. "Copy that." He ran back to Brian's car and handed him the driver's license. "It's your lucky day." Within seconds, the trooper sped off, with the siren blaring and blue lights flashing.

"That was damn close," Jack said tensely. "You have no registration with the car?"

"I thought I had it. It's in my mother's name anyway."

"Once he ran your license through, you know, it's possible you might have come up as a wanted man."

"I guess we'll never know that now," Brian said, shrugging his shoulders. He started the car and rolled out onto the open freeway. "I don't know about you, but I need a drink."

"You think that's a good idea?"

"Well, have you looked at your face in the mirror lately, Jack?" Brian said with a chuckle. "I'm thinking nobody is going to recognize you out here."

"Yeah, I guess."

Brian drove down the highway for another twenty

minutes, before taking the Spokane exit. They drove another few miles until they came to a cluster of shops and restaurants located on a main street. "That pub called O'Malley's looks as good as any," Brian said, pointing in the direction of a pub set among a group of small retail shops.

The evening sun had set. Brian eased the car into an empty parking spot in the rear of the building. They both got out of the car and Brian stretched his aching body.

Jack's face showed the results of the recent battering he had taken. The swelling had subsided but his face was still sore and the black-and-blue shiner gave him the look of a boxer who had lost a fight.

They walked together into the pub and found a couple of stools at the end of the bar, close to one of the small screen TVs overhead. The place was pretty busy, with waitresses scampering about carrying trays of drinks and food. The conversations were loud and boisterous. Music blared in the background.

Brian signaled to one of the bartenders, who came over to greet them. They ordered food, beer, and a couple of shots of O'Malley's best stuff. Jack kept a low profile, not wanting to draw attention to himself.

Brian was his usual outgoing self, making conversation with anybody who was interested. Jack just observed the people in the bar, while slinging back a whiskey shot in one gulp and chasing it with a beer. He watched the news on the flat screen TV in front of him.

CNN was recapturing the day's events and playing back the FBI press conference that was held earlier in the day in Bismarck, North Dakota. Jack asked the bartender to put up the volume. Brian, busy yacking it up with the townies, seemed oblivious to the news.

"The dead serial killer's name was Rex Saxton, a loner who went from state to state, picking his victims at random," the lead agent stated, with no further details. "We believe from the information we now have that he was involved in a series of murders."

Jack continued watching as the press conference continued, then leaned in to hear if the authorities would furnish any information about the two men who had saved the two young women. The authorities would surely go back and check video footage from the gas station, and Brian's face surely would be big as life on the video. *But would they be able to put the two of them together?* Jack rubbed a hand across his brow. Then again, maybe they would just keep it quiet.

He continued to listen and watch as the lead agent talked about a written list that was found at the house of possible locations of other victims. He talked about the deceased older couple found in the house. They had been married for fifty-two years and were part of the community for the last fifty, living in the same house where they were found. The reporters yelled out questions, and one asked if the agent had any idea who the two men were who had rescued the women. The FBI agent answered predictably, "We're working on it."

Brian got the bartender's attention and ordered a few more drinks for his new friends.

Jack nudged Brian in the back.

"What the hell?" Brian sputtered.

"Look what's on the screen."

Brian glanced at the screen. "Well, there's nothing to see. Even if they can identify us, they're not going to mention us. We're the bad guys in their eyes. They can't badmouth good guys in public."

"You think it's wise to draw attention to ourselves?"

"You know, Jack," he said in a low voice, leaning in. "You worry too much. Nobody here is going to recognize us. Loosen up, have some fun."

"Easy for you to say, Brian," he muttered.

The bartender delivered an array of drinks and placed them on the counter. Brian wasted no time passing out glasses to the rowdy group of revelers behind them. His *life of the party* persona had been turned on. He had the small crowd around him in stitches. He acted as if he had known them for years.

In battle, Brian was a cool character, unfazed by the mayhem around him. But one time that over-confidence worked against him on a mission in the Wardak Province in Afghanistan, a raging hellhole of insurgent activity. When Brian and a few other Navy SEALs were lured into an ambush to save a couple of young children in harm's way, disregarding orders to stand down, that stubbornness nearly cost him his life and the lives of the SEALs who followed. Good intentions that went terribly wrong. That act was the beginning of the end of his Navy SEAL career, even if he didn't realize it.

Jack was becoming amused by the situation. Here they were, sitting in some bar in Spokane, Washington, acting as if they were normal people with normal lives. If the patrons only knew who these two crazy guys at the end of the bar really were, the place would be surrounded by police. He smiled in a sad way to himself, shaking his head, as he reflected on the events of the past week. He'd been broken out of prison. He was nearly killed by a Mafia hit man. He shot a senator's son. He robbed a Mexican cartel. He returned a deceased former Navy SEAL to his dad. He made a deal with an attorney to enable the release from prison of a guy he had never met but who he thought was innocent. He survived an attempt on his life by henchmen of the government. He laundered nine million dollars in a triple A-rated, good old Midwestern bank. He ended a serial killer's rampage. And, through all of this, a massive manhunt for him was ongoing. Jack just shook his head and slugged another shot of whiskey to calm his nerves while Brian continued to captivate the bar patrons around him.

Brian, rising from his stool, continued to entertain while Jack sat off to the side. The alcohol was beginning to take its toll. He couldn't help but think how nice it would be to just go out with close friends, have a real job, a family, talk about current events, sports, or whatever came to mind. It was funny how the mind worked. Now, he just wanted to forget the past and move on to a calmer world, a place where he could live a normal life. And the more he thought about getting Jeff Keller out of prison, the more he thought about being free himself. The pressure was beginning to get to him.

Jack scanned the pub as if he were looking for hostiles, while Brian was unconcerned. He was having too much fun. Jack hoped he wouldn't start singing. If he did, they'd both be in trouble.

Brian's energy level was fading as the night wore on. The alcohol took over, and he finally sat down and took a break next to Jack, throwing his arm around him and shaking him like a lost teddy bear. "What's happening, buddy?" he said with a big grin.

Two plates of pub food consisting of big juicy hamburgers and thick flat fries were placed in front of them. They both dug in.

"You're wrecked, aren't you?" Jack said jokingly.

"I'm...just a little bit," he said, in between bites. "But you need to loosen up, Jack," he replied warmly, throwing his arm around him again.

"I'm a little nervous about giving myself up."

"Canada is just a few hours away, Jack. The hell with Keller," he spat.

"You keep saying that," Jack replied. Two more beers were delivered by the bartender and placed in front of them.

"That's great service," Brian said to the bartender, reaching into his wallet to pay for them. "I was thinking about another beer and here it is."

"They're paid for," the bartender replied.

Jack and Brian looked at each other when the guy sitting next to Brian on the left spoke up and said. "The beers are on me."

"Well, thanks," Brian said.

"My name is Chris Baron," he said, turning his chair toward them.

"How the hell are ya, Chris," Brian said with a smile and a handshake. "I'm Brian. This is my buddy, Jack."

Jack nodded, forcing a smile.

"You look like a regular," Brian said, looking at Chris.

"I come here all the time. I live just a few streets over. A nice easy walk," Chris said, staring straight ahead. "I know who you are, Jack."

Jack tensed. "I think you have me confused with someone else."

"I don't think so," Chris said. "Your last name is Bolton, right? It was pretty hard to tell at first because your face is a little beaten up, but there was something about you two, and then I overheard Brian mention that he's a former Navy SEAL. That's when it hit me who you were, Jack."

Brian's smile quickly disappeared.

"Hey, I'm not going to say anything," Chris said. "You know, I was a SEAL myself at one time."

"You were, huh?" Brian said with a smirk.

"Yeah, I don't care if you believe me or not. It really doesn't matter."

"Who was your commander? When did you serve? What team? Where did you train?" Jack bombarded the man with questions.

Chris downed a shot of whiskey and followed it with a swig of beer, staring straight ahead. "I was officially court martialed quietly about nine months ago. I didn't have to serve any time as long as I kept quiet. That was the deal. So the media never knew about it."

"Why all the secrecy, huh?" Brian asked, eyes narrowing in suspicion.

"Why would the media care that you got court martialed?" Jack added. "And you haven't answered any of my questions."

"Your questions don't really matter. Because nothing really matters, does it, Jack? I don't need to prove anything to you and I don't care to get an 'A' on your quiz."

"So, then, why were you court martialed?" Jack asked, looking at Brian with a roll of his eyes.

"You really want to know?" Chris asked with a small chuckle, putting the shot glass to his mouth and downing it.

"Yeah, we both do," Brian, said. Creases of doubt appeared on his forehead. He obviously agreed with Jack that Chris was just another wannabe SEAL telling stories. But they were forced to listen because the last thing they needed was a scene.

"About a year ago, there was a helicopter that was shot down over the Wardak Province."

"What about it?" Brian asked with a skeptical look.

"I should have been on it," Chris replied looking straight at each of them.

"Come on, Chris. Why the hell are you making up crap like this?" Brian said, tired of listening to bullshit from a stranger.

"You know, I don't care if either of you believe me." He leaned in, softening his tone. "Hell, I could have called the cops hours ago. There's a two hundred thousand dollar reward for your capture, Jack. So maybe you guys could give me a little courtesy and hear me out."

"You're right," Jack said warily. "Finish your story."

"Prior to taking off, I noticed we had no air support, which went against protocol. I know the Chinook is a sitting duck out there and it was only a matter of time before one of these things was going to get shot down over the Wardak Province. I looked around and figured something was out of sync, twenty-five SEALs sitting in a Chinook. I had never seen that before. Usually, we would be in smaller groups. Here we had twenty-five Navy SEALs sitting in this large helicopter used for transporting troops, not for special missions. My gut was screaming at me to get the hell out of there. And it didn't stop there. Command decides to switch out six members of the Afghan forces at the last minute. Most of the SEALs were checking their equipment. I was in a panic. I went to the lieutenant and told him I had a bad feeling and I didn't see any air support and asked about the change of Afghan troops at the last minute."

"What did he say?" Jack asked, still wondering if this guy had read the story from the Internet and was just a good bullshit artist.

"He said, sit down. I went back and sat down, but I didn't sit for long. I got up and went to the lieutenant again and told him I couldn't go and I didn't care what they did to me for refusing to go."

"What happened next?" Jack asked.

"Military police came aboard and escorted me off the helicopter. I remember sitting in the brig and then the news came that the Chinook was shot down. It was the worst day of my life. Most of those guys were my friends, and they were all gone. It was like a knife to the heart and I felt as though I betrayed them.

"I was court-martialed quietly, served six months in the brig, and was sent home with instructions to keep my mouth shut. Nobody knows I was on that helicopter except you guys."

"Well, that's a nice story, Chris," Brian said, finishing his last bite.

"I believe you, Chris," Jack said sincerely. "You must have an opinion of why it happened."

"You want to know why it happened, Jack?" Chris paused, belting down another shot and turning toward Jack. "It was payback for the Bin Laden raid and I'm going to leave it at that."

Jack kept his opinion to himself, but his thoughts were the same as Chris's. Somebody had sold out the SEALs. He gazed intently at Chris and saw a man tormented by the events of that day. "Let's have a toast to a better future," Jack said. The three men banged their bottles and raised them to their lips for one big swig.

Chapter 36

The surveillance on the Cap residence had never completely ended, even with the deaths of George and Joe Cap. The high priority status was now downgraded to low by the NSA in Maryland. After months of surveillance, nothing had been uncovered that warranted further investigation. The fear of George Cap leaking incriminating information about Gus Banner's Phoenix Project seemed to be fading fast as the weeks went by.

George Cap had gone to his grave without a chance to tell his story or bring down the people at the top of Banner's inner circle. Gus Banner's years of experience had trained him to always be prepared for the unexpected, even if it meant wasted man-hours and resources.

An NSA technician by the name of Wendell Smart stepped into his small cubicle. He was a recent college graduate who majored in computer science and he surely looked the part with his coke-bottle glasses and a real zest for computer games. He still lived at home with his parents. He was low man on the totem pole with bottom-of-the-rung clearance, and he worked the late-night shift.

Wendell's job consisted of data mining flagged individuals from the Internet cesspool, which was basically analyzing data from different perspectives and summarizing it into useful information for the CIA. He secretly reviewed phone conversations, scanned the Internet, read emails, tweets and any other garbage he came across relating to an assigned list of people. He never knew why, and he never asked - not that he would be told why these people were under surveillance. He just did his job, day in and day out. In fact, he never even knew if any of the information he uncovered actually made a difference. He just passed it on to his superiors. Nobody ever came by and patted him on the back and said "Great job, Wendell." But he liked the thought that maybe his nightly searches of data stopped the bad guys.

Tonight, he was going down the list of his assigned clientele, as he liked to call it. Nothing seemed to jump out at him until he came to the Cap file. He did the daily routine search. As usual, there was nothing on the Internet, not even any emails or tweets. These people didn't even use the Internet, which sure was smart, especially if they feared that somebody might be monitoring them. Wendell sometimes wondered who they were and what they did to get on his special clientele list. That made him wonder if there was another group of people monitoring him. Of course, watching him living at home with his parents and playing hours of video games sure would bore anyone to death.

He leaned back in his chair and grabbed his usual snack of peanut butter crackers, rinsing it down with a six-ounce carton of milk. In the next part of his job, he got to listen to phone calls, which he considered to be the best part. Much of the drama that was part of people's daily lives was revealed in their phone calls. They were always complaining about their problems and their ailments. Some were having secret affairs. So many soap operas, Wendell thought. He listened to one call where the guy was hiring someone to kill his wife for the insurance money. It was pretty crazy. He reported it but never knew what happened.

He wiped bits of peanut butter from his lips, adjusted his ear set, and began listening to the phone calls. The Cap phone calls were few and non-eventful. But there was one strange call that came in from Multibank of Washington. The bank called looking for a payment for George Cap's safe deposit box. George had used his father's address when he set up the box. Carl Cap explained that his son had passed away. The bank employee explained that they would need to put a freeze on the safe deposit box until they got letters of administration from the courts. Wendell wrote it all down and passed the information on to his superiors. He had no idea what he had just discovered. He went on to the next person on his list.

***

Gus Banner walked into his office around 8 a.m.
Before he had a chance to sip his coffee, a package was
delivered to him from the NSA. He opened it while
sitting at his desk. The George Cap file slid out. He
flipped open the vanilla folder and scanned the contents
with burning eyes. The document, which would appear
harmless to most people, was setting off alarms in his
head.

He got up from his desk and paced around the office,
not sure what to do. Maybe this wasn't a problem after
all. Perhaps he was overreacting. But there was
something strange about this. What was George Cap
doing with a safe deposit box in Washington State when
his main residence was in Virginia? And, ironically, the
bank was across the street from the main office of First
Rate Bank of Washington, which was also Sam Atkins
brother's bank, a player in the secretive foreign cash
transaction. He needed to act immediately and resolve
this issue quickly.

He pushed a few buttons on his smartphone, put the
phone to his ear, and gave a team of two CIA associates
their marching orders. They were to take a private jet to
Seattle immediately, visit the downtown Multibank
office, and return with the contents of George Cap's safe
deposit box. They would do whatever it took to get
access to the box, whether it meant showing a forged
search warrant or using the Patriot Act to confiscate it

under the guise of national security. Of course, there was no law on the books that gave them the authority to use the Patriot Act to search a person's safe deposit box. However, Gus fully expected that they would report back in seven hours that the contents of the safe deposit box had been secured.

Chapter 37

The early morning sun broke through the gap in the motel curtains, waking Brian. Jack was already awake, dressed, and ready to go. He had been up for an hour, unable to sleep. While he waited for Brian to get ready, he drank his homemade brew of morning coffee and shook the cobwebs from his head. He sat looking out the window, contemplating his future. He was tired of being on the run, looking over his shoulder, and wondering if this was the day he would be caught or shot.

"Let's get on the road, Brian," Jack said. "We've got a four- hour drive ahead of us."

"Hold your horses," Brian snapped, throwing on his jeans and combing his hair back. "What's the rush?"

"I'm anxious to find out what's in George Cap's safe deposit box."

Brian had gotten himself together and finally was ready. He was a little hung over from the night before but ready to roll. They both got in the car, with Jack taking the wheel, and left Spokane around 7 a.m., heading west on I-90, a two-lane highway.

As Jack drove, he was surprised by the similarities in terrain between Afghanistan and eastern Washington State. At least it appeared that way, the same flat land

and miles of sand. "Hell, this looks like Afghanistan in places, a barren desert," he remarked.

Brian, slumping and nodding off at times, suddenly sat up straight. "Well, thank God it isn't. But don't worry, as we get closer to Seattle, the weather will be downright crappy with plenty of trees to make up for all this barren land."

"Thanks for the update, Brian." Jack said, taking a sip from his coffee.

"Hey, we never really talked about the other night, that serial killer." Brian said, looking out the window.

"What about him?"

"Well…I'm just curious. What made you shoot him?"

"You really want to know?"

"Yeah." Brian asked, turning his head, waiting for an answer.

"He talked me into it, but he was right." Jack paused for a moment and took another sip of coffee. "He said he would plead insanity and that eventually the court system would let him out and he would do it all over again."

"Well, if it makes you feel any better, if you didn't do it, I was going to," Brian said calmly.

Jack just shook his head. He couldn't help but chuckle at their situation.

"What's so funny, Jack?"

"Us," he said. "Me and you. I just realized it's like

we are still in Afghanistan. Except we're just two partners in crime, driving across America, with three million dollars each to our names. The world wants us dead or in custody and we're taking the law into our own hands."

Brian sat staring ahead and started to laugh. "I see your point. You know, you might be onto something. We should be able to sue the government for our actions. They created us. It's their fault. We need some counseling or maybe some therapy," he said, choking on his laughter while Jack joined in. After the humor of the moment died out, the conversation faded and their minds wandered back to their own internal demons.

***

After four hours of driving, falling rain and gray clouds filled the sky. Brian was right with his forecast. The desert now had become the rainforest. The car splashed through the mist and puddles, stopping at a roadside motel ten miles outside of Seattle. They unloaded their gear. The dreary conditions made them just want to forget about the day, but there was one big task that needed to be settled. What was in George Cap's safe deposit box that might have cost him his life?

Once the car was unpacked, they got back into the vehicle and found a local place to eat. They entered the establishment and settled into their chairs as the hostess left a pair of menus at their table. Jack went over the plan to access George Cap's safe deposit box. Jack had barely digested his food when Brian needed to ask him about the plan again.

"Can you go over the plan just one more time, Jack?" he repeated for the second time, in between swigs of water. He played with the crumbs on his plate.

"I knew you weren't listening. You were too busy checking out the waitresses and stuffing food into your face," Jack said, a little annoyed. "You need to take this seriously, Brian."

"Okay, okay. I get it. I'm sorry. Go ahead."

"All right. The bank is located at 1201 Third Avenue in downtown Seattle. Now, you'll park the car about two blocks from the bank and wait for me to return. I'll go in as a new customer, looking to open a safe deposit box. While being shown the safe deposit area, I will order the manager, by force if necessary, to accompany me to George Cap's safe deposit box. I'll put in the key, grab the contents in the box, and then force the manager to his office, close the door, duct tape his month, and handcuff him to something sturdy. Then I'll be on my way."

"Sounds like a plan, Jack," he said, leaning on his elbow to pick his teeth.

"It shouldn't be hard."

"What about security?" Brian asked.

"I'll do a little due diligence before I apply for a safe

deposit box. I don't think we have to worry about security. It will work out fine."

"Let's do this," Brian said.

They got up from the table, left cash to cover the bill and the tip, and headed out the door.

It was 12:50 p.m. They were ten minutes away from the bank as they drove through the Battery Street Tunnel north, following the GPS. Brian slowly pulled off to an empty parking spot on a side street, a block and half from the bank. "You okay to do this?" Brian asked, studying the street around them.

"Well, after this last week, I'm prepared for anything." Jack looked at Brian with absolute confidence.

"I hope it's all worth it." Brian said with a smile.

"Yeah, me too. Now, if I'm not out in fifteen minutes, you should leave and I'll meet you at the McDonalds down the road."

"I'm not leaving," Brian said, his voice raised. "If you're not out in fifteen minutes, I'm going in."

"Okay." Jack packed his MK25 handgun, lifted the door handle and got out of the car. He signaled a thumbs up and closed the car door as the drizzle continued to fall. He was wearing a nondescript gray sweat jacket with dungaree pants and a funny looking baseball cap to hide his face. He tucked the handcuffs into his sweat jacket left pocket and stuffed a plastic bag and duct tape into his right pocket. He strode north for thirty yards, turned onto First Avenue to walk west. In another fifty yards, he was in front of Multibank. He walked in as if he did it every day, but he felt more like a bank robber than a customer.

He casually looked around and checked the colorful retirement brochures. The bank was quiet, foot traffic was light, and a couple of tellers sat up front at the cashier windows, bored from lack of business. He calmly walked over to a receptionist sitting at a corner desk. She greeted him with a smile. He told her that he would like to open a safe deposit box. She immediately got up from her desk and grabbed the manager.

"Can I help you?" asked the friendly manager as he walked over to greet him.

"I would like to open a safe deposit box."

"Sure, are you a customer?" he asked.

"No."

"Okay, I'll just need you to fill out some paperwork. How about following me over to my office?"

As he followed the manager, he asked, "Can I see where the safe deposit boxes are located and what they look like?"

"Sure. Follow me," the manager replied. He led Jack through a side door to a room lined with safe deposit boxes on each side. They stood in the center of the room admiring the rows of safe deposit boxes.

"Now, don't worry," he said boastfully. "We've never had anyone's safe deposit box broken into. If you lose your key, you will need a locksmith to get into it. The bank doesn't have access to the box. So don't worry about an inside job." The bank manager chuckled, while Jack just smiled and nodded.

"There's a yearly fee, which can be paid quarterly," he continued. "The boxes are all numbered and that coincides with your name on the bank records. So, when we give you a key for your box, the number is specified on the key to match the box. As you can see, the numbers start at the low end on this side and the high numbers are on the other side," he said, pointing to the wall of boxes.

Jack walked around the room until he came to box 242. His heart pounded and his mouth went dry. The moment had come. "I'm sorry I have to do this," Jack said. He pulled the gun out of his side pocket and grabbed the manager with one hand while holding the gun close to the man's head.

"What are you doing?" the manager said choking.

"Just do what I say and you won't get hurt." He pulled the manager close and took out the key to Cap's box. He slid the key in and pulled the box out, keeping one eye on the manager. He set the box on the table. It was almost empty, except for two small USB Flash Drives. Jack quickly put both drives in his sweat jacket side pocket and realized he could just handcuff the guy right here, which would be easier than going to his office.

"Sit in the chair," he ordered.

"I have two young kids," the manager pleaded nervously.

"Just keep your mouth shut and I'll be gone, and you can go on with your life." He took the handcuffs from his side pocket.

"What are you doing?"

"Get out of the chair," he demanded, then yanked the manager to the floor. "I need to handcuff you to the heating pipe running along the back of the wall."

Jack didn't have time to be gentle. He needed to get the hell out of there. He had almost completed his task when two men in trench coats entered the bank, looking for exactly what Jack had just put in his pocket.

Jack finished handcuffing the manager, took a small roll of duct tape out of his pocket, ripped off a piece, and planted it firmly over the manager's mouth. "Sorry, but I think you need to change your security procedures," he said, and exited the room.

He peeked quickly around the corner. A rush of adrenaline pumped through his body. From the corner of his eye, he noticed two men wearing trench coats, who were talking to the receptionist at the corner desk. They weren't customers, and they surely weren't cops from any world he knew. There was something about men who worked under the radar, fighting in secret wars or on the front lines of terrorism or bringing down third-world dictators all in the name of democracy. Whether it was Special Forces or CIA, it was as if they gave off some type of signal. These government henchmen were there for the same reason that he was, but he had beaten them to the punch.

Both men followed the receptionist. Jack clutched his gun as the eyes of one of them locked on him. He had walked past them when a woman's voice rang out, "Sir, sir, you dropped something."

Jack turned back, looked at the henchmen, and then glanced at the floor, noticing one of the flash drives. He bent over and picked it up. "Thanks," he replied, as one of the henchmen opened the door to the safe deposit room.

Jack scurried out the front door of the bank. He heard something behind him, looked back for a quick second, and caught a glimpse of the two henchmen running out of the building in hot pursuit. Jack accelerated from a slow trot to a sprint down Main Street. He turned the corner in a full dash. Brian was clambering from the car as Jack approached on full throttle, with two guys sprinting after him.

Jack hollered, "Brian, get back in the damn car!"

Brian slid back into the driver's seat and started the car. Two seconds later, Jack jumped in and pulled out his gun. The two henchmen were only a short distance behind. Brian hit the gas and the car peeled out into the open traffic.

***

Gus sat in his office, waiting for the men to report that the safe deposit box had been secured. His smartphone buzzed. It was the call he was waiting for. He listened as they explained what happened and then slammed the phone down on the desk, breaking it into a million pieces. He looked out the window from his office, exhaling deeply. He had a big problem now. It was time to take the gloves off. Jack Bolton had become enemy number one. Whatever was on the flash drives could be damaging information, not only to him, but also to anyone connected to it, including Senator Atkins.

Gus pulled himself together and sat down at his desk. With a few keystrokes, he brought up the Jack Bolton file. While reviewing it, he came across the latest file report and was amazed to discover that Jack Bolton was turning himself in - five days from today at "The Cup of Joes" in downtown Seattle. He smiled wryly and shook his head. He couldn't believe his good fortune.

Studying the agreement, Gus noted that Bolton was doing it for Jeff Keller, which was strange anyway he looked at it. Bolton was giving himself up for Keller - such a gentlemanly thing to do - because he thought Keller had gotten a raw deal and the Senator somehow was behind Keller rotting in jail.

Gus's mind was working overtime. The world had no place for guys like Jack Bolton. Their values and ethics couldn't be controlled. They marched to their own drummer, doing what they thought was right. He leaned back in his chair and began to develop a plan. He sat forward to study Bolton's file more closely. The Mafia wanted him dead. This would be perfect. If it failed, he would make sure that one of his own men was there to finish the job. He just needed Bolton to fulfill his end of the bargain and not get cold feet.

Chapter 38

Sam Atkins paused, waiting for his cue to take the podium. He had been invited to be the guest speaker at a Democratic National Committee fundraiser held at the Pearl Function Hall in downtown Washington D.C. It was the beginning of his run for president. He was the outright favorite to win the Democratic nomination.

He walked to the podium as a rowdy crowd of Democratic committee members, donors, and campaign workers gave him a standing ovation. The crowd settled back into their chairs around circular tables covered in white, satin-edged tablecloths. Waiters and waitresses wearing black slacks and white shirts went about their business, serving food and drink to the enthusiastic, hard-core, Democratic Party supporters.

Sam adjusted the height of the microphone to meet his six-foot frame. This was the beginning of his ride to the presidency and, today, he was in the friendliest of camps. They would clap at every statement, cheer whatever he said, and nod their heads in agreement. But the best part was that they would donate to his campaign without hesitation.

After the applause died down, Senator Atkins took a sip of water and looked out at the two hundred or so supporters, each confident he could change the world. They couldn't see his flaws. His womanizing and ruthless ways were under lock and key. He was a man of great wisdom, ready to bring America back to greatness. That was what his supporters wanted to believe, and Senator Atkins would not disappoint. In fact, it really didn't matter what programs or statements he advocated. All that mattered was that people believed. He knew it was all about saying whatever he needed to say in order to get elected.

He extended his arms wide and opened his hands. "Fellow Americans, let me begin by saying we have an opportunity before us today to make our country great again, and I have a plan to make that happen."

Loud and thunderous applause followed.

"Profound and powerful forces are shaking and remaking our world, and the urgent question of our time is whether we can continue to make those changes to keep us number one in the world. This new world has already enriched the lives of Americans who are able to compete and win in it. But when most people are working harder for less, when others cannot work at all, when the cost of health care devastates families and threatens to bankrupt many of our enterprises, great and small, when fear of crime robs law-abiding citizens of their freedom, and when millions of poor children cannot even imagine the lives we are calling them to lead, we have not made change our friend.

"We know we have to face hard truths and take strong steps. But we have not done so. Instead, we have drifted, and that drifting has eroded our resources, fractured our economy, and shaken our confidence.

"Though our challenges are fearsome, so are our strengths. Americans have ever been a restless, questing, hopeful people. Our goal must be to bring the vision and will of those who came before us to today and to those who will come after. From our country's great beginning to struggles like the Great Depression and the yearning for equality, our people have always mustered the determination to construct the pillars of our history from these crises.

"Thomas Jefferson believed that to preserve the very foundations of our nation, we would need dramatic change from time to time. Well, my fellow Democrats, this is our time. Let us embrace it. Our democracy must not only be the envy of the world but the engine of our own renewal. There is nothing wrong with America that cannot be cured by what is right with America. And so today, we pledge an end to the era of deadlock and drift. A new season of American renewal has begun. To revitalize America, we must be bold. We must invest more in our own people, in their jobs, in their future and, at the same time, cut our massive debt. And we must do so in a world in which we must compete for every opportunity. It will not be easy. It will require sacrifice. But it can be done and done fairly, not by choosing sacrifice for *its* own sake, but by choosing it for *our* own sake.

"We must provide for our nation the way a family provides for its children. Our great forefathers saw themselves in the light of posterity. We can do no less. Anyone who has ever watched a child drift into sleep knows what our future must hold. Our children are the world to come, the world for whom we hold our ideals, from whom we have borrowed our planet, and to whom we bear sacred responsibility.

"We must do what America does best: Offer more opportunity to all and demand more responsibility from those who have shirked their duties for far too long. It is time to break the bad habit of expecting something for nothing, from our government or from each other. Let us all take more responsibility, not only for ourselves and our families but for our communities and our country.

"To renew America, we must revitalize our democracy. This beautiful capital, like every capital since the dawn of civilization, is often a place of intrigue and calculation. Powerful people maneuver for position and worry endlessly about who is in and who is out, about who is up and forgetting about who is down, forgetting those people whose toil and sweat sends us here and pays our way. Americans deserve better, and, in this city today, there are people who want to do better. And so I say to all of us here, let us resolve to reform our politics so that power and privilege no longer cloud out the voice of the people. Let us put aside personal advantage so that we can feel the pain and see the promise of America. Let us resolve to make our government a place for what Franklin Roosevelt called 'bold, persistent experimentation,' a government for our tomorrows, not our yesterdays."

The crowd rose to their feet, clapping and cheering.

Senator Atkins smiled at the response and waited for the audience to be seated. He continued, "I propose that we begin in our most depressed cities by rejuvenating them through what I call 'economic zones,' where corporations will be enticed to create jobs by paying lower wages to employees, who in return will get government subsidized housing and healthcare."

The crowd roared their approval.

"I believe the time has come to revamp our educational system, which is stuck from policies created six decades ago. It's time to bring our education system into the twenty-first century by installing computer software and Internet learning programs in our schools, along with a push for higher competency in English and practical math and consumer law courses that our students can understand and use in everyday life."

His supporters nodded in agreement.

He was on a roll. "Good paying jobs will allow our young citizens the ability to start their own families, which, in turn, drives the real estate market, creating jobs and a stronger economy. Now, another way of creating jobs is to reduce the tax rate to zero for manufacturing corporations who keep eighty percent of their jobs in America.

"We also need to cut down the inner city violence that plagues our cities, and the best way to do this is to get our youth to understand the importance of education and how this is a way out of poverty. Knowledge is power in this world. Once we train our youth to believe in this concept, we will begin to cut down on inner city violence." He stepped back from the podium briefly to take a sip of water, basking in the audience's adulation.

Gus, who had arrived five minutes earlier, took a seat at the side of the stage and watched Sam work his magic. The country needed jobs and Sam was proposing marvelous ideas to get the economy going. The audience was swallowing every word. Sam soaked up the euphoria of the moment.

A sly smile emerged on Gus's face, as he watched Sam mesmerize the audience. He remembered what Sam had told him in conversation one time: "Tell the people what they want to hear and they will follow." He knew voters had short memories. The beauty of Washington was that a politician could say anything and blame the other party for the failure of legislation. Sam played that game better than anyone

"Finally," the senator said, "I would like to add, the time has come to revamp our tax code. It is too complicated and burdensome, not only for the taxpayer, but for the IRS itself.

"So, I would like to leave you this evening with ideas to ponder and hope for the future. These ideas are just a sample of what we can do to bring this country back to greatness. It is up to all of you to get on board and take this campaign to the White House. Thank you for inviting me tonight."

The audience rose to their feet, giving him a boisterous ovation, as if he were a Caesar, leading the Roman Empire. He slowly walked to the side of the stage where he was greeted by the Democratic Party handlers. The smile faded from his face the minute he saw Gus, from the corner of his eye.

Exiting the auditorium, he greeted everyone with a smile and shook hands with many of his supporters. Stopping for a quick second, he exchanged a handshake with Gus. He leaned in to whisper "Meet me at my son's grave in forty minutes." Then he chuckled, as if they had shared a private joke, and continued to work his way around the room.

***

The evening sun was fading fast. The cemetery was deserted except for a few crows gliding in the air. The fall air was crisp, but refreshing. Senator Atkins stood in front of his son's grave as Gus's car rolled to a stop on the side of the road, thirty-five feet from John Atkins's gravestone.

Gus emerged from his car, clapping his hands while he walked toward Sam. "Bravo, great speech. Where's the secret service for our next president?"

Sam turned, "I declined the secret service. It's a good symbol for my campaign. Let's walk."

Gus stopped and lit a cigarette.

"When are you going to quit that bad habit?" Sam asked.

"I don't know, probably never."

"When I saw you there this evening, I was thinking, what in the world would bring Gus out to listen to my campaign rhetoric? The funny thing that came to mind was Jack Bolton. I don't know why, but the guy seems to have nine lives."

"Well, you're right about Bolton."

"I'm damned right about Bolton, and if your men did their damn job, I wouldn't be talking about him."

"Hey, my guys thought Butler was still at the motel. I guess the question is how did he know where to look for Bolton, unless he followed one of the cars or, worst-case scenario, there's someone on the inside."

"That would be a big problem, Gus," Sam said sternly.

"So far we haven't found a leak. But that's not why I needed to meet with you today."

"I don't even want to guess."

"Well, it has to do with Bolton."

Sam smirked and shook his head. "It's the damn Phoenix project, isn't it?

"Yeah."

Sam calmly said, "What should I be worried about?"

Gus flicked his cigarette as they walked, then stopped and reached into his top pocket and pulled out another Marlboro. He lit it and pressed the cigarette to his lips, exhaling a puff of smoke. "I won't bother you with all the details, Sam, but we had a very low level of surveillance on the Cap residence. In fact, it was at the point that we were going to end it. It was absolutely a waste of time. But a phone call came in from a bank in Seattle looking for a safe deposit box payment for George Cap."

"Let me get this right…Cap had a safe deposit box in a bank in Seattle, and he lived in Virginia, Ohio, or wherever. The guy has a sense of humor, don't you think?"

"Yeah, so I had two men check it out today and Jack Bolton beat us by a couple of minutes. He handcuffed a bank manager, but he had a key to the box."

"What the hell was in the box?"

"A flash drive," Gus said nonchalantly.

"Do you understand what's at stake here, Gus?" Sam said through clenched teeth. "This isn't just about you and me. It's about the people behind me, the ones who bet on a sure thing. They put a lot of money on a horse; they research it to death; weight the odds and pick their winner."

The two walked to the highest point of the cemetery. The light from the receding sun was barely evident.

"Sam, I have a lot to lose here too."

"I'm not here to argue about who has more to lose, Gus. We need to take care of this problem by any means possible, and quickly."

"I have a plan to solve our problem, Sam," Gus said, exhaling a puff of smoke.

"What is it?"

"Well, it appears that the Virginia Commonwealth's Attorney has made a deal with Jeff Keller. In return, he gave them information about where Bolton will be on October 8th."

Sam just shook his head. "How in the world would he know where Bolton is going to be?"

"It doesn't matter, Sam," Gus said, trying not to agitate the senator. "I'm sure Bolton somehow came across the story about Keller and how Laura worked in your office. I guess he has a soft spot in his heart for the guy and a lot of hatred for you. But this is going to be his downfall."

"I told you never to mention her name," Sam said in an agitated tone.

"Sorry," Gus said. "I didn't mean anything by it."

"How do you know he'll show up?" Sam asked, moving on.

"Oh, he'll show up. Trust me on this one. From what

I'm told, he was involved in killing that serial killer in North Dakota. Bolton's weakness is he sees himself as some sort of vigilante."

"Look, you can't let the feds take him in," Sam said, his voice a shade stronger. "Is that the plan?"

"Of course not. You know me better than that, Sam."

"How are you going to do it, Gus?"

"It's a beautiful plan. Listen, that Mafia fellow, Gallo, wants him dead, right? We tell him where Bolton is going to be. He sends his goons to kill Bolton. They kill him and nobody will question it. Perfect, right?"

"You are going to count on them with the feds everywhere." Sam asked in disbelief.

"Come on, Sam," he said with a grin. "Now, if that fails, I'm sending my own guy who will have orders to kill him. So, either way, Bolton is going to be dead at the end of the day."

"I'll believe it when I see it," Sam said. "And how's your guy going to get close enough to kill Bolton with federal agents right there?

"I met the lead agent, a guy by the name of Ryland. He tries to act smart, but he can be easily controlled. He won't be a problem."

"What about Bolton's buddy?"

"Butler? We'll take care of him and the rest of them, in due time. Let's just focus on Bolton first."

They walked back to their parked cars, shook hands, and drove off into the night.

Chapter 39

Gallo's, an upscale restaurant in Manhattan, opened every morning for breakfast at 6:00 a.m. and served the Wall Street and fashion industry regulars. Frank Gallo ate his breakfast at the same table every morning at seven sharp and read the Wall Street Journal and the New York Times. He paid some bills and took out a black book used to track the real profits of the organization - those the IRS didn't know existed. There was the drug money, the gambling money, and the extortion fees that shop owners paid for protection. Gallo was old school. He was feared and unloved, just the way he liked it. People came to him for favors, but any favor granted usually came with a price down the road

Frank sat at the table, his mood somber. He could sense his own demise. The feds were circling him like sharks circling a hapless seal. If they took him down, the New York Mafia would crumble. He was a big fish on the verge of extinction, all because Joe Russo was ready to sing like a canary.

Gallo's attorney had flown to Boston a day earlier to talk to Russo. Russo refused to talk to him. He had his own lawyer, the type of lawyer who makes deals with the feds that enable his clients to enter the witness protection program.

Frank stared ahead, thinking it was just a matter of time before the feds would be back to read his Miranda Rights to him. Russo was a big rat, a killer, and the guy who could bring down the whole New York Mafia. Ironically, he would walk free, a guy who was involved in more Mafia killings than any member in the last twenty years.

A short, skinny, well-dressed, middle-aged man followed the hostess until she came to a corner table and placed a menu on it. He sat down at the table and a smiling waitress came over to serve him.

"Good morning. Can I start you off with a cup of coffee?" she asked, smiling, her voice gentle and polite.

"Yeah, I'll take a cup of coffee for now. Oh, one more thing…" He reached into his pocket. "Please take this note to Mr. Gallo."

"Certainly, sir."

The waitress walked over to Frank Gallo's table at the far end of the restaurant and stopped. He looked up, pleased to have a distraction from his thoughts, and asked, "Tory, what can I do for you?"

"One of my customers, a fellow at table twenty-three, gave me this piece of paper to give to you," she said shyly. Gallo turned his head and looked over his shoulder. He didn't recognize him.

Frank opened the piece of paper. The stranger

wanted to meet with him on a matter of some urgency. Gallo signaled to two of his lieutenants who escorted the man to the back room. A few minutes later, Frank entered.

One of his lieutenants said, "He's clean, Frank."

Frank stared at the skinny man, opened his hands wide, and said, "So what brings you here to my lovely establishment, and what's so urgent this early in the morning?"

"We can't talk here."

Frank just laughed. "What, you think the feds might be listening?"

The lieutenants joined in the laughter.

"Okay, you don't want to talk here. I have a soundproof room in the cellar, but it better be important."

The four men walked down a flight of stairs and entered a room with padded walls. It looked more like an interrogation room, a place from which no screams could escape. The four men sat at a table.

"Your two buddies need to leave," the skinny man said.

The two men looked at Frank.

"Alright." Frank directed the men to wait outside. "This better be good and, by the way, who the hell are you?"

"It's better that you don't know who I am." The man said, sitting straight up across from Frank.

"You know who I am and I don't know who the hell you are?" Frank asked angrily.

"Mr. Gallo, I've been sent by people who share a common interest with you."

"And what could that be?"

"Jack Bolton."

"Did you say Jack Bolton?"

"Yeah. We have the location of where Jack Bolton will be in four days. We just need you to take care of him."

Frank just smiled. "Like tuck him in or take him out for an ice cream?" he said with a snicker.

"You know what I mean, Mr. Gallo," the man said with no hint of a smile.

The smile left Frank's face and he leaned in. "I want him dead, so you came to the right place. But I have to ask: Why get me involved. Why don't you do it yourself?"

"It would be better if you did it."

Frank leaned back in his chair, rubbing his chin. "Give me a moment to think." He wanted Bolton dead as much as anyone, but he wasn't going to be some set-up guy for whatever motive was behind these people wanting Bolton dead. Maybe it was Senator Atkins who wanted him dead for all he knew. Then again, maybe there were other reasons, unknown to him. Frank had sidestepped the law many times because he knew when to walk away. This was surely one of those times. But, then it hit him… He was in a desperate position. The feds were closing in. Maybe this guy had the power to take care of his big problem. If he could get rid of Russo and get Bolton, it would be like winning the daily double. Frank leaned forward, "I will do it under one condition. I have a little problem."

"What's the problem?"

"I have an associate that the feds are holding in Boston by the name of Joe Russo. I need him to have an accident, maybe a heart attack or something like that."

"I'll have to make a phone call."

"Sure, the men have your phone outside." The man got up from the table and exited the room.

Frank sat back, patiently waiting for the mystery man to return.

A few minutes later, the man entered the room. He plopped back down in his seat. "We'll take care of Russo. To show our good faith, it will happen today. But if you don't keep your end of the bargain, Mr. Gallo, there will be consequences."

Frank hated being dictated to. "You just worry about taking care of Russo," he snapped back. "I'll take care of Bolton. I don't go back on my word."

"Well, Mr. Gallo, it was nice doing business with you." The man got up from his seat and pulled an envelope from his pocket. "Here is the information on where Jack Bolton will be on October eighth."

"What if he doesn't show up?"

"Then you got a pretty good deal." The man said as he walked out of the room.

Chapter 40

Jack rose from his bed at 5:30 a.m. in the rundown motel they had found off the freeway. They had bought an Apple laptop the night before and decided they would wait till the morning to view the contents of the flash drive. Jack felt like a kid at Christmas, waiting for everybody to wake up. He sat at a desk staring at the laptop, flash drive in hand. He couldn't wait any longer. He turned on the laptop and pushed the flash drive into the back port. An array of files came up. There were jpeg files, word files, and spreadsheet files. Nothing, to his surprise, had been encrypted.

The first file he opened bore the heading *The Phoenix Project.* It was a highly classified document that certainly wasn't meant for public viewing. In 2012, Congress had appropriated eighteen billion dollars for the rebuilding of Iraq. The administration flew eighteen billion dollars of shrink-wrapped cash into Iraq on pallets. The funds flown into the war zone were made up of funds from the U.N.'s oil-for-food program, as well as money from sales of Iraqi oil and seized Iraqi assets. Officials were supposed to distribute the money to Iraqi government ministries and U.S. contractors tasked with the reconstruction of Iraq. The money was supposed to be safeguarded by American forces. Instead, it disappeared. The U.S. conducted three audits and no trace of the money could be found. The U.S. blamed corrupt Iraqi officials, saying it had been used to line their pockets. Some believed that U.S. officials absconded with the money. Once the story died, so did the investigations and the audits.

Jack leaned in as he scanned different documents. He was like a person watching a close call on an instant replay. He finally knew why George Cap lost his life.

The truth of what happened to the money was that the CIA, without authorization, ordered the money to be transferred into secret off-shore accounts to be used for the following defense and CIA projects: advanced drone development, biometrics, robotics, laser weapons, weather control, espionage, the funding of a secret delta force, the negotiation of swapping political prisoners, deal-making with terrorists, buying off foreign government officials…the list was endless.

Jack leaned back in his chair to give his eyes a rest and to digest the significance of what he had just read. Clearly, the people behind this could never let it get out. They had misused a Congressional appropriation for their own unauthorized objectives and God knows how high up this went.

Brian awoke from his slumber and rolled over in his bed. "Hey, Jack, I thought we were both going to look at it together."

"I couldn't wait."

Brian sat up. Half asleep, he walked in slow motion over to the table and sat heavily in the chair next to Jack. He rubbed his face, trying to get his eyes to focus on the task at hand. "So they took Iraq's money and decided to use it for better things. Bravo."

"You're looking at this all wrong, Brian. These guys stole the money for their own purposes. When some drone is chasing you down the street, you'll be thinking differently."

Brian looked closer at the computer screen. "Hey, do you think we could make the delta force?"

"You aren't taking this seriously, Brian." He used the big-brother tone of voice that he knew could make Brian feel a bit guilty.

"I'm sorry, Jack, you're right."

"Look, if the people knew the CIA or whoever else is behind this, stole this money for other purposes, it makes our whole Constitution worth shit. What the hell are we fighting for, Brian? If these guys are just using us for their own benefit and lining their own pockets, we are no different than any third-world hellhole. These same people don't even care whose side they're on."

"You done with your rant, Jack?"

"No, I'm just getting started. I'm pissed off, actually."

"Does that mean you won't turn yourself in now?"

Jack ignored the question. "You should be pissed off

too, Brian. How many guys did you see get killed over there, huh? What was it for?"

"Jack, all I want to do is start my boat business on a nice small island. You're not going to change anything. In fact, if you turn yourself in, most likely they are going to kill you. Now that you know what happened with the missing money, I would say you aren't going to make the life expectancy tables."

Jack didn't answer. He started opening more files.

As each jpeg file came up, one after another, the guys eagerly scanned them. Many of the photos were pictures of money, showing the serial numbers. Then pictures of First Rate Bank of Washington came up. The two looked at each other, not sure what that meant.

Jack opened another file. "Here's something. The bank received a three hundred-million dollar transaction processing fee."

"So they got a fee for laundering the money," Brian replied.

"So where's the money exactly?" Jack said.

"I don't know; maybe if we open more files we'll find out."

"Wait a minute. Let's look up First Rate and see who the top dogs are," Jack stated. He maneuvered the mouse, Googling the Internet for financial information on First Rate Bank and, to his amazement, Walter Atkins was listed as the CEO.

"Brian, do you see who the CEO of the bank is?"

"Yeah. Wikipedia it."

Jack pressed a few keystrokes on the laptop and instantly Walter Atkins's bio came up. To neither man's surprise, it revealed that Sam Atkins was listed as Walter's brother.

"What a coincidence," Jack muttered.

A few more pictures came up of different people. Jack froze a picture in which the guy looked familiar. After a long moment of staring at the screen, he recalled where he had seen the face before. "The guy in the background with Atkins is the guy who was in the abandoned warehouse."

"You sure?" Brian asked.

"Yeah, I'm sure." Jack said with lines of wrinkles across his forehead.

"He has to be someone high up if he's hanging around with Atkins...maybe CIA." Brian said, focusing on the screen.

"Let's see if we can look on the Internet and find out who he is."

"Is there anything in any of the files, Jack?"

"I don't know." Jack Googled photos of the current CIA Director. He stared at the photos intensely. He shook his head. "Incredible. The CIA director was Atkins's partner in crime the night they tried to kill me, and now Atkins is running for president with his own private hit man on the side."

"The guy's name is Gus Banner," Brian said. "Look,

we are in way over our heads here. It's one thing to be playing around with the Mafia and a Mexican cartel. It's a whole different ball game playing against these guys. I can see why they took care of Cap's brother. If this stuff ever got out, Banner is gone and Atkins, with his connection to his brother… Well, let's just say it sure ain't going to get him elected."

"It's already too late; we're both dead men," Jack concluded.

"Not necessarily. They don't know what we have. They're as much afraid of us as we are of them."

"Yeah, what's your point?"

They opened up another file that contained several Cayman Island accounts where the money was held. It also included account numbers, pass codes, and pass keys.

"So it looks like the money went through First Rate, with good old Walter getting a piece of the action and, from there, it got transferred to the Cayman accounts."

"I've seen that look before. What are you thinking, Brian?"

"This is actually funny, Jack"

"Well?"

"Okay, let's just say they take you in. I can blackmail them, once Atkins becomes president. Threaten them that if Atkins doesn't pardon you, I'll offer this information to the media. That should get their attention," Brian said. He then let out a deep laugh. "He pardons the guy who killed his son. Wouldn't that be great P.R?"

"Yeah, great P.R.," Jack said, rolling his eyes. "I'm just thinking that Atkins as our next president and Banner working with him is a very scary thought."

"Maybe a better option is that I use these pass keys and pass codes to transfer the money from their Cayman accounts to some Swiss account through my contact in Indiana. How's that sound?" Brian asked with a wicked grin.

"You're computer illiterate, remember?" Jack teased, smiling back.

"These files talk about some lone wolf, so I'm guessing there's somebody else out there who might know about the money. I would have to find him or maybe he finds me."

"Maybe you already found him."

"What do you mean?" Brian asked. His brow furrowed.

"You know, the guy who knew where I was and just so happened to know where to call you about my dire situation."

"Oh, that guy. Maybe you've got something there."

Chapter 41

Agent Ryland walked around downtown Seattle under an afternoon drizzle, observing the area around the coffee shop where Jack Bolton would surrender in a few days. He studied the downtown buildings and wondered if Jack would show up. Part of him hoped he wouldn't. The other part wanted him to show up just to end the madness. Yet, he couldn't help but think there was more to all this. What if Jack's team of professional soldiers got involved again once he was captured or transferred to Boston after Jeff Keller was freed?

A few more FBI agents joined him now in front of *Cup of Joes*, as they discussed the strategy for bringing in Jack Bolton.

One of the agents stepped forward. He wore an overcoat that hid his tall lanky frame. His military haircut made him look like he just got out of the marines.

"Agent Ryland," he said, offering his hand.

"Do I know you?" Ryland asked, shaking his hand.

"I don't think so. I'm Special Agent Mike Weldon. I've been working overseas on special assignments here and there," he said, smiling. "The director sent me just to provide extra support and another set of eyes to make sure we get our man."

"Well, I think I can handle it, but this is a special situation, right?"

"I just take orders, Agent Ryland."

"Excuse me for a minute, Mike. My phone is buzzing." Agent Ryland pressed the button on his phone and put the phone to his ear as he moved to a quiet corner of the coffee shop. "Agent Ryland."

Agent Hawkins was on the other end. "Paul, you won't believe this."

"What?"

"Russo had a heart attack this afternoon."

"What? You sure it was a heart attack?"

"Well, I was right there when it happened. He was in the conference room with his lawyer. I was sitting across from him and he was ready to spill his guts about Gallo and the New York Mafia. Then, all of sudden, he clutched his chest, his face turned pale white, his eyes rolled up, and his head did a free fall and bounced off the table. The officers tried to resuscitate him, with no luck. The guy was dead before his head even hit the table, Paul."

Ryland, with his phone to his ear, walked out of the coffee shop and moved under a storefront. He looked out at the drizzle, wondering about the timing. "What a coincidence: to drop dead when you're about to take down the New York Mafia."

"My guess is that he had a massive heart attack,"

Hawkins said. "I ate lunch with the guy and his lawyer prior to the meeting. Russo sure had an appetite. The funny thing, a few minutes before we were going to take his statement, he was joking with me, grinning from ear to ear, telling me that we weren't going to believe all the stuff Frank Gallo and the New York Mafia did. The guy was so excited to tell his story and retire from the Mafia."

Paul thought about how they had Frank Gallo right where they wanted him and the guy still managed to slip through their fingers. "I've never seen a luckier guy than Gallo. I can't believe this. Was Russo under twenty-four hour watch?" Ryland asked.

"He sure was," Hawkins replied, sitting in front of his computer screen. "If you're thinking that somehow Gallo and his men got to him, there's no way."

"I just can't believe Gallo is going to walk again."

"We'll get him someday, Paul."

"Yeah. Hey, what's the story with those former Navy SEALs?" Ryland asked, looking out at the street.

"We've had surveillance on them for a week now and they're just going through their usual routine, nothing out of the ordinary," Hawkins explained on the phone. "Milton works on antique cars, Brady is going through a divorce, and Rodriguez is busy with a landscaping business. If these guys made a big score in Mexico, they sure aren't showing it. No large purchases. Just ordinary phone calls, texts, and emails. There's no contact with either Bolton or Butler. You would never know these guys actually broke Jack Bolton out of prison and hit a cartel."

"They've been told to keep a low profile, and it sounds like they're doing just that." Ryland reasoned. "So it looks like these guys are staying put. What about Brian Butler?"

"We were able to get a photo of Butler at that gas station where the girl was abducted."

"So we have no idea if he's with Bolton now?" Paul asked, leaning against the side of the door front.

"Yeah. But my guess, if he's gone this far, he's probably still with him."

"I agree. Any good news?"

"Well, we started finding bodies from that Saxton letter, if you consider that good news."

Agent Ryland's phone buzzed again; he glanced at the screen. It was his wife's number. He hadn't been able to answer her earlier calls. "Hey, thanks Alex. Let me know if anything comes up. I've got another call coming in."

Chapter 42

A cool night breeze blew from the trade winds off the Gulf of Mexico. She had finally gotten up her courage to flee. She had planned it with the help of one of the women villagers. Tonight was the night. Her heart was racing, but her mind was made up. She could no longer stay here as a captive and chose to ignore any thoughts of retribution if she were caught trying to escape.

After two years, she had gotten to know the villagers as if they were family. The majority of them tilled the fields for a Mexican cartel, producing opium poppy and marijuana for export simply because they had no other good alternative. Those who didn't till the fields made pottery or supported the men out in the field. Dozens of armed men roamed the area and made sure the product was in good order while protecting it from Mexican authorities, hoodlums, and other cartels.

She was treated well. Strangely, nobody tried to force themselves on her, even though some of the armed men were of despicable nature. They feared something much greater.

The villagers were generous, hardworking, down-to-earth people, who were stuck in a place with no future. They took orders from the armed men, who at times treated them harshly. They worked the fields twelve hours a day in the hot sun. She would supply them with water during the day and teach them to read at night with the little free time they received. The field hands' pay wasn't much, but it was enough for them to get by.

The village, located at the base of a mountain, was made up of small wooden structures. Electricity came from generators. As for plumbing, there wasn't much of it. Water came from the mountains. The bathroom commode was a bucket. Food came from the land or was purchased when someone made a trek to the closest market. But the people never complained; they were happy with the little they had. There was no Internet, and there were no computers or smart phones. It was a world where families focused on each other and did the best they could with what they had.

She slipped into a white dress that had seen better days and tied her long black hair into a ponytail. No makeup was required for this trip.

A long cloth reaching from the top of the doorframe to the floor separated her small bedroom from the main room. She pushed the cloth aside and tiptoed to the fragile, wooden, outside door and eased it open. She ran silently, so as not to disturb the sleeping villagers. A village woman by the name of Carmen waited for her at the outskirts of the village. Carmen made a spot in the back of the wagon for the young woman, hiding her under bags of pottery and a blanket so the armed men wouldn't notice if they bothered to check the wagon.

Carmen flicked the reins, and the mules responded to her command by lumbering forward, hauling the wagon behind. A few armed men watched her pass but let her go unmolested. She had done this so many times before that it was routine in their eyes. She was going to the closest town to sell her pottery and bring back fresh meat that the armed men enjoyed. They didn't know that, this time, she had a passenger - the young woman whose presence there had never been explained to them.

After seven miles, the wagon stopped in a small town on the outskirts of Oaxaca. Carmen took off the blanket and moved the pottery. The young woman bounced up from her position. She had barely moved in the last few hours, too scared she would be detected. A man with an old Chevy pick-up truck waited for her. The young woman hugged Carmen as if she were leaving her mother to go on a long trip. She couldn't thank her enough for her courage and generosity in helping her to escape.

The hour of driving seemed like five. Finally the truck stopped in front of a bus station. She boarded the bus that said Mexico City. Her ticket was paid for. The three-hour bus ride would take her close to the U.S. Embassy.

She sat quietly in the middle of the bus, not looking at anyone, terrified that someone would take her back to the village where she might have to pay the consequences of her actions. An hour had gone by and she wished the bus had arrived already. The thought of freedom swirled in her mind. Her mouth was extremely parched and she longed for a sip of water.

The bus slowed down abruptly and pulled to the side of the road. She thought nothing of it until she heard a commotion outside and saw armed men at the front of the bus. She got very small in her seat, hoping the men wouldn't notice or that they were looking for something else. Maybe they were here just to rob everyone, which would be better than the alternative. Her greatest fear was that they were looking for her.

Two armed men slowly shuffled down the aisle of the bus, passing people as they went. She looked down, hoping the men would keep walking, but they stopped at her seat. She looked up and the men grabbed her by the arms. Her heart skipped a beat, her body shook, and her mind went blank. They dragged her from the bus. She was thrown in a car and driven back to the village.

That day she sat in her small structure, too scared to go out. A group of men she had never seen before showed up at the village. They walked over to her place. Two men came in as the others waited outside. A well-dressed man with a manicured beard wearing an expensive suit began to talk.

"Do you know who I am?" His voice was loud and authoritative.

"No," she murmured, her palms sweaty, her throat

dry, and her heart pounding.

Both men laughed. "Well, it really doesn't matter. I run this place. My name is Jose Moreno," he boasted. He pulled a few pictures from his pocket. "Do you recognize any of these pictures?"

She stared at the pictures. "What are you doing with these?" she asked nervously with tears in her eyes.

"The next time you try to escape from our great hospitality here, I will kill one of your family members," he said with no emotion. "That's what I do to people who don't listen to my warnings. Do you understand?"

Tears began to roll down her cheeks. "Yes."

"This is business. That's all it is.'"

A man walked in holding Carmen by the arm.

Moreno turned toward the woman. "Did you help her?" he asked sternly.

Carmen said nothing, too afraid to answer.

Moreno reached into his side pocket and, with one swift movement, pulled out a gun and shot her in the side of the head. Blood exploded against the wall. Carmen fell to the floor. The young woman started screaming hysterically.

"Calm down," Moreno said. "This is what happens when you do things you are not supposed to do. Do you understand?"

She nodded, trying to hold back her screams, while her legs wobbled.

Two men came in and took the body away. Moreno

and his partner turned and started walking away.

"Why are you doing this to me?" she blurted out.

He stopped in his tracks, turned towards her and chuckled. "You screwed around with the wrong man."

***

She woke abruptly in a cold sweat from a nightmare she couldn't shake. Once a month, her body wouldn't let her forget that ugly day that happened four years ago. Laura Weston couldn't shake it from her mind. Guilt plagued her about Carmen whose kindness had caused her to lose her own life. After that horrific day, she had never seen Moreno again, nor did she want to. But the thought of escaping had been forever removed from her mind.

Laura stared at the mosquito net that draped above her, thinking of her past life. Tears trickled down her cheeks. She had shed enough tears to fill a small swimming pool over the last six years. There was no communication from the outside world. She had no idea how her family was doing. She wondered if her sisters had gotten married or had kids and how they were getting along in life. She wondered how long they looked for her after she went missing. By now, though, they all must have thought she was dead, a victim of foul play. She couldn't imagine how her parents dealt with her disappearance. She was their youngest child, the one who had participated in dance recitals, which the whole family would show up for. She was daddy's little girl. The suffering of her mother and father must be excruciating. She could only hope they were well.

When her thoughts shifted to Jeff, she would sob silently. She wondered how he was doing. Was he married? Did he have a family? He was probably a senior partner now in the law firm. He most likely had a young family with some lucky woman. He was a great catch, good looking, smart… he was a really, really great guy. She missed him so much. He was the one and only love of her life. What was she thinking, getting involved with an older man like Sam Atkins?

It made her sick now, thinking about it. She got caught up in the Washington whirlwind. What started off as a subtle flirtation turned into something that got out of control. Jeff was so busy with his job and she missed his attention. The good-looking, larger-than-life senator just sucked her in. He made her feel like an important member of his team, complimenting her at every opportunity. Before she knew it, she was lying in bed with him. It was a horrible decision. She was too young, inexperienced, and naïve in the ways of Washington, where she was just another "piece of ass" that got played by a powerful, ruthless political figure.

She often replayed the memory of that last night with Jeff at the restaurant - the awful argument, the embarrassing scene, her scratching him on the face, and the two of them arguing endlessly at her apartment. She looked back now and realized how cruel she had been. He never deserved that betrayal. Tears rolled down her checks as she thought of him. She loved him so much and wished she could take it all back.

Laura thought back to that one moment when her life changed forever. She heard a knock on the door, thinking it was Jeff coming back. She opened it to two strange men. She had no recollection of what happened after that. All she remembered was waking up in a medical clinic somewhere in Mexico. She knew right away that her fetus had been snatched away. A painful ache radiated from the pit of her stomach to her pelvis. After half a day at the medical center, a few men came and took her away, blindfolding her for a journey she didn't understand.

She had come to the conclusion that she was in this place because of Senator Sam Atkins. She believed that he was afraid that she was going to destroy his political aspirations. He emphatically told her to get an abortion, that he would pay for it. She refused because she didn't believe in it. That was the last conversation they ever had.

Political figures rarely survived "the other woman" scandals, especially ones where the other woman was carrying a child. Media coverage sucked every ounce of the politician's soul, and it usually led to a messy divorce. It was political suicide, while opponents sat back and enjoyed their challenger's self-destruction.

Laura tried to go back to sleep but sometimes she couldn't escape the past. Little did she know that, like her, Jeff was a captive and paying the price for her mistake as well.

Chapter 43

Watching peeling paint at 6 a.m. wasn't something Jack did unless he couldn't sleep and had a lot on his mind. Hands folded behind his head, he stared up at the ceiling.

"What you thinking about, Jack," Brian asked from the other single bed.

"I'm wondering how the hell I got here, in some motel outside Seattle, waiting to turn myself in." He exhaled deeply. "Why couldn't I just lead a normal life, you know, like everyone else? Why did I lose my family the way I did? Why couldn't I have a normal job with a normal girlfriend? Why couldn't I just sleep at night like everyone else? Belong to a fantasy football league? Be able to go out at night and enjoy myself, not looking over my shoulder?"

Brian just shook his head. "Look, you can have all that. Just go to Canada and start your new life. It's not too late. Who the hell you trying to please?"

"I have too many sins, Brian. I'm doing the right thing. You just don't see it."

"You're right, I don't see it and I never will, Jack."

"That guy, Gus Banner, the CIA director. I might have been working for that corrupt patriot if nothing had happened to my sister. George Cap worked for the guy and it cost him his life. To tell you the truth, I don't even think there are any good guys anymore."

Jack rolled out of bed. After a quick shower and shave, he pulled on his dungarees, threw a red polo shirt over his head, and pushed his feet into white socks and slid them into a pair of sneakers. "So how do I look, Brian, for my big day?"

"You look a bit underdressed. Maybe we should get you a suit." Brian said from his bed.

Jack chuckled. "You're pretty funny, Brian," he said, sitting down in the chair closest to the window. He slid the curtain to the side while watching the drizzle sprinkle down from the overcast skies above. "It's a perfect day to be arrested."

They bantered about life as they cleaned up, packed, and got ready to check out.

"Hey, Jack, you don't want to be late," Brian said with a wide smile.

"You'll never change."

"I hope not," Brian hollered back on his way out to the car. He opened the trunk. In his bag of tricks was a beautiful CIRAS bulletproof vest. He walked back in, tossing the vest to Jack, who was sitting on the bed.

"Good idea. Thanks." I was going to ask you what you might have in that truck."

"You haven't seen the half of it."

"Now, I'll need a trench coat or something like it."

"Well, we'd better be on our way if we're going to pick one up."

They checked out of the motel and made the fifteen-minute drive to downtown Seattle. They made a quick stop at a men's store for a trench coat. Out in the parking lot, Jack pushed his arms through the bulletproof vest and secured it tightly, before shrugging into the overcoat. He buttoned it snugly and tugged on a baseball cap.

Conversation faded into thoughtful silence as they got closer to downtown Seattle. Brian pulled the car into an empty parking spot a few blocks from the coffee shop.

"Well, this is it, Buddy. Final stop. It's not too late to change your mind," Brian said, climbing out of the car.

"I'll be okay," Jack replied, standing outside the car.

"It's been a wild ride."

"It sure has, Brian."

"Give me a hug?" Brian asked, trying to keep his emotions in check.

"Look at you. You're getting all emotional on me," Jack said. He pulled his friend into a bear hug, silently patting him on the back.

"Yeah, can't help it. Just don't tell anyone," Brian said with a smirk, trying to hold himself together.

Jack smiled warmly. "Hey, I can't thank you enough for everything... breaking me out of prison, saving my life, giving me a lot of laughs, and making me a millionaire."

"That's me," Brian responded. "Hey, I wouldn't be standing here if it weren't for you, Jack. I'm going to get you out of this. When Atkins becomes president, I'm going to blackmail the son of a bitch for your release."

"Well, that's our ace in the hole, huh?"

"It sure is. You ready for this?"

"As ready as I'll ever be."

"I'm a little worried about you, Jack. Take this," Brian said, pulling out a 9MM handgun. He handed it to Jack.

"You really think it's a good idea to have a gun on me?"

"Let's just say it's an insurance policy."

"All right. Let's do this."

One last handshake and Jack slipped off to his final destination.

Jack sauntered through the streets of downtown Seattle, in no hurry to get to the coffee shop. His stomach felt queasy, as if he was going under the knife.

The downtown clock read 9:20 a.m. He stared up at the buildings, looking for a sniper like he was back in a war zone. The last few months had taken their toll.

He was tired of being hunted in a country which he had risked his life to defend. He was sick of the senseless killings. There was nothing to run from or to come home to. He had resigned himself to whatever would happen. He couldn't tell Brian that he had thrown in the towel. Maybe he knew. Brian was still fighting the good fight.

Jack accepted the fact that he was going to prison for the rest of his life, but at least Jeff Keller would be able to get a fresh start. That was the ultimate sacrifice, as if he were a soldier who threw his body on a grenade to save everyone but himself. He was now ready to go back. He accepted his fate.

People were walking in all directions. Jack mingled in, keeping his head down until he entered the coffee shop. He found a center table and took his cap off, signaling to anyone who was watching or cared that he had arrived. Now it was just a matter of waiting for the feds to come out of their hiding places and whisk him off.

***

The FBI had the area under surveillance, but Jack was able to elude their scrutiny until he made himself known. Agent Ryland, sitting in a van across the street, got word that Bolton was in the coffee shop.

The van was central control, watching every angle of the coffee shop. He had hoped that they would get an opportunity to intercept him before he got inside, but clearly they had missed their chance.

Ryland had three agents in the coffee shop, as well

as two in the back of the building and two more in the front. It appeared Bolton was here to turn himself in as promised, he thought, relieved that the case was finally coming to an end. The team now waited for his signal to take him down.

Ryland looked at his smart phone, and waited anxiously for the time to strike 10 a.m. At that precise moment, they would place him under arrest, escort him quietly out to the waiting vehicle, and transport him back to Boston under heavy guard. He would be arraigned for the murder of John Atkins, which was basically a formality since he was already serving a life sentence with no chance of parole for the murder of Nick Gallo.

In ten minutes, it will all be over. Jack Bolton will be back in custody. He would send a message to Mr. Greenberg that his client was a free man and he would accompany Jack back to Boston. Then he would race home to see his family.

***

Sometimes it's better to be lucky than good. Art Glover planned robberies the same way he lived life. He was a brilliant strategist, who left nothing to chance. He chose to live a very regimented single lifestyle. He worked out every day, kept his weight within a ten-pound range, ate healthy food, and went to bed around the same time every night. He lived in a well-to-do neighborhood in Colleyville, Texas. His neighbors thought he was some kind of hedge fund manager; little did they know that he was a modern-day bank robber.

He viewed his work much like a stock analyst. If he did his research correctly, the payday was big. His goal was twenty banks before he officially called it quits. Just five more banks and he could retire at the young age of forty-seven. He had amassed a nice nest egg of fifteen million dollars, certainly enough to retire on. But the adrenaline rush from the challenge of beating the system kept him in the game. His crew had fifteen successful and lucrative bank heists to their credit. At some point, luck runs out. He just hoped it would come later rather than sooner.

Timing is everything in life. For Art's crew of ex-military men who were highly trained, experienced, and heavily armed, today was not the day to be robbing a bank in downtown Seattle.

The five-man crew had spent their lives robbing one or two banks a year around the country. They would spend months researching the bank to ensure it was an ideal candidate to be robbed. That required a risk-reward in their favor. Art's crew wasn't run-of-the-mill bank robbers. They left no stone unturned in their preliminary evaluation. If there was too much risk, they walked. Even though they were heavily armed, they never fired a shot in the ten years they had been robbing banks.

The FBI had offered a nice reward for any leads into these particular bank heists, but nothing ever came in. The main reason was the keen discipline of Art's crew and the people who backed them. It was a ten-year mystery that the Feds had yet to solve.

Art and his crew, through months of observation and recon, had identified a lapse in security at First Rate Bank. Every Thursday around 9.55 a.m., an armored car would drop off bundles of cash, which would be transferred to the vault. It was at this split second in time before the vault was closed that they would hit the bank and four duffle bags of cash would be loaded into a waiting SUV. It would take them approximately three minutes to load the duffle bags and drive away from the bank. By the time the police arrived, they would have switched getaway cars and been long gone.

***

Cup of Joes was bustling with people going in and out. Jack sat back, waiting for the feds to come out of the woodwork. He glanced at the clock: 9:58 a.m. *Come on, let's get this over with.* He looked around, trying to figure out where the FBI men were sitting. Two large men wearing overcoats, stopped at his table. "Jack Bolton, FBI."

"Yeah, it's about time," he replied. Jack began to get up with his hands held out in front of him in surrender.

371

One of the men pulled a gun out from his side pocket. In a single motion, he pulled the trigger. The bullet struck Jack squarely in the chest. The force of the blast caused him to tumble back into the booth.

Reflexively, Jack pulled out his gun and fired at the two men. Gunfire exploded throughout the coffee shop. Hit, both men crumpled to the floor.

Jack sprang up and hopped over the two men. Running low to the floor, he heard bullets whiz past his head. In all the confusion, he wasn't sure what was going on. Patrons were scrambling to the nearest exits, screaming as they fled. He made it through the back door, feeling the rain on his head one second and then a blow to the head the next.

***

Brian watched from the side street in disbelief as the situation unfolded in front of him. Gino's men had quickly neutralized the two feds at the back of the coffee shop, knocking Jack unconscious as he fled through the exit. Two Mafia men instantly picked up the unconscious Jack and threw him into the back row of their Suburban. Within seconds they were squealing out of the back parking lot onto a side street toward University Avenue.

The feds came running out of the back exit, led by Special Agent Mike Weldon - the mystery agent sent by

Washington – who could only watch as the Suburban turned out of the parking lot. Agent Weldon called Ryland. "A Suburban is heading toward University Avenue with Jack Bolton in it. We also have two agents down."

Sitting in the passenger seat, Gino looked back at the unconscious Bolton lying in the third row seat. *This could work out better than planned.* A bigger payday awaited if he could get Bolton back to Frank Gallo alive and in one piece. But it was a fleeting thought. As the vehicle turned on to University Avenue, Brian crouched low, aimed, and fired. Bullets tore through the tires of the Suburban.

The driver lost control of the car and wandered into the opposite lane where Art Glover and his crew's Suburban was just exiting from the First Rate Bank in a hurry with a boatload of cash and alarms going off. The vehicles swerved out of control, crashing into storefronts on opposite sides of the street.

Brian took a moment to observe the chaotic seen. Sirens were blaring. Blue lights could be seen in the distance. People were running from the sound of the gunshots, as if they were being chased by a bull through the streets of Barcelona.

Brian got to within twenty yards of the Suburban driven by the Mafia and tossed a flash grenade. Gino and his men were still shaking off the impact of the crash, when the grenade detonated, producing a blinding flash of light. The loud blast caused more panic in the street.

Brian moved quickly towards the wreckage with an MK25 handgun in one hand and another semi-automatic handgun in a side holster. Gino and his men stumbled from the wreckage, temporarily stunned by the explosion. They struggled to regain their senses.

Brian opened the tailgate of the Suburban and gun-butted the two groggy men flanking Jack, who was still unconscious. Brian reached into his pocket, to retrieve smelling salts.

"Come on, Jack. We are going to be dead men if you don't come to fast." Brian mumbled. Time was running short. Glover's crew opened fire from the other side of the street, holding the FBI and police at bay.

Jack eyes shot open and he shook his head to clear the smell of the ammonia compound. Sitting straight up and inhaling, he exclaimed, "What the hell happened? Where am I?"

"I'll explain later. Take the handgun," Brian snapped. "Let's go."

Jack stumbled for the first few yards until he got his footing. They got about another fifteen yards when bullets starting flying in their direction. They ducked down behind a row of cars. Brian popped his head out to get a better idea of what was going on. Police had closed off the street about seventy yards ahead. The FBI and police were held up in the rear by the Mafia, who were now firing high powered semi-automatic weapons at the police. But there was another group of shooters in the equation. Glover's crew was fleeing on foot with duffle bags of money. All hell was breaking loose from all directions. A running gun battle was playing out in downtown Seattle.

Jack and Brian crouched low as they scrambled along the sidewalk behind the row of parked cars. They exchanged gunfire with Glover's crew as they made their way down the street. They glanced back to see Mafia thugs coming up fast from the rear, slowed only by the FBI and the police who were hunting them.

Jack and Brian darted into an empty yogurt store for cover. Brian stepped out of the doorway and unloaded a clip of bullets at the Mafia in an effort to slow down their advance.

"This is absolutely crazy, Brian," Jack yelled, as Brian darted back into the store. They both hit the floor to take cover from the hail of bullets.

"Yeah, but we can use all this confusion to our benefit," Brian said, wiping sweat from his brow. "Listen to all that gunfire out there. It's like a war zone."

"It sure feels like we are in some third world hellhole, huh?" Jack retorted, rubbing his neck.

"You okay?"

"Yeah, my head hurts, though."

"You know we've got to get out of here before the SWAT team gets here?"

"Let's think about this. I'm a little tired of being pushed around. It's time for some pay back," Jack said, his voice gruff with anger.

"Jack is back," Brian exclaimed. "Let's get you to Canada."

Jack kept low and peered out the door, firing his semi-automatic handgun at Gallo's goons in the rear, keeping them pinned down.

"We've got the police in front of us, the Mafia and the FBI in the rear. Then we have, I think, a bunch of bank robbers shooting at anything that walks," Brian surmised, snapping a cartridge into his weapon. "We have Fifth Avenue up about twenty-five yards. I say we make a run for it, take a right, and see what we have in front of us from there. But I'll throw another flash grenade as we turn the corner to buy us some time. I parked the car on Third Avenue, so we'll need to backtrack. They won't think we'll do that."

"You ready, Jack? On three."

They came out guns blazing, running with lightning speed, firing as they went. Just before Sixth Avenue, Brian tossed the flash grenade at the blockade of police cruisers. It went off, stunning the officers. The two turned down Fifth Avenue but the Mafia men were in hot pursuit, following their lead.

As Jack and Brian sprinted down the street, pedestrians scurried in front of them, trying to find cover. The bank robbers indiscriminately fired at Jack and Brian, who returned the gunfire, crouching from car to car. Ahead of them about forty yards was another police blockade. Behind them, Mafia thugs were shooting at them.

Jack and Brian slid between two cars and opened fire on the approaching Mafia thugs. Two of them dropped to the ground. Gino and the others dove into a store. Meanwhile Glover's crew continued to shoot at them from the other side of the street. Bullets ripped through cars and store windows. Glass exploded all around them. The police at the barricade were shooting at both sides of the street, not sure exactly who the bad guys were.

"Jack, this is unbelievable. I feel like I'm one of those western sheriffs, trying to fight his way out of Dodge."

They both snapped another clip into their handguns. Automatic weapon fire could be heard from behind them, in front of them, and to the side of them. The drizzle continued to fall, making it hard to see where the shooters were.

"We can't stay here much longer," Jack said.

"Yeah, I know."

"You have another flash grenade?"

"One more," Brian replied.

"Seneca Street is coming up, but they're going to have that closed off." Jack surmised. "We have to get by the police blockade and take the next street after that to get back to your car."

"So you want me to throw this flash grenade at the police barricade?"

"Yeah. I think that's our best chance of getting out of here, Brian."

"Okay. That SWAT team is going to be here shortly, so we've got to move fast."

They both got up and started running, dodging bullets as they went. Just as they passed Seneca Street, a couple of FBI Agents appeared on a side street. A horrific gun battle ensued. The bank robbers fired at the approaching agents. The Mafia fired from the rear. Caught in between, Jack and Brian leaped into a small shop for cover as the police from the blockade opened fire on them.

Brian slid against the wall, sat up, and caught his breath. Pain radiated from his chest. Two bullets were wedged in his vest. He yanked them out, opened his vest and saw two large black and blue marks starting to form. He shook the glass from his head and saw blood on his arms.

Jack rinsed the flesh wounds he found on his arm and leg, which were not serious in his eyes. He found a mirror and noticed a slither of glass in his shoulder. He grimaced as he pulled it out and yelled, "Shit."

Jack looked around the shop. Some people sitting in the back silently observed the crazy guy digging bullets out of his vest. They were too frightened to say anything.

"Hey, we're sorry. Here's a few bucks for the damage. I'll leave it on the counter," Jack offered.

Brian poked his head out from the doorway and studied the landscape for a few seconds. "This works, Jack. You cover me while I throw this flash grenade. Then we'll run as fast as we can past the blockade, and we're home free."

"What about the people behind us?" Jack asked.

"It's a hell of a firefight between the Mafia, FBI, bank robbers, and the police. They won't even have time to respond."

They crouched low in front of the bay window.

"On three."

This was where their years of being SEALs worked in their favor. There was chaos in the streets, but they were calm and collected, making good decisions as they maneuvered the streets of downtown Seattle to freedom.

Brian stepped out of the shop and, in one motion, lobbed the flash grenade at the four police cruisers blocking the road. A flash of light and a loud explosion rocked the street. As Jack stepped out and took a quick look behind, he noticed Agent Ryland twenty-five yards in the rear. He saw him pulling the slide on top of the barrel several times. His gun was jammed. Two of his men were down. The Mafia hit men were charging Agent Ryland's position with their guns blazing, while Glover's crew from the far side of the street were firing relentlessly at the authorities.

Brian yelled at Jack, "Let's go."

Jack pivoted in the other direction. Without hesitation, he charged toward Ryland, as if he was back in Afghanistan trying to save his team from an ambush. When he got within ten yards of Ryland, he abruptly stopped, arched his back, aimed and fired at the approaching Mafia men, stopping them in their tracks, and knocking off two of them. From the corner of his eye, he sighted one of the bank robbers, calmly turned, and pulled the trigger, shooting him down. Turning quickly, he dashed for the perimeter.

Art Glover, kneeling down behind the hood of a car, watched in horror as his brother fell to the ground in between two abandoned cars ten yards to the right of him. He knew from the motion of his head that he was gone. His face turned red. Veins in his neck bulged. Anger exploded inside him. He clenched his teeth, his forehead wrinkled. He stood up in the middle of chaos with no fear. His eyes caught the man responsible for his brother's death. He fired his semiautomatic rifle relentlessly at Jack, as he ran through the street.

Jack sprinted, covering his head from the onslaught of lead. He could feel the breeze from the bullets zinging by his head, arms, and legs. Glass was breaking all around him. When he ran past the barricade the police officers were just regaining their senses from the after-effects of the flash grenade.

Agent Weldon, accompanied by police and a few

more agents, got to Seneca Street - where Ryland was located - just as Jack and Brian breached the perimeter. Weldon sprinted after them.

Jack, huffing and puffing, caught up with Brian, who waited a short distance outside the police perimeter. They jogged their way into a crowd of people running from the gunfire. They watched from the crowd as two armored vehicles containing SWAT teams raced down the road. Jack and Brian ran down Spring Street and cut back to Third Avenue. The street in front of them was deserted.

"Where's your car?" Jack asked.

"Right up here."

They dashed into the car just as bullets began flying from behind them.

"Shit," Brian said, as both of them ducked under the dashboard for cover. He started the car and swerved it around while Jack hung out the window, empting his clip to nullify Weldon's chance to get a good shot off. They sped by him as Weldon ran out into the street, shooting wildly until his gun emptied. But they were long gone.

Chapter 44

The clock showed 1:50 p.m. There was a three-hour time difference. Jeff Keller quietly sat with his lawyer, Aaron Greenberg, in a private room that the warden allowed them to use while they waited for the news that Jack Bolton had been captured. Aaron checked the Internet news outlets for any sign that Bolton had been captured, but nothing showed up.

"Anything?" Jeff asked.

"Nothing yet," Aaron replied.

"What are the chances he actually shows up?"

"We'll just have to wait and see, Jeff."

Jeff pushed out his chair and took a nervous stroll around the room. "I'm never going to get out of here, Aaron."

"Look, I have a little more faith than you, Jeff. I think Jack Bolton is going to turn himself in."

"You know, Aaron, my family is all excited about this, but I told them I'll believe it when I see it. Since that night that Laura told me she couldn't marry me, it's been a living nightmare. Do you realize I'm in prison for something I didn't do?" Jeff asked rhetorically, pacing the room. "I would have never thought in a million years that I would be spending the rest of my life in prison."

"I know it's a bad deal, Jeff."

Jeff scoffed, "The funny thing, I miss Laura so much. I still love her. There's not a single day that goes by I don't think about her." His eyes began to well up. "I'm sorry."

"It's okay, Jeff."

"If Laura never met Senator Atkins, this all would be so different. The scary part is that the guy is running for president and he's a murderer. If that wasn't enough for these people, they framed me for her murder, not caring what happened to me or, for that matter, Laura. And it's all because the guy wanted a young piece of ass. You know, I'm glad Bolton killed his son. He was going to be just like his dad and what goes around comes around." Jeff rambled, running his hands through his hair, and then took a seat across from Aaron.

Aaron watched Jeff. He knew this was all so hard on him. It would be hard on anyone framed for a crime. He had been through the ringer. Sometimes, hanging on to one little ounce of hope can drive a person mad.

"I'm sorry about the rant, Mr. Greenberg. I didn't mean what I said about Atkins's son."

"Jeff, I know. Forget about it. Let's hope we get some good news here."

Aaron took another quick look at Fox News on his smart phone and saw a late breaking news alert flashing on the screen: *BREAKING NEWS: 9 DEAD, 15 INJURED IN BLOODY SHOOTOUT IN DOWNTOWN*

SEATTLE.

Aaron studied the headline. If Bolton was killed in a shootout, it was still part of the agreement. Aaron turned on a TV in the center of the room.

"Why are you turning on the TV?" Jeff asked.

"Well, there's breaking news coming out of Seattle." He found a major network where a reporter was talking to witnesses to the shootout.

"So what did you see?" the reporter asked.

"It was surreal," the witness said, his voice still shrill. "I'm sitting there in Cup of Joes coffee shop with my girlfriend just talking, when I notice these two guys out of nowhere pull out guns and shoot this guy in a booth. Then these other guys, I think they were FBI, start shooting at those two guys and everyone's screaming and panicking. I run out with my girlfriend and we head down University Ave, but then there's an explosion and gunfire erupts and everyone starts running the other way. It was pretty scary."

"Thank you," the reporter said. "I have here Chris Mathews, who had a close up view. What did you see?"

"I've never seen anything like it," Chris nervously explained. "I got trapped on Fifth Avenue and the bullets were hitting everywhere. It seemed to last forever. So we're in Frank's Café, a bunch of us just taking cover in the back, when these two guys come flying in. I mean these guys are taking bullets out of their vests and glass out of their arms. They got flesh

384

wounds and blood all over themselves. So one of these guys tells us he's sorry and he even leaves some money on the counter. I thought that was so strange. And then they just run out of the café with guns blazing and there's a loud explosion and twenty minutes after that the SWAT team comes in and rescues us."

"Any idea what happened to the two guys?" the reporter asked.

"I don't know," Chris said with a shrug.

"Thank you. We'll have more details as we get them. This is Tammy Smith from KBG news in Seattle."

Jeff glanced at Aaron. "What is going on?"

"I don't know."

Aaron's phone buzzed. "Agent Ryland, good news I hope." He listened to the reply and, after a few seconds, quietly pressed it off.

"Well?" Jeff asked.

"Jack Bolton is still a free man. I'm sorry, Jeff," Aaron said sadly.

Jeff put his face in his hands.

Chapter 45

Driving at seventy-five miles an hour on I-5, they weren't too far from Peace Arch Crossing.

"I need something for my splitting headache," Jack said, rubbing his head.

"It's probably a good idea that we stop and clean up a little bit and get something to drink," Brian replied. "I'll take the next exit."

"That sounds good, Brian. Hey, what made you stick around?"

"I don't know. I just figured if something bad happened, maybe I could help. Once I heard the shots, I thought you were dead."

"You know what was strange, Brian? These two guys came up to my booth and said 'Jack Bolton, FBI,' and I started getting up, thinking they were there to take me in. Suddenly one of the guys pulls out a gun and opens fire. Luckily, the bullet hit the vest. I instantly fired my gun, striking the man. Gunfire erupted from everywhere, or at least it seemed that way. I remember heading out the back door and that's about all I remember until you woke me up in the back of the SUV."

"You know, it would seem that someone told the

Mafia that you were turning yourself in."

"I know."

"These government henchmen usually have a plan B."

"It probably was that asshole chasing us up Third Avenue," Jack said, leaning back and laughing.

Brian laughed along. "I'm too sore to laugh." He turned the car off the highway into an area with restrooms and food.

They both headed to the restrooms, where they washed their faces, cleaned glass out of their arms and hair, attended to their flesh wounds with antibiotics, and changed into fresh clothes. Jack emerged from the bathroom wearing a flannel shirt to cover his cuts and wounds, dungaree pants, and a baseball cap to help shield his face.

Jack strolled to a convenience store located in the block of stores. He paid for a bottle of Advil and a couple of bottles of water. He popped two pills and chased them down with a big gulp of water.

He walked into a gift shop and looked around, waiting for Brian. He noticed a man in his eighties, still in quite good shape for his age, wearing a U.S. Marine cap. He walked over to him. "Sir, were you once in the U.S. Marines?"

"I sure was. I fought in the Korean War. Earned a Purple Heart, but that was a long time ago. People tend to forget," he said, shaking his head.

"Wow. My name is Jack... Jack Riley, he said, putting out his hand. He hated to lie about his last name.

"My name is Al Reece," he said proudly, gripping Jack's hand. Did you serve?"

"I was a Navy SEAL for seven years. I earned a Purple Heart as well. Let me show it to you." Jack said, recalling how lucky he was that prison officials allowed him to carry it. He took it out of his pocket and showed the old timer.

Al returned the favor, showing Jack his Purple Heart.

The two men bantered back and forth for the next ten minutes. An instant bond was struck between the two of them.

"Well, it was nice meeting you," Jack said. "I have to get going. I'm being dropped off at Peace Arch Crossing. I might have some walking to do once I get over the border."

"Hey, I'm going in that direction as well. I'm on my way to Vancouver, so I can give you a lift as far as there."

"Um...I might take you up on that." Jack paused and thought about the offer.

"Come on, take a ride with us, if you don't mind hanging in the back seat with my grandchildren and, of course, there's my beautiful wife of sixty years."

"You know, I'm going to take you up on that. I'll pay you."

"I don't want any of your money." Al said politely.

"Are you leaving now?" Jack asked with anticipation.

"Yeah."

"Where you parked?"

The man walked over to the entranceway and pointed to a Honda Pilot in the parking lot.

"I'll be back in a few minutes ready to go," Jack said.

"Okay, we'll see you in a few minutes."

Jack jogged over to Brian's car. "Brian!"

"Where the frig have you been?"

"I've got a ride to the border."

"With who?"

"An old army veteran," Jack said with a slight smile. "It's perfect. You know they are going to be looking for us at the border and they probably have a pretty good description of your car. But they aren't going to be looking for me in a car with grandparents and a couple of grandkids."

Brian stood back and thought about it. "You are one smart guy, Jack. So I guess this is the end of the line for a while?"

"Yeah, I can't thank you enough for everything you've done. You're like a brother to me." Jack's eyes filled up.

"Oh, man. I'm going to miss you, Jack. Everything we've been through. It's amazing we're still alive."

Jack chuckled. "No shit."

"Come here, give me a big hug." Brian said, as the two hugged like lost war buddies. "Jack, I'm going to Antigua. That's where I'm going to start my boat business."

"Well, good luck, Brian."

"I wish you the best, Jack. Find a good gal and forget about the past," he said with a sad look. "Hey, before you leave, I have a place you can go if you need somewhere to stay."

"Where do you find all these people?" Jack teased, rolling his eyes.

"I've got a crazy uncle who lives outside of Vancouver."

"You don't say."

"The guy kind of hates the U.S. government, so he went to Canada to live off the land."

"It doesn't surprise me he's related to you."

"No, seriously. He's a pretty smart guy and was a Marine during the Vietnam War. But he did a lot of drugs back then." Brian wrote down his address and handed it to Jack.

"Well, hopefully, I won't get a chance to meet your crazy uncle," Jack said with a half-smile. "What do you want to do about the flash drive?"

"Well, I think we should let things calm down for now. Lull them into believing there's nothing on the flash drive and, when they least expect it, we get a little payback or we have it if we get in a pickle."

"That sounds like a plan. How are we going to keep in touch?" Jack asked.

His brow furrowed for a moment before he snapped his fingers. "I've got it. Six months from today, April 8th, we meet at 10:00 a.m. on the Grouse Mountain Skyride in Vancouver. Of course, you've got to make it past the border first." They both shook hands and gave each other one last hug.

"Good luck, Jack," Brian called, watching Jack throw his backpack over his shoulder and jog over to the old Marine veteran's car.

Chapter 46

Border security was heavier than usual as they approached the crossing.

"Hey, Jack. I hope you have your passport," the old veteran asked from the driver's seat.

"I sure do, Al," Jack replied, glancing out the window. He saw a cluster of flashing lights near the crossing. The authorities were looking at every car with a meticulous eye. The traffic crept at a snail's pace as their car moved closer to the border. Jack could see that border agents were walking along the middle of the road, peeking inside the row of cars as they slowly passed.

As the car crept forward, Jack exhaled nervously. The last thing he needed now was getting caught at the border. His gaze followed the FBI agent, who was now walking right down the middle row of cars, glancing in at the occupants of every vehicle.

The FBI agent's distinctive haircut gave him away as the guy who chased them down on Third Avenue. He tilted his head down as Agent Weldon approached the driver's side window of the Honda Pilot.

"Good evening," Al said.

Jack had one hand on the door handle. He wasn't

going to use his gun, not with little kids around. He would hightail it through the border crossing on foot if he had to.

"Sorry to bother you, but…." Before he could finish and get a good look inside, Agent Weldon's attention was drawn to a black Chevy Impala a few cars farther back in line. He turned abruptly away from the Honda Pilot.

Jack breathed a little easier. They got to the crossing. Border security checked each person's passport and looked through the car. Jack and Al's family were asked to wait outside until they had completed their inspection. It felt like an eternity before the all-clear signal came through that they were approved to pass.

Jack was officially in Canada. He had made it. He looked back at the crossing as they drove away.

Mr. Walsh drove a few miles. "Jack, there's a great place up here for dinner. Everybody comes here. You hungry?"

"Sounds good," Jack said. He was extremely tired. A good meal was surely needed at this point. The clock showed 4.30 p.m. The day had been the hardest and longest of his life, and that included all his Navy SEAL missions, even the one where he was captured.

The friendly older couple and their well-behaved grandkids were such a drastic change from the mayhem he had experienced just six hours earlier. The restaurant was already rocking, with waitresses and waiters scurrying around delivering food and drinks. They were directed to a booth by a row of windows, which faced the bar. The establishment had been recently remodeled. The red cedar wood stain and the high ceilings gave it an old country feel that added to the family atmosphere.

A waitress with a big smile greeted them at the table. The flat screens showed clips of the wild gunfight on the streets of downtown Seattle. In fact, he could hear people talking about it all around him. Little did they know, it all centered around him. There were two photos on the screen. One was a nice picture of him, while the other showed that Brian had made the cut. But who would ever suspect a fugitive was sitting among them? He looked like a nice family guy, taking his kids out for dinner along with their proud grandparents. The only thing that was missing was a beautiful wife. He thought how nice all this was for a moment. This was what he was missing in his life and Al, unknowingly, had given him a glimpse of the missing piece of the puzzle. He was technically a trained assassin created by the U.S. government, not that SEALs were considered that, but that was the next step in the progression, at least for some of them.

Jack sat quietly, finally letting his guard down. While eating a hot bun, and observing the patrons, he noticed three men sitting at the bar. They must have just arrived. But maybe they knew he was here. Maybe the place was surrounded. Or maybe it was simply that the restaurant's great reputation had enticed Agent Ryland and two other agents for a quick bite to eat. Regardless, he was going to have to forego his dinner with Al and his lovely family.

"Pardon me for a moment, folks, I need to use the restroom," he said, trying to appear calm as he got up from the table and grabbed his backpack. Jack walked past a few booths and went right by the agents who had their backs toward him, as they sat at the bar looking forward at the news on the flat screen TVs. Jack turned the corner and saw a back door exit next to the bathroom.

***

Agent Ryland got off his bar stool and headed quickly to the restroom. He pulled out his gun as he entered and checked under the stalls. There was nobody there. He immediately pushed out the exit door. He initially thought the man sitting next to the two little kids was Jack Bolton, but he had dismissed the idea. But something about the man had piqued his suspicion.

Agent Ryland dashed down the stairs with his gun drawn. He assessed the surrounding area and saw a path into the woods. The drizzle had stopped, but the damp cool evening chilled his bones. He hurriedly followed the path along a river, having no idea where he was going or if Jack Bolton even followed the path. He flat-out pushed his tired body half a mile until, to his surprise, Jack Bolton appeared fifteen yards ahead of him.

Ryland drew his gun, "Jack Bolton, stop and put your hands up."

Jack turned. "How did you know it was me?"

"We needed to eat, this is the place everybody goes, but you probably didn't know that, Jack," Ryland said, not believing he had the elusive Jack Bolton right in front of him. "You are one smart guy, Jack. Who would have thought you would be with some family? I don't know how you pull it off. When I saw you at first, I dismissed it because you were sitting with a family. But when you walked by, I knew at that moment it was you."

"Well, what are you going to do now, Agent Ryland?"

"I'm going to take you in."

"Here we are in the woods, just me and you. I'm not going back, Agent Ryland," Jack said. "Even if I wanted to go with you, I wouldn't make it back to Boston. And, for that matter, neither would you."

"And why is that?"

Jack laughed out loud. "It's been a long day for both of us. I'm sure you're exhausted like I am. You've been a pawn from the start. You have a nice family, Agent Ryland. Go back to them. They're the only ones who care about you."

"I'm just doing my job."

"Ask yourself, Agent Ryland, how did the Mafia know I was here? Can you answer that question? In fact, I'm the only guy who has been playing by the rules. The two guys who approached me in the coffee shop knew I would be there and they knew the FBI would be there. Any thoughts on that?"

Agent Ryland paused.

"That's what I thought. Now, the only way you're taking me in is if you kill me and, if you kill me, like I said, you won't make it back to Boston." Jack paused and pulled a flash drive from his pocket and waved it in the air like a flag on Independence Day.

"What's that?"

"It implicates the CIA Director, Gus Banner, Sam Atkins's brother, maybe even Sam Atkins himself and probably a bunch of other top dogs."

"Where did you find that?"

"I got this information from Joe Cap's brother's safe deposit box at Multibank on University Avenue in downtown Seattle. You know, Cap's brother once worked for the CIA and just happened to have an accident."

"What's on the flash drive?"

"You don't need to know, Agent Ryland. It's better that way."

Agent Ryland's mind was going a thousand miles an hour. He had a real dilemma on his hands. *Could he do the unthinkable and just let Bolton go?*

"Agent Ryland, I've never killed anyone who didn't have it coming to them. And today, in all the chaos, we never shot at the good guys or, if we did, it was to miss them."

"You just can't go around taking the law into your own hands, Jack."

"Both of us have been playing by the rules, Agent Ryland. What about Keller, huh? The guys in the game are making up their own rules as they go. So don't give me a speech about taking the law into my own hands."

Ryland aimed his gun. "You need to come back with me, Jack."

"I'm sorry you feel that way. But I'm tired of the killing and the running. I'm not going back to prison now, Agent Ryland, and after all the shit I've been through, it's no longer on the table. So I'm walking, unless you want to do something about it."

Jack turned and started marching his tired legs up a small hill along the path.

Chapter 47

The overcast, wet miserable day couldn't end soon enough. Yellow police tape decorated downtown Seattle. As of 6:45 in the evening, one FBI agent and two police officers were listed in critical condition while three additional FBI agents and six police officers were listed in serious condition. A handful of individuals were being treated at local hospitals. Miraculously, however, nobody from the FBI or the police or any people caught in the crossfire had succumbed to their injuries yet. The story was different for organized crime and the group of bank robbers. Ten bodies had tarps draped over them, waiting for the medical examiner to examine. Forensic teams could be seen throughout downtown, gathering as much evidence as possible. A few of the armed men had managed to escape during the fierce gun battle.

In the shadows, Agent Ryland looked out at the downtown area. Usually a place of bustling activity, it was quiet, except for the authorities doing their investigative work. The whole day had been like a scene out of a movie. The surreal running gun battle earlier in the day had left dead bodies scattered here and there, rounds of bullet holes lodged in storefronts, broken glass littering the streets, and shot-up cars abandoned in all directions.

He wondered how many of the bad guys Bolton and Butler had killed. He had seen, firsthand, Bolton's ability, in a situation of extreme chaos, to easily gun down three bad guys in the blink of an eye. He could see how the guy had been awarded a Purple Heart. The man had no fear.

Outside the police perimeter of yellow tape, Multibank was still open for business. Before meeting with his team, Agent Ryland walked into the deserted bank and found that a couple of bank clerks were tending the open windows. He walked by the glass windows until he came to the bank manager's office.

The manager looked up. "Can I help you?" he asked. "We are closing in a few minutes."

"Yeah, I'm Special Agent Ryland, FBI," he said, pulling out his badge and flashing it to the manager. "I just wanted to talk to someone about George Cap's safe deposit box."

"I was here the day it got robbed," the manager explained. "I was showing a guy our safe deposit room and he pulled out a gun and handcuffed me to a metal pipe in the room and unlocked George Cap's safe deposit box. He grabbed what was in it and ran out. It was kind of strange, though."

"What do you mean?"

"Well, right around the same time, these two men

came in looking for the same safe deposit box, and they immediately ran out after the guy who had grabbed the contents. Then they came back asking questions about Cap's safe deposit box. I showed it to them, since they flashed badges and said they were from the Department of Homeland Security. They took a quick look at the box and left."

"That's it?" Ryland said, wondering if the men were from Homeland Security.

"Yes."

"Do you know what was in it?"

"I think it might have been a flash drive, but I don't know exactly."

"Well, thanks for your time."

Ryland emerged from the bank and listened to a message on his phone informing him that after the news conference the FBI director wanted to see him in Washington. He figured it probably wasn't good news.

Drizzle began to fall again. Portable but powerful floodlights illuminated the downtown area as the FBI crews continued working into the night. Paul found a diner and grabbed a cup of coffee before roaming downtown. He walked in between forensic teams, who were wearing yellow raincoats over white lab coats, sifting through the tiniest bit of evidence from the deadly shootout.

Thinking about Jack Bolton, he didn't have the will or the heart to take him in. The guy had saved his life, and there was an even bigger force at work that had tied him together with Jack Bolton and his partner Brian Butler.

Ryland reviewed it all in his mind, more convinced than ever that Senator Atkins had the Weston girl killed years ago and framed Jeff Keller. But that was just the tip of the iceberg. He thought back to his first meeting with Bolton. A decorated Navy SEAL, who gave everything for his country, he had returned home to find that his sister had been brutally murdered. His quest for justice had set off a chain of events that led all the way to downtown Seattle. Now, there were a slew of dead bodies littering the street, with more than half of them probably killed by Bolton and Butler.

The rain was falling a little bit harder, Ryland continued to walk the street, the rain saturating his raincoat and hair. He had begun to connect some of the dots in this sometimes puzzling chain of events. The question he couldn't seem to answer was why a CIA director got involved in a murder investigation and a prison break. It appeared from what Bolton had said, that Atkins and Banner were tied together in some way.

Regardless of that, it was becoming clear. The surveillance bug that Carl Cap showed him had been placed to determine if George Cap might have leaked out information about what was in the safe deposit box. This information had come to the attention of Bolton, who now had it, presumed to be a flash drive at this point, in his possession. Banner's surveillance on the Caps must have uncovered the SEALs plot to break out Bolton. It may have been after the fact, but it became personal to Senator Atkins when his son was killed by Bolton. In a strange twist of fate, Joe Cap gave Bolton the safe deposit box information that his brother had given him. The CIA was able to track the safe deposit box, but Bolton beat them to it.

This put the hit on Bolton in play. Who better to do this than Gallo who already wanted him dead? And Gallo was in a bind. One of his most trusted men, Joe Russo, was going to turn state's evidence, which surely would have taken him down. But, conveniently, Russo has a heart attack. More likely, he was poisoned by a government henchman, and the autopsy would never reveal the true trigger.

A mysterious FBI agent by the name of Weldon coincidently comes down from Washington. *Why?* In case the Mafia screwed it up. But Weldon failed as well.

The technicians were busy hooking up wires, positioning the podium, and hanging up a canvas tarp to cover the reporters and the cameras.

Finally, the clock struck 8:30 p.m. in downtown Seattle. Rain pelted the canvas above and six-foot floodlights beamed. Ryland, standing at the center of the podium, was surrounded by a contingent of police, FBI, and government officials. He taped on the microphone and began the press conference in front of a swarm of media members, both local and national. Rows of satellite trucks lined the streets, ready to transmit the information around the world.

Chapter 48

The next day, at 35,000 feet altitude, Agent Ryland found himself sitting in coach. After eight days in Seattle, he couldn't wait to get home and hug his family, but first he had to see the FBI director in Washington. He had no idea why he was being called to Washington. He had concerns about his future with the FBI. He was worried about his marriage. Then, there was the conjecture about Banner and Senator Atkins, who could possibly be the next president. It was scary just thinking about it, but what made it even worse was the idea that he had to keep this dark presumption to himself.

***

Frank Gallo sat at the bar in the backroom of his club. He was having a little celebration in honor of the passing of Joe Russo. Gallo had won the battle as the feds, once again, had failed to get something on him. The little, skinny man who had come to the restaurant had taken care of business just as he said he would.

Frank hadn't forgotten about Jack Bolton. He was going to get him if it took his entire lifetime. He couldn't believe how it played out in downtown Seattle. The news video was quite entertaining. The authorities had guessed that at least a thousand rounds of ammunition had been fired. Frank couldn't figure how Bolton and Butler had escaped that onslaught. Nine men had been sent and only three managed to get out of there in one piece. The authorities believed that Bolton had slipped through the border to Canada, and Gino was going to continue his search there.

***

Jose Moreno, the leader of the Moreno cartel, enjoyed the beautiful view of his lavish ocean villa overlooking the Pacific Ocean. It was a beautiful sunny day. He had watched the news clips showing the wild gunfight in downtown Seattle and was impressed by the men who had escaped that madness. He commented to some of his foot soldiers that he wished he had men like them. Little did he know that the men who killed his brother and ripped him off were the same men who impressed him.

His lawyer, dressed in a fancy white suit and an Indiana Jones-style hat, joined him out on the terrace.

"So, Miguel, what do your friends from Washington say? Who robbed us and killed my brother? It's been a few weeks now," Jose said, staring at his lawyer.

"They tell me to be patient. They will give us the names shortly," he said, sipping his cup of coffee.

"I pay you a lot of money, Miguel. I expect answers,

not excuses. Have they forgotten what I have done for them?"

"Jose, trust me. We will get the names," he said. "And many favors down the road, especially if their man becomes president."

"I hear you, but I want those names."

"Jose, just be a little more patient. We will have their names and addresses in due time."

***

Early morning on a beautiful fall Saturday, Atkins and Banner walked along a narrow road in the cemetery where the senator's son was buried.

"I don't understand, Gus. How did this get screwed up again?" Sam said.

"My man tells me the Mafia had a clear shot at him, except they shot him in the chest and, of course, he must have been wearing a vest."

"What do you mean, Gus? I read somewhere a thousand rounds of ammunition were used, and nobody can kill these guys?" Sam said, frustrated with Gus's excuses.

They walked until they got to the top of the hill overlooking his son's grave.

"Look, the Mafia decided they were going to take Bolton home with them. I don't know what they were thinking, but these guys robbing a bank at the same time just threw a monkey wrench into everything. These bank robbers were ex-military and were shooting at everything."

"I saw the video, Gus. You don't need to make excuses."

"Bolton and this guy Butler are not your average guys with guns, if you know what I mean. They're very good at killing people."

"Yeah, my son is lying down there because of these animals," Atkins said, irritated by Gus's response, pointing to his son's grave.

"I'm sorry, Sam. I didn't mean to say it that way. Look, they can't hide forever. We will find them. And I have an idea how to flush them out."

"Well I hope it's better than the last two," Atkins said with a disgusted look. "I worry about what they might have on that flash drive. I can't have anything derail my campaign."

"We'll get them, Sam. I promise you," Gus said, lighting up a cigarette.

***

The seven-by-ten-foot cell was something Jeff Keller never really got used to, nor the sound of metal gates closing and opening endlessly every day. He didn't belong here, and he wanted out. He was just a man who had been waiting to get married to the love of his life.

Instead, he was condemned to prison by powerful, corrupt government men with an agenda. He prayed that somebody would say it was all a mistake or a bad dream.

Laura continued to occupy his daily thoughts, as well as his dreams. He realized now that he was here for life, something he had never accepted before. He began to think about how to change that. He was a pretty sharp guy and everything had a flaw or a weakness that could be taken advantage of.

He observed everything and anything. He worked different work details. He watched delivery trucks when they made deliveries. He learned how the laundry was cleaned. He watched the guards' shift changes. If there was a weakness in this prison, he was going to find it. And once he escaped, they were never going to find him again. Only one convict had ever escaped from this prison. He planned on making it two.

***

The sun was fading behind the trees as Laura watched another sunset descend. She saw her life slipping away. She wanted a family. How long could she go on like this? Six years of the same daily routine. She was shut off from the outside world. If only her family knew she was still alive. She rubbed the tears away as her mind wandered to Jeff; she just wanted to be by his side, to see his smile, hear his infectious laugh, observe his confidence. He was always there for her, even the night she turned on him like a traitor, realizing only later how foolish she had been. She had the man of her dreams but had been too blinded by ambition to see it. Now, paying for her sins, she prayed every day that someone would rescue her from this nightmare.

***

A private plane touched down on the small island of Antigua. Art Glover stepped off the plane on a beautiful, crystal clear, sunny day - a far cry from the dismal conditions of Seattle. A villa retreat awaited him.

It was late afternoon when he sat on a terrace couch overlooking the bay. He had a beer in his hand, and a cool breeze blew in from the ocean. The usual ritual after a bank job was broken. His brother wouldn't be joining him for a few beers, laughs, and a good time entertaining attractive women. Life had been good until Jack Bolton gunned him down right in front of him. He had worked with the same four men for ten years, but they were all tragically shot down in that chaotic scene.

He never forgot a face. The news media showed Bolton's face over and over again. Art made a few calls when he got everything packed away. He talked to his well-connected sources and let them know that he wanted to know everything about Jack Bolton from the day the guy was born. During this time, his plan was to lay low until the authorities were no longer motivated to investigate the people responsible for the mayhem that took place in downtown Seattle.

***

Buck Airlines, as Buck would call it, had one passenger. Brian Butler was on his way to Antigua to start his boat business. He couldn't believe that his dream was about to become reality. It was touch-and-go there for a while in Seattle, but they had survived. He wondered how Jack was doing. He must have made it over the border or it would have been headline news.

The plane landed in late afternoon and he found a hotel overlooking the crystal blue ocean where mantra rays could be seen from his balcony. He made himself a drink and sat out on the balcony, enjoying the stunning view. He was a millionaire. Tomorrow, he was going to start his boat business and relish the good life in Antigua.

***

Water dripped slowly from the faucet as Jack moved the shaver around his face. He decided a crew cut was in order. He might have made it over the Canadian border, but he had to make sure he wasn't recognized by anyone. He had found a bed-and-breakfast outside of Vancouver and planned to stay there for a few days until he regained his strength. He needed some time to figure out the best course of action.

A quaint little town in Canada seemed like the way to go. A place where nobody would question his identity. A place where he could assimilate into the daily routine of a small town, not as Jack Bolton, fugitive and killer, but as Jack Riley, a hardworking, regular, nice guy.

Watch for the sequel to

Slip of the Hand

coming in 2015